About the Author

Beth Corby started out in a small Welsh mining village, and pursued her interest in music through to a PhD. Finding academic writing constricting, she embraced creative writing and fell for comedic storytelling at the first pen stroke. Beth relishes time writing, daydreaming, plotting and capturing those moments when her characters misbehave. Her debut novel, *Where There's a Will*, published in 2019; *Leave It to Fate* is her second novel.

To get to know Beth better, follow her on Twitter: @BethCorby1.

BETH CORBY

Leave It to Fate

HODDER

First published in Great Britain in 2020 by Hodder & Stoughton
An Hachette UK company

1

Copyright © Beth Corby 2020

A CIP catalogue record for this title is available from the British Library

Paperback ISBN 978 1 529 35960 2
eBook ISBN 978 1 529 35961 9

Typeset in Plantin Light 10.75/13.5 pt by Palimpsest Book Production
Limited, Falkirk, Stirlingshire

Printed and bound in Great Britain by Clays Ltd, Elcograf S.p.A.

Hodder & Stoughton policy is to use papers that are natural,
renewable and recyclable products and made from wood grown in
sustainable forests. The logging and manufacturing processes are expected
to conform to the environmental regulations of the country of origin.

Hodder & Stoughton Ltd
Carmelite House
50 Victoria Embankment
London EC4Y 0DZ

www.hodder.co.uk

For my husband and children,
and also for Nanna

I

The Yoghurt of Doom

I want many things in life: an end to world hunger; all wars to cease; a definitive answer on whether that dress was really blue and black or white and gold. But most of all, right now, I want whoever keeps stealing my yoghurts to STOP.

We're adults in a London office, not teenagers, and yet for three weeks now, someone has gone to the fridge and pinched my yoghurt. And it's not a mistake, because I've lavished half a sharpie on them, writing everything from 'Ella's – Hands Off!!!' right through to 'Thrush medicine' – which admittedly got me some funny looks, but even *that* yoghurt was gone by lunchtime! Whoever it is must have a strong stomach as well as no conscience.

That's why I've finally decided to follow Jenny's advice and do something about it. Last night I peeled back the corner of my cherry yoghurt, squirted in some hot sauce, added a few dried chilli flakes, and stuck it down again. It's in the fridge right now, waiting for the culprit. Trouble is, the kitchenette is down a side corridor, together with the toilets and the photocopier, and I've just 'been to the toilet' for the third time, and the yoghurt's still there. Maybe whoever it is doesn't like cherry, which is a shame, because I do, and unsurprisingly I don't fancy it any more.

Over at the next desk, Jenny taps her pencil urgently on

her keyboard and gives me a keen look. I shake my head to show the trap hasn't been sprung and she rolls her eyes. I pull a face in agreement and we get back to work.

I plough through some emails, and pull up the next set of design layouts advertising villas. *While away the warm summer evenings with a cocktail and a swim in your own private pool, surrounded by the beautiful Italian* . . . blah blah. The page has dry text and a few glossy photos. It's my job to liven it up by inserting blocks of colour to 'heighten the reader's sense of engagement and immersion'. Usually in pastel shades – nothing inventive or avant-garde, because if you notice I've done it, I've failed, apparently. It's your standard thankless task, but I don't mind. Well, not really. I mean, it is a bit of a comedown from managing my own team at the call centre, both financially and status-wise, but I knew I'd have to work up from the bottom when I took this job. It's the price I have to pay to get back into art and design, and soon enough I'll be one of a team over in the glass conference room, throwing about ideas and doing proper design work, like the Eau de Parfum Team brainstorming in there now. They're gesticulating and laughing, drinking coffee from the Gaggia coffee machine, happy, enthused and energetic as they take turns to air their ideas for the next big ad campaign.

I try a few shades of aqua, some slightly bluer tones, but it's difficult to focus *and* keep an eye on everyone heading down towards the kitchenette end of the office. Though, to be fair, with Sexy Tom going that way, I'm not the only one looking. Tom's on the Fashion Team and his metrosexual good looks, dove-grey suits and hair graded to nothing at his collar, draw eyes like iron filings to a magnet. He *is* pretty, if a little too self-assured for my taste and I bet his make-up bag is better stocked than mine, but he has a certain something. Not that he'd look twice at me. To him I'm just another mid-height, pretty but non-remarkable junior member of staff, with feathered and highlighted brown hair, wrap-around dress and boots. Although, now I think about it, he'd probably just stop at 'junior member of staff'. But I have to admit, I'd much rather be doodling a pencil drawing of him than arranging pastel-coloured blocks behind text.

I reread the brief: 'Sun, sea and sand colours, with a hint of coral'. I bring up some pictures of coral, which seem to come in as many shades as paint, and try to decide what colour the sun is as I've never looked at it myself.

I try pastel yellow and peach, adjust them to the glorious tones of Italian buildings in the evening sun, lighten them and—

'Pssst!' Jenny tips her head to indicate the people jostling at the end of the kitchenette corridor. 'Do you think . . .?' she whispers, and triumph zips through me.

Very possibly. We hurry over, and I stand on tiptoes and crane my neck to see over the heads of the people standing in the kitchenette doorway. Sexy Tom is scrubbing at his tongue with a blue paper towel. I shift slightly, and catch a glimpse of my cherry yoghurt on the countertop beside him. It's denuded of its 'Do not eat!' lid.

'What's going on?' cries someone from behind us.

'Tom's been poisoned!' calls someone nearer the front. 'We've called an ambulance.'

Jenny gasps, and my stomach drops.

Oh shit.

'It could be cauthdic thoda, or athid, or bleatth,' pants Tom, his mouth under the tap. A co-worker repeats his every word into her mobile, and Jenny grabs my arm to pull me away.

I shake her off and try to push forward, but I can't get through. 'No! It's just chilli,' I call, but no one listens. 'It's just chilli,' I repeat.

Tom clutches at his throat, his eyes wide. 'God! Am I dying?'

'You're *not* dying. It's chilli. Just chilli, that's all.' I'm squeezed in beside the person on the phone. I lean my head into her line of vision, but all her focus is on Tom. I push forward again, but the knot of people is so tight, all I get is glares and I'm forced to watch as three women minister to him in the confined space: one filling a cup, another applying a wet towel to his forehead, while a third flaps at the rest of us stuck in the doorway.

Tom hangs his head and grips the countertop, shaking. 'Tell them to bring an antidote.'

'It's not poison, it's chilli!' My words are lost in the shocked gasp as Tom collapses to the floor. His acolytes prop him against a kitchen cupboard, his face upturned like a fish on a hook, and I savagely elbow my way through, crouch down next to him, take his face in my hands and peer into his half-open eyes. 'YOU HAVEN'T BEEN POISONED. IT WAS JUST CHILLI, THAT'S ALL. I WAS JUST TRYING TO STOP SOMEONE STEALING MY YOGHURTS.'

He looks into my eyes for the first time, probably ever, focuses, and glowers. 'You *poisoned* me?' he asks incredulously.

'No, I—'

'Ella poisoned Tom,' says someone behind me, and her comment is relayed back.

I close my eyes, ready to explain yet again that it was just sodding chilli, when a quick-response paramedic pushes through and kneels down beside me.

'What's he taken? Narcotics? Poison? Chemicals? Do we know?' He looks from me to Tom, and pulls up Tom's eyelid.

'Chilli,' I say, now heartily sick of the word.

The paramedic frowns. 'Chilli?'

'Hot sauce. I put it in my yoghurt because someone's

been stealing them and . . .' I hold out my hands to present Tom. Tom glares wonky-eyed daggers at me, and the paramedic lets go of his eyelid and joins Tom in glaring at me. 'It only had two out of three chillies on the label! Sorry, I didn't think it would cause this much fuss. Sorry,' I repeat, though actually, I think Tom should be the one apologising.

The paramedic relaxes onto his heels and pulls his radio off his belt. 'Call off the ambulance. False Alarm. Just someone playing silly-buggers with hot sauce.'

'Roger,' says someone at the other end, and he clips it back on his belt. He takes Tom's wrist in his hand. Probably checking the time rather than Tom's pulse, but it goes awfully quiet. Everyone glares at me, except for Jenny who studies her shoes.

'I'm sorry,' I apologise to the room at large. 'I didn't mean to scare anyone, but someone's been stealing my yoghurts, and I needed to find out who.' The room erupts. It seems *everyone else* would rather supply Tom with his daily snack than harm a hair on his immaculate, thieving head.

Rob, my boss, rests his chin on his fingertips and studies me across the wide expanse of his desk. 'So, a prank gone wrong?'

'No, nothing like that. I was just trying to stop my yoghurts being stolen.'

Rob's eyebrows shoot up. 'By Tom?'

'Yes, as it turns out.'

Rob presses his lips together and air jets out through his nose. He looks down at his desk and shakes his head sadly before looking back at me. 'Tom has made a complaint, and I might have been able to explain away a prank gone wrong – but an intentional trap, Ella? That's more difficult, and might I add, not very nice.'

My insides squirm. 'It was just meant to stop him taking

my yoghurts, and I've tried everything else.' Rob's frown doesn't budge. 'And some might say stealing someone's lunch day after day isn't very nice, either. Thou shalt not steal, and all that.'

Rob sighs and pulls a file out from his desk drawer. He places it between us, so I can read 'Ella Tate', written in pencil on the top corner. 'I'll be dealing with Tom's stealing separately, don't you worry. But that's not the point. This is a very *serious* situation, Ella.'

'But it was just—'

'Let me finish. You have caused another employee emotional anguish and to fear for his life, and he has formally complained. There must be consequences.'

'Fear for his life?' Seriously? Who does Tom think he is – James Bond? I try to look contrite. 'But he just ate some chilli. Nothing dangerous. Nothing weird. I even wrote "Do not eat" on the lid. I mean, would you be having this conversation with the cleaner if he drank hand soap?'

'The cleaner had no reason to think he would drink hand soap. You, on the other hand, had every reason to believe your yoghurt would be eaten and yet you still tampered with it.'

'Not in any dangerous way! He just ate some chilli! Chilli! He got a hot tongue. The cure is yoghurt, and he was already eating that! People do it all the time. It's hardly the crime of the century.'

Rob massages his temples and breathes out. 'I'm disappointed you can't grasp the seriousness of the situation, Ella.'

Believe me, I'm grasping it! What I don't get is why it was apparently hilarious when Matt drew a spider on the toilet roll and Claire freaked out, and why when Karen concussed John with a metal bin full of ping-pong balls propped on top of a door, she got a pat on the back, but this is too much? 'I don't see why we can't just move on.'

'Because he's contacted Human Resources,' Rob says calmly.

'Oh.' My heart thuds to the bottom of my boots. It's gone inter-departmental. And I'm guessing that's where Tom used the words 'emotional anguish' and 'fear for his life'.

'Someone will be up shortly to speak with you. I just wanted to hear your side of the story before they arrived. Am I right in thinking you are coming to the end of your three-month trial period?'

Heat courses through me, leaving me strangely cold. 'Yes.'

'And you are . . . how old, if I might enquire?' He tags on a smile.

'Twenty-nine.'

The smile vanishes. 'So, not fresh out of university?'

'No.'

He breathes out heavily as my defence of youthful exuberance floats away on an ebbing tide of yoghurt.

'And what is it that you bring to the department?'

Is he talking about my lunch? 'Erm?'

'What are your skills? What do you bring to the table? Why should we keep you on?' He's waiting for my answer.

'I do design choices . . . support the process,' I say weakly. It's not even good English. 'And I work well with my colleagues?' Not Tom, obviously, but I have no idea what Rob's looking for.

He nods slowly, and there's a gentle knock at the door. 'Go and wait at your desk, please, Ella.'

I sidle out past Mr HR, who looks down at me with interest, and return to my desk.

Jenny taps her keyboard with her pencil. I give her a clipped shake of my head.

'What happened?' she hisses, refusing to be put off.

'Tom complained,' I whisper. 'I explained about the yoghurts and why I did what I did.' I'm careful to add a lot of 'I's so she knows I didn't mention her. 'But it doesn't look good.'

She bites her lip. 'They sent Tom home to recover.'

'Oh God!' I look anxiously at her. 'I only put in a few drops. Do you think he's allergic?'

'No, he's fine – no hives or anything, and he sprang up off the kitchen floor pretty damn fast; even checked his suit for signs of dirt before he rushed off to the toilets. It was only when he came out that he staggered about like an old man.'

'Delayed shock?' I offer.

Jenny shakes her head. 'He was milking it for everything he's worth – sorry for the dairy pun.' She giggles, but stops as Rob opens his door and beckons me back with his head.

'Good luck,' she mouths, and I get up and walk over, trying to ignore the ceremonial drums beating in my head.

'Close the door, please, Ella. Sit down,' says Rob.

Mr HR is perched on Rob's desk with his arms folded, so I take the chair. I grip the edge of the seat and cross my fingers under the folds of my dress, even though the troubled look in Mr HR's eyes and Rob's throat clearing tells me it's a lost cause.

It doesn't take long. They put on a good show full of we-regrets, unfortunatelys and out-of-our-handses. Rob even pinches the bridge of his nose as he calls down to security for someone to escort me from the building, and we sit in uncomfortable silence until Stan, the cheerful security guard, opens the door and grins at me.

'Ah hello, pet! Leaving, are we?'

'Yes.' What else is there to say?

'Ah well, let's get you on the tube before rush hour.'

Stan follows me to my desk and waits, like a human billboard, broadcasting my fate. Blushing furiously I log off my computer, slurp down my cold coffee and dry out my Secret

Santa 'Let's get Graphic' mug before stowing it in my bag along with my lip balm and mints. I look around, but even though it feels like every eye in the office is on me, Jenny's the only one who meets my eyes, and she's biting her thumb-nail.

I smile at her and shrug. 'It's just a job.' And it is. It's just a job. It was supposed to be The Job, but clearly that's not going to happen.

She smiles back sadly.

Stan steps back to let me out and I wave my fingers at her. She holds up a hand, but she's the only one. Everyone else types frantically, glued to their computer screens, deter-mined not to make eye contact. I'm almost tempted to shout an exuberant goodbye, saying I didn't want to work here anyway – but for one, Stan is holding his arm out directing me towards the lift, and for two, it isn't true. I gave up a lot for this job – gambled everything on it in the hope that it would lead to the life I wanted.

I pick up my coat and take one last look at the glass conference room, where one of the designers is pitching her ideas to the mobile phone company she's been assigned to. She's smiling and talking animatedly to a rapt audience and, as Stan clears his throat encouragingly, they applaud her.

I sigh and follow Stan to the lift. We wait, with him wheezing even after only that small distance, and I glance at the stairwell, tempted to make off down the stairs just to see if he follows me. I'm betting he'd take the lift and hope to catch me at the bottom, or else radio in for backup.

We step into the lift and Stan presses the lobby button.

'Soon be Valentine's Day,' he says.

Now I really wish I'd taken the stairs. Thankfully, we're only three floors up so the doors slide open before he can say more. I hand him my pass and he waves as the glass doors swing closed between us: him in the warm, me in the wilderness . . . well, on the London street, anyway. Though it could be the Arctic tundra, given the way the February wind is slicing through my clothes.

I pull my coat a little tighter and stare about helplessly. A tide of people usually carries me towards the tube station, but right now the expanse of paving is empty. Apart from the crow. It gallops over and tips its head and looks up at me inquisitively.

'If you're an omen, you're late!'

It looks at the ground as if to acknowledge this sad fact and bounds off on its next prophetic mission, while I button up my coat and set off for the tube station.

2

'Don't Pass Me By'

The tube station concourse feels wrong. My footsteps are too loud and echoey, the lights are too bright and the ticket barrier clamps closed behind me like an industrial press. I slide my Oyster card back in my pocket and I'm so cold, the warm, stagnant air from the tunnels is almost welcome. I try to breathe it in, but knowing this is the last time I'll come through here, my breath hitches. I try to swallow, but there's a traitorous lump at the back of my throat and my eyes start to sting. I close them and count.

In, two, three, out, two, three.

I know from experience I just need to pinpoint the feelings and tamp them down long enough to get back. So what are they? Anger? Upset? Anxiety? They don't quite fit this glacial half-panic. Am I in shock? That's closer. Bewildered? Yes. Lost? . . . Heartbroken that I've just lost the job that could finally make sense of me, my life and who I am? My breath hitches. That's the one, but labelling it isn't helping. If anything, it's making it worse and I have to squeeze my eyes closed to keep the tears from leaking out.

Someone barges into the back of me, and a man glowers at me as he accelerates past and onto the escalator. In an instant, he's gone, but the shock is enough to get me moving.

I step on the escalator and breathe careful, measured breaths as the escalator emits eerie, ghostlike groans.

It scrapes me off at the bottom, and I take the tunnel towards my platform. One foot in front of the other. Still breathing, but even though I know it's coming, I stop short in front of the cat food advert designed by our office. Tears blur the cat, but I really don't want to cry – not here. People will think my cat's died, and I really don't want to have to explain I don't even have one.

I stumble onwards and an unseen train sends dirty air up the tunnel, blowing my hair away from my face. I wipe my coat sleeve across my eyes, and—

I'm only metres away from the tattooed busker who always plays Beatles tunes, whose pitch is by the blocked-off tunnel junction. Luckily he hasn't noticed me – he's just setting up, tuning his guitar, but as I half turn, ready to creep past, he puts aside his guitar and makes a fuss of his dog. He smiles indulgently as the sweet brown mongrel sprawls on its blanket, front paws like a meerkat, basking in having its tummy scratched. It would be a good time to slide past, but I'm caught in their moment. So much so, I can't help smiling as its tongue lolls, and as I do, the constricted feeling in my chest loosens. With relief, I take a deep breath and dry my tears with the back of my hand, then feeling some sort of thanks is in order, I pull a five-pound note from my bag. I drop it into the collection pot, and to my horror the tattooed man glances at the pot and looks up.

'Are you sure, love? I'm not even playing . . .' His eyes narrow. 'Or is that the point?' I almost shrink back, but he grins and I smile weakly.

I indicate the dog. 'It's just nice to see someone happy. I needed that.'

'He's a happy soul – good to have around. Tough day?' he asks softly.

I bite my lip. 'Is it that obvious?'

He smiles. 'People rarely stop unless something's knocked them off course . . . or if they're on holiday,' he adds grudgingly.

'Not on holiday.'

His eyes are kind and his tone is gentle. 'I didn't think so.'

'Actually, I've just lost my job.'

He smiles sympathetically. 'And you found yourself staring at a happy dog . . .'

'. . . wishing my life was that simple,' I agree sadly. 'Not that I want my tummy scratched.'

He laughs. 'Oh, for the simple pleasures in life. Did you like your job?'

'What do you mean?'

'I mean did your life revolve around your work? Did it make you feel valued, important . . .' He shrugs. 'Did it give you a sense of achievement?'

I want to say yes, but his earnestness invites me to be truthful. 'I was hoping one day it would.'

'Ah. You were trying for your dream job,' he says with sympathy.

I picture some of my friends whose art has taken off and who have their own studios. 'Well, maybe not my dream-dream job, but it was something I'd hoped I could be proud of.'

He nods. 'And the people you worked with? Will they stay in touch?'

'My friend Jenny might.' Though now I think about it, I doubt she will if she's afraid it's her fault. Survivor's guilt, or something? But like the old saying says, 'If I told you to jump off a cliff . . .'

He smiles. 'Well, that's something.'

I manage a half-smile. 'Silver linings? Or is this where we talk about closing doors and opening windows?'

He frowns. 'Well, I suppose we could, but I find it better

to remember success comes in different guises: more than you can possibly imagine, and you can't possibly see all ends. For example, this may be an opportunity to follow your actual dreams.'

'I suppose,' I say, unwilling to admit I've already spent years doing that; touting my drawings to agents, galleries, card companies and gift shops, even to the extent of having stalls at festivals and Christmas fairs. I'm not sure I so much followed that dream as trampled it to death, but nothing came of it and in the end I gave up. 'But that only works if you have dreams to pursue.'

He winks at me. 'Surely there's something you want?'

I look up the tunnel to avoid his gaze. 'I wouldn't mind a fairy godmother plopping down and presenting me with a winning lottery ticket, if that's what you mean?'

He assesses me for a moment. 'No, but there's definitely something,' he persists, even though I smile apathetically to dampen his interest. 'Closet ballerina, or a secret Fat Duck chef?' he offers playfully. 'Pocket Pavarotti?'

I laugh. 'Maybe in the shower,' but I shake my head. 'Why are you so certain there's something?'

He smiles at me. 'Because Fate or Destiny or whoever clearly has you marked down for change, otherwise why would you be here?'

'Fate?' I ask. I can't go with Destiny, because she's always struck me as a stripper, spreading clumpy fairy dust about like glitter. Fate, however, has a solemn life-choices vibe about her. 'Are you saying Fate made me lose my job, today?' It sounds better than yoghurt, but still . . . 'Why would she do that?'

'Maybe she reckons it's time for a change. Maybe she thinks you're destined for something better. Maybe she thought you should chat to me?' His wide grin shows me he is, to some extent, joking.

'That's a lot of maybes.'

'Maybe.' He smiles.

'But what if a London design job was the pinnacle of what I could achieve?'

'Then I think she'd have left you to it, don't you? But maybe . . .' He smiles wider. '. . . she has something better planned for you.'

'I wish she'd tell me what it is.'

He chuckles. 'I don't think that's her style.'

'Then what is?'

'You have to give her legroom, keep your eyes open for opportunities. Maybe even think outside the box and not head straight back into your old routine—'

'So you're saying I shouldn't apply for a similar job?'

He laughs. 'That's up to you. It's your life.'

'But if you were me?'

He holds my gaze for a long second. 'Let me show you something— No, don't look like that, it's nothing weird. I want you to see exactly what *I* see every day.' His eyebrows flick up in challenge, reminding me of my old A-level art teacher when he was about to suggest something radical.

'What do I have to do?'

'Just stand there and watch the rush hour come through, that's all. Just see what I see.'

I check my watch. Five o'clock isn't far away and the number of commuters is already picking up. He picks up his guitar, slings the strap over his head and starts playing a rendition of 'We Can Work It Out'. He winks at me. Funny. I bend down and stroke the dog, who nuzzles my leg. A gust of warm air announces the arrival of another train somewhere down the tunnels, and after a minute, the air sucks away with its departure.

As he plays the last few chords, the busker jerks his head back. 'Stand against the wall, well out of the way, and listen.'

At first I think he means I should listen to 'Help!', but as he moves on to the chorus, his head nodding to the rhythm, a strange, low patter funnels down the tunnel. It grows in volume, until a stream of people turn the corner and course through the narrow tunnel towards us. It's almost an onslaught, or a charge, and I flinch as the odd coin lands in the busking pot and guitar case like stones kicked up by a panicked herd. I press myself back against the wall, glad of the extra space provided by the blanked-off tunnel, and watch mesmerised as they condense and compress, until they merge into a single sinuous entity, slithering past, their footsteps echoing off the tiles like the rattle on a snake, bizarrely accompanied by the cheerful melody of 'I Want to Hold Your Hand'. And just when it seems like they're a never-ending tide, the flow decreases, and the mass relaxes and gradually reverts to individual people, still hurrying and busy, but no longer that shocking beast.

He strums his final chords and turns to me. 'That's what's been carrying you along all this time. Where could Fate fit in amongst that? She'd be trampled to death by your timetables, charts, appointments and meetings. No, Fate would have to do something pretty drastic to even separate you.'

'Like make me lose my job?'

He winks. 'Now you're getting it. You asked what I'd do? I'd give Fate a chance, after all she's put a lot of work into getting you here.'

It would certainly help explain the ridiculousness of what happened. I almost like the idea. 'But don't I get a choice?'

His eyebrows meet. 'Of course you do. You can plough straight back into the rat race if that's what you want. But do you really want to, now that you've seen it?' He glances at the people still streaming past us, but it's like we're in a different dimension: invisible and unheard – the ones who've 'seen it', not quite *The Matrix*, but close. 'I certainly wouldn't go back,' he says softly.

'But isn't leaving it to Fate scary?' My pension, food bills and rent all hurl themselves against a glass wall in my mind.

'I guess that depends on your definition of scary. Is uncharted scary? Is trying something new scary? Is learning what you want and becoming who you want to be scary?' He pauses significantly. 'Or is settling for stagnation and a less-than-wonderful life the real nightmare? I guess you have to decide whether what you have now is worth settling for.'

Our eyes meet. What do I have now? Apart from a few friends and some savings, just my flat, which is rented, my roommate, who I'm avoiding right now, my mother's respect, which I'm not sure I've ever had, and a head-start on getting another job.

He smiles at me. 'Just think about it,' he says gently.

'I will. Thanks,' I say, meaning it.

'My pleasure,' and giving me a small wave, he plays me out to 'Hello, Goodbye' and I carry on along the tunnel in a daze of new ideas.

3

Gravel-rash Friends

Three trains squeal to a halt, load up and leave. Part of me wants to climb on, go back to the flat, crawl under my bedcovers and sleep, but the sane part knows that won't happen. I'll actually just end up listening to my flatmate and her boyfriend exploring the early stages of their new relationship, which I don't begrudge, but it's a little off-putting when you're trying to eat, sleep or figure out what to do with your life.

No, what I need is a friend – a good friend who'll give me some proper honest advice, and that means Vivienne, because no matter how painful, she always speaks her mind. Decision made, I get on the next train, switch tube lines, and head for Vivienne's shop in Notting Hill.

Vivienne's shop is tiny, but glorious. It's a cluttered Aladdin's cave of glistening curiosities, chock-full of Vivienne's own amazing handcrafted wire, wicker and bead-work birds, some as tiny as hummingbirds, others as huge as herons, and her partner (both business and wife) Clara's beautiful copper and enamel jewellery, which has graced both catwalks and magazines. The shop strikes a happy medium between tropical bird emporium and Moroccan market, and stocks both their work and pieces by other artists they admire. They sell mostly via the Internet, with Vivienne's Christmas tree robins, decorated with anything from sequins to real diamonds, sometimes fetching thousands. This little shop, however, as well as being worthy of a place on London's list of must-see attractions, earns its keep, and provides them with a workshop out the back.

The bell on the door tings and Vivienne comes through from the back dressed in bright jumpers, scarves and jeans, and wearing dragonfly earrings made by Clara.

'Ella! It's been weeks!' She grabs my hand and leads me through to the back to make us chamomile tea. 'What news?' she demands as she flicks the switch on the electric kettle, and I tell her about my yoghurt, the chilli sauce and my swift exit from the company.

She blows out a breath and gives me a one-armed hug. 'Jesus! It sounds frickin' hilarious, right up to the point they sacked you. What on Earth's the matter with them?'

Relief floods through me. 'I know, right?'

'But seriously, don't you have some recourse? Unfair dismissal or something? I thought the best thing about working for these corporate giants was the job security?'

The irony isn't lost on me. 'In theory, if I'd got past my three-month trial period, then yes, they'd have had to go through the whole "first warning, second warning" thing. But as it is, they can say I wasn't suitable and that's that.'

'How long until the three-month point?'

I wrinkle my nose. 'Six days. I know, I know. If only I'd been a bit more patient—'

'Stuff that, he stole your yoghurts!'

'Yes, he did! But no one seems interested in that part. It was all "Tom had a near-death experience", "Tom feared for his life", when he could have just laughed it off.'

'Hmm. He was probably embarrassed and wanted to deflect the attention onto you.'

She might have a point. 'But to go so far as to get me sacked?'

Vivienne shrugs. 'Don't underestimate the power of embarrassment. It's a highly under-rated emotion.'

'I suppose.' I picture Tom lying martyred on the kitchenette floor. He really went for the Oscar.

'What about your mum. Can't she help?'

I sip the scalding-hot tea and wince. 'No, she mainly deals in conveyancing, not employment law.'

'And you don't want to tell her, anyway?' Vivienne guesses shrewdly.

'You've got it.' I rub my tongue on the roof of my mouth.

The door tings and we make our way back into the main shop. We perch on the bar stools behind the counter as a lady browses.

'So what's the plan?' asks Vivienne.

'It only just happened!'

'Yes, but the world hasn't stopped turning. What are you going to do?'

This is exactly why I came to see Vivienne – she can be like a hundred-mile-an-hour gravel rash, but she makes you face facts. I sort through my options. 'I could ask about my old job at the call centre? They were genuinely sorry when I left.'

'Is that what you want to do?'

I shrug. 'It's a job with a pay cheque.'

'That's not what I asked. I asked if it's what you *want* to do?'

I hold up my hands. 'That's the problem. I don't *know* what I want to do!'

'I only ask because now could be a good moment to make a change. It's not like when the call centre offered you that promotion and you went bananas about being stuck in the same depressing job for the rest of your life. This time you have nothing to lose.'

I almost laugh.

Vivienne frowns. 'What?'

'It's just that a busker I met on my way here said pretty much the same thing. He said Fate is giving me a chance to do something different.'

Vivienne leans forward. 'What else did he say?'

I shrug, skipping over the pocket Pavarotti comment and the slithering basilisk of people. 'That I could step out of the rat race and see what happens – maybe even leave it to Fate. He was quite compelling about it, actually. I was almost tempted.'

Vivienne's eyes narrow. 'Really? That doesn't sound like you.'

'I know! I've always been sensible and taken the next logical step; worked at one job while trying to get my drawing off the ground in my spare time, but look where that's got me.'

'Up yoghurt creek without a spoon?'

'Exactly! And now I'm not so sure I want any of it any more, or if I ever did!'

'You wanted to draw when you went to art college,' Vivienne reminds me, which is true. I fought tooth and nail for it back then. I didn't even back down when Mum brought out the big guns and accused me of being just like her sister Gillian.

'You're right. I loved it, and I'm sure I still would if I'd had even an ounce of success, but despite really, really trying, I haven't, and to be honest, I don't think I feel the same about it any more. In fact, I think it's time to admit defeat and try something new; find something fresh I really want, because I'd *love* to feel that spark again – that excitement of wanting something so much I'd do almost anything to get it,' rather than the stomach-churning anxiety I get every time I look at a sketchpad.

'So, what you're saying is: you want to *want* something new?' checks Vivienne, boiling it down.

'As ridiculous as that may sound, yes! And I want it to be fulfilling, worthwhile and enjoyable.'

She nods thoughtfully. 'OK, it's a place to start.'

'Do you really think so?' I stare at her uncertainly as the customer shyly puts her purchases on the counter. Vivienne wraps the three wire birds in newspaper, pops the necklace into a velvet pouch, and takes her money. We wait for the customer to leave the shop, and Vivienne leans on the counter and props her chin in her palm as she studies me.

'Are we just talking about your job here, or living arrangements and relationships, too?'

To be fair, none of them are in that great a shape, and I'd love not to go on any more disappointing Tinder dates. 'Everything,' I say, even though my stomach contracts.

Vivienne looks me in the eye. 'Everything?'

'Yes,' I repeat more confidently. 'Because look at what you've achieved since art college –' I indicate the shop in all its Bohemian glory – 'whereas I've ended up in this weird non-happening rut. Maybe I *should* give Fate a chance?'

Vivienne nibbles her thumb for a second and nods. 'All right, but I think you need a plan.'

'A plan? Isn't "planning" and "Fate" a contradiction in terms?'

She presses her lips together. 'You want to *want* something, right?' I nod. 'Then you should practise.' She says it like it's the most obvious thing in the world.

'Practise what?'

'Asking yourself what you want and following through on it. After all, how do you figure out what you want if you don't start looking, and what's the point of wanting something if you don't actually get it? You could start right now. What's the one thing you want *right now*? I mean *really* want.' Her challenge escapes into a smile.

'Such as?'

'Anything: as ridiculous as you like. Just name it.'

Cream cake? A date with someone fantastic? Then I think about the next few days and shudder. 'I don't want to spend Valentine's Day in the flat with Lindi and her boyfriend.'

'OK, there you go. Now make it positive.'

'I want to spend Valentine's Day somewhere else.'

She holds out her hands in a 'ta-daa' move. 'There you go. Now all you need to do is make that happen. And each time you think of something you want, write it down and work on it.'

'So that's how you'd plan for Fate?' I ask, slightly thrown. It's practical, I'll give her that, and I really would love to be out of the flat on Valentine's night.

'Well, it can't hurt, can it? They say that God helps those who help themselves, and I don't see why Fate would be any different. Plus, you'll be giving her a place to start.'

'That's true.' I examine my fingers, feeling faintly ridiculous. 'But I can't help feeling this is all just an overreaction to losing my job.'

Vivienne brings up the search engine on her phone.

'What are you looking up?'

'"Should I re-evaluate my life?",' she enunciates, taps enter and scans the entries. 'Answer these questions – "What would you do if money were no object?"'

'Go back to art college,' I say without thinking.

Vivienne frowns. 'Really? After everything you just said?'

I try to think. 'I loved art back then. I loved being with creative people and trying out new things, and I loved having time to . . . play.' It sounds frivolous, but it's true. 'Why, what would you have said?'

Vivienne's eyes widen. 'I don't know . . . I'd probably go on a buying trip to Cambodia, Thailand and Morocco with Clara.'

'And then?'

'And then come back here and sell the stuff in the shop.' Vivienne smiles, content with her life. I push down my envy as she checks her phone for the next question. '"What are you most afraid of regretting at the end of your life?"'

That's trickier. 'Of not being missed, I suppose.' It's how I feel right now, and it's scaring the hell out of me.

Vivienne's mouth tightens, but she doesn't comment. 'And "Describe yourself in three words".' She pins me to my stool with her eyes.

'Aimless.' That's pretty obvious. 'Lonely.' Shit, that's bleak, but given I'm here avoiding my flatmate's exuberant love life, it's probably true. 'And . . . bored, I suppose. Not in a bad way,' I add as Vivienne's eyebrows meet in the middle. 'It's just . . .' I squeeze my hands together. 'I want something exciting to happen.'

Vivienne gives me a nod. 'OK. Well, let's nudge Fate into action, then.' She checks the time and pulls a face. 'It's closing time. Come back for dinner?'

I shake my head. 'No, thanks. I've got leftovers in the fridge.'

'OK,' she says, perhaps sensing I need some time to think. She gives me a comforting hug. 'Phone me if you want to. And make a list of things you want. It'll give you a place to start.' As she empties the till, I wander back to the underground, deep in thought.

Back in the flat, things are just as cosy as I expected – Lindi and her boyfriend are snuggled up on the sofa watching TV. I get changed into some sweats, collect a pen and a pad and take a seat at the kitchen table as yesterday's lasagne rotates in the microwave.

I stare at the pad.

What do I want from life?

God, it's like an exam question.

I push my hands through my hair and jot down *What do I want?* I resist the urge to write 'be somewhere else for Valentine's Day', in case Lindi comes in and sees, and put the pen down.

What does anyone want?

I pick up the pen and draw over the question mark a few times. Thankfully, the microwave beeps. I take my dinner out, get a fork and sit down again. I take a bite and chew.

Maybe I should try to picture my ideal life?

Do I want kids? A husband? A house? Career? Penthouse flat? Castle? Cottage with roses around the door? Igloo? . . . I let out a sigh. I can't picture myself with any of it . . . Do I want money? Fame? Success? Do I want to reject the world and move to an island in the Philippines and spear fish for my dinner half-naked for the rest of my life?

I snort and take a forkful of lasagne, burn my tongue, already rough from the chamomile scalding, and breath fast in and out to cool what's in my mouth.

Lindi giggles in the living room.

I pick up the pen.

1. A place of my own. OK, that's a start, and that means:

2. A career. Not just a job, but something I can get really excited about and can't wait to get up for each day.

I take another bite of lasagne.

So *3. Fulfilment? Or at least be able to feel proud of myself.* I have no idea what that entails, but I'm hoping it might be covered by 2? . . . I'll come back to it.

4. . . . Even just thinking about it, I have to take a deep breath. *To find some way of putting everything bad that happened with my drawing behind me.* Anything to stop me feeling sick whenever I think about it, although maybe that's something I'll have to come back to in a few years' time, when it's not so raw. I draw brackets around it.

And then there's relationships. I'm done wasting time on

dates that go nowhere, so he would have to be something special – considerate, confident and kind, and not fixated on football, rugby or golf . . . or himself. I've already been on too many Tinder dates where I haven't got a word in edgeways. My pen hovers over the page. What the hell – it's only a list, not a contract.

5. *A man who actually wants to spend time with me, who's interested and interesting, and who's there when I need him.* After some of the dates I've been on that's like asking for a knight in shining armour.

My pen hangs, poised to scribble it out. Trouble is, I don't want to be lonely, either. I think for a second. *(or a cat)*, I add.

And, last but not least, the elephant that's been in the corner of every room for as long as I can remember:

6. *To find out who my dad is.*

When I was little, Mum maintained he was a sperm donor, but when they changed the law so you could apply to find out who donated, that changed to him being an unofficial sperm donor. She said he was 'kind-of married' and 'best to leave it alone', so I did. I didn't pester her, or try to find out, but it does bother me. It has for a long time, and it's funny how often, when you're making life decisions, not knowing leaves you feeling unanchored. And though, at times in the past, I was almost scared of finding out the truth, now I'm older, I think I can handle it . . . even if he's a mass-murderer. At least I'd know. And if it's some dreadful mistake with a friend's husband? I could ask some basic health questions, find out what he did for a living, his interests and move on.

I finish the lasagne, put my plate in the dishwasher, and reread my list.

It's a start.

I tear it off the pad, tuck it inside my phone case, and go

to my room. I sit on my bed and survey the books and DVDs on my bamboo shelves. Oddly, there's plenty that's applicable on there. Perhaps even a theme – Elizabeth Gilbert, Hugh Fearnley-Whittingstall, Ben Fogle. They all dramatically changed their lives. Even my DVDs shout change with *G.I. Jane*, *Shirley Valentine*, *We Bought a Zoo*, *Erin Brockovich* . . . even *The Matrix*. Perhaps I've been feeling this way for a while without even knowing it?

Next door, Lindi's bedroom door clunks closed and Ed Sheeran fills the flat.

I take out some headphones and put them on.

Vivienne's right – I need to think how I'm going to get away for Valentine's Day.

4

Fate's Emissary

A week later, and I've determinedly looked at jobs and courses, as well as countless web pages on finding myself, self-improvement, finding my true calling, and releasing my inner child. I've also tried exercise, mindfulness and positive thinking, but no matter what I do, I'm still no nearer finding out what I want from life or any further on with a Valentine's escape plan. In fact, I'd go as far as to say I've gone back-wards, because in a moment of desperation – OK, panic – I went to see my old boss at the call centre and asked for my old job back. On the plus side, she was only too happy to have someone she could bring in without training. On the minus side, I'll be going back at a lower level than when I left, answering calls while another girl goes on maternity leave. And on the seriously negative side, it goes against everything I said and completely against allowing Fate some legroom.

But as I sit on Vivienne's sofa, holding a glass of white wine and admit what I've done, as usual, Vivienne's reaction surprises me.

'Obviously the job's a copout.' She taps her bottom lip thoughtfully, and moves up the sofa so Clara can sit down. 'But when does it start?'

'First week in March.'

She does some counting on her fingers. 'So, you've bought

yourself just over two guilt-free weeks to follow your under-ground guru's advice?' She stares at me expectantly. 'So, had any ideas?'

'I could take a holiday?' I offer, nonplussed.

'Really?' Vivienne's unimpressed, and Clara tactfully goes back to the kitchen.

'Yes. I have a little money put by. I could book somewhere; have a rest . . . get some perspective on my situation . . .' I try, but Vivienne's still frowning.

'Well, I've been thinking. Remember what you said about going back to art college? How about you take some evening classes – try pottery and put your illustrative skills to use that way? Or silk painting, or Chinese calligraphy? You did beautiful work, and you're so talented – it seems a shame to waste it.' She looks at me sadly. 'Are you sure you don't want to try the illustrator route one last time?'

Even Vivienne doesn't know the full extent of my efforts since art college. Over the years I've tried hundreds of agents, galleries and shops and received everything from a flat two-word 'not interested' through countless variations on 'not the kind of thing we're looking for', to a two-page diatribe on why one agent could no longer face dealing with illustrators. But none of that was as bad as the unscrupulous agency who requested a set of drawings, scanned them and tried to sell my designs to a card company without a contract or my permission. I had a nasty time, and even had to hire a solicitor before they were stopped. Luckily they'd done it to several others, so my costs were eventually covered, but even though I pretended to everyone – even Vivienne – that I was fine, it was still a vile seven months, and I've felt sick picking up a pencil or a paintbrush ever since.

I blow out a sigh. 'You know I tried, but short of finding a decent agent to take me on, I don't see any way of making that work.'

'Then how about you get a body of work together and do an exhibition?' persists Vivienne. 'Word would get around about how good you are.'

'And live off what?'

'Get a bank loan – that's what you told me to do.'

I smile at her. Vivienne doesn't realise how special she or her birds are. 'I don't have the bejewelled chicken or the orders you had, let alone your balls-to-the-wall courage,' I add.

'As I remember it, you made me stay up all night doing costings, business plans and future designs so the bank manager didn't laugh me out of there,' protests Vivienne.

'Just to bolster your case, but even he had to recognise you're something special.'

'So are you!' Vivienne tries to hold my gaze, but I look away. 'All right then, what are you doing about getting away for Valentine's Day? I'm not saying a holiday will solve anything, but I agree it'll give you some room to think.'

'And give Fate some elbow-room,' I add.

I'm joking, but Vivienne pauses. 'Fate,' she says thoughtfully. 'OK, how about we find six places, roll a dice and let Fate decide where you're going? Good places, fun places, scary places—'

'Why don't we go the whole hog and put visiting Mum on the list,' I suggest.

Vivienne shudders. 'Have you told her about your job, yet?'

I shake my head, and ominously, my handbag starts to ring.

Vivienne hands me my bag. 'I don't remember saying her name three times!'

'Once is apparently enough.' I hold up my phone to show it's 'Mum'.

Vivienne bares her teeth. 'The force is strong in that one!

Get it over with, and I'll find more wine.' I open my mouth to protest. 'And stay the night,' she adds.

I smile and touch the green icon.

'Hi, Mum.'

'Oh, you're there.' Mum always starts like that, no matter where I am. 'You'll never guess who phoned me – your Aunt Gillian!'

'Really?' They're estranged, so that's odd for a start.

'Yes, and you won't believe what she wanted.' I open my mouth to say I haven't the faintest clue. 'Help! Can you believe it? From me! Like I owe her anything after all these years. I'm astonished she has the temerity to ask, and yet here she is, perfectly happy to yank on the family ties now that it suits her, and all because she fell down some steps and ended up in hospital.'

'Oh God! Is she all right?' I smile at Vivienne as she tiptoes out, leaving me to it.

'Yes! I told her the hospital is the best place for her and she should stay there! Rest, get better, consider herself lucky she has a hospital bed and count her blessings it was only a mild concussion, a knee ligament injury and a fractured wrist! But oh no! Apparently hospital's not good enough for Gillian! Gillian doesn't *want* to be in hospital. Gillian *wants* to go home, and she wants me to drop everything and rush up there! Can you believe it?'

How hard did Aunt Gillian knock her head?

'And why she wants to go home, I have no idea!' continues Mum. 'She should be grateful for a decent bed and three square meals a day. But oh no, not Gillian! Gillian's determined to go back to her hovel with no mod cons, no matter how much it puts everyone else out, even though she's clearly not safe to be there by herself.'

Vivienne puts a pile of pillows and sheets on the sofa arm and winks at me before going into the kitchen.

'Mum?' I try gently, embarrassed to be keeping them from their living room.

'I told her straight. I told her, now Mike's dead, she should find somewhere more suitable, somewhere closer to the shops, and do you know what she said to me? You won't believe it! She told me to *sod off*!'

I stifle a laugh – I'd have loved to be a fly on that wall.

'When she's asking me for help! And yet I'm supposed to rush up there—'

Vivienne peeks her head around the kitchen doorway and nods encouragingly.

'Err, Mum?' I try.

'—like I've no life of my own, just to look after her. Have you ever heard of anything more selfish?'

'Mum, I've lost my job,' I slide in and wince. I could have chosen a better spot than after 'more selfish'.

Mum breathes out and readjusts her annoyance. 'When?'

I feel myself flush. 'A couple of days ago.' OK, more like a week.

'Were you sacked or made redundant?' she asks, becoming scarily businesslike.

'Neither, really. It was more of a misunderstanding than anything.'

'Tell me.' Her tone is resigned, which ironically is the one option she didn't give me.

'Well, it was stupid really. My yoghurts kept going missing, so I put some chilli sauce in one, and well . . . it just got out of hand and someone complained.'

Silence. Mum's worked at the same solicitors' office since before I was born, so her disappointment is implicit. 'Did they follow procedure?'

'Given that I was still within the trial period, yes, I think so. And I already have another job,' I offer brightly. 'Where I used to work?'

'The call centre?'

'Yes.'

'Ah. What are you doing this evening?' Her change of subject isn't subtle, but seeing as there's nothing either of us can do . . .

'I'm over at Vivienne's, having dinner and staying the night.'

'Oh, is she still with . . . Clare?' I'm not sure if she disapproves of Vivienne or her relationships, but the one time they met, Vivienne maintained an attitude of silent defiance, and Mum's lips were so tight they almost turned white.

'Clara, Mum. And yes, they're still together.'

'Well, that's . . . good. In that case, I'll wish you a pleasant evening.'

'You, too.'

'Hardly! I still have to sort out Gillian.'

In theory I could say 'OK, good luck', but my conscience tells me I shouldn't. 'I thought you weren't going?' I say instead.

'I'm not, but I'll have to come up with something or be branded the evil sister. Ironic, considering the opposite is true!'

'Perhaps Aunt Gillian could hire some home help?'

'No, I suggested a community nurse, but apparently her house is too remote – which is all the more reason to move, in my opinion.'

'So what are you going to do?'

'That's the question, isn't it? I'm not about to condemn myself to several weeks in the middle of nowhere, living amongst a bunch of reprobates who've supposedly escaped the rat race!'

'Rat race?' That's the term the busker used.

Mum breathes out heavily. 'Yes, back in the sixties, all these hippies migrated to Wales to opt out and explore their inner self, or some such nonsense. Thought themselves very clever, but in reality they were just a bunch of degenerates, smoking dope and expecting the state to support them.'

Escape? Opt out? Inner self? They've all cropped up in my Internet searches over the last week, along with Gandhi's advice on achieving inner peace through helping others. When you add my need to get away for Valentine's Day . . .

'How about I go?'

'What?'

'How about I go and look after Aunt Gillian?'

Mum gives a harsh laugh. 'You can't, Ella – it's in the middle of nowhere, and you haven't got a car.'

That's a good point. 'I could hire one?'

'You haven't driven in years and it's halfway up a mountain. And why would you *want* to?' she asks, like I've lost my mind.

'I just thought it would be nice to get away somewhere a bit different.'

'"Somewhere a bit different"?' she repeats in disbelief. 'The place is unlivable!'

'But she needs someone.'

Mum goes quiet, and when she speaks again her tone is severe. 'No, she doesn't. Not really. She *should* be in hospital. And besides, the place is ghastly, it's also a long way away and Gillian's a nightmare. Do I need to remind you she swore at me? She'll swear at you, too, and you won't get any thanks!'

From Mum, or from Gillian? 'I wasn't expecting any.'

'Well that's good, because in all the years I've known her, she's not thanked me once!'

I bite back a smile. 'But if I go, you'll be absolved of your obligation to her. That has to be a good thing, doesn't it?'

Mum hesitates. 'Why are you so determined to go?' she asks, suddenly suspicious.

If I tell her about Fate and tattooed buskers, she'll think

I've gone mad. If I tell her about Lindi and her boyfriend, she'll tell me to get over it. If I tell her I feel lost and need time to think, she'll laugh in my face – well, ear. 'I've got some spare time before I start at the call centre, Aunt Gillian needs help and, at the end of the day, she's family.'

Mum snorts. 'Gillian opted out of our family years ago. We don't owe her a thing.'

'But I'm at a loose end,' I point out.

Mum takes an audible breath. 'Well, if you're determined to go, then go.'

'OK.' I'm not sure if I've just won the argument or shot myself in the foot.

'And I'll let her know you're coming.' Mum sounds irritated.

'I'll have to sort out a car first. It might take a few days.'

'And no doubt you'll come to your senses in that time, but I'll call and get you some directions.'

'A postcode will do. I'll use the satnav on my phone.'

Mum lets out a derogatory laugh. 'I doubt you'll get a signal, but all right, I'll get you that, too.'

'Thanks.'

'Just don't complain when you hate it!'

'I won't,' I promise, and with a clipped goodbye, she hangs up.

Clara comes in with a handful of knives and forks, and Vivienne comes over and tops up my glass like it's medicinal.

'So?' she asks.

'I'm going to Wales.'

Vivienne stops mid-pour. 'Really? I didn't even know that was an option.'

'Nor did I. But then . . . I don't know what happened.'

Vivienne laughs. 'Fate?'

'Possibly, if Fate's intent on burying me in a backwater with my most hellish relation.'

35

'How hellish?'

'Well, put it this way: everyone in the family hates her.' That only includes Mum, and Granny and Grandpa when they were alive, but still. 'Have I made a huge mistake?'

'I don't know. Does it feel like a huge mistake?'

'I don't know.' I stare at Vivienne. 'I have to get a car, so, on balance, yes, I think it might be.'

Clara looks up from laying the table. 'Why not take ours? It's not like we use it much. It spends most of its time getting in the way parked behind the shop.'

'It's true, we hardly use it thanks to the bloody congestion charge. And parking is always a nightmare, so it's easier and cheaper to take public transport.'

'But I haven't driven in years,' I remind them. 'I'm not even sure I remember how. And considering my aunt lives halfway up a mountain, it could take a battering.'

Vivienne flaps her hand. 'It's ancient and I was thinking of selling it to one of those buy-any-car websites, anyway. So what do you know about your aunt?'

'Not much, except Mum always said I'm a lot like her. Though, now I think about it, she only said that when I did something bad.'

'Sounds promising.' Vivienne grins. 'Might she know something about your dad?'

'It's pretty unlikely. Mum had me after Aunt Gillian left the family.' I sip my wine. 'But it might be interesting to find out more about her. How far is Wales?'

'A couple of hours along the M4.'

I scowl. 'Motorways,' I mutter darkly.

Vivienne nudges me playfully. 'Wuss! Try the car in the morning, and if you're interested, we'll add you to the insurance.'

'Thanks.'

Vivienne sighs contentedly. 'Fate takes a hand, and you

have to admit, a quiet rural retreat in the beautiful Welsh hills sounds like heaven.'

I shake my head. 'From what Mum says, it's more like a hovel in the depths of depravity.'

Clara raises her glass. 'Well, cheers to that, then. And Fate, too!'

We chink glasses and I wonder what the hell I've let myself in for.

Early the next morning, and suffering from a fairly decent hangover, Vivienne and I stand in front of their little red Clio. The car is quite old, but it looks friendly. I even like the colour, which for someone who wears a lot of brown, blue and black, isn't the most obvious choice. I try to squeeze around it to get a better look, but it's difficult with the trailing brambles and the boarded gate almost touching its rear. Vivienne unlatches the gate and pushes it open. She reverses the car out and leaves it flinching between the toothy, wide-mouthed grilles of a Mercedes and a BMW.

I stroke its front wing. At least it would be somewhere to sleep if I don't get on with Aunt Gillian. In fact, I could happily curl up in the back right—

Vivienne elbows me. 'Take it for a test drive.' She tosses me the keys and luckily I catch them, but then I remember I haven't driven in ten years, and my heart starts to pound. Vivienne gives me a shooing gesture.

I get in, adjust the seat position, the mirrors and glance over all the buttons and levers, and turn the key. The engine roars loudly, or maybe that's just the hangover. I clonk the gear stick into first, struggle to balance the clutch with the accelerator, put on the indicator, lurch out of the space and kangaroo off around the block. It takes a good few minutes and a lot of hesitation at every junction, but I come back doing a creditable impression of someone who drives, and find Vivienne sending away an Audi A1 who wants to park in the gateway.

Vivienne winks at me as I pull in. 'Looking good.'

'Are you sure you don't mind me borrowing it?'

'Not at all. In fact, look at this space! We might even put a table and chairs out here.'

I hug her. 'Thanks.'

'You're welcome. Let's go and sort out the insurance. Then I must take over from Clara, and you must go home and pack, especially if you want to get away before tomorrow night,' she says, referring obliquely to Valentine's Day. 'And take your drawing stuff,' she adds. 'Inspiration might strike once you're there.'

'I hope you're right.' After all, I haven't been able to draw in a long time.

'Always,' she says, giving me a reassuring grin, and I follow her into the shop.

5

Bared Teeth

There's nothing more motivating than the idea of being stuck with a loved-up couple on Valentine's. When Lindi confirmed last night she and her boyfriend would be spending it in the flat, after my initial reaction of a scream emoji, I got moving. I called Mum for the name of the hospital, Gillian's postcode and dire warnings, and called Vivienne to let her know I'd collect the car. This morning, I packed, though I couldn't quite bring myself to pack my drawing stuff, collected the Clio and in the end I left the flat, to both Lindi's and my relief, just after lunch. It felt like a grand escape, but I've been sitting in the slow lane for almost three hours now, and after a few early hair-raising forays into the middle lane, it's been tedious more than anything.

I pass under a *Welcome to Wales* sign and onto the giant bridge over the estuary. A few fat raindrops spatter across the windscreen. I try various levers, accidentally indicate, and turn on the wipers just as a deluge hits the car so violently, they strain under the weight of water. Catching only glimpses of the lorry in front between wiper-beats, I slow down. Another squall billows through and the lorry brakes, turning my entire windscreen red. For a split second I think I'm going to be concertinaed flat by the lorry behind, and . . .

Nothing.

I kick-start my breathing and move off with the lorry in front.

Jesus – Welcome to Wales! Avoiding Valentine's Day had better be worth this.

'Take the next exit,' commands my phone's satnav app. I take it, and pull over into the next lay-by. For a full twenty seconds I rest my head on the steering wheel, then take out a limp sandwich and check my phone. Vivienne's sent a gif of some sheep. If only that was all I had to contend with! I send one back of billowing rain.

'I won't see them coming. Baaa . . . aaargh!' I type.

Vivienne replies with a running person followed by three sheep.

I smile down at my phone, but as the car's steaming up, I crack open a window and set off at a more sedate speed.

It's dark and drizzling as I pull into the utilitarian hospital car park, and it's packed. I tail someone walking back to their car and sit eyeballing anyone who dares even glance at the space. With a grateful wave, I pull in, grab my purse and head into the bleak concrete hospital building.

Several people try to direct me through the maze, until a nurse finally takes pity and shows me the ward, and with a distrustful glower, the ward matron points at a bed with her pen. I approach quietly as the woman lying in it is asleep. She's more robust than I expected. I was expecting someone more like my mum – built like an ostrich, with a scrawny neck and broad in the beam. And, to be fair, the parallel doesn't end there as Mum has a piercing look, a lot of mascara and a peck as hard as a rap on the knuckles with a spoon. This woman, however, looks shorter, has iron-grey hair tied in a bun and no make-up.

I glance at the nurses' station, but the matron's busy castigating a nurse.

I suppose this woman's injuries are consistent with a fall. There's yellowish bruising around her cheekbone and her wrist is strapped up, but her leg isn't slung from the ceiling as I was expecting. The chart on the end of her bed is typically indecipherable, but that's definitely a G—

'I'm not on bloody show!' I jump about a foot in the air, and her eyes bore into mine. 'Go on! Sod off and find your own damned relation!'

Yes, that's her, although I'm almost tempted to do as she says and see if anyone else *would* like a visitor. I smile awkwardly at the other patients.

'But I'm Ella,' I say, returning my attention to Aunt Gillian.

There's no snatched inhale of recognition.

'Or Eleanor?' I offer. 'Marion's daughter?'

Her eyebrows shoot up. 'She said you might come. Not that I believed her, the way she said it. She said you'd come to your senses and cry off – and she said it would serve me right.' Her eyes narrow, like I should explain myself for keeping my word.

'I was only unsure because I didn't have a car. I borrowed one this morning.'

'Oh! Well, then, what are you waiting for? Let's get me out of here!' She sits up and surveys the ward, ready to make a break for it.

'Isn't there some kind of procedure? I'm guessing it's not as simple as tipping someone out of their wheelchair, strapping you in, and racing for the door. Don't we at least have to tell someone?'

She snorts out a laugh, but as she deflates back into her pillows, the dark circles under her eyes make her look vulnerable. 'Probably. But see what you can do,' she says, rallying.

'I want to get out of here. I'm sick of being prodded and poked, and Gwenda here is a bloody malingerer.'

Gillian gestures to the old lady dressed in a pale-blue bed jacket to her right, who's been eyeing me suspiciously since I arrived. I attempt a smile, but neither Gwenda nor her female visitor smile back. 'Twenty visitors a day,' whispers Gillian. 'Not a moment's peace.'

'Jealous,' mouths Gwenda, with a self-satisfied snake's smile on her lips. 'My daughter comes in every day.' Gwenda's daughter, her hair scraped back into a tight, greasy ponytail, nods. 'And my friends all come, but no one ever visits *her*. Makes you think, doesn't it?'

I want to pull the curtain closed between us, but I settle for a hard stare.

'And Janet snores,' continues Gillian, pointing to a tiny woman blinking owlishly at us through enormous glasses from across the way. 'Not that it's her fault, but you can't get a decent night's sleep if *she* is.'

'I do snore,' agrees Janet with a girlish giggle. 'My Arthur always said I did. Enough to wake the dead, he said, but sadly that wasn't true.' She shakes her head mournfully.

I smile weakly, and turn back to Gillian.

'She's all right, but every conversation circles back to Arthur,' Gillian murmurs. 'It gets bloody wearing after a while.'

Janet nods, clearly aware of her shortcomings. 'He was my life,' she explains.

'I don't know why she bothers with you,' cuts in Gwenda, determined to gatecrash our conversation. 'No one likes Gillian: nurses can't stand her, and Matron *hates* her.' Her daughter nods and Gwenda gives me a simpering smile, which I wouldn't be surprised to see a forked tongue escape from.

Gillian's eyes meet mine, her mouth twisting. 'Matron and I had a disagreement,' she confesses reluctantly. 'But why say something *may be* a little uncomfortable when you're about to scream out like a stuck pig? And why can't they use my name? And if that matron tells me once more not to raise my voice and "bother the other patients" when I'm desperate for the loo, I'll give her something to bother about!' Gillian folds her arms, leaving her injured wrist carefully on top. 'At least, I would if I didn't know she would just order some other poor sod to clean it up!'

There's a sea of tutting from around us.

'Hospitals are very short on funds and staff,' I begin, but tail off as Gillian cocks an eyebrow.

'I do *realise* that! Two seconds of watching the news and any imbecile knows that, but I don't see why that means I have to be patronised! I'm not simple, I'm not anyone's "dear", I'm just old.' Her look of irritation sweeps the entire ward. 'And I want to go home.'

'That would be best for everyone,' agrees Gwenda.

'I didn't ask you,' snaps Gillian. 'In fact, I'd go so far as to say I value the air most without your opinion in it!'

Gillian's tone is so sharp the ward sister's head snaps up. She stalks over and treats Gillian to a look of pure loathing. 'I've told you before – this is a hospital, not a rugby match. Keep your voice down,' and seeing Gwenda's water jug is empty, she indicates to a nurse that it should be refilled.

Gwenda smiles unctuously at her. 'Oh Matron, you are kind, but Delyth will do that.'

Matron smiles, saving a parting scowl for Gillian, and Gwenda's daughter gets up and resignedly picks up the water jug.

'And do my teeth,' gripes Gwenda. 'But do them properly with a tablet this time.' There's a sickening un-sucking noise, and Gwenda lands them in her daughter's palm. She smiles thinly at me. 'Gillian's shown my Delyth how good she's got it. Didn't know, did you, that anyone could be so foul?'

Delyth walks off without comment, and I turn back to Gillian, no longer surprised she called Mum to get out of here. In fact, I give her full credit for not having committed neighbourcide.

'What do I need to do?' I ask, blocking Gwenda from view.

'You need to assure them I won't be on my own and that everything social services recommended is fitted at home. Say it is even if it isn't,' she whispers firmly. 'Then agree to everything they tell you, sign the form and get them to damned well discharge me! Go on,' she orders, gesturing for me to hurry.

Fortunately, Matron seems just as keen as Gillian, and calls around to arrange everything. I sit on a plastic chair, just within her scowling distance, while opposite me, Gwenda's daughter scrubs her mother's teeth in the patient kitchen. She's using dirty washing-up water, and both hers and the false teeth are gritted. It seems Nemesis is alive and well and living in Wales, but I'm glad Matron comes back before she notices me.

I'm led to a doctor and then a physiotherapist. I'm given instructions on what medications Gillian has to take and when, what exercises she will need to do, what she shouldn't do, side effects, risks, appointments, walking aids, when Gillian can drive, pain management, how Gillian should and shouldn't twist and danger signs to look out for. I agree to everything and say everything is in place, even though I haven't the faintest idea whether there is a downstairs bedroom or not, and come out with enough leaflets to start a small fire. I stand in the corridor with my head spinning, and a young nurse with a nervous smile beckons to me.

'You're here for Gillian?' Her soft Welsh accent bounces over Gillian's name. I nod, and she lays a hand on my arm. 'Look after her. That Gwenda's been getting inside her head.

Nasty, she is, muttering away into the small hours. I heard her tell Gillian no one cared for her. Cruel, she was, and what with Gillian having so few visitors . . .'

'Not many people have come, then?'

She shakes her head. 'No, it's a shame.'

'But you like her?' I ask, surprised.

She looks up and down the corridor and lowers her voice. 'She stood up for me with Matron, when . . . well, when one of the patients wet the bed. They complained I didn't get them the bedpan on time, but it wasn't true. She didn't even call!' I'm willing to bet anything it was Gwenda. 'But Gillian's nice. She tells the truth, and I thought you should know.'

She glances up and down the hall again and scurries off without a backwards glance.

I stumble back to Gillian's bedside feeling like I've been through the spin cycle on a washing machine.

'Done?' asks Gillian, her eyes alert.

I nod. 'As far as we can be. Hospital transport will bring you home tomorrow.'

Gillian's face falls. 'Not tonight?'

I shrug helplessly. 'They said, what with your leg, you should be transported in an ambulance. And perhaps it would be a good idea if I made sure everything's ready?'

A look of concern, or perhaps anxiety, flits across her face. 'Yes. Can't be helped, I suppose. And if I'm leaving tomorrow, that's something. Oh *Lord*!' she mutters as Matron strides over.

Matron points at the clock like a Victorian school mistress. 'Visiting time's over.'

Gillian leans over to her bedside cabinet, while on the next bed, Delyth obediently kisses her mother's cheek. For a second Delyth's eyes meet mine, and I feel a chill.

Gillian lands her bag on the bed, rummages inside and

thrusts some keys into my hand. 'I'll see you tomorrow,' she says, like it's a pact. I nod, and as Matron hurries me out of the ward, Gillian calls, 'Look after the cat!'

I give her a confirmatory nod over my shoulder, but it's only as I emerge into the badly lit hospital car park, still clutching the leaflets and Gillian's keys, that I realise we haven't discussed anything about my being here. We haven't agreed how long she needs me or how long I'm going to stay.

I type Gillian's postcode into my satnav app. Forty-five minutes. As if today weren't long enough already, I'm not going to get there before nine. I start the engine, and as I pull out of the half-empty car park, the rain pelts down again.

I just hope the windscreen wipers hold out.

6

Ditched

The drive to Gillian's could start any self-respecting horror movie: it's dark, the wind's hurling the rain about, the empty, saturated villages are even more eerie than the empty roads and my phone's satnav's been quiet so long, I'm starting to wonder if it's nodded off. I peer through the windscreen at yet another dreary village, and almost pass clean through the roof as the satnav demands I take a side road. I take it, and as it climbs past some terraces and the village peters out, I'm reminded of all the tales where people end up in rivers, or drive off cliffs, just because their satnavs told them to.

The road continues to climb. Thankfully, there are one or two lights in the distance, but even they disappear as the road dips to skirt a river. Trees crowd the road, and just as I slow to tackle a narrow hump-backed bridge set almost at right angles to the road, lights swing sharply across from the other side, a horn blares, I'm blinded by their full-beam and *thunk!* My car falls off the edge of the road, stalls, and I'm left with the sound of the other car accelerating away.

Bastard! I mean, what are the chances? Not a car for miles, but just as the road hits its narrowest point . . .

I take a deep breath and wait for the bright circles in my vision to clear. I turn the key and mercifully the engine starts, but as I try to drive out, there's ten feet of progress, a grating noise, and I'm left revving, going nowhere. I put the car into reverse, but it's too late – I'm beached, and now I'm blocking the bridge, too, and to top it all my phone has no signal. Not that I have breakdown cover, but the satnav might have proved useful – I could have walked to Aunt Gillian's. As it is, I don't even know which direction it's in, and it's not like I can try Gillian's key in every random front door until one magically opens.

I turn on the hazard lights and rub my eyes.

What are my options? It's a quarter to nine, it's dark, it's raining and I'm stuck in a hole, both literally and metaphorically. I suppose I could try pushing the car out, but it's raining so hard it's practically hailing. I could go for help or at least try to find a phone signal. Or, I could stay here and hope help comes to me? In survival programmes they always say stay with the vehicle, but I think that's more for deserts and the Australian outback than Welsh hillsides.

I take out a biscuit and munch on it.

Stay or Go? Since Fate's the one who's landed me here, I suppose I could ask her? I take a two-pence piece out of my purse, and turn it over like I always do to check the sides are different. 'Heads – I go out to find a house or a phone signal. Tails – I stay here.' I say it out loud just in case Fate's hanging about, and then I flip it.

Tails. Very damsel in distress. But as the rain puts on an extra burst of energy and clatters across the car, I nod. 'Good call.'

I drop my head back against the headrest and let my eyes close.

There's some distant beeping, and after a moment or two someone hammers on my window. I prise my eyelids open, swallow with difficulty and open the window a crack. Rain spits at me through the small gap.

'What the bloody hell are you doing stopped here?' demands an angry man. From his accent, he's English, but thanks to his wax jacket's rural-grim-reaper hood, and the fact he's highlighted from behind by his headlights, I can't make out much else.

I roll the window down a little further, and find myself spattered with both rain and gruff swearing.

'I'm stuck. A car ran me off the road.'

'And you thought you'd just sit here?' he asks, his voice rising a complete octave.

'Well, I can't move. So, yes, until the rain stops.'

'You *do* know we're in Wales, right? This could last for days!'

'Then I'll be here a while!'

It's just possible he's smiling, but it's difficult to tell under the hood. 'But you're blocking the road, and I'm in a hurry.' Not smiling, then. 'You can't just sit here!'

I look around dramatically. 'What else do you suggest I do? Levitate the car, conjure a genie, or perhaps turn into the Hulk and push?' The dark space inside the hood fixes on me. Perhaps sarcasm wasn't the best idea. I take a calming breath. 'Look, I'm sorry. I know it isn't ideal, but this wasn't exactly my grand plan for the evening, either.'

He looks back at his car, his face and stubble briefly illuminated. He sighs, but seems to take my point. 'Where were you heading?'

'Achub yr Angel,' I say, no doubt massacring the pronunciation.

His head tilts. 'Obviously – it's the only place up here. I meant, who are you going to see?'

I open my mouth and hesitate. 'I'm not sure I should tell a stranger that. Not on a lonely road, in the middle of the night. You might do anything!'

'Like what? Help?'

I glare at him. 'Like do the opposite of help,' I say carefully. I don't want to give him ideas.

His hood tilts. 'Seriously? On a good day this place has a population of about twenty. It couldn't support a milkman, let alone a serial killer.'

I stare at him, not budging.

He sighs again. 'I just thought, since you're stuck here and I'm not getting past you, I might do the *neighbourly* thing and drop you off!'

'Then why are you snarling at me?'

'Because you're very irritating!'

Cheek! 'Thanks. So are you!'

Our disgruntled silence holds for a few seconds, and he laughs. I try to glare, but a smile sneaks through.

'So . . .?' he asks in a softer tone. 'On the promise that I'm not about to re-enact some grizzly scene from whatever horror film you've seen, would you like a lift?'

I weigh up my options. They don't amount to much. Also, it's not like he can make a getaway with my car blocking the road. 'OK then. Yes, please,' I add, finding my manners.

'So who are you going to visit?'

'My aunt.'

'And she is . . .?' he asks with exaggerated patience.

'Gillian Tate.'

His hood jerks. 'Gillian is your aunt?'

'Yes.'

'Then you're out of luck – she isn't here.'

'I know. That's why I've come.'

His hood tilts irritably. 'How about you run that past me again using different words. More of them, preferably.' Next he'll be telling me to use my indoor voice.

'I mean, I'm going to her house. I know she isn't there, and if you're offering me a lift – that's where I'd like to go.'

'Without her being there?' he checks. The disapproval

given off by his dark hood is oppressive, but it doesn't change the facts.

'Yes.'

'You're going to sit on her doorstep?'

His tone is just this side of exasperation, but I'm not about to tell him I have keys. 'If I am, is that a problem?'

'If I'm aiding and abetting a dodgy character by taking her to an empty house and leaving her there? It could be.'

'But I thought you were offering?'

'Yes, because I can't just leave you *here*.'

We stare at each other, locked in some weird kind of stalemate. He cracks first and looks up and down the road, probably willing someone to come and take me off his hands, but Fate doesn't seem inclined to help him.

He stares at me for a long second, inhales deeply, straightens up and holds his hand out, twirling it obsequiously. 'Excuse me, miss. If I may politely enquire, why are you going to Gillian's when she isn't there, and, perchance, are you a burglar?'

'Why, sir, not that it's any of your business, but no, I'm not a burglar. I'm here to look after her when she comes out of hospital, so you see I wasn't *expecting* to find her at home as that would defeat the purpose of my visit.'

'Well, hallelujah! Some sense at last,' he cries, saluting the sky.

'Glad you're happy. Now, are you going to help me, or should I wind up the window? Because I'm getting wet.'

'*You're* getting wet?' He looks down at himself exaggeratedly.

'Yes.' I bite back a laugh.

'You really are the most exasperating—' He looks away and takes a deep breath. 'Since you asked so nicely, get what you need and put it in the back of my car.'

'Hallelujah,' I say drily, and pick up my purse.

It takes us two waterlogged minutes to pile my things into the back of his estate car, and as he sets up our warning triangles, one on either side of the bridge, I climb into his front passenger seat. There's a scrabbling sound from behind me and a little white dog pops its head through from the back seats. I hold out my hand for it to sniff and it nuzzles my fingers, pushing under them so I stroke its head. I think it's a Bichon Frise, which is not at all the type of dog I'd expect my gruff rescuer to have – he seems more of an Irish Wolfhound or German Shepherd kind of person.

He gets in, throws back his hood to reveal a stubbly chin and dark disarrayed hair, to which the red dashboard lights lend a dash of B-movie horror, and points at the little fluff-ball of a dog. 'Aren't you worried she'll have your hand off?'

She pants happily at me.

'Be serious. She's more likely to trip me up wanting a belly-rub.'

'I just wondered if distrust was a part of your nature.'

'You really think it's odd for a single woman not to trust a stranger on a lonely road at night?'

He gives me a hint of a smile. 'Perhaps not, but this isn't exactly the murder capital of Wales.'

'I know, but "Stranger Danger" and all that,' I quote.

He switches on the engine and reverses over the bridge. He pulls back deftly into a field gateway and puts on the handbrake. 'If by stranger you mean we haven't been introduced yet: I'm Joe.' He holds out his hand. 'That is, presuming introductions aren't an intimacy too far?'

'No, I'm sure they're fine,' I say, holding out my own hand. 'Now that I've seen your dog.'

He shakes my hand, but raises an eyebrow. 'Should I have held her up at your window?'

'The conversation would certainly have gone differently.'

'Like, for example, "Why are you holding that poor dog at my window?"'

'Perhaps,' I concede, laughing. 'She is suspiciously sweet.'

'But savage if you confront her with a hairbrush.'

The poor thing *is* styled to within an inch of her life. 'Why do you brush her, then?'

'*I* don't,' Joe says, so I'm guessing there's a woman in his life.

'Well, I'm Eleanor . . . Ella,' I amend, not sure how Aunt Gillian might have referred to me . . . or if she ever has.

'Nice to meet you, Ella.'

'I'm afraid I can't give you directions.'

'No need, I know the way.' He gives me a sideways glance and we set off. 'You haven't been to your aunt's house before, then?'

'No, never. In fact, I only met Gillian today.' I picture her, fed up and abrasive in her hospital bed.

'And you've just driven up from . . .?'

'London.'

Joe looks confused. 'But, if you live so far away and she doesn't even know you, why are you here?'

'She called my mum asking for help, and I was at a loose end.'

A pub we're passing illuminates the road, the car and Joe's sudden frown. He glances at me suspiciously and I shift my gaze to the pub's hanging baskets swinging wetly in the rain. The pub's called Achub yr Angel.

'We weren't that far from the village, then?' I say, hoping to bring back the easy banter, but instead of smiling, his lips tighten.

'It's hardly a village. Don't expect any shops or anything.'

'I wasn't "expecting" anything,' I protest, a little stung at his change of manner.

'Still, in my experience, you city girls in your high heels –'

I glance down at my sodden flats – 'with your online shopping and Uber apps can find this place a little . . . challenging.'

'I'm sure I'll manage,' I say stiffly. But as we turn up a track and leave the welcoming lights of the pub behind, his doubtful look leaves me feeling nervous.

We splash in and out of potholes – the little dog presumably bouncing around the back seat like a pinball – and just as I fear we're heading for a disused quarry, we pass a modern bungalow with a solitary lit window and a five-bar gate barring admittance. The curtain flashes briefly aside, only to fall back again, proving to me just how unusual it is for someone to come up here. We don't stop, but carry on up the track, and worryingly, there isn't a single light ahead. I peer into the darkness, but the headlights only reach the drystone walls hemming us in. After only a few hundred yards, though, we pull into a yard and are industrially illuminated by floodlights worthy of a prison yard.

'Bloody hell! They're new,' mutters Joe, shielding his eyes.

He pulls up against a long, blindingly whitewashed outbuilding, and after some blinking, I get out and look up at the main house. It's a grotty, dark and four-square farmhouse. Net curtains hang limply in the windows, and the front garden's straggly and overgrown. If asked, I'd swear the place was abandoned.

The little dog gives out a high-pitched yap, adding to the desolation, particularly as the only sign of life is an old Land Rover parked against the yard wall.

'Well, this is it,' says Joe, getting out. He throws open the boot.

'Are you sure?' I manage to keep the tremor out of my voice, but Joe nods, and I feel my stomach sink.

He passes me my tote bag and I get out Gillian's keys. Sure enough, they fit the lock, but the front door doesn't open far. I give it a shove, but like my car, it seems to make the situation worse, so I reach an arm in, feel the wall and flick on a light. I then crouch down and reach around behind the door and feel a surprising build-up of post. I pull it away, handfuls at a time, and finally push the door open the rest of the way.

The stone-flagged hallway offers little in the way of home comforts; only coat hooks hung with limp waterproofs, a row of wellies and shoes, three doors and some narrow stairs worthy of a miserable nineteenth-century drama. My nose wrinkles at the smell of damp, but now I'm here, I have to go in. I dump my bag in the hall and open the solitary door to the left, turn on the light, and— my mouth falls open.

The room's a sea of ghastliness. The smell alone could knock someone out, and there's junk everywhere: dirty crockery strewn across every surface, newspapers, letters and jars crowding out an over-laden table, and although I can make out a sink, fridge and cooker, which tell me that this is a large kitchen-cum . . . hellhole, it more closely resembles a set from *Steptoe and Son*. There's even a couple of armchairs, near-camouflaged under piles of paperwork and books, set ready for a couple of old geezers to sit griping at each other, with a pine dresser and possibly a coffee table beneath a tide of debris and—

I freeze as something shifts on the kitchen table. Turning slowly, I'm caught in a pair of unnerving, unblinking green eyes and . . .

Oh, thank God – it's just a cat. Admittedly it's no fluffy Tiddles – more of a brazen, black, muscular witch's familiar of a thing, but at least it's not a rat. I yank my eyes away before it hypnotises me, but unfortunately the rest of the room doesn't bear looking at. It's clear no one has cleaned, washed or put the bins out in a very long time.

I turn tail, and returning outside, I take a few deep breaths. Joe gives me a funny look. He hands me a carrier bag, takes out my holdall and slams the boot before following me in. He gives the hall a cursory glance, lowers my holdall onto the stone flags, strides into the kitchen and . . . stops.

He closes his eyes for a second before he looks at me, and I can tell from his expression that I was right: this is far from OK. Neither of us says a word, probably because there isn't much to say beyond swearing, but weirdly, it's a relief to know this isn't what he expected either, though what it says about Aunt Gillian, I'm not sure.

Joe turns, his mouth a hard line, and strides back outside. I scuttle after him, wanting to say something, anything, but there are no words. At his car he looks at me, opens his mouth and closes it again, before he gets in and slams the door.

Shit. I resign myself to a pitiable wave from the doorstep, but as I step out, I kick a saucer I hadn't noticed by the front step. The cat!

I flap my arms, and summon a pleasant expression as Joe winds down his window.

'Do you know the cat's name?'

'Boswell,' he says quietly. 'Bozz for short.'

'Bozz,' I repeat, committing it to memory.

'Good luck,' he adds, staring into my eyes with deep concern, but I'm determined not to be wimpy about this.

'Thanks. And thanks for the lift.' I try to say it lightly.

He nods and pulls away. The little dog peers forlornly at me through the rear window. Feeling the same, I give her a little wave, and to my surprise, Joe raises a hand out of his open window and waves back.

7

Unfamiliar Familiar

Back in the kitchen, Mum's harsh words no longer seem so far off the mark. Especially as some bluebottles have woken up and are cruising the room like World War II bombers.

I walk through the mess, cataloguing what needs to be done, and bleugh! Just to crown this *Hammer House of Horror*, there are some mouse entrails on the floor in front of the fridge.

Bozz looks over the edge of the table at them and back at me.

'Are those yours?' I ask, pointing at them.

Bozz gives such a pathetic, high-pitched peep of a meow, I can't help smiling.

'I guess I wouldn't blame you for going feral, but the gory entrails don't help, you know.' We maintain eye contact, but he'd win if this were to become a staring contest. 'You think about that!'

I leave him in possession of the kitchen and check the rest of the ground floor.

Across the hall, there's a small living room with a dusty sofa and armchair, a Victorian fireplace with art deco tiles up the sides and an empty grate. There's also a dusty but empty occasional table, which tells me Aunt Gillian spends very little time in here.

The other downstairs room is the bathroom. There's a cast-iron bath, a pedestal basin in a squared-off art deco style and a toilet. It's OK, but could do with a deep clean. I tear off a few sheets of toilet roll and, like a revolted dog walker, go back to the kitchen and pick up the mess. I stumble back to the toilet, retching all the way, and hastily flush it away. But after two minutes waiting for the hot tap to warm up, I give in and scrub my hands on the withered bar of soap under the cold water. I forgo the greying towel, and while drying my hands on my trousers give myself a long hard look in the age-spotted mirror.

It's time to face facts: Mum and Joe were right. I had *no* clue what I was letting myself in for, because, even though I wasn't expecting mod cons exactly, I *was* expecting liquid soap, warm water and clean floors. But then, Joe didn't seem to be expecting this, either.

I splash some cold water on my face and, just too late, remember the grey towel. I stumble into the hall, dig through my things and pull out my fluffy blue one. I breathe in the 'summer fresh' fabric softener, and giving my towel one last sniff, drop it back in my bag.

OK. So, where to start? The smell. That's the biggest assault on the senses, and heading back into the kitchen, I open the flip-top bin in the corner and the smell almost knocks me off my feet.

'You have got to be kidding me!' I raise my eyebrows at Bozz, but he doesn't comment. I hastily tie the bin bag and, seeing a doorway through to a recess beneath what must be the stairs, find the back door complete with key in the lock and dump the bag in the wheelie bin outside.

I come back in, and my phone buzzes in my pocket. Surprised it has a signal, I take it out and stifle a groan as I press the call accept button.

'Hi, Mum.'

'So you're there?'

'Yes, I am.'

'Wouldn't it have been nice to let me know you'd arrived safely?'

Nice isn't the first word that springs to mind. 'Actually, I've only just arrived, and since Vivienne's car's stuck in a ditch outside the village, I haven't really.'

'"Haven't really" what?'

'Arrived safely.'

Her silence suggests I'm being awkward. 'Hmm. Did you see Gillian?'

'Yes, I dropped in at the hospital on my way here.'

'And how was she?'

Scary, rude and fed up mostly. 'Glad to be coming home.'

'And the house? How bad is it?'

I slump against the kitchen counter and stare at the damp patch on the floor. 'Pretty bad.'

Mum's derisive snort blasts down the phone. 'Well, I did warn you. Gillian never was one for housework. Said it wasn't the key to a happy life – but there's nothing happy about botulism or salmonella.'

She has a point, but there's also no sign of Gillian being happy, either. In fact, it's as if the place has been stripped of all homely comforts. 'When did Mike die?'

'What? Oh, I'm not sure – eighteen months ago, I think?'

A fly settles on a mug. 'I think she's been struggling.'

'Well, wash everything, even if you think it's clean. She won't object to *you* cleaning. It was always just laziness, you know. Right, I must go.'

'Well, thanks for phoning.'

'I thought I should,' Mum says pointedly, and hangs up.

Bozz picks his way across the table to stand on the nearest edge, and stretches his mouth wide in a passable impression of Munch's *The Scream*.

'Exactly,' I agree, but taking his actual point, I pick up an open cat food tin . . . and almost drop it. It's writhing, and is probably the source of the bluebottles. Giving up the spoon for dead, I rush out and dump the whole lot in the wheelie bin.

'Fresh one?' I ask glibly on my damp return, and Bozz brushes his side along my arm. Armed with a clean saucer and a new tin, I pull the ring-pull and spoon out some cat food, while Bozz purrs like a band-saw. It's a surprisingly comforting sound, and I stroke his back as he tucks in. It rises up under my hand, but his face doesn't shift from his dish.

I take out my phone to text Vivienne, and pause. I'll tell her about the car tomorrow when I know more.

'Arrived in Hell. Seems to be raining! X'

As I clear the sink, my phone pulses.

'Ask Fate for an umbrella. Wine and sofa here if needed. V xxx.'

Thank heaven for Vivienne. I put the kettle on to boil and start on the washing-up.

I've never been a big fan of housework, but there's something cathartic about stacking a draining board with clean mugs and clearing enough space to make tea. It would be even better if I actually had some milk.

I've just finished my first stint and pulled the plug on the sink, when there's a knock at the front door.

Bozz and I look at each other, and I check my phone. It's well after ten. I suppose it could be a nosy neighbour noticing the lights, but it could also be that under-utilised serial killer Joe was talking about. I tiptoe to the front door and open it a crack. A tall, hooded figure with rain bouncing off its hood reaches out to push the door open. I open my mouth to scream, and—

—realise it's Joe.

'Oh! It's you!' I swallow my heart back into my chest and stand aside so he can stride in out of the pelting rain. I quickly close the door. 'Did I leave something in your car?'

'No,' he says, bending down to let the little dog out of his coat. She trots into the kitchen. There's a hiss and a yowl, but she doesn't shoot back out again, so I'm guessing she's all right . . . unless Bozz has her pinned under a weighty paw.

I summon a smile. 'Then to what do I owe the pleasure?'

'Pizza,' he says, holding out a carrier bag. 'And wine,' he adds, pulling a bottle from a surprisingly deep pocket.

'Great!' I stand back as he shrugs off his waxed jacket, and follow him into the kitchen. 'I've cleared up a little,' I point out. Although, coming from the hall, it's obvious the smell hasn't quite cleared. Bozz glares from the kitchen table and the little dog stands happily on a pile of papers like she's won them. She circles three times and settles down.

Joe grunts noncommittally. 'It must be tricky to know where to start.'

'Actually, it wasn't. I nearly stepped in some mouse entrails, so I started there, and the bin almost knocked me out, so I chucked that outside, together with the maggots in the cat food. I fed the cat and started on the washing-up.' I frown, disappointed he can't tell.

'I stand corrected,' he says, smiling. 'The place is transformed! Let's get the oven on.'

'Do we need to?' I have the oddest feeling animals might be nesting in there.

Joe raises an eyebrow. 'Unless you want to gnaw on a frozen pizza.'

'Oh. It's not delivery?' Even as I say it, I wish I hadn't.

He smiles. 'There's no speedy pizzas up here.'

'Are you sure? I was once told that if you're trapped on a mountain, it's best to call pizza delivery, because they'll get there quicker than the mountain rescue . . . and bring pizza.'

Joe laughs. 'I'm guessing someone in London told you that?'

He crouches down in his old jeans, well-used walking boots, thick plaid shirt and dark hair that's been mussed up by his hood, to light the gas oven. He looks rugged and capable, whereas I feel useless and insubstantial next to him, which is probably the exact impression he's got from my trousers, flats and pretty top, make-up and manicure.

'Baking tray?' he asks, having succeeded with the oven. He unwraps the pizzas.

'Don't they go directly on the oven shelf?' I ask.

'Probably, but looking at the place . . .'

He doesn't need to say more. I choose a low cupboard and start searching. In the third cupboard I find pans and trays. I rinse two and hand them to him so he can slide the pizzas into the oven.

'How come you came back? Not that I'm not grateful – I really am!'

'No, well, I thought I'd better make sure you didn't starve. Especially as you don't have transport.' He half smiles, and the way his eyebrows arch make my fingers itch for a sketch-book and pencil. The impulse surprises me, and I push it away. 'But also I felt bad for leaving so abruptly.'

'I sort of figured the place wasn't what you were expecting?' I guess.

He nods and glances about anxiously. 'The last time I saw it, it was covered in throws and full of art, with the smell of cooking, tea, oil paints and linseed oil permeating through everything.'

It's like he's describing a different house.

'Well, thanks for coming back, and especially for bringing food. There doesn't seem to be a lot in the cupboards. At least, not that's in date.' I pick up a mug I missed. 'Although there might be something in the freezer.'

'Possibly, if you're partial to a bit of blue tit, squirrel or fox.'

I stare at him. 'I was thinking more of chicken nuggets or fish fingers . . .'

'Not unless they died on the road.' His head tips thoughtfully. 'But there might be a pheasant in there.'

'Oh God! Gillian isn't one of those people who lives off road kill, is she?' I saw a programme once, about a man who travelled around with a shovel and a plastic bag in his boot, but thankfully, Joe's laughing.

'No! People brought them for Mike to paint. You know, dead voles, kingfishers, finches – things you can't paint easily in the wild – but he didn't always have time, so he froze them. I got the shock of my life when I found a dead badger in there once!'

'But surely Gillian's got rid of them?' Eighteen months is a long time to keep a flock of corpses in your freezer.

Joe's eyes stray around the kitchen. 'You think so?'

I blow out a breath. 'Perhaps not. This place is . . . out of hand.' Understatement of the century. 'I think Gillian needed help long before she fell down those steps.'

Joe looks around with concern. 'Me too, not that she said a word.'

I'm suddenly reminded of the first-aid course I took for work, where the instructor taught us how to triage roadside casualties: 'Ignore the screaming ones, they have the energy to make noise. It's the quiet ones you have to check,' and looking at the state of the place, Gillian's been very quiet indeed.

The oven timer beeps, calling time on our concern.

'Right,' he says, crouching down in front of the oven – not

that it's possible to see anything through the grimy window. 'Plates? Or are you happy to eat off the cardboard?'

'Cardboard – I've had enough of the cupboards.'

Joe looks up. 'Is it the spiders?'

'There are worse things than spiders!'

'Such as?' His eyes crinkle at the corners with lines that would translate beautifully into a sketch. 'Do you reckon Red Rum is hiding in there as well?'

I laugh. 'You may joke, but I dare you to open the fridge after what you said about the freezer. Go on,' I prompt.

He looks at the fridge-freezer, which looms at us like a stable door to hell.

'Perhaps that one's best left for daylight,' he agrees, and I can't help giggling. 'But I'll brave the cupboards if we do it together? We'll need wine glasses, anyway.'

'Are you sure she has any?'

'An artist without wine glasses?' he asks, like I've gone mad.

We soon find plates and glasses, along with some very healthy spiders and their winter store of cocooned woodlice, and while I wash the glasses, Joe piles the things on the table at one end. Bozz stalks about on the space like it's a novelty.

Joe raises an eyebrow. 'Come on, Bozz,' and he lifts Bozz onto the Welsh dresser and grins at me as he gives Bozz a quick stroke. 'Everyone talks to Bozz – he expects it.'

'I know. We chatted earlier,' I agree, but I'm caught by the ease with which Joe handles Bozz. I wouldn't dare be so casual. 'So I'm guessing you know Gillian quite well, then?'

'Pretty well,' he replies. He finds an oven glove and takes the pizzas out of the oven. They smell glorious, and I remember I've only eaten biscuits and a sandwich today. He slices them with a bread knife and hands me some on a plate.

I sigh as I bite into one. 'Thanks.'

'You're very welcome.'

I clear the armchairs with one hand, dumping the slippery-windowed envelopes on top of the overloaded coffee table, and wince as they cascade to the floor.

The little dog's head jerks up, and Joe shakes his head and takes a seat. 'Now you've done it – you've made the place all messy.'

I laugh and collect the wine glasses. Joe rests his plate on his knee and tackles the seal on the wine bottle. He pours some into the glasses I'm holding out, and takes one.

'So this place must be quite a comedown from where you normally live in London?'

'This place would be a comedown from a rundown housing estate,' I point out.

Joe nods sadly. 'Why did you agree to come?'

'For one thing, I didn't know the state the place was in—'

'Would that have stopped you?' he interrupts.

Would it? I picture myself gooseberrying Lindi and her boyfriend, and Gillian's disappointment when I couldn't bring her home with me. 'No, I don't think it would. Although, I might have packed a hazmat suit and wellies if I'd known what lay ahead.'

Joe relaxes, although a small crease remains between his eyebrows. 'So why did you come?'

I shrug. 'I needed a change of scene, time to re-evaluate my life, and this seemed as good a place as any. So what's Gillian like?' I ask, hastily changing the subject.

Joe pouts in thought. 'You've met her. What do you think she's like?'

'I met her in hospital, where she was angry and cursing the world. I'm asking what she's like normally?'

'Exactly like that.' I raise my eyebrows and he bows his head in submission. 'OK, before tonight, I would have said she was proud, strong, straight-speaking, decent and not likely to suffer fools gladly. But now?' He looks at the room. 'Your guess is as good as mine.'

'How close were you?'

His eyes meet mine and stay there. 'Pretty close. I'm Mike's nephew.'

I'm surprised. I guess I thought Mike would be just as cut off from his family as Gillian is, but I suppose there's no reason he should have been. 'And what was Mike like?'

Joe frowns. 'Apart from being a very talented and much sought-after painter, he was amazing, exciting and charismatic. He had this boundless energy and he was full of ideas and plans and always working on something. It shocked everyone when he died.'

Looking at the kitchen, I can see it affected Gillian. 'How old was he?'

'Seventy-four – ten years older than Gillian, not that he seemed it. He had this vitality that made us all think he would go on forever. Even though he was older than Gillian, I think she was often more of a grown-up than he was, but they fitted, somehow. And you could tell they really loved each other. It was there in the way they looked at each other; how they always laughed at the same moments and glanced at each other before anyone else whenever anything funny, odd or surprising happened.' Joe swallows and smiles awkwardly. 'How come Gillian and your family aren't close?'

I shrug. 'Mum always said Aunt Gillian broke Granny and Grandpa's hearts by moving in with Mike . . . but if they'd got on, I doubt that would have been the deal-breaker it was, so who knows? As it is, my mum and Gillian are barely in contact.'

'And yet *you* still came?'

I nod. 'She didn't break *my* heart. But then again, if Gillian's harbouring some festering resentment towards my family, who knows what will happen when she comes out of hospital tomorrow?'

Joe smiles. 'I doubt she'll hold it against you. How was she, by the way?'

'Honestly? Extremely fed up, but I reckon she's finding hospital worse than her actual injuries.' I smile. 'I guess we'll find out more tomorrow . . . if they don't whisk her away as soon as they see the state of this place.'

'Yes, I wouldn't fancy explaining this mess to a health professional.'

'No. I'll scour the place in the morning so that they don't paint a red X on the door.'

'Hmm,' he says, his brow furrowing again.

'So, how come you were on the bridge earlier?' I ask quickly. 'And how come you helped me out?'

'Good Samaritan?'

I chuckle. 'Roaming the mean streets of Achub yr Angel looking for damsels in distress? Be serious.'

He laughs and pours more wine. 'When I saw you in the ditch I had a pretty good idea how you got there.' I raise an eyebrow, and Joe looks suddenly sheepish. 'I knew Petra must have come through there, and it wouldn't surprise me to find she drove you off the road.'

'And who's Petra?' I ask.

'My little sister.' Ah! The brusher of the little dog. 'We had a row. She stormed out, drove off and—' He takes a heavy breath.

'—I'm in a ditch,' I finish, though why I'm smiling, I've no idea. I still have to explain to Vivienne and Clara what I've done to their car. 'And you were following her?' But as I say it, I realise he was nearly half an hour behind her.

'No, I was on my way to see Gillian, actually. We'd just found out about her accident, and I was on my way to the hospital when I found you blocking the road.'

'And that's why you were so abrupt?'

His mouth twists and he glances at the little dog. 'Yes, that and because I'd just spent fifteen minutes trying to coax Pompom out from under the kitchen table.' Joe sits back and looks at me over his glass. 'How come you're at a loose end to look after Gillian?'

I avoid his gaze and take another bite of pizza. 'I lost my job a week ago. I have another one lined up, but it doesn't start for a couple of weeks.'

'Lucky for Gillian. Were you disappointed about your job, or was it by design?'

I smile at his unintended pun. 'Not by design, and it's not ideal as I'm going back to my old job, which feels like a backward step, but beggars can't be choosers.'

'What kind of work is it?'

'I *was* doing graphic design, but I'm returning to a call centre. What do you do?'

'I'm an author, actually.'

I stare at him. I'm not sure what I was expecting, but it wasn't that. 'What kind of thing do you write?'

'Thrillers.'

'Would I have heard of you?'

'I write as Jordan Remus.'

Oh my God! I've never read any, but I've seen them on supermarket shelves. He's watching me carefully, though, so I school my face into blankness. 'So what's it like being an author?' I ask casually.

'Great, mostly. Except . . .' He sighs heavily. 'Have you ever been defined as something to the point you've felt constricted?'

I think for a moment. 'Not really. I've been stuck in a job that didn't give me any satisfaction. Does that count? The one I'm going back to, actually.'

'I guess,' he agrees, nodding. 'You see, everyone says if

I'm onto a winning formula: why rock the boat? And I take their point, but what if I *want* to write something else? What if I *need* to? Because right now, I don't seem to be able to write anything at all.'

'Tricky.'

'Very,' he agrees. 'And it's making me reckless.' He leans forward and lowers his voice. 'I've been considering killing off my main character.' He sits back heavily. 'But . . .' He holds up his hands in defeat.

'You're afraid to close the door on them entirely?'

Joe nods. 'What if I can't write without him?'

'Has he been with you for a long time?'

'Twelve books.'

'Jeez! Well, have you thought to ask him what he wants?'

Joe stares at me, puzzled. 'Who? My main character?' I nod, and his gaze moves to the middle distance. 'No, I haven't.' He sips his wine, and his hand strays to his mouth. What I wouldn't give for a pencil and paper right now. I nudge my plate onto the overloaded coffee table, and Joe smiles. 'Sorry, I get caught up. It drives people mad.'

'Actually, I was thinking I'd like to draw you,' I admit. 'People find *that* disconcerting, too.'

Joe's smile widens. 'Back when I was a child, Mike used to sketch me in the evenings. He'd draw, I'd get on with doing whatever I was doing – jigsaw, whittling or whatever – and Gillian would be sorting through negatives or figuring out how to frame a photograph. It was nice.'

'It sounds it. Did you come here a lot as a child?'

'I used to stay here all the time. I had the little bedroom at the front.'

'And your sister?'

'She came once and *hated* it: made a huge scene, and after that stayed with Dad's relations in London.'

'But you liked it?'

Joe nods. 'I made friends with a kid up the valley and we had tons of freedom. To me, it was heaven.'

'And you still live around here?'

Joe's expression clouds and he gestures vaguely with his hand. 'Mike left me and Petra a cottage across the valley.'

I look at him questioningly. 'Then why did Gillian need me?'

'Because we don't actually live here. I live down in Exeter. In fact, I recently bought a house down there, and Petra's been staying with me since she broke up with her boyfriend. We only came up to look into putting the cottage up for sale.'

'Oh.' I'm not sure what to say.

His eyes meet mine and there's embarrassment in them. 'Petra needs the money, and I'd buy her out, except all my money's now tied up in the new house . . .' He holds his hands out helplessly. 'And being an author isn't as lucrative as you'd think. And since things haven't been great between me and Gillian since Mike died . . . well . . .' He lets his hands fall. 'Anyway, long story short, we arrived this afternoon, found a rat had died of gluttony in the pantry, and we were all set to have done with the place, when a neighbour told us about Gillian's accident, and . . .' Joe looks at me ruefully.

'You changed your mind?' I guess.

He nods. 'I told Petra we should at least make sure Gillian's all right; but Petra decided it was just another excuse to dig my heels in. We had this blazing row, she got in her car, and—'

'—drove off at speed, not stopping for anyone,' I finish for him. Although, by the sounds of it, I'm lucky she didn't stop.

Joe tops up our glasses, emptying the bottle, but as I'm already pleasantly fuzzy, I leave mine on the coffee table.

'She'll calm down,' he says, more to himself, I think. 'But

as you can imagine, I'm glad I'm drinking wine with you, rather than dealing with a dead rat or a livid sister.'

'There are worse places to be,' I agree, watching him stroke Pompom, who's sneaked up onto his knee.

'Such as?' he asks teasingly.

'Stuck in a ditch for one . . . or trapped in my room, while my flatmate and her new boyfriend christen every surface in our flat in honour of Valentine's Day.'

His eyes widen. 'Blimey!'

'My sentiments exactly.'

He raises his glass. 'Then let's toast to a very unexpected evening.'

I pick up mine. 'And thanks for rescuing me.'

We each take a sip, and he carefully nudges his glass onto the coffee table. He frowns at his watch, and checking my phone I see it's almost midnight.

'Have you found somewhere to sleep tonight?' he asks. 'Because I have a spare room now that Petra's gone?'

I smile at him, but shake my head. 'I need an early start on the cleaning. And besides, what if Petra comes back and finds someone sleeping in her bed? Very Goldilocks.'

He tips his head. 'Or just deserts, but I take your point.' He gets up, still cradling Pompom, and shuffling her from arm to arm, puts on his coat. I struggle out of the low chair and watch him, feeling a little awkward. I'd normally hug a friend, or kiss their cheek, but Pompom's between us.

'Thanks for a lovely night,' he says softly.

'Good night,' I say. 'And Happy Valentine's Day.' I don't know why I say it, but he smiles and very gently leans in and kisses my cheek. The prickle of his stubble tickles, and the smell of his waxed jacket mixes with the wine in a way that's strangely pleasant.

'Happy Valentine's Day,' he murmurs, and pulls back.

'Thanks,' I manage, and follow him to the front door.

I wrap my arms around myself and watch him walk across the yard. He puts Pompom in the back of his car.

'Thanks for the pizza,' I call.

He raises a hand and gets in. I wait for his tail lights to bump out of the gateway before I close the door.

It's too late to call Vivienne, but I tap in a quick text.

'Valentine's Day successfully avoided!'

Who am I kidding? – it was the most interesting Valentine's Day I've ever had!

My phone bleeps.

'Well done! Time to figure out what you want next.'

A faint waft of waxed jacket nudges my thoughts, but it's quickly banished by the ominous gloom of the steep stairs.

Somewhere decent to sleep would be nice, so I push Joe to the back of my mind, take a deep breath, and start up the dark, narrow staircase.

8

The Platform Toilet

A chink of sunlight burns its way through my eyelids and I yank the blanket over my head. Smelling dust, I throw it off again, and the bed creaks as I reach for my phone.

It's seven forty-five. I stare up at the old glow-in-the-dark stars on the ceiling and give the blanket another experimental sniff. That settles it. What I want next is a clean bed.

I sit up and look around blearily at what must have been Joe's room. Several things give it away – the world map over the bed and the posters of cars for a start, and opposite me there's a bookcase full of boys' adventure books, toy cars, a ratty teddy and an old biscuit tin too full of Lego to close. On the mantel over the tiny Victorian fireplace is a collection of bird skulls, along with jam jars of marbles and pens. I chose this room because I didn't want to intrude on Gillian's privacy by using hers, and out of the other two, this was the only one that looked even vaguely habitable. Also, knowing it was Joe's is actually quite comforting.

I glance at the old Lloyd Loom chair in the corner where Bozz is curled up on the clothes I took off last night.

'Hmm,' I say, unimpressed, and Bozz opens one eye, fixes me with it, and closes it again. I wouldn't mind, except I have some serious cleaning to do, and it seems like sacrilege to put on clean clothes only to instantly ruin them. Still, it looks like I don't have much choice, and maybe I should be glad he didn't join me in bed, because thanks to the freezing night, it's draped with all my clean clothes, while my pillaged bags lie deflated on the floor.

Glad of my cotton pyjamas, I shiver as I slip on my shoes and my coat, and patter downstairs to clean my teeth. Returning, I root through my clothes and look regretfully at Bozz. Bozz, perhaps realising he's won the ones he's slept on, jumps onto the floor, washes his chest and looks up at me reproachfully.

'Breakfast?' I ask, like I didn't know, and checking over his shoulder that I'm following, he leads me down the stairs.

The kitchen is no better in daylight – in fact, it's worse because Bozz has left another set of animal entrails. Honestly, why people feed him, I don't know! Bozz fixes me with a look, flicks his tail and jumps onto the kitchen table, presumably to get a better view of me clearing them up.

I come back from the bathroom and glare at him. 'You eat those *outside*; not inside. Out-side!' He blinks, scratches his chin and looks pointedly at his empty saucer. 'I mean it!' We both know I don't, so I mumble a few choice words containing 'f's and 'k's, and fetch the cat food tin.

'Not that you deserve it,' I mutter as I spoon some out, but the little git's too busy purring to notice. I make myself a black coffee and munch on a few biscuits while Bozz finishes his breakfast. Leaving his bowl licked clean, he slinks out through the catflap, presumably to catch a squeaky second breakfast, and I stare helplessly at the kitchen.

The trouble with a mess of this magnitude is where to start.

Where do I want *to start?* I mock, and spotting the washing machine in the small area by the back door, I know exactly where. I strip both Gillian's and my beds, carry down everything washable, including my blanket, dump it all on top of the washing machine and put the first load on to wash.

Next, I tackle the sink and the draining board, and as I throw away the old bottle tops and jam-jar lids, discard the perished elastic bands and put all the bottles and jars in a box for recycling, I look out of the rear window at the back garden. The garden reaches up the side of the valley to the fast-moving clouds above, and what's more important, there's a washing line.

I scrub the sink with toilet bleach and slosh some into the toilet for good measure, and as soon as the sheets finish their cycle, I hang them on the line. I put the washing machine straight back on, and collect up all the towels and tea towels ready for load number three. That done, I bravely turn to the kitchen table. The kitchen table is like that point where all the oceans' junk collects into a ghastly floating island, and the only thing to do is extract items by type and deal with them individually, so I put the washing-up by the sink, stack the post in a pile and investigate the jars one by one. Most are congealed, crystallised or moulding. I empty jar after jar, wrapping and rolling the contents in old news-papers, fill the food waste bin with the squidgy packages and put the empty pots to be washed, all while fighting the urge to bin the lot. As it is, even though I know it's beyond retrievable, I'm hoping Aunt Gillian won't mind my intrusion if I tell her I've disposed of it responsibly.

Half an hour later, I've freed up almost half the circular table, but if I'm ever going to get some milk, I need to tackle the fridge.

I stand in front of it.

I've never been scared of a fridge before, and I've lived in student accommodation. This fridge, however, has history, and as I open the door, the off-dairy smell sends me lurching for the bin. I remove the old packets of curled-up ham and dry cheese, the out-of-date eggs and some ghastly-looking pâté, dump the congealed bottle of milk and put the salad drawer of primordial ooze by the sink. On the plus side there are no dead animals, but the use-by dates tell their tale. This fridge hasn't been cleaned in a *very* long time, and if I was a social worker, I'd declare Gillian incapable of looking after herself.

By half past nine, the fridge smells clean thanks to a YouTube tip about bicarbonate of soda, and I've earned another black coffee. But as the weak sunshine serves only to highlight the remaining mess, I turn the key on the back door and take my mug out into the garden. It's freezing and windy, and the sheets I put out are raging almost horizontal on the line, but it's also invigorating. There's an ancient wooden bench that looks protected from the wind by a wall, so I make my way up the steps and sit, trying to ignore the damp slats and the gunshot whip-cracks of the sheets on the line. Bozz stalks through a graveyard of abandoned house plants with weird, fat, alien-like roots, and sits beside me. He extends a long hind leg in the air, gives me a charged look, and washes his bottom.

I can't believe I ever wanted a cat. He's not cute or fluffy, but maybe that's just Bozz.

'Hello?' calls Joe, coming around the side of the house.

I stand to show him where I am, and shade my eyes against the wind. 'Long time no see.'

'I knew you couldn't have gone far. Do you fancy getting your car out?'

'Yes, please. I could do with some milk.' I hold up my mug. 'I'm fed up of black coffee.'

'And it would have the added benefit of clearing the road so other people can get in and out of the village,' he suggests.

'Yeah, that, too,' I agree sheepishly.

'Any one of them might not have milk,' he adds solemnly, and I grin at him.

I put my mug inside, collect my keys and lock up. Pompom is waiting in Joe's car, and I stroke her head as I get in.

'In the back,' orders Joe. For a second I think he means me, but Pompom hops between the seats.

'I thought she wasn't your dog?'

'She isn't, but Pompom and I have an agreement – I don't brush her, and she does as she's told.'

'If only all relationships were so simple,' I say, thinking of Lindi.

'If only,' he agrees heavily, presumably with his own person in mind.

We bump down the track, passing the bungalow, and this time there's an old gent, who looks to be in his sixties, leaning on the gate. There's a collie at his side, and a sign saying there's camping in the field, but unsurprisingly, there isn't a single tent.

Joe raises a hand, and the old gent watches us slide by with scepticism.

Joe glances at me. 'That's Bryn. His family used to own Gillian's house back when it was a farm.'

I look back. Bryn is still watching us like he's making sure we don't stop anywhere on the lane. I sink a little lower in my seat. 'Do you always wave?'

'Always,' says Joe.

'Does he ever wave back?'

'No.'

We pass the pub and reach the bridge, where a muddy, battered 4x4 is pulled up, its driver standing on the verge, contemplating my car like it's an alien spaceship.

Joe winds down his window and pulls to a stop. 'Hi, Huw!' He gets out, pleased to see his friend – or maybe just glad of the extra help.

'Ah, Joe, new girlfriend?' asks Huw, looking at me approvingly.

I flush slightly as Joe shakes his head. 'Huw, Ella, Ella, Huw. Huw has a sheep farm and a gorgeous family up the valley.' Huw, who's tall, attractive and in his mid-thirties, nods cheerfully. 'Ella is Gillian's niece.'

'Ah! There's lovely.' Huw nods delightedly. 'I'm glad someone's come to help her. How is Gillian?'

'Hating hospital, but coming home today, we think.'

Huw raises his eyebrows. 'Bet there's been hell to pay in there!' He grins, clearly comprehending the nightmare combination of Gillian, enforced rest and strict matrons.

'It hasn't been good,' I confirm, easily returning his smile.

'So, this your car, is it?'

'Yes.' We all look at the car, which looks drunkenly abandoned. 'Some lunatic forced me off the road last night,' I explain.

Huw glances at Joe for confirmation, and Joe nods. 'Petra,' he says succinctly.

'Ah!' Huw nods. 'Well, let's get it out for you, then,' and he pushes up his sleeves and joins Joe in examining the front of the car.

It doesn't take long. With three of us lifting and shoving, it soon comes free, and we push it back far enough for Joe's car to squeeze past. He attaches a tow rope and pulls it out the rest of the way, while I sit in the Clio and make sure it doesn't roll back into him. Within minutes we're done, and as if on cue, the post van crawls by, the postman examining the state of my car with amused interest.

Joe detaches the tow rope, checks nothing is damaged or leaking, and has me try the engine. It rumbles obligingly into action.

Huw gets into his 4x4 and pulls up next to my open window. 'Check your tyre alignment,' he advises, and explains how I'll know if anything's amiss. 'Take it to a garage if you're worried, and tell me if Gillian's tyres are flat again – I'll come by and pump them up.'

'Are they often flat?' I ask.

'More often than they should be,' he agrees. 'And come up to the farm. Seren would love to meet you.'

'I will, thanks,' I say, and he speeds off, giving a happy bip-bip to Joe as he passes.

I reverse a little further and cross the bridge, ready for the whole car to lurch uncontrollably to one side, but it feels just the same as it did yesterday. Having seen me safely across the bridge, Joe overtakes, gives me a thumbs-up and drives off without giving me a chance to thank him. Left on my own, I drive slowly and carefully up the track, and I'm just bouncing up past Bryn's bungalow, when he holds out a finger for me to stop. I pull over, put on the handbrake and get out.

'Hello,' I say, perhaps a little too enthusiastically.

'You're staying at Gillian's?' he asks. His accent is quite thick, and together with the flat cap and his wary expression, I feel I should explain myself.

'Yes, I'm her niece. I'm here to look after her. She comes out of hospital today.'

He juts his head in acknowledgment. 'Staying in the house?'

'Yes.'

'For how long?'

'Not sure. Maybe two weeks? It's up to Gillian, really.' I pull a worried face, and he grunts, but whether in amusement or agreement, I can't tell.

'Feed the cat,' he says, and with a nod, he stops looking at me. He doesn't go anywhere, or turn away, but the conversation's definitely over. I get back in the car and jolt up the last few yards of track.

That was definitely weird.

I park up and quickly check Gillian's tyres. They seem fine to me, but it's worrying that they're regularly flat . . . unless it's a slow puncture? I've heard that can happen, but wouldn't they be flat now?

I push the front door open against a new tide of post – far more than is reasonable. I collect it up to add to the pile in the kitchen and find Bozz parked on my clean section of table, primly washing his paw.

'If I discover you're not allowed on the kitchen table, we're going to have words.'

His eyes lock with mine defiantly, and I almost leap out of my skin as someone knocks hard on the front door. I open it, heart fluttering, but rather than Bozz summoning the armies of evil, there's a portly man and a young lad standing there.

'All right, my love?' asks the portly man in a broad Welsh accent.

'Yes, thank you,' I say, struggling with his over-familiarity.

'We're here for the toilet.'

I'm no clearer. 'To take it away?' I hazard.

He glances at his clipboard and then back at me. 'No! Social Services we are, love. Here to put in handrails and an elevated toilet seat.' He holds out his clipboard for me to see. 'For your mam, is it?'

'Err no, my aunt, actually. Come in.' I hold the door open so they can troop in, and I point to the bathroom. The portly man mutters a few things in Welsh, and the young lad nods and goes back to their van. 'Tea?' I ask the man who's now staring into the toilet. He smiles hopefully. 'But I haven't got any milk,' I remember.

His smile fades. 'No, you're all right, then.'

Embarrassed, I retreat to the kitchen and make a list of supplies: milk (obviously), food, cleaning supplies (including a large pack of rubber gloves as my hands smell funny from the bleach), and some basic jeans and trainers if the super-market has any.

There's some drilling, but they're done quickly – maybe because there's no tea on offer – and after twenty minutes he's back at the kitchen door holding out his clipboard.

'Sign here, love,' he says, and after admiring their handrail and platform-shoes version of a toilet-seat, I sign and see them out.

But as I stand in the doorway, waiting for them to drive safely out of sight, I have to admit I'm uneasy. There's something wrong here. Something more than Gillian being a hermit and which has nothing to do with the two men who just left. Too many things don't add up: the post, the tyres, the floodlight and Bryn. I'm not sure what it all adds up to, but I don't like it, and until I find out, London rules apply. I lock up carefully, leave a light on and make sure no one sees me leave . . . except Bryn. To his utter indif-ference, I wave at him, and it's not until I'm pulling in to the supermarket that I realise I've left Gillian with no means to get in.

9

Flowers and Grapes

I needn't have worried. It's dark by the time the ambulance pulls into the yard, and I've shopped, washed up, done three loads of washing, made beds, cleaned, stacked, mopped and dusted. I've even called Vivienne and told her about the car, not that she was bothered – 'so long as it still runs and there's no obvious signs of damage, don't worry about it' – all while Bozz watched me from the kitchen table.

As the engine outside cuts, I pull open the front door and the burly driver greets me cheerfully.

'Evening,' he says to me. But as he opens the back doors of the ambulance, he shakes his head at Aunt Gillian's energetic volley of swearing.

'. . . so if I want to bloody-well walk into my own house, I will!' she scolds someone presumably stunned into silence during the course of their long journey.

'Oh no you don't, missus!' says the driver, winking at me as he steps up into the ambulance. He pushes Gillian in a compact wheelchair onto the tailgate. 'More than our job's worth to let you go slip-sliding about in the dark. Now, you stay there, and we'll wheel you in.'

Aunt Gillian swears loudly, competing with the tailgate's whine, and her voice rings clear as it stops.

'. . . bloody embarrassing being treated like an invalid,'

she tells him, but since she doesn't object to his large hand on her shoulder, I reckon she likes him. If she didn't, I wouldn't put it past her to bite him.

I step forward, but the driver shakes his head. 'Leave this to us, lovely,' he says cheerfully. 'Bit of a handful, this one.'

'You wish!' grunts Aunt Gillian. 'You couldn't handle a handful!' and she swears colourfully, rendering us all dumb with her inventive use of language as the wheelchair grinds over the uneven ground. They wheel her into the hall and then into the kitchen, and Gillian falls silent at the sight of it before rounding on me.

'What the bloody hell have you done to my—?' She glances at the driver, and her lips snap shut. 'Well, get the kettle on,' she says instead.

'Cup of tea?' I ask the ambulance men, pleased to have milk at last, but the driver declines.

'Best be getting on. We have three more to get home tonight, although I expect they'll be more grateful than this one.' The driver smirks at Gillian as he transfers her to an armchair.

She glares at him. 'Is it *too* much to ask for you to be on time?'

The ambulance driver chuckles and raises his eyebrows at me. 'Yes! Best of luck to you. She's a right one, this one, and no mistake.' He nods at the other paramedic, who props some crutches, along with Gillian's bag, in the corner.

Aunt Gillian's scowl deepens. 'At my age I'm entitled to be bloody-minded, *particularly* when people call me "dear" like it's a space-saver for something *rude*!'

He laughs, shaking his head. 'Just like my ma,' he says, and skilfully folding up their little wheelchair, he gives me a cheerful wave and follows his colleague out into the night.

'Thank you!' I call after them, and he obligingly closes the front door behind them.

The ambulance rumbles away and leaves a hollow silence as Gillian's eyes roam over everything I've done.

'Now, girl, what the hell happened to my kitchen, and why's the heating not on? It's brass monkeys in here!'

'Heating?' I ask, and Gillian looks at me like I've got a screw loose.

'Yes! It's not the dark ages. There's a combi-boiler in the cupboard upstairs.'

I stare at her. I'd assumed, after everyone's talk of no mod cons, that there wasn't any, but now I'm looking, there's a radiator right behind her. I try not to grind my teeth at having washed, cleaned and mopped using kettles of hot water and spent a whole night trying to keep warm.

Gillian smirks. 'I got the ambulance men to turn it off when they picked me up – no point wasting energy. Top of the stairs in the old airing cupboard. Flick the switch to "on",' she instructs, and I go upstairs and simply 'flick the switch to on'.

'That's better,' says Gillian as I come back in, and relaxes as if the heat's already reaching her, which it can't possibly be. She treats me to a long, hard look. 'So, where are they, then?'

Given the number of things I've washed up, put away, thrown away or just jammed in the dresser cupboards, she could be talking about anything. 'Where are . . . what?'

'My flowers.'

'I didn't buy any.' To be honest, I didn't even think of it, and right now I'm not sure she deserves them, anyway.

Gillian gives an amused snort. 'Grapes?'

'Nope . . . Sorry,' I tack on, though I'm not sure I am, really.

'No flowers, no grapes,' she grumbles. 'I am an *invalid*, you know!'

Is she testing me? The look in her eye tells me she is, but

I'm too tired to deal with it. 'But I thought you didn't want to be treated like one?' I ask pointedly. 'Or was that all just bluster? How about you start behaving like one, and I'll treat you like one? Would you like that?'

Gillian frowns, but looks at me with a new respect. 'I'm not sure I would. All right, what *have* you bought, then? You must have bought something, because there was damned-all left in the place when they took me away.'

'I bought milk, bread, cheese, tomatoes, pasta, pesto, toilet rolls, teabags, biscuits,' I list. 'Washing-up liquid, sponges . . .' I slow down. '. . . rubber gloves, washing powder,' I add heavily. 'Wine, which could count as grapes, I suppose?'

'Yes, it could,' she agrees. 'As for the rest, far more practical. But what on earth have you done to my bloody kitchen?' She regards it like I've dressed it in doilies, twee crockery and fake flowers.

'Cleaned? Washed up? Fumigated?' I offer. If Gillian's allowed her rough brand of speaking, I reckon I am, too. 'It was dis-*gust*ing,' I add, making sure to smile so that she knows I'm not angry.

Gillian pouts. 'A few germs never hurt anyone. Scientists have said they're fine.'

'Not when they've formed a gang and are moving the furniture about!'

Gillian's glare reaches about a 4.0 on the outrage scale. I brace myself, but she snorts out a laugh. 'All right. You'll do,' she mutters. 'Glad you're not as vapid as you look.'

'Thanks . . . I think!'

'You're welcome,' she says, ignoring my sarcasm, and winces as Bozz jumps on her lap. She holds out her hand to prevent me taking him, and lets out a slow shuddering breath.

'Hello, old friend,' she says warmly, and tickles him behind his ears. He sniffs her face, pushes his head up under her chin and jumps down again. He hops up onto the Welsh dresser and purrs at us from on high. He's clearly not the submissive curl-up-on-your-lap type, but he's glad she's home.

Gillian gives him a fond smile, then hones back in on me. 'Now, make us both a cup of tea, and then you can tell me why you're here.'

I open my mouth to say I'm here because she needs me, and close it again. That's not what she's asking, and if I say anything like that she'll be calling me worse things than 'vapid'.

I boil the kettle and open the box of teabags, playing for time.

Honesty seems like the only path. Anything else and she'll land me bum first in the yard. So the truth.

I place a mug beside her, and sit down in the other armchair.

'So what happened?' she asks. 'You might as well tell me, because Marion wouldn't have sent you unless you'd *really* blotted your copy book. In fact, she'd have advised you against it. So what's the story? Come on, I want all the gory details.'

I chew my lip. 'Actually, Mum didn't send me, and when I said I'd come, she *did* advise me against it.'

Gillian's eyebrows flick up. 'Then why are you here?'

I frown at her. 'Because of a tattooed man on the underground.'

Gillian splurts out her tea, glances down at herself in surprise, puts her mug down and reaches for the clean tea towel I've left draped over the back of a kitchen chair. 'I wasn't expecting that,' she admits, patting herself dry.

'No.' I hide my smile behind my mug.

'So?' she prompts. 'What happened?'

'I lost my job.'

'And the tattooed man?'

'I was travelling home afterwards, feeling rotten, and I got chatting to this busker on the underground—'

'A tattooed busker?' checks Gillian.

'Yes, a tattooed busker, and he suggested Fate was trying to tell me something.'

'What?'

I shake my head. 'No idea, but he suggested she must have plans or I wouldn't have lost my job, and maybe I should keep my eyes open for opportunities and give her some legroom.'

Gillian looks sceptical. 'What? So you just sit about until something crops up?'

'Not quite. To begin with I looked into different jobs, anything to do with my art college qualification, meditation, hobbies, but nothing appealed.'

'Then what did you do?'

'To be honest, I cut my losses and went to see my old boss, who offered me a job at the call centre starting in March.'

Gillian frowns. 'So how did that lead you here?'

'My friend Vivienne suggested I had two weeks to try something different, and what with not wanting to spend Valentine's Day with my loved-up flatmate and her boyfriend, I thought I might go on holiday. We were just deciding where I should go, when at that exact moment Mum called mentioning –' complaining – 'that you needed help, and I wondered if Fate was finally taking a hand.'

Gillian looks doubtful. 'And what did your mum say when you told her?'

I nearly spit out my own tea. 'I didn't! I just told her I was at a loose end, but when you asked why I'm here, I assumed you really wanted to know.'

'I do. And I have to give you credit – that's too far-fetched to be anything but the truth!' She adjusts her position so she can reach her tea, and takes a sip. 'So, given that you're relying on the universe to cosmically arrange itself around you, does that mean, by logical extension, I had to fall down some steps for you to . . . what? Find yourself?'

I cringe as Gillian's frown deepens. 'No, that's not what I—'

'Which makes me, at best, Fate's tool to further your cause, or, at worst, expendable? Does that sound right to you?' Her bright eyes suggest she's teasing me.

'Perhaps it's just that Fate likes me better than she likes you?' I hazard, and bite my lip on my grin.

Gillian's eyebrows descend into a deep V. 'Quite possibly!' she agrees solemnly. 'She's been a bit of a git of late, so I wouldn't put it past her to scrap me for parts and use me as a pawn in someone else's life.'

'But if that's the case, why did *I* lose my job, and why was *my* life put on hold for me to come up here?' I challenge. 'I might be the pawn.'

We stare at each other, unsure of the cosmic plan, our ratings within it or which of us is the intended target. There's evidence to say we both need a bit of help, but if it were a competition, I'd say Gillian would win.

I shift uncomfortably, and throw caution to the wind. 'Well, seeing as we're being honest with each other, can I ask what happened here?'

Gillian hefts out a breath and regards me severely. For a second I think she's going to tell me to sod off again, but then her eyebrows flick up. 'I needed some time to myself, that's all: time to recover. And I've kept my distance from people so I didn't drag everyone down with me.'

I sense that she's not telling the whole truth, but I nod because she's watching me. 'It doesn't look like it's been very . . . comfortable for you.'

'No, well. What would have been? Boring everyone to tears? Depressing everyone? And time alone never hurt anyone.'

The joyless room disagrees.

'And nor does a bit of dirt,' she adds, misinterpreting my glance.

I smile at her. 'A *bit* of dirt?' I ask. I collect a packet of Hobnobs from the kitchen table, open it and hold it out to her.

'Yes,' she says, accepting one, taking a bite and puffing out crumbs.

A knock at the front door has us staring at each other. It clicks open, and Gillian's eyes glitter with anger at the temerity of whoever has decided to let themselves in.

'Anyone in?' calls a lilting Welsh male voice. Having expected it to be Joe, I'm a little disappointed, and Gillian's jaw clenches in irritation.

'In here,' she calls. 'Fate had better have a damned good excuse for this one,' she mutters, and a tall and very attractive man, maybe a few years younger than me, strides in.

Despite the cold weather, he's dressed in artistically ripped jeans and T-shirt, and has a shark's tooth on a leather lace around his neck. This, together with his floppy hair, suggests he's a surfer, but where he'd surf around here, I have no idea.

He gives us a grin. 'Da saw the ambulance and sent me up to see if you need anything, Gillian, but I see you're not on your own?' His grin widens as he assesses me head to toe.

Gillian rolls her eyes, but seems to let go of the majority of her outrage. 'Ella, this is Gareth. Gareth – Ella. Ella's my niece, Gareth's parents run the pub.'

I get up to shake his hand. 'Hello.'

'Come to help Gillian?' he asks, smiling warmly.

I nod. 'Sounds like you've been sent on the same mission.'

Gillian gives us a sour look. 'Yes, yes. Everyone's come to help the poor old lady who's had a fall. Aren't we fantastic!'

'Cup of tea?' I ask, ignoring her.

Gillian's mouth falls open. 'Hang on a minute, if he's come to help, he can damned well earn his tea.' She gives me a piercing look. 'Have you organised where I'm going to sleep, yet?'

'I've made your bed, upstairs?'

Gillian purses her lips. 'And what am I supposed to do when I need the loo in the middle of the night? Fall down the stairs and break my remaining limbs? No, thank you! I need a downstairs bedroom, as the doctor must have told you, which means converting the sitting room.' Gillian raises her eyebrows at Gareth. 'Gareth can help.'

'I'm happy to move furniture about,' he agrees obligingly.

'I should think so, strapping lad like you with two good hips.' Gillian looks me up and down.

I hold up my hand. 'If you mention my hips, you and I are going to have words!'

'Wasn't going to, but the sofa needs to come in here, and that's going to take two of you.'

Gareth smirks, like he's thinking of other things that take two of us, but I'm more concerned about the space under the window. 'Are you sure it'll fit?'

'It'll fit, smarty-pants,' says Gillian. 'Now, go upstairs and strip my bed. Gareth, you start bringing the sofa through.'

'On my own?' he asks.

'I'm sure you can manage the odd cushion,' she says witheringly, and picking up her mug, she relaxes back into her chair. 'Hop to it,' she says, her mouth twitching, and I follow Gareth into the hall.

'Want to come and help me with the sofa?' Gareth's voice is warm and velvety.

I give him a quick grin. 'No, it'll be quicker to do as she says,' and matching the action to my words, I take the stairs two at a time.

'Let's hope it's just a single,' he calls up after me.

'Hmm,' I agree, even though I know it isn't.

I open her bedroom door and sag. Everything in Gillian's bedroom is enormous, from the dark Victorian chest of drawers and matching wardrobe to the large wooden ottoman under the window, and the bed is no less substantial. But that's not the only issue – I'm starting to regret my earlier decision to respect Gillian's privacy and not touch too much in here. I quickly bundle all the dirty clothes into the laundry hamper. I strip the clean sheets ready for the move and pile up the books. I then check the bed's construction and collect up the stash of dirty mugs I find underneath.

Gareth meets me at the foot of the stairs with a solitary sofa cushion. 'So, is it a single?' he asks, following me into the kitchen.

I dump the dirty mugs in the sink.

'Of course it isn't a bloody single,' snaps Gillian, watching him add his cushion to the growing Jenga pile. 'I'm not a child.'

I smile at him, hoping to soften Gillian's words. 'The good news is that the base is in two halves, so it's just the mattress that's going to be difficult.'

'Shall we start with the mattress?'

I ignore his wink. 'Sofa first, then base, or we'll end up in a jam at the foot of the stairs.'

He follows me into the hall. 'I love an organised woman,' he whispers, his mouth a little too close to my ear, and I move away.

'If you've *quite* finished flirting,' calls Gillian, who must have the ears of a bat, 'perhaps you could move some furniture? Just a suggestion!'

I almost laugh, but Gareth's jaw clenches, so I chuck the remaining sofa cushions on the floor and lift one end, indicating he should take the other.

Between us we heave the sofa just shy of the floor and stagger through, avoiding swinging doors, grazing off door jambs and knocking down several coats on the way. After shifting everything, including Gillian, we finally manoeuvre it into position.

'It looks quite good there,' she says approvingly. 'Apart from the mess you've made bringing it in.' She smirks at my scowl. 'Now the bed,' she prompts, and just about managing not to swear at her, I follow Gareth up the stairs and into Gillian's bedroom.

Gareth looks around critically, his hands on his hips. 'God, it stinks in here.'

He's right, but it irritates me that he's pointed it out.

I start taking the bed apart. 'Yes, well things haven't been easy for her.'

His nose wrinkles. 'I know, but . . .' I raise my eyebrows at him, daring him to complete his sentence. Thinking better of it, he kneels down to find the catches that hold the base together, and we deconstruct the bed almost in silence. As I work, I think about how squalor, like trust and secrets, is one of those intimate things you can only share with certain people. I'd give almost anything to be doing this with Vivienne . . . or Joe.

10

Flying Beds and Whiskey Truces

We're just struggling down the stairs with the second half of the bed base when there's another knock at the front door. This time, Gillian yells through that it's open.

Joe lets himself in and glances up at us. 'Need a hand?' he asks as Pompom trots straight into the kitchen.

'No, we're fine,' says Gareth. 'We've got a system, haven't we, Ella?'

I shrug. It's not so much a system as me directing.

'In that case, I'd better make my peace.' Joe slides a bottle of whiskey half out of his coat pocket for me to see, and with his shoulders slightly hunched, walks into the kitchen.

I just catch Gillian snarling, 'Look what the cat's dragged in,' before the door clicks closed, and I bite my lip.

'Problem?' asks Gareth, looking up at me.

'Not sure,' I say, frowning.

'Oh, come on! I thought you girls were all women's lib these days, but if you want him to take over, just say.' Gareth's clearly mistaken my concern about the tension between Gillian and Joe for irritation at Joe not taking over from me.

'No, it's fine,' I assure him curtly, and we assemble the bed base in silence. The mattress, however, which is both heavier and double the size, takes a lot of negotiation just to get upright, and we're halfway down the stairs when it wedges itself firmly between the steps and the lintel over the stairs.

'It's stuck,' says Gareth. He stands back to show he isn't holding it.

I kick the mattress, but it doesn't budge. 'It must go down if it went up,' I reason.

'I'm telling you, it's stuck.' He stares past each side. 'Maybe they took out a window to get it in?'

'And brought a crane up the lane?' I ask, my sarcasm getting the better of me.

Gareth frowns.

Joe opens the kitchen door and leans against the door jamb. 'Tip it,' he suggests, and seeing what he means, I tip the top of the mattress to one side, and it instantly cascades down the stairs and sweeps Gareth off his feet. Luckily he lands firmly on its cushioned surface.

'Sorry!' I squeak.

'Never turn your back on a woman,' Joe advises Gareth, and I give him a dirty look, but ruin it by smiling.

Gareth grins. 'No harm done. Care to join me?' He looks up at me and pats the mattress beside him. Joe's eyes meet mine for a nanosecond before he steps back in the kitchen and closes the door.

'Don't be silly,' I say briskly. 'Now, let's get this bed together.'

'Did you say get into bed together?' asks Gareth.

I leave a scornful pause. 'No.' I take a firm hold of the corner of the mattress.

Gareth gets up. 'Well, let's get on with it, then,' and looking more sulky than sultry, he helps me dump the mattress on its base, and without even squaring it up, goes to join Joe and Gillian in the kitchen.

Feeling thoroughly Cinderella-like, I collect Gillian's mattress protector, pillows and eiderdowns. I collect her clean bedding and I'm just stretching the fitted sheet over the mattress when I catch Joe watching me from the doorway.

He holds out a glass of whiskey. 'Take a sip and I'll give you a hand?'

I stretch my back, then take the glass. I sip it and close my eyes, relishing the burn on my throat, and smile at him as he puts our glasses on the windowsill. 'Thanks.'

He stretches the sheet over the corner nearest him. 'How's the car?'

'I drove it to the supermarket, and there didn't seem to be any issues.'

'Good. And you got some milk?'

'Yes,' I say, smiling. 'How did it go with Gillian?'

His mouth twists and he stuffs a pillow into its case. 'She told me to go home.'

'And you said?' I ask, confident there's more.

'I told her I'd do no such thing; that I'm here to help and she has to put up with it. Then she swore a lot, I gave her a glass of whiskey and she sent me out here to help you.'

'Sounds like she's pleased to see you,' I say drily.

'Actually, it went better than I expected. She must be relieved to be out of hospital.'

'I think the feeling was distinctly mutual.'

Joe chuckles. 'Yes, well . . . I doubt the NHS has a manual on dealing with someone of her calibre.'

'No,' I agree, thinking of guns rather than intelligence. 'But frank speaking seems to be the key.'

'Yes, and not speaking down to her.' Joe gives the kitchen a telling glance, and as if on cue, Gareth scurries out. He pauses in the doorway, his cheeks flushed.

'Better be getting back,' he says. 'Now that I've checked on poor old Gillian.'

Joe's lip barely twitches.

'Well, thanks for your help,' I say, careful to keep a straight face.

'My pleasure,' says Gareth, his face suddenly radiant, which is quite sweet considering he hasn't had the best of receptions. 'Perhaps we could meet up for a drink sometime?'

'Perhaps,' I agree. 'Although I'm really here to take care of Gillian, so—'

'Don't bring me into it! Your sex life – your business,' Gillian shouts through from the kitchen.

I force a smile onto my lips. 'In that case, that would be lovely.' There's not a lot else I can say, but Gareth's face lights up a little too brightly for my liking.

'I look forward to it,' and giving me a cheery wave and Joe a nod, he closes the front door behind him.

'Shit,' I mutter, and plump up the pillows a little more viciously than is necessary. I can feel Joe watching me, and I sneak a glance at him. He's holding out my whiskey.

'Anything else need doing?' he asks gently.

'No, I think it's pretty much ready for her ladyship.'

'Then come and sit down. From what I've seen of the kitchen, you've been on your feet all day. Are you all right with whiskey, or would you prefer a cup of tea?'

I want to hug him. 'I'd *love* a cup of tea.' I follow him into the kitchen and he puts the kettle on, indicating I should take a seat on the sofa he presumably assembled.

'Already got them lining up,' comments Gillian as Pompom hops up onto my knee. Bozz glares at me from the dresser.

'Don't start. I might have got away with saying no, if you hadn't started shouting about sex lives!' I shake my head at her.

'Shouldn't have brought me into it, then, should you?' she says.

'Maybe not, but where's your family loyalty?'

Her eyes fix me to the seat. 'Flushed down the toilet, as your mother should have told you.'

Like Bozz's ghastly offerings. 'Well, get your rubber gloves on – we might need to find it if he comes again.'

Gillian chuckles. 'Not attracted, then?'

'No, I'm not into sleazy young men.'

Joe is pouring milk in my tea and Gillian catches me looking at him. 'Oh, I see!'

I feel myself flush and glare at her. 'No, you don't. Stop making trouble!'

'All right, all right!' She chuckles to herself and leans over to get Joe's attention. 'This one's got attitude.'

He nods. 'Don't I know it – family trait by the looks of it!'

I roll my eyes at him and Gillian frowns as she turns to me. 'Speaking of which, do you know what your mother said to me?' I shake my head. 'She told me to find somewhere more suitable to live! "More suitable for what?" I asked. "Someone my age," she said! The cheek of the woman! She's only five years younger than me, which makes her sixty if she's a day, and yet she thinks she can challenge me about my age! What a self-righteous arse!'

My mouth drops open.

'Don't you defend her,' warns Gillian, but I hold up my hands. I've been on the rough end of Mum's comments myself.

Joe smirks. 'Don't worry. You should hear some of the things she says about *my* mother. They could strip paint.'

'Well, *your* mother—' begins Gillian.

'Shut up, and drink your whiskey,' says Joe. 'I knew you shouldn't have started on it so early.'

She salutes him with her glass. 'Making up for lost time. But honestly, *his* mother's a complete airhead,' Gillian whispers.

'That's it, I'm confiscating your whiskey,' says Joe, coming over with my tea.

Gillian clutches her glass to her chest. They eye each other warily, then Joe sits down beside me and Gillian relaxes.

'So, how come you spent so much time here as a child?' I ask.

'It's where I spent my holidays from boarding school,' he says.

'Not his sister, though. Hated it,' says Gillian. 'Came once, had the screaming abdabs and refused to come again.'

I seem to be hop-scotching from one tricky subject to another.

'Why did you go to boarding school?'

Joe stares into his whiskey. 'My parents travelled a lot.'

Gillian flicks her eyes heavenward. 'Oh, get over yourself, Joe. His parents are hippies – always off to some retreat or commune to *commune* with nature.' Joe raises his eyebrows at her. 'Well, they are!' Joe's eyebrows climb even higher and she purses her lips.

'They're wellness gurus,' he explains. 'And when I was young, they were often asked to speak, or run courses at retreats around the world.'

'In places like Jordan,' says Gillian.

'Like Jordan,' agrees Joe, his eyebrows knitting together. 'I'm called Joe, short for Jordan, because that's where they were at the time. They loved it so much they went back year after year, and that's why Petra is called Petra after the Rose City. Then, unusually for hippies, they travelled the world and made a lot of money teaching spiritual health and well-being.'

'They now own a luxurious, five-star retreat in the Caribbean. Celebrities can't get enough of the place,' says Gillian scornfully.

'But as you can imagine, growing up with them travelling

wasn't conducive to getting a decent education, so they sent us to boarding school.' Gillian rolls her eyes in disapproval.

'And that's why in the holidays you came here,' I say, finally understanding.

Joe nods. 'If they were in India or Indonesia, for example, it was impractical for us to join them, so I came here. And I *loved* it.' He looks fiercely at Gillian. 'I loved roaming the hills, painting with Mike, visiting the farms and playing with Huw.' His attention shifts back to me. 'The farmers would let us help with the animals, and Gillian was always here with food and hugs. It was home.' He smiles at the memory, and so does Gillian, though more covertly into her whiskey.

'And after school?' I prompt.

'I went to university in Exeter and came here when I needed a break. Then life just got complicated, I suppose.' He glances at Gillian.

Her mouth tightens and she looks away. 'Speaking of complicated, how is that sister of yours?' she asks, changing the subject.

Joe frowns suspiciously. 'Fine,' he says guardedly. Gillian glowers at him, and he relents. 'Her relationship went sour and she's been living with me. We came up yesterday to sort out the cottage, had a row and she drove back to Exeter last night.'

'Fast,' I add, with feeling.

Gillian's attention flicks to me, and I wrinkle my nose guiltily at Joe.

'We think she drove Ella off the road,' he explains. 'And I was on my way to visit you in hospital when I found Ella stuck in the ditch by the bridge. Apparently Petra took the bridge at quite a lick and Ella had to swerve to avoid her.'

'And since Joe couldn't get past, he had to stop and help me.'

'I didn't have to,' he protests. 'I was being a gentleman.'

'As I remember it, you stopped to demand what I thought I was doing. You even told me to move my car!'

'Yes, because you were asleep behind the wheel! I thought you were drunk!'

I clear my throat and glance significantly at Gillian, who's watching us avidly.

Joe grins. 'Anyway, when I figured out what had happened, I brought Ella up here—'

'And that's how come you already know each other,' says Gillian, light dawning. 'Nasty hole, that. Surprised you didn't see it.'

'I might have done if it hadn't been dark and raining . . . and I hadn't been dazzled by ten thousand watts of Petra's headlights!'

But Gillian's already moved on. 'So what was your row with Petra about? The cottage?' Joe stares tellingly at his hands and Gillian turns to me. 'Petra doesn't understand why Joe keeps it when he no longer has any family here. And since she can't stand me and wants the money . . .' She holds out her hands to show the rest is obvious.

Joe's eyes move guiltily to the floor. 'Well, you have to admit you haven't made it easy for her to like you.'

'Why should I? She was the one determined to hate me.'

'When she was about eight!'

'Still, she started it, and she never changed her mind, did she?' She looks him in the eye. She slumps, but not in submission. 'I'm tired. Hardly slept a wink in that bloody hospital. Is my bed ready?'

I nod and spring up. 'I'll just get your bedside lamp from upstairs.'

Joe stands up, too. 'And while Ella does that, let's get you ready for bed.' He shakes his head as I start to offer help. 'Bathroom first?' he asks, and at Gillian's nod, supports her out of her chair with considerably more care than I'd manage.

Not sure what else to do, I run upstairs and collect the lamp. I connect it up in her makeshift bedroom, but as they're still in the bathroom, I wander back through and start cleaning up the kitchen.

'She's in bed,' he says, coming in twenty minutes later. 'She can manage a lot herself, but sleeves, socks, twisting and manoeuvring seem to cause her problems, and that annoys her. My advice is to let her tell you what she wants and block your ears to the swearing.'

I smile, easily imagining the scene. 'OK, thanks.'

He shakes his head to show it's nothing. 'I should have been here months ago. If I'd realised how bad things were . . .' His jaw clenches for a second.

I lay a hand on his arm. 'She didn't want people fussing over her, that much is obvious.'

'I know, but I of all people should have—' He stops and takes a deep breath. 'It's just it's hard to see her like this when she's always been so capable. I never thought it could come to this.'

I can see his inner turmoil and I want to hug him, but I don't quite dare. 'Grief's weird – there's no telling how people will react.'

'Amen to that. I just wish I knew why she didn't ask *me* to bust her out of hospital.' He shakes his head at himself. 'Mike would be appalled!'

I smile sadly, but I don't have an answer for him. 'You're being very hard on yourself. I only came because I was at a loose end.'

'I'm not sure that makes it better.'

'Perhaps not, but we can make it up to her.'

'You're right.' He smiles. 'And I shouldn't be ranting at you – sorry.'

'That's all right. I know you're worried. So am I.'

Joe looks deep into my eyes, checking I mean it, and I feel a flutter deep in my stomach. He smiles, almost like he's amused at himself. 'You should catch up on some well-earned rest.' He sighs. 'And I should phone Petra to see what she wants me to do with her dog.' We both look at Pompom curled up on the sofa like a fluffy white cushion. 'I'll drop by tomorrow.'

'Great. Gillian will like that.'

'You think so?' he asks, regaining his sense of humour. 'Come on, Pompom.' Alert to her name, Pompom jumps up and races into the hall. Joe follows her, but turns as we reach the front door. 'Oh, and I've been meaning to thank you.'

'What for?' I ask, intrigued.

'Last night.' My eyes widen, and he grins with embarrassment. 'I mean, what you said about my main character. You were right – he has his own plans for the future, and they weren't anything like I'd thought they'd be.'

'No sudden death?'

'No, he vetoed that one,' Joe agrees. 'He wants to retire, but like a doctor, people come to a detective's door regardless.' He takes my hand and gently presses it to his lips. 'Thank you,' he says again, and with a sudden blazing smile he lets himself and Pompom out, quietly closing the door behind him.

I have to resist the urge to open the door and watch his tail lights meander down the track. Instead, I peek in on Gillian. She's snoring with her mouth wide open. I lean in to turn off the lamp and smile before I go into the kitchen.

I'm actually glad I came.

11

Petra-fied

It's so much better to wake up in clean sheets, and it makes me wonder what I want next. I stare up at the outlines of Joe's glow stars, and realise what I really want is to know why Gillian is the way she is. That, and why she receives so much junk mail!

A vehicle rumbles into the yard and I roll out of bed to look out of the window. It's drizzling outside and Joe, his hood up against the rain, is trying to cajole Pompom into his arms. She's not interested, and slips through his fingers to leap into a puddle and bound around the yard in delight. Joe watches her for a moment, his hands on his hips, but his quaking shoulders suggest he's laughing, and I can't help laughing, too.

He sets off towards the front of the house, calling to her, and I drop the curtain and run down the stairs to let them in.

'Come on, scamp!' he calls as he steps inside, and Pompom races straight through into the kitchen leaving wet footprints behind her. Joe raises his eyebrows at my pyjamas and I blush faintly, glad that I chose my full-length cotton ones again.

'Thought I'd help get Gillian up,' he says.

I haven't had a chance to clean my teeth yet, so I just nod. There's a hiss from the kitchen, and Pompom scampers out like she's having the best day ever.

I quickly check Gillian's happy for Joe to come in, and trot back upstairs to get ready.

It takes them a while to sort out Gillian, so I put some of Gillian's clothes on to wash, feed Bozz, give Pompom a few cat biscuits, which she wolfs down, and spend the next few minutes checking my phone to see whether they're bad for her. Deciding no harm's done, I make us all a cup of tea, and when Joe finally comes in I've moved on to emptying yet more jars of mouldy jams and chutneys I found in a cupboard, and I'm lining up the empties on the draining board.

'Ten green bottles?' asks Joe. He inspects the mould ring inside one.

'Very green,' I agree, and running the tap, he starts to rinse them out. We work in companionable silence. I hand him the jars, and giving him the last one I lean against the table and assess the kitchen. 'Why aren't there any of Mike's paintings on the walls?'

He pauses. 'Are there none upstairs, either?'

'No.'

Joe scrapes under a jar rim with his fingernail, but I suspect his frown has nothing to do with that. He finally puts it in the box and looks at me. 'Mike's paintings used to be everywhere. Gillian must have taken them down.'

'Too painful a reminder, do you think?'

Joe shrugs. 'Possibly, but I thought grieving relatives wanted to keep things the same?'

'Not always. I've heard some people sell up and move on.' Like in *Sleepless in Seattle*, and *We Bought a Zoo* – not that I'm going to reveal my movie-based sources. 'What kind of thing did Mike paint?'

Joe gestures towards the window. 'Large, sweeping mountain-scapes, mostly. That's why he moved here. He found it "inspirational". And after his first big sell-out exhibition in London, he had the money to go practically anywhere.' Joe smiles. 'He could have gone to the Mediterranean or the Caribbean, but he wanted to pace the craggy peaks with huge canvasses, and in the end it was a toss-up between here and the Lake District.'

'What made him choose Wales?'

'He said the Lake District was too popular, almost a cliché, while there weren't enough giant canvasses of Wales.'

'And that's what hung on the walls in here?' They'd swamp the room.

'No, no. These were smaller hill-scapes, along with a few intimate portraits and a couple of pictures by friends. There was a lovely one Mike did of Gillian in the hall.' He glances at the kitchen's front window. 'I suppose they're in the studio now. At least, I hope so.'

'There are a few paintings in the spare room upstairs, but I haven't seen any others, and I think I've vacuumed, scrubbed and cleaned most of the rest of the house.'

Joe smiles. 'You're not scared of hard work, I'll give you that. But you should see his paintings – they're amazing. Do you want to take a look in the studio, now?'

'Do you think Gillian would mind?'

'Maybe, but what she doesn't know won't hurt her, and it makes sense to check the place is OK – no leaks in the roof or anything. There should be a key under the plant pot outside.'

'Actually, I think it's on the ring with the back-door key, now.'

He goes to the back door, pulls the key out of the lock, and looks down at the accompanying key marked 'Studio'. 'All right, let's go and look,' and we head out of the back door, followed by Pompom.

The long, low studio that forms one entire side of the yard probably at one time housed sheep, pigs, feed and tools, all in separate little rooms, but now its windows and all but one of its doors are bricked up and painted white. The remaining door is wooden, and it's obvious from the scratches on the brass key plate and fresh gouges in the wood that someone has tried to get in – probably quite recently.

Joe examines the scratches with a frown, and we both wince as Joe steps onto the twin paving slabs that form the front step, and they knock together loudly. We glance back at the house, but there's no sound from Gillian, so he tries the door handle. It doesn't open.

'That's something, at least,' he says, but his expression clouds as a black Audi sports car pulls into the yard behind us. He hands me the keys and folds his arms. 'Looks like you're going to meet Petra,' and I have to admit, I'm curious to meet the woman who ran me off the road.

Her door swings open to let out high heels, sleek legs, tailored black dress, cinched-in maroon leather jacket with matching lipstick, sunglasses and silky dark brown hair cut into a perfect bob. Her look shouts Rodeo Drive, but as I compare her with Joe, and picture their New-Age parents, it also screams rebellion. Pompom looks from me to Miss Shiny, and sits at my feet.

'I thought I might find you here,' she says to Joe, sauntering over, and turns her gaze on me. 'I don't believe we've met?'

I resist the urge to introduce myself as the person she ran off the road and put on a businesslike smile. 'I'm Eleanor.'

'Charmed. I'm Petra, Joe's sister.' She turns to Joe, but a small frown puckers her forehead and she turns back to me. 'You're not related to Gillian, by any chance?'

'Yes, I'm her niece.'

'Niece!' She bestows a smile on Joe. 'See? I told you there would be someone to look after Gillian.'

Joe's jaw muscles tighten. 'I never said there wouldn't be. I only said I wanted to be here if she needs me.'

'And does she?' Petra sounds sceptical.

Joe meets her eyes with a steady gaze. 'Yes, she does.'

'Really? Since when?'

'Since she fell. You know she fell. You were there when Bridget told us.'

Petra glances at me. 'And now it's, what? Business as usual? All forgiven and forgotten like she didn't shut you out for eighteen months?'

'If I'm needed, I'm going to be here,' says Joe firmly.

I try to back away, but Petra smiles at me. 'So, how's the patient doing?' Joe rolls his eyes and Petra pouts. 'Don't look like that, Joe, I'm really asking!'

'Fine. Cantankerous, but fine,' I say, and smile at Joe, but he's staring hard at Petra.

'See?' says Petra like I've just supported her in some long-running argument.

'Oh, I like Gillian,' I say quickly. 'But I know she's an acquired taste.'

'Like Marmite!' huffs out Petra. 'But you really *like* her? Honestly?'

I nod. 'I do. I find her refreshingly honest, once you get used to her turn of phrase.'

'That's true – I could never fault her honesty,' Petra concedes, and turns to Joe. 'I left my cottage key behind. Can I borrow yours?'

I take the opportunity to head inside, and find Pompom hard on my heels.

'Who's here,' demands Gillian from her makeshift bedroom. 'I heard a car.'

'Petra,' I say, going into her room.

'Ah, the glamourpuss returns. Help me up; I'll come through to the kitchen.'

Thanks to Joe, she's already dressed, and using me and

a stick for support we make laboured progress through to her chair in the kitchen. She subsides into it like a slow-motion sack of potatoes.

'Knew she'd be back,' mutters Gillian.

I fill the kettle. 'Should I make Petra a cup?'

'Don't bother, she won't come in,' says Gillian, managing to imply both that she's not welcome and that Petra wouldn't have the decency to come in anyway. Two minutes later, though, Petra pops her head around the kitchen door and comes in, followed by Joe, who looks more dark and brooding even than when he met me on the road. To her credit, Petra's smile doesn't falter as she greets Gillian.

'How's the invalid? Better?'

Gillian bridles. 'Better than you! But then, I haven't had my brain replaced with silicon.' Wow, no wonder Petra can't stand her!

Petra nods pityingly. 'If I had, I still wouldn't be stupid enough to like you.'

'Touché,' mutters Gillian, and Joe's eyebrows flick heavenward. 'Well, at least you've got some colour in your cheeks, if not your personality.'

'Oh, that's painted on, just like my smile,' replies Petra tartly, and grins at me.

'Actually, you do look more . . . healthy, Petra,' says Joe thoughtfully. 'Not so stick-thin.'

Petra flushes, and to my surprise Gillian glares at him. 'What are you talking about? If she ate peas, she'd look like a snake that swallowed a pearl necklace.'

Petra pouts becomingly, but doesn't seem to have a handy retort, possibly because, like me, she can't figure out if Gillian just came down on her side of the fence.

'So, why are you here? Joe, I presume?' asks Gillian.

'Of course! I didn't drop by for the joy of a tête-à-tête with you.'

'Tête-à-tit, more like,' mutters Gillian, a smile curling her lips. 'But feel free to drop by from *any* height you like.'

Petra stretches her mouth wide. 'Sounds like you've had more practice than me. Or did you throw yourself down the steps to have everyone at your beck and call?'

'Everyone? I don't remember asking *you*.' They glare at each other, while Joe stands by looking tense.

'Tea?' I interject feebly.

Petra drags her eyes away from Gillian and eyes the tea caddy like a mouse might pop out of it, which it won't – I've checked. 'No, thanks.'

Joe pulls his keys out of his pocket, and extracting one from the ring, holds it out to Petra.

'I'll see you later. Make sure you're around when I need to get back in.'

Petra takes it in her perfectly manicured hand. 'Have you decontaminated the pantry?'

'Yes.'

'And don't you think we have a few things to discuss?' she asks pointedly. 'I've been to see the solicitor.'

Joe looks guiltily from Gillian to me.

'Oh, go with her if you're stupid enough,' growls Gillian, but Joe's eyes are fixed on me. I give him a half-smile to say it's fine, and dipping his head he calls Pompom to heel, and they both follow Petra out.

I finish making the tea as the two cars pull away, and put a mug down next to Gillian. I sit quietly on the end of the sofa and cradle mine.

'So what's the story there?' I ask.

Gillian looks at me. 'Pph! She's a scheming little cow – always has been, always will be, but Joe's her big brother so there's no shaking the woman loose.'

I sip my tea. 'Neither of you seem to have an easy relationship with Petra.'

'No, well, it all stems back to her gargantuan hissy-fit when she was little. Though, perhaps I should have expected it, what with the lure of "Daddy's posh relatives in London". It was a mistake to send them there that first half term. We just couldn't compete with the money and bright city lights, in Petra's eyes at least, so Joe came here, and she went to London.'

'Odd to split them up, wasn't it?'

'Perhaps, but he didn't like London.'

'Yes, it's not always all it's cracked up to be,' I mutter, half to myself.

'Hmm.' Gillian assesses me with pursed lips. 'Speaking of which, how's your personal quest going?' I look at her blankly. 'Has Fate made another appearance?'

'Oh, that! No, she hasn't.'

'Have you figured *anything* out?' I don't think she means to sound condemning – it's just the aftermath of her irritation with Joe and Petra, but it still makes me feel frustrated.

'Just that I'm better at cleaning than I thought.' Gillian frowns at me. 'And I'm quite enjoying your no-holds-barred manner of speaking.'

'I don't beat around the bush, if that's what you mean.'

'Yes, that's *exactly* what I mean,' I agree.

'Well, what the hell have you been doing, then?'

'I've been polite.'

Gillian stares at me. 'And that's worked for you, has it?'

Has it? No fulfilling job, no lasting relationships; just politeness and never saying what I really want. I meet her eyes. 'No,' I say. 'No, it hasn't. Not at all.'

'Then perhaps you should work on that.'

'That's what I'm starting to realise.'

She chuckles. 'Your mother will say I've rubbed off on you. She won't like that!' No, she won't. 'Good thing to learn, though. Cathartic.'

'Hmm,' I agree. 'And less frustrating, I imagine.'

'Yes,' she agrees. 'But you have to temper it. You have to know what you can get away with and with whom . . . unless you don't give a damn, in which case, fire away.'

'I'll take that as *carte blanche*, shall I?'

'Take it how you like.' Gillian breathes out and surveys the room. She glares disconsolately at the books on the coffee table. 'Looks like we're on our own for the day . . . unless you have plans?'

'Not me. I don't know anyone around here except Joe.'

'And Gareth. Didn't he invite you out for a drink?' she asks, her eyebrows raised.

I frown at her. 'He did, but I don't want to encourage him. I reckon he's a give-an-inch, take-a-mile kind of person.'

'Hmm,' agrees Gillian. 'Well, in that case, perhaps you should get on with figuring out what you want from life, while I read a book.'

'I might see if I can find anything on my phone,' I agree half-heartedly. 'But actually, I was thinking of making a start on your post. You get a hell of a lot of junk mail. Did you request any of it?'

'No, it just started to arrive after Mike died. It increased week on week, and now it's an avalanche through the letter box each day.'

'You didn't request *any* of it?' I check.

Gillian shakes her head. 'Not as far as I remember. I just assumed one company sold my details to all the others. I get a lot of sales calls, too. That's why the phone's unplugged.' And explains why the phone hasn't rung once since I arrived, which it should have done if people have heard about her accident and that she's now out of hospital.

'Hmm,' I say, hiding my concern at how isolated she is. 'Well, if you don't want the junk mail, I'll return it to sender. Chances are they'll remove you from their list if it keeps coming back.'

'Could work,' she admits grudgingly. 'All right. You do that, and I'll read a book.' She pokes again at the books I've left stacked on the coffee table like a witch probing in entrails. 'Not that I haven't read these several times!' she says, casting aside the top three.

'Actually, I can help with that!' I run upstairs and come back down with my e-reader, and hand it to her. 'Try this.'

She turns it over in her hands. 'What is it?'

'An e-reader – lots of books stored on one device.'

'I've heard of those. Do you have any classics on here?'

Taking it back, I download some free ones by Dickens, Jane Austen, the Brontës and Jules Verne, and show her how to use the menu screen and turn pages.

'Hmm.' She chooses one of the titles, scrolls forward a few pages and back again. 'Right, that'll do nicely.'

Taking advantage of her absorption, I open the dresser cupboard and retrieve all the paperwork I stashed in there. I start to make a massive pile of junk mail, and a pitifully thin pile of actual mail.

A while later, bored, I take a break, and seeing my phone has a signal I quickly look up 'finding myself'. There are a lot of step-by-step guides, which, now I look at them, could apply equally well to someone who's grieving . . . after all, Gillian's just as much at a crossroads in her life as I am. The only question is how to get Gillian to try a few of these ideas with me? Be straight or be sneaky?

Gillian looks at me with suspicion. 'What are you smirking at?'

'Nothing! Just an errant thought,' but as I scribble out Gillian's address on a few more envelopes, I try to think how I can get her to participate.

12

A Square on the Wall

By mid-afternoon, I've sorted out what post can be returned. Gillian, meanwhile, has taken to my e-reader like the proverbial duck, and as she carefully hides the screen whenever I pass, I reckon she's found my racy romances and thrillers. I'm glad, because now in unguarded moments, she looks furtive and absorbed, rather than tired and anxious.

Seeing me stretch, Gillian puts the e-reader aside and tries to lift herself out of the chair.

'Want some help?' I ask.

Gillian shakes her head, but demands her crutches with an outstretched hand. 'Might as well learn to do this myself, while you're still here to pick me up off the floor.'

I hold out the crutches ready for her to grab. 'There's no rush, I don't need to be back in London for . . .' I do a quick calculation in my head. '. . . twelve days.'

Gillian raises an eyebrow, but whether she doubts my staying power or thinks me presumptuous of my welcome, I'm not sure. She makes it upright and hobbles painfully out to the bathroom.

I listen out for any obvious sounds of distress and after a few minutes, the toilet flushes, but she doesn't come back. I check the hall, and find her standing in front of a blank section of wall where a picture used to hang.

She scuffs away a tear.

'Where's the painting?' I ask quietly.

'In the studio, with everything else.' Everything else of Mike's, I'm assuming.

'Wouldn't it be better to have it hanging there, rather than just imagining it?'

Gillian looks down, teeth gritted, half angry, half upset, then returns her attention to the wall. She slumps slightly over one crutch, her mouth moving around like she's sucking a boiled sweet. 'I took them down when Mike died,' she says finally. 'But I still see it there . . . and that's worse, somehow. Why is that?'

I stare at the wall, too. 'Maybe the empty wall shouts louder that he's gone than the picture would?' I'm scared I'm being too blunt, but she doesn't react. 'And it not being there doesn't mean he never existed.'

'No, but I thought taking it down might erase the hurt. The trouble is, nothing does that, and whoever said time heals all things . . .' Gillian's bottom lip quivers. '. . . lied.'

I want to take her hand, but I'm almost certain she'd hate that. I bite my lip and search for something comforting, but not trite, to say. 'I watched a woman talk about grief on breakfast television once. She said you can never get back to normal. The only way through is to find a different "normal". A decent, manageable normal,' I add, in case Gillian thinks the squalid, lonely normal she's settled for counts.

'Hmm,' she agrees grudgingly. 'There's some sense in that, I suppose, but what's your point?'

'I suppose, in specific terms, my point is that you can't take the picture away and not replace it with something.'

Gillian's lips draw tight, but she doesn't disagree. 'So . . .?'

'Either you hang a new picture there, or put the old one back. Having nothing is—'

'Denial,' Gillian finishes for me.

I was going to say 'not a good option', but her word's better. 'So what do you think? Do you want me to find the old picture? Or should I put something new in its place?'

'Like what?'

'I'll do you a nice pen-and-ink drawing of Bryn glaring over his gate, if you like?'

Her lip twitches. 'I don't want that old sod watching me every time I go to the loo.'

'Or we could get you a poster of a kitten hanging from a tree with "Hang in there" written on it?'

'Pph!' Gillian looks at me for the first time. 'Or a trite verse telling me to live life to the full?' she asks scornfully.

'Or a calendar of naked men,' I counter with a grin. She shakes her head, her lips pursing against a smile. '*Or* I could go to the studio and find the old painting?'

'You wouldn't know which one it was. There must be over two hundred paintings in there.'

I feel a little dart of triumph: that's not a no. 'You could describe it to me?'

Gillian stares at the wall and takes a jagged breath, but after a moment she nods. 'The sky in the top left corner is a wispy blue, but the fine weather is being chased away by a flurry of heavy rain clouds. The sheep in the near hills are hunkering down against a drystone wall, dark in the shadow of the approaching squall, while the far ones just catch the last of the evening sun. The drystone walls slice through the landscape as far as the eye can see, and the sparse grass doesn't look rich enough to support the flock. There's a stoicism to the painting, and he was so pleased with how he caught the light just before the rain hit that he came home soaked to the skin because he used his coat to protect the canvas. He was smiling from ear to ear. I lit a fire to warm him up, and we sat in front of it, the pair of us sipping whiskey and toasting our toes.' She's still staring at the wall. 'The key to the studio is with the key to the back door.'

Leaving her there, I collect the key and take it out to the studio, praying the moment won't be ruined by a comedy parade of almost identical paintings . . . or worse, that the person who gouged the door got in. I jump as the rocky paving slab knocks its neighbour, and with a flit of nerves, I fit the key in the lock. Unsure what to expect, I push against the resistance of the door's draught-excluding brush, and gasp.

The studio's so amazingly bright it almost takes my breath away. For although there isn't a single window in the place, skylights run the full length of it, flooding it with sunshine, and the light bounces around the plaster-boarded, white-washed walls and the bare concrete floor like it's a mirrored box. It's like stepping inside a cathedral full of sunshine, except here, the pews are deep shelves made from pallets holding dozens of upright canvasses, and the stained-glass windows are paintings stacked on the floor, leant face to face, but with the odd one visible. The ones I can see are astonishing, sweeping expanses of mountains; the weather rich in every brush stroke. They're so evocative of the day they were painted I feel like I was there. I step inside the studio to get a better view, but the floor is so littered with cluttered trestle tables, smaller tables holding brushes and tubes of paint and paint-daubed easels, one holding an unfinished picture of the valley, that I have to pick my way through. Over in the far corner, a daybed is strewn with sheets, and it's easy to imagine a tortured artist working into the small hours and getting up at first light to continue. Everything rings with that story, except for the untidy heap of belongings by the door: clothes, books, toiletries, even a chess set – its pieces scattered across the floor. They tell a very different tale.

I tiptoe around it, careful not to tread on the escaped pawns, and crouch down next to the untidy batch of paintings that are leaning against the wall. I tip them back one by one against my knees, and stop at the third painting. It's a small canvas of about 30x40cm, and it evokes an oncoming storm in the hills with a flock of sheep about to have a very wet night. I know it's the one Gillian described, but I check the others just to make sure, and pause over a two-tone oil study of Gillian in brown and white. It's beautiful; so human, with her a lot less weathered and sceptical than she is now. Her eyes look warmly into mine.

It's lovely, but it's not why I'm here, so I extract the landscape and tip the rest back as they were. I lock up the studio and carry it inside, and find Gillian is still standing where I left her. She doesn't move as I slide the painting onto its hook and step back.

There's no outpouring of emotion. There doesn't need to be. Her mute nod and uncomfortable swallow tells me everything, and hobbling back to the kitchen she sits heavily in her chair and picks up the e-reader.

'Time to start dinner, I think,' I say gently. I make sure I don't look at her.

'Yes, I think so,' she agrees, and I open the fridge to see what we can have.

After dinner, Gillian settles back into her chair with the e-reader. I half-heartedly pick up a biro and a pile of envelopes that need returning and settle myself on the sofa. It's going to be a long task, but rather than scribble out Gillian's address, I doodle big daisies across the bottom. I put in a trellis behind them and draw on some roses, and off to one side I add in spires of foxgloves, and a butterfly for good measure. Then, seeing as I can't get the idea out of my head, I turn over the envelope and start a small, loose pen drawing of Bryn staring dourly over his five-bar gate on the back. My pen bumps over the joins in the envelope, but I keep going. I add the collie, just visible between the bars, peering through with intelligent eyes and one ear cocked. It's not in my usual style – I used to draw highly detailed pictures that took weeks. No, this is something new, and I'm enjoying it!

I add the camping sign to the gate, put it down on the coffee table and stare at it feeling slightly stunned, unsure if it's a breakthrough or an aberration. Gillian peers over the e-reader at it and nods.

'Decent likeness,' she says.

'Thanks,' I say, because given her brazen honesty, I'm flattered.

'I have to say, I'm surprised,' she adds.

So am I, but I think her surprise is that I can draw something recognisable, not that I've drawn at all. 'Why? I did go to art college.'

'Well, for one thing, Marion doesn't have an artistic bone in her body, and for another, I've learnt qualifications mean very little when it comes to art.' I glance up at her, tearing my eyes away from Bryn's likeness. 'Of course they can teach you method,' she grants, 'and allow you to explore styles, but some of the so-called "professional artists" we had up here . . . well, one look at their work told you they'd completely missed the point of doing it.'

'And what, in your opinion, is the point of doing it?'

She looks at me as though I'm stupid. 'Expression and enjoyment, of course! Art should be fun – bring joy and emotion, not be so far up its own arse it takes three pages and an "expert" to explain it. It's time people realised, that when it comes to art, there *are* no rankings. Whether it's the process or the finished product, it should make people *feel* something, otherwise what's the point?'

She's right, and I've been missing that point for a very

long time as I tried to claw my way towards some kind of success. So much so, I'd lost my love for it while trying to make money out of it, and stopped doing it. Whereas this drawing of Bryn – even though it's on the back of an envelope with a crappy biro, and will be of little interest to anyone who doesn't know him – I drew for me, and is the most enjoyable and satisfying thing I've drawn in years. And, what's more, I can't stop looking at it.

'It's one of the things they said at art college – don't forget that a child's picture can be more valuable to someone than a Rembrandt or a Van Gogh,' I say, remembering.

'Exactly! Everything else is just visual clutter and self-aggrandisement!' she says, and I reach out and pick up the drawing again. 'Mike and I used to discuss that kind of thing all the time.'

'The value of art?' I ask.

'More like what is art, and what is an artist. He hated the idea of artists locked away in their ivory towers torturing themselves.'

That isn't the impression I got from his studio, or from Joe, come to that. 'But isn't that why he moved up here? To stalk the hills, brooding and tortured, clutching canvases?'

Gillian half smiles. 'Maybe to begin with, but he quickly moved on to championing the principles behind the Arts and Crafts movement. He thought there was a lot to be said for sharing ideas and techniques, inspiring people and getting everyone involved in art. He really believed in the health and dignity acquired from creating something, and frequently quoted Salvador Dalí, saying: "A true artist is not one who is inspired, but one who inspires others." I'd even go as far as to say he was quite the idealist by the end.'

'He sounds exciting to be around.'

Gillian hesitates, and the enthusiasm dies in her eyes. 'Yes,' she agrees, her voice flat. 'But enough of the past.' She nods at my phone. 'Have you figured out what to do with yourself using your phone?' It's an obvious change of subject, but since she's already opened up more than I expected, and it brings up a subject I've been wondering how to broach, I let her have it.

'It's a multistage process, by the looks of it.'

'Like the twelve steps for AA?' she half jokes.

'Something like that. Otherwise there's Gandhi's path.'

'Which is?'

I look it up on my phone so I get the words right. '"The best way to find yourself is in the service of others." I'm doing that already, so job done, do you think?'

I am, of course, joking, but Gillian shakes her head. 'I doubt the road to enlightenment has shortcuts, and besides, with that advice you'd end up as a bloody doormat!' I frown at her. 'Not that he wasn't a great humanitarian,' she concedes.

'Then we're back to the multistage process, only . . . I need you to do it with me.'

Gillian's mouth drops open. 'Why? I don't need to find myself! I know exactly where I am.'

'Maybe you do, but I need a partner to stop me deluding myself, and I can't think of anyone better for that than you.' I grin at her and her mouth twists. 'And it's not like you have anything better to do,' I add daringly.

Gillian's gaze hardens, but then something in her demeanour changes and she smiles. 'All right. Where do we start?'

I'm not sure I trust her expression. There's something almost dangerous in it, but I pick up my phone and find the web page. 'Vivienne asked me three questions.'

'And they were?'

'"What would you do if money were no object?"'

'Move to the Seychelles.'

I want to ask why, but perhaps it's best to keep going

with the questions while she's willing to answer them. '"What don't you want to regret at the end of your life?"'

'Choices I made.' Her unwavering stare forbids me to ask for details.

'And "What three words would you use to describe yourself?"'

Gillian's eyes narrow. 'What words did you use?'

I hesitate. I don't want to say, but if I don't, she won't open up. I take a deep breath. 'Aimless, lonely and bored.' I wait for Gillian's scathing assessment, but she only raises her eyebrows.

'Hmm, well, if we're being honest, I'd say gullible, angry and . . .' She looks around the room. 'Put angry twice.'

'So gullible and double angry?' I check.

'Yes.' She holds my gaze. I have so many questions! Gullible suggests she was duped, but by whom? And 'double angry'? But her eyes are almost glittering with defiance.

'OK, some stuff for both of us to work on there,' I say timidly.

She turns on the e-reader, and puts her glasses back on to show we're done. I pick up my drawing of Bryn, but Gillian's 'gullible and double angry' has me intrigued. Something must have happened, but what? The pile of Mike's stuff in the studio suggests it had something to do with him, but I know so little about him, I daren't even guess, and I'm not sure this is something I can bring up with Joe.

I move to put the stack of junk mail back on the dresser and Gillian looks at me over her glasses. 'When you're done, I think I'll go to bed.'

It's only half past eight, but I can see she's tired. I am, too, but my mind's whirring. Perhaps I'll go to bed with a good book. Not the e-reader, obviously, but I found a copy of *Dracula* while sorting through the post. Lonely castle, middle of nowhere, two lone occupants, secrets and mystery – quite appropriate, really. I take another look at my sketch of Bryn and warmth washes through me, partly because I've finally drawn something, but also because it's good! It has something of a sentry or a sentinel about it . . .

'Can you hurry up, I need a wee,' Gillian grumbles.

'Will do,' I say, and putting the drawing back down on the coffee table, I offer her my hand.

13

Tempestuous Times

Unsure whether to expect Joe after his swift exit with Petra yesterday, and having heard Gillian shift restlessly, I go down to help her get up. It takes a fair bit of grumbling and swearing, but we manage it and she's sitting in her armchair with my e-reader, sipping tea and unconsciously munching her way through a packet of bourbon biscuits when Joe finally knocks at the front door. I'm just straightening up Gillian's makeshift bedroom, so I shout through that it's open and I'll be out in a minute. A few minutes later, I come out and almost trip over Joe standing in front of Mike's painting.

'Good morning,' I say cheerfully.

For a second he doesn't move. Then, breaking free of whatever spell the painting has cast over him, he turns, takes my hand and looks fervently into my eyes. A smile radiates across his face, and before I can collect my thoughts he walks into the kitchen and greets Gillian.

'How's my most belligerent aunt today?'

I follow him, and grin at Gillian as she assesses him severely over the top of her glasses.

'Bloody-minded,' she replies. 'How's my recalcitrant nephew and his dim-witted, hoity-toity sister?'

'We're both fine.'

'Come to any decisions?' Her expression hasn't softened one iota.

'No. And she's not a dimwit.' He doesn't refute the 'hoity-toity' bit, though, I notice.

'Good!'

'That she's not a dimwit?' I check as I skirt around them to check if the washing cycle I put on earlier has finished.

'Yes!' She turns her attention to me. 'There's no challenge if she's stupid.'

Making use of her inattention, Joe tries to tip the e-reader screen to see what she's reading, but Gillian yanks it back.

'Mind your own business,' she snaps. 'Now make us both a cup of tea. Ella's had to take up *all* the slack while you've been gone.'

Joe's lips tighten, but he nods. He turns to me. 'Would you like one?'

'I'd love one.'

'Then sit down and take a break. She's hard work.'

Joe pulls a face at Gillian, and she holds up a finger in warning. 'Watch it. You're not too old to put across my knee,' she warns.

'You'd have to catch me first,' and he switches on the kettle with a flourish.

Gillian shakes her head in disgust. 'Taking advantage of an old lady's decrepitude. You should be ashamed!'

Joe grins. 'And yet, I'm not!'

'Scamp,' mutters Gillian darkly. 'So, how's the duchess settling in up at the cottage?' Joe's brow furrows a little, and Gillian sighs. 'Let me guess: it's too small, has no modern conveniences and it's a social wasteland.' Joe nods, while Gillian shakes her head. 'Of course it bloody is – that's the point! It's a haven for people to work on their masterpieces . . . or grand opuses,' she adds in deference to Joe.

'That's not much of a bonus for Petra,' says Joe.

'Of course it isn't, considering her creativity is limited to styling that poor dog! But having somewhere quiet to work is important to you, isn't it?' Gillian watches him carefully, and I can't help feeling sorry for him.

'Gillian . . .' Joe closes his eyes in exasperation, and I glance at the washing machine, hoping to escape out into the garden, but it still hasn't finished its cycle.

Gillian sighs. 'Look, Joe, I know she wants to sell. She said as much at Mike's wake.'

Joe presses his lips together. 'I didn't know you'd heard her,' he says quietly.

'Well, I did.'

'Then you also heard me telling her I wasn't even going to contemplate selling.'

'I did, but I also know she can be very persuasive. I'm sure she's been telling you Exeter is better, that it's expensive to maintain a cottage, that I'm not really a relative. How long before you decide she has a point?'

Joe's eyes meet mine guiltily as he hands around tea. 'I've told her we're not selling right now. That's why Petra drove off the other night . . . and why Ella landed in a ditch.'

'But you've considered it.' Gillian's statement hangs in the air. Joe's face colours, and he suddenly turns on his heel and walks out of the kitchen holding his tea.

Gillian rubs her forehead anxiously as the front door slams. 'Bugger, I thought so.'

'Should I go after him?' I ask.

She sips her tea, winces at how hot it is, and puts it down. 'Yes, go and get him. Tell him we'll change the subject.'

Joe took his tea, so I don't think he's gone far. I pick up mine, and head out to find him leaning on the bonnet of his car, staring out across the valley deep in thought. I perch next to him and sip my tea.

'She's scared,' I say, not looking at him.

'I know.' He exhales. 'But I couldn't stay in there – not when I'd agreed, no matter for how short a time, that I'd sell.'

'Why did you agree?'

Joe shrugs. 'Petra needs the money. I've used up all my capital buying the house, and when I've been up here recently, Huw's been busy on his farm, and what with Mike gone, and Gillian shutting me out . . . the valley just didn't hold the draw it once did. I found it too lonely, and if we're not using it . . .'

'It's difficult to justify keeping the cottage,' I finish for him.

'Exactly, and to be honest, if Gillian hadn't fallen, I *would* have sold . . .' Joe runs his hand distractedly through his hair. '. . . even though Mike would have hated that.'

'But if Mike wanted you to keep it, why didn't he just leave it to you in the first place?'

Joe scuffs the ground with his boot. 'Because Mum said it was favouritism to leave it to just me; it had to be both or neither of us.'

I blow out a breath. 'And has Petra always been in favour of selling?'

Joe nods. 'Pretty much, but when she was happily settled in London and the housing market wasn't that great, she agreed to hang on to it. However, now she's single and needs the money to put into her eBay business selling knick-knacks . . . and since the cottage is half hers . . .' He shakes his head at the impossibility of it all.

'What happens if you refuse to sell?'

'She'll never forgive me. And if I upset Petra, Mum will be furious.'

'And your dad?'

'Dad will be very Zen about it, then, like a feather landing on a balance, come down on Mum's side.'

'And if you do sell?'

'Gillian will never forgive me, and what's more, I'm starting to wonder if I'll ever forgive myself.'

'Jeez. Damned if you do. Damned if you don't,' I sum up, and Joe nods. We stare out across the valley. The clouds merge, and the opposite hillside turns monochrome and dark. 'If it's just about money, could you or Petra get a loan?'

'I already have a mortgage, and Petra doesn't have a hope with her financial record. Credit cards,' he adds by way of explanation.

'Hmm.' It's easy to imagine Petra laden with expensive paper and rope carrier bags, flashing her teeth and her credit card with gay abandon. 'What would you do with the cottage if it was just yours?'

A humourless smile graces his face. 'A few days ago, I'd have happily sold it, but now Gillian's talking to me again? I don't know. I might have kept it, but then again, maybe the place has changed too much, and considering it isn't the same for Gillian, either, maybe we should both consider moving on.' His voice is wistful, but the way he writes off Gillian's wishes puts my back up.

I frown up at him. 'To what, exactly?'

'What?'

'What should Gillian move on to? Or are you thinking along the same lines as my mum: she suggested that Gillian should go into sheltered accommodation, or get a nice little flat somewhere near the shops.' The bitterness in my tone surprises even me.

'What? No! I was just thinking of a fresh start somewhere new. Why? What did Gillian say when your mum suggested it?'

'"Sod off," I think! And I'm betting the paint blistered around where Mum takes phone calls, so I'd think carefully before you make a suggestion like that, because Gillian sees herself *here* in ten years' time!'

'How can you possibly know that?'

'Because I asked.'

Joe looks at me incredulously. 'You've known her less than three days and you asked her that?'

I nod.

'Huh,' he says thoughtfully. He puts his mug down on the bonnet and folds his arms, both mirroring and challenging me. 'All right, seeing as you seem to have been the one asking pertinent questions, what do *you* think I should do?'

I feel myself blanch. I don't know what I'd do, and truth be told I'd hate to be in his position. 'It's your decision, but if you really want to know what I think, I think you should at least make sure Gillian's in a position to cope. That way, she'll be fine whatever you decide.'

Joe tips his head. 'Fair point,' he concedes, and a ray of sunshine sheers through the clouds to illuminate the far hilltops. 'I'd still like to know what you'd do, though.'

I worry at my bottom lip with my teeth. 'I'd stall,' I say truthfully, 'until I figure out what I want.' Ironic, considering 'figuring out what I want' seems to also be my eternal question. 'And I'd help Gillian and Ella as much as I could,' I add seriously.

He tries to hold back a smile. 'I'll do that, then.' He gets up off the bonnet, picks up his mug and offers me a hand up. 'And what if I decide to sell?' he asks. 'Gillian's going to fight me every inch of the way.'

'I'd say, if that's what you want to do, "Lay on, Macduff".'

'"And damned be him that first cries, 'Hold, enough!'"?' he says, continuing the quote.

'You know your *Macbeth*!'

'Of course,' he says in surprise. 'I studied it, *and* it's one of my favourites.'

'Mine, too! Along with *The Tempest*. I did illustrations for them at college.'

'"Why, thou deboshed fish thou." But don't test me. I only remember that phrase because I liked the insult.'

'I always liked "I do begin to have bloody thoughts."'

He pulls a face. 'Sounds like Gillian. Speaking of which, perhaps we should go in.'

'Perhaps,' I agree, and I follow him inside.

14

Backchat

'You took your sweet time,' Gillian grumbles as we come back in.

Joe glares at me as I slide past them both to the washing machine, leaving him to contend with Gillian by himself. 'Venting about you *takes* some sweet time!' he says, rallying. 'And don't act all affronted, you knew it would be a tricky subject when you brought it up.'

'Well, excuse me for mentioning the elephant in the room! Next time I'll just sweep it under the carpet and pretend it isn't under there, sneezing, shall I?'

'I'm just asking you not to ride about on it setting off fireworks, that's all.'

'I wasn't. I was discussing it calmly. *You* were the one who stormed out.'

Joe sighs, and I can feel him watching me as I tip Gillian's wet clothes into a laundry basket. 'All right, maybe I was. But I've had enough of talking about it, so how about this? When I make a decision, I'll discuss it with you.'

'Promise?' she asks.

'Promise. Now let's change the subject.'

'Yes, let's,' she agrees, and confident they're fine again, I slide on one of Gillian's coats and escape out of the back door.

I hang Gillian's clothes on the line, and as the sun's come

out, I perch on the wall and check my phone. There's a text from Vivienne.

'How it's going? Vxxx.'

I quickly choose her number, and she picks up almost immediately.

'Hi, Ella,' she says cheerfully. 'Just wondered how your aunt's doing?'

'Better, now she's out of hospital.'

'Good. What's she like?'

'Wonderful, terrible, rude,' I offer, plucking words out of thin air.

'Fabulous – how rude?'

'Utterly forthright, blatant and without any kind of filter. You'd like her.'

Vivienne laughs. 'I love her already! So what's the story? How come she needed you?'

'Actually, I'm not a hundred per cent sure. I mean, I know she's grieving, but I'm getting the oddest feeling there's more to it,' and I tell Vivienne about the strange excess of post, the disconnected phone, the scratches on the studio door and the flat tyres. 'Then, on top of that, Gillian refuses to discuss the past.'

'That's not so odd, surely,' protests Vivienne.

'Maybe not, but . . . I don't know, I can't put my finger on it.'

'You have a feeling there's something more?'

'Yes. Particularly as she described herself as gullible and *double* angry.'

'Gullible sounds suspicious, but isn't anger one of the stages of grief?'

I sigh. 'Yes, but . . . you know when there's something someone's not telling you?'

'Yes,' agrees Vivienne. 'Perhaps it's to do with the family rift and she doesn't want to put you in a difficult position?'

'It's possible, I suppose, but I don't think that would stop Gillian. Not unless it was something *really* bad.'

Vivienne pauses. 'Might your mum know what happened?' I hear a ting in the distance. 'Shit! That's a customer,' says Vivienne, and for the customer's sake, I hope Vivienne's said that out of earshot. 'Phone your mum and let me know any revelations. Love you!'

'You, too!'

Vivienne disconnects and I stare out across the roof of the house, then quickly scroll down to Mum's number before I chicken out. After three rings I almost hang up, but then Mum answers.

'Ah, Eleanor, had enough already?' she asks.

'No, no, everything's fine,' I say quickly. 'Actually, I'm phoning to ask what happened between Aunt Gillian and Granny and Grandpa all those years ago. I thought I'd better check so I don't tread on any toes.'

'Oh, I wouldn't worry – Gillian was never one to waste time on other people's feelings.'

'Still, seeing as I'm going to be here for a while, wouldn't it be a good idea if I knew?'

Mum sighs. 'What do you want to know?'

Everything, but I don't want her to clam up. 'What was Gillian like?'

Mum lets out a half-laugh. 'Gillian was selfish, right from a small child. Wilful they called it back then, but it boils down to the same thing: selfish and inconsiderate. Granny and Grandpa had enormous trouble with her.'

'What kind of trouble?'

'Associating with the wrong children, playing in the woods, always filthy with no regard for time or what people thought.

She had no concept of propriety and Granny and Grandpa were beside themselves trying to keep her under control. Whatever rules they laid down: she broke. Whatever punishments they gave: she flouted. And when they grounded her, she unscrewed the blocks they put on her window to stop the sashes going up.'

I can't help admiring Gillian a little, because Granny and Grandpa always terrified me, with their posh house full of china ornaments in glass-fronted cabinets and their constant frowns. I remember sitting very upright at their kitchen table, struggling with outsized cutlery under their watchful gaze, forbidden from their posh dining room with all the photographs of Mum growing up. I snuck in there once. There were silver-framed photos of Mum in her tennis whites, Mum at ceremonies, Mum in the garden, Mum at family weddings, but now I think about it, there weren't many of Gillian, and those that there were, included Mum.

'So she was rebellious?' I ask.

'That's putting it mildly,' agrees Mum. 'She didn't study or tidy her room. She wouldn't wear skirts. The arguments were endless, and the worst came when it was time to apply to secretarial college. She flatly refused to go! Of course, Granny and Grandpa insisted, but the next thing we knew she'd run off to London to become a photographer, and living with hippies, smoking pot and weed—'

'Aren't they the same thing?'

'I don't know! Ask Gillian! What I'm telling you is that she broke their hearts.'

'So how did Gillian meet Mike?'

'She was sent to photograph his work, I believe. I don't know the details, but she moved in with him pretty damned quick, and when she said she didn't even intend to marry him – it was the final straw.'

I bet Granny's pruny features sucked in even tighter, and Grandpa's puce face looked fit to burst. 'Did Granny and Grandpa ever speak to her again?'

'No.' Mum's tone is oddly closed off.

'Did you try and persuade them?'

Mum hesitates. 'I did visit Gillian once. I begged her to have a registry office wedding if they must, but Gillian refused, so there was nothing left to talk about.'

I struggle to imagine Mum begging anyone for anything. 'What was it like when you came here?'

'Primitive. So much so, I almost wondered if Gillian was doing it to spite us. Granny and Grandpa certainly thought so. They said Mike would leave her and she'd come crawling back, penniless and pregnant . . . and in a roundabout way, I suppose they were right.'

'Mike died, Mum. There was no crawling, no baby.'

Mum goes very quiet.

'What did you make of Mike?' Mum goes so quiet, I wonder if we've been cut off. 'Mum?'

'Not sure, really,' she says coldly. 'Driven. Obsessed with his art. So obsessed I don't think he even noticed Gillian half the time. That's why I found it so difficult to understand. If he'd adored her that would be one thing, but . . .' Mum peters out. I wait, but she doesn't continue.

'Well, thanks. It's good to know what happened.'

'If you say so. Now, I must go. I *am* at work,' she points out. 'Goodbye, Ella,' and with an irritated sigh, she cuts the line. I check the phone screen to make sure she's disconnected, and gaze at the opposite hillside picturing Gillian's childhood.

'Hi, Eleanor.'

I jerk out of my reverie. Petra's standing on the path looking pristine, whereas I'm sitting on a wall in Gillian's old coat. I smile politely, unsure how much of my call she might have heard. 'Hi, Petra. Would you like a coffee, or are you here to see Joe?'

She glances uneasily at the back door. 'Actually, I came to see you – and at the perfect time, by the looks of it.' I give her a blank look. 'Seeing as you've been driven outside by the Auntichrist.' She smiles, proud of her pun.

'Oh, I'm just out here because I get a better signal.' I hold up my phone.

'God, I know. This place is the back of beyond. Even the satellites don't pass over it,' she says, unperturbed. 'Anyway, I came to see if you want to come out for a drink tonight?'

'Oh! Well, I shouldn't really – I'm here to help Gillian,' I say, uncomfortably aware that Gillian will brazenly expose me if she hears.

Petra flaps her hand. 'Joe will stay. He said you deserve a break, and it's only down the track. And wouldn't it be good to get to know each other, since we're *almost* related? Go on, please?' She pouts endearingly.

The '*almost* related' bit has me, and I'd quite like to hear more about Mike and Gillian. 'All right,' I agree, smiling despite myself. 'But only if Joe says it's OK.'

'Of course he will! See you at eight?' She's so pleased it's hard not to grin back at her.

'Eight, it is.'

She glances unwillingly at the back door. 'And could you tell Joe we're on for this evening?'

'Sure,' and with a little wave, she goes back around the side of the house.

Joe's in the kitchen as I let myself in. 'Was that Petra?'

'Yes, asking me out for a drink. Was that your doing?'

'Partly. I think she finds it a bit lonely up here. Did she tell you I'll stay with Gillian?'

I nod. 'Thanks.'

'No problem. Besides, Gillian and I have a few things to thrash out, and that's probably best done in private.'

'Probably,' I agree, and together we start on lunch.

After lunch, I sit at the kitchen table and sort through Gillian's bills. Fortunately most of them, like the electric and water bills, are paid by direct debit, but the TV licence has expired, which explains why it's dumped in the spare bedroom, and more worryingly, given the state of the lock on the studio, the house insurance needs renewing. There are also some letters with a solicitor's logo on, so I slit open the earliest one and hand it to Gillian.

Gillian frowns as she reads it, and calls Joe. 'Is this anything to do with you?'

There's a warning in her tone, and as Joe reads it, his expression clouds. 'Nothing, whatsoever.'

He hands it back to Gillian, who passes it to me. There are two more letters with the same logo, and I hand them to her in exchange.

'Read that one,' she instructs, and I skim-read it until I come to the nub of the matter:

'It has come to our attention that certain aspects of your partner's will have not been attended to. Various interested parties have requested that, should the money not be put to its intended purpose, steps be taken to ensure the funds pass on to the family, as per the "remainder of Mike Masters' estate clause".'

I lay the letter on the table. 'What do they mean by "intended purpose"?'

Gillian rubs her forehead and glances at Joe. 'Mike wanted me to establish an artistic retreat here at the studio. I don't know, something about living on in posterity, inspiring artists of the future, with the Mike Masters Institute for Artistic

Excellence, or some other self-aggrandising title over the door. I think he did it almost as a joke, thinking he'd write another will before he died, but here we are, and it's left for me to deal with.'

'And who benefits if you don't do this?'

'Joe's mother, who doesn't need the money . . . and by extension, Petra.' Gillian looks up at Joe, who's as taut as a bowstring.

'Is it a lot of money?' I ask.

Gillian dips her head. 'Near enough a hundred thousand.'

'Jesus! And the other two letters?'

Gillian drops them on the coffee table. 'Demanding a reply, and "wishing to hear my plans at my earliest convenience". Well, they can all go whistle – I'm not interested in any of them!'

Joe looks daggers at the floor.

'All right, then let's get the house insurance sorted,' I suggest, as I have no intention of getting in the middle of any dispute between Gillian and Joe's family.

'Yes,' agrees Gillian, and as I pick up the house insurance documents and plug in the phone, Joe quietly pockets the solicitor's letters, his eyes warning me not to say a word.

15

Rum Talk

I release my hair from its clip and run my fingers through it. I apply some mascara and lip gloss, and before I can think too deeply, I take my purse and head downstairs.

In the kitchen, Joe and Gillian are settled into the armchairs and Joe is reading aloud as Pompom snuffles for crumbs under the kitchen table.

Joe looks up and smiles. 'You look lovely.'

My eyes meet his and stay there. 'Presentable enough for a drink with Petra?'

'More than!'

'Thanks.'

Gillian nods approvingly. 'Have a nice time. Just don't come back thinking I should be euthanised. Petra's a dab hand at brainwashing people into thinking I'm the Wicked Witch of the West.'

Bozz blinks at me from the dresser, the very image of a witch's familiar.

I grin. 'Too late, I already found your broomstick and wand.'

'If I had one, I'd have used it,' Gillian mutters darkly. 'Given her a wart.'

'Keep it nice,' warns Joe. 'Or I'll stop reading this to you.'

I wink at Gillian. 'What's the book?'

He holds it up. It's a P.D. James detective novel. 'Inspiration for me, and entertainment for this one to stop her snacking on small children.'

Gillian smirks. 'I'm good with children: fricassee, barbecue, stew.' She chortles happily to herself, while Joe shakes his head and checks his watch.

'Hadn't you better get going?' he asks.

I check my phone and he's right – I'm late. I wave my fingers at them, and with my car keys in hand I head out the door.

The pub is nothing like the 'country pubs' in London, with their wooden floorboards, screwed-down watercolours and *objets d'art* glued to every surface. This one has authentic scarred furniture, sticky carpets, real nicotine-stained ceilings, genuine faux-leather banquette seating and a fruit machine that's probably older than I am.

Petra hails me from a corner table. I thread my way over to her, the locals monitoring my progress with one outright staring, and take a seat.

'Ignore them,' Petra hisses as I give them a sideways look. 'They don't get many visitors. Fancy a drink? I'm buying. Word to the wise: don't touch the white wine – it's worse than vinegar.'

'What are you drinking?'

'I'd recommend rum and Coke. I haven't had it since my teens, but needs must.'

'Same then, please,' I agree.

She goes to the bar commendably unfazed, puts in my order and gestures to our table. The man serving, presumably Gareth's dad, gives a small suspicious nod, while the woman, who I assume is Gareth's mum, smiles at me as Petra comes back.

'This place is the back of beyond,' she whispers, sitting down. 'You can't imagine how pleased I was to find *you* here.'

That wasn't my first impression. 'Don't you have any friends up here?'

'No, everyone's either ancient or so ensconced in the "lifestyle" they might as well be. You know, farming . . .' she whispers scornfully in answer to my blank look. 'Or art.'

'Joe has some friends up here, though?'

'Yes. He and Huw played together as kids. Huw lives with Seren at the top end of the valley, but like I said, he's a farmer and she's into quilting and kids.' Petra pulls a face at one, two or all three of these things. 'And then there's Bridget. She's old like Gillian and . . . well, she's into felting and disapproves of me.' Petra pouts.

'So what do you do?' I ask, changing the subject.

'Internet retail.' She looks haughty for a nanosecond then grins. 'I have a business selling things on eBay.'

'What kind of things?'

'You know how some people love owls? Others love cats, dragonflies, avocados, sloths?' I nod, even though avocados are a new one on me. 'Well, I find suppliers who make ornaments, cushions, earrings, scarves depicting those things and I categorise them by theme to make present-buying easier. And I seem to be doing something right, because it's doing brilliantly.'

'Wow!' I'm impressed, despite myself. 'I wouldn't know where to start.'

'No, well,' she says modestly, but her eyes stray to Gareth, who arrives with my drink plus one for himself.

'Ladieez,' he says with a lazy smile that would make Vivienne shudder. 'Good to see you. Is it girls' night or can anyone join?'

'No, join us, Gareth,' says Petra. She shifts along the banquette so he can sit beside her. 'You don't mind, do you, Eleanor?'

'No, of course not – and call me Ella.'

'Gareth, this is Ella —' begins Petra, but Gareth holds up a hand.

'No need. Ella and I are old friends, aren't we, Ella? There's already been some bed action.'

Petra freezes. 'Oh?'

I roll my eyes. 'He helped me carry Gillian's bed downstairs, that's all,' I say, quickly pruning any thoughts in that direction.

Gareth subtly tenses his muscles. 'Always ready to help a woman in distress.'

'I bet you are,' says Petra, smiling broadly.

'I'll tell Gillian,' I say, toasting him.

Petra sips her drink. 'I didn't realise you knew anyone up here.'

I smile at her. 'I don't, not really. In fact, I only met Gillian the other day. Family rift,' I explain in response to her enquiring look. 'And I never met Mike at all. Although I've heard he was quite a character.'

'Yes, he was, but then I never spent much time with him, either,' admits Petra.

Gareth laughs. 'There's funny – two of you related to the man, and I probably knew him better than either of you!'

It's not that funny, but I smile anyway. 'So what was he like?'

'Single-minded – spent most of his time painting, but when he came to the pub he was the life and soul of the party.' Gareth shakes his head in admiration. 'People loved him – came from all over the country to take his classes, and they stayed here in the pub, or camped in Uncle Bryn's field.'

'Bryn's your uncle?' It's funny to think of easy-going Gareth being related to Bryn.

Gareth nods. 'Yes, Mam's brother. Those artists were a

funny lot, though. They'd spend all day getting soaked in the hills, then come back like drowned rats and drink. And they *really* could drink,' he says appreciatively.

'So lots of artists used to visit?' I ask.

'Not just artists – friends, buyers, models, fans. They all stayed here, and then Mike died, and Gillian sent them all packing!' He shakes his head at the loss of business.

'You make it sound very sudden,' I say, surprised.

'Overnight,' agrees Gareth. 'Night of the wake, it was. One night it's business as usual and the next the place is a ghost town – no one staying, no one camping, no parties, no artists, no drinking the night away, and all because Mike had a brain haemorrhage in the hills.'

Poor Gillian! I hadn't dared ask, and Mum didn't know. It must have come as a real shock. 'I hadn't realised it affected the valley so much,' I say, trying to cover my irritation at his narrow outlook.

'It did. It's only a matter of time before we lose the pub,' which I suppose explains why the people at the bar are giving me such searching glances.

'And what about Gillian? Did her friends rally round?'

Gareth nods. 'They tried! But after the wake, Gillian wouldn't let anyone in, and no one had a clue why.'

'Do *you* know why?' I ask Petra. She's bored and drawing circles on the table using the condensation from her glass, but even though she shakes her head, I'm too interested to change the subject.

'It was *weird*!' says Gareth. 'Even at the wake she wasn't right, and when people went up afterwards to see if she was OK, she sent them away. Swore at them, even, and everyone was so shocked they didn't celebrate Mike's life like we expected them to; just raised a glass and went to bed.'

'It *was* a funeral,' I point out.

Gareth shakes his head. 'Before the service, we were

expecting a rowdy lock-in, but afterwards it was as quiet as the grave . . . and has been ever since – no offence.'

'And I thought this place was dead *before* Mike died,' says Petra.

Gareth and Petra start to discuss the valley's shortcomings, but I'm still stuck on Gillian – it sounds like she snapped. But why? Was it just Mike's death hitting her? I've heard that burying a loved one can act as closure and help people move on, but this sounds like the opposite.

'Ella?' prompts Petra, and I realise I haven't heard a word.

'Sorry, miles away. What?'

'I was saying we should go out one night; visit the local town, go dancing. What do you think?'

I smile half-heartedly. 'I'm here to look after Gillian, but you two should go.'

Petra's eyes flick to Gareth and back to me. 'Surely you deserve a night off.'

'Yes, but what if she falls?'

'Joe will watch her. Honestly, you'll be doing him a favour – he's been feeling guilty about selling the cottage. Go on. It'll be fun.'

Gareth's mouth drops open. 'You're selling?'

'Yes.' Petra nods, like it's a done deal. 'We had an estate agent up a few weeks ago. He couldn't give us more than an estimate because I couldn't get up here with the keys, but he looked around the outside.'

'Oh!' says Gareth, light dawning. 'It was your place he was talking about! He came in here complaining that he couldn't get inside the property because the woman asking for the valuation couldn't let him in. We thought he was talking about Gillian's!'

'I hope he valued the right cottage,' says Petra, annoyed. She searches her bag like she's set to phone him right now, even though it's well out of office hours.

Gareth looks at me. 'Well, we should definitely all go out before you leave me here all by myself!'

'Yes, we definitely should. How about it, Ella?' asks Petra, abandoning her search.

'I'm not sure how long I'll be staying, and I really should make sure Gillian—'

'Oh, for God's sake, you're coming. I won't take no for an answer,' growls Petra. She smiles cheekily at me.

'And I'll drive!' says Gareth.

They're both so eager, it's almost impossible to go up against them. 'I'll see, depending on when you want to go.'

'Yay!' cries Petra, squeezing Gareth's hand, and he gives her a warm look.

I shake my head at them. 'So, tell me who lives up here,' I say. 'I need to sort out some visitors for Gillian,' and Gareth starts listing the residents of the upper valley.

'Originally there were two sheep farms – the one up the valley is now run by Huw and Huw's old dad, Daf.' He glances towards an old man at the bar.

'I met Huw when my car got beached,' I agree. I glance at Petra, but she doesn't show the faintest unease.

'Then there's the four summer cottages,' continues Gareth, 'mostly owned by artists. They're empty most of the year, except for Bridget's. She lives here year-round, while the others just come up for the odd weekend.'

'And Bridget is Gillian's friend?' I check. I seem to remember Joe mentioning her.

'They *were* friends,' says Petra. 'But from what I've heard, even she hasn't seen Gillian over the last eighteen months.'

'Then there's Joe and Petra's cottage,' lists Gareth. 'Gillian's farm, which used to belong to my grandparents, and their parents before them, and their parents etc. etc.' He leaves a significant pause. 'And Bryn's bungalow, which my grandparents built when they found out neither Mam nor Uncle Bryn wanted to be farmers.'

'And they sold the farmhouse to Mike?' I ask.

Gareth nods. 'Mam got the money to buy the pub, Uncle Bryn moved away to work for the council, and the rest of the land went to Daf. Then, when my grandparents became ill, Uncle Bryn moved back with his wife, Mair. She left, they died, and now it's just Bryn up there.'

I'm not sure I needed that much detail, but I smile with polite interest all the same. 'So there aren't many people up here?'

'No, and apart from us at the pub, that's about it,' admits Gareth.

'Then where do your customers come from?' I indicate the small crowd of elderly gents at the bar.

'There's Bryn, of course.' Bryn turns at the mention of his name, and I quickly look down. 'And Daf, Huw's dad. The rest of them come from the lower valley: the pub down there closed. In the summer we get a lot of hill walkers, but it's not the time of year for them now.'

Feeling awkward, I indicate our empty glasses and both Gareth and Petra nod, so I collect them together and take them to the bar. Gareth's dad glowers as I put them down.

'You're Gillian's niece. Staying long?' he asks, not quite conversationally, and Bryn's head lifts.

'A week, maybe two?' I try a smile, but it falls on stony ground, partly because he's bustled out of the way by Gareth's mum, whose hair is a vivid shade of brown for someone who's about sixty.

She smiles wide enough for both of them. 'Hello! That's George and I'm Dolores.'

'Ella.'

She holds out her hand and I offer mine. She shakes it

with three fingers in the way we're told posh people drink tea. 'Same again?' she asks.

'Yes, please.'

She takes some tall glasses from beneath the bar and reaches for the rum bottle. 'So, you're Gillian's niece?' she asks, and I notice she puts rum in only one.

'Yes,' I agree, and she plunges the glasses under the Coke dispenser.

'Nice, that – her having family around. Not that I've seen you here before, mind.'

'No.'

She looks me in the eye, until it's clear she's not going to get more of an answer. 'She up to visitors, then? Or is it still a no?'

'Err, the occasional one, I think?' I swallow uncomfortably.

'Oh lovely. We've been that worried about her, haven't we, boys?' The men at the bar murmur agreement. One even raises his pint. 'Been very worried,' she repeats. 'Tried to look out for her, didn't we, boys, but she wasn't having any of it. Slammed the door right in my face.' Her smile doesn't flicker. 'Not that we hold it against her. No, no. Not considering.' She fills a pint for Gareth, even though I only remember him having a half last time. 'Odd though. Didn't see you at the funeral?' She tips her head as if a different view of me might change that.

'No. Gillian and my mum don't get on.'

'That'll be it, then. Family rift.' She nods as she takes my money, puts it in the till, but she keeps my change in her hand. 'Awkward for you, though, Gillian being as difficult as she is.' She smiles, perhaps waiting for me to agree. I don't. 'Never mind. If she gets too much for you, there's plenty of room here.'

The grim George leans in on his way past. 'Reckon she's best off staying where she is.' He gives me a stern look, his English accent strangely at odds with his wife's Welsh one.

Dolores pats my hand as she finally relinquishes my change. 'Don't listen to him,' she whispers. 'You're always welcome, and I'll be sure to come up and see Gillian soon. Oh, and that one's Petra's,' she says, pointing to the rumless Coke. I look over at Petra, but she's deep in conversation with Gareth. I suppose she must have told Dolores she'd go alcohol free on her next drink.

I pick up all three glasses, and walk carefully back to Petra and Gareth. They're laughing and joking, but as I look back at the bar, something about George's demeanour has me spooked. Sure enough, he's smiling and joking with his other customers. I sip my drink and nod as Gareth and Petra chat about films I haven't seen and places they'd like to visit. They're happy in each other's company, so I don't feel guilty as I guzzle my drink and fidget to show I'm getting ready to leave.

'You're not going?' asks Petra, watching me put on my coat.

'Yes, I'm afraid so,' I say, trying to sound regretful. 'I'm tired. Thanks for the drink, though, Petra.'

'My pleasure, and thanks for mine.' She indicates hers, which she's hardly touched. Gareth raises his and turns back to Petra before I've even returned the gesture, and I let myself out of the pub with no regrets.

16

Put in the Picture

It's so cold outside, the evening air freezes my lungs like menthol, but since I've had two rum and Cokes, I do up my coat and leave Vivienne's car in the car park. I plod along the road, but as I clear the lights from the pub, all regret disappears as a firmament of stars stretches into the distance above me. It's a 3D landscape of clouds and stars, and a kaleidoscopic gift compared to anything I'd see in London. I stare up, meandering along the road until I turn up the track to Gillian's, and almost fall over, tripping on a wok-sized pothole. Glad there's no one to see, I concentrate more on the ground, and start to make steady progress up the hill.

Staring at the dark ground, images of everything I heard at the pub flash through my mind: Gillian happy, parties and art classes, Bryn's field full of tents and the pub heaving. It sounds magical, but can one man really support a valley? Can he really make that much difference? If he did, then no wonder he left such a hole behind, and no wonder Gillian's grieving.

. . . So why doesn't that sit right with me? 'Gullible and double angry', for one. And then there's all the other things.

I trudge past Bryn's. The curtain of the single lit window twitches as the collie smears its nose across the window. I wave at it, but it pulls back like an embarrassed curtain twitcher, and I carry on up the track. I pass the two fields, one empty apart from a standpipe and tap, the other with fruit trees and the remnants of a vegetable plot.

I pass through Gillian's gate and the yard light blasts on, which is another reminder that something isn't right, and a feeling of foreboding pricks at me. I shade my eyes and let myself in, keen to check everything's all right, but as I take off my coat, Gillian's snoring tells me everything is fine. I relax a little and find Joe in the kitchen, settled in an armchair, a drink at his elbow and with Pompom on his lap. As I come in, Joe puts the detective novel face down on the arm of the chair and smiles so warmly, all my concerns wash away as Pompom springs off his lap and rushes around my feet.

'Nice time?' he asks.

'Yes, thanks.' I pick up Pompom, laughing at her enthusiasm. 'Everything all right here?'

'Yes, after a few chapters read in a dull monotone, Gillian said she'd had enough of me draining all the emotion out of decent prose and went to bed.'

'Did you do it on purpose?'

'Might have done,' he says, his lips twitching.

'I wouldn't have let you off so easily – I loved being read to as a child. One or two of my infant teachers really brought books to life, and I still love a good audiobook.'

Joe nods. 'Mike used to read to me in this very room: on that very sofa, in fact.' He glances at it fondly. 'Gillian would be washing up or tidying the kitchen, pretending she wasn't listening, but she always laughed in the same places we did. It was nice.'

'It sounds it,' I say sincerely.

'It's good to have it back in here – and well done for getting the picture back up, by the way.' He gestures towards the hall.

'She missed it, so it wasn't that difficult.'

'Even so, you did well. And it's lovely to have him and his art back in the house.' Something about his words ring true.

It *was* like she evicted him. 'Which reminds me,' he says, reaching over to something beside his chair. 'Gillian asked me to find you these.' He hands me a sketch pad, a tin of pencils, some drawing pens, a bottle of ink and some brushes. 'They were Mike's. She said you might find them useful.'

I take them, my fingers shaking. On the cover of the sketch pad an unfamiliar hand has scrawled a message: *You need to start drawing again! Love Gillian.* I open the cover, and the pages are blank, but I find my sketch of Bryn tucked inside.

'It's good,' Joe says, indicating my drawing. His smile confirms he means it. 'And Gillian said you need to do some drawing to get yourself back on track. She said it's important.'

Tears prick my eyes. I clutch the art materials to my chest, and Joe holds up his glass to offer me one. I nod mutely and swallow with difficulty. He comes back with two glasses, and hands me one. I take a swift sip, and after a few settling breaths I smile at him.

'Thanks. Gillian saw more than I thought,' I explain.

Joe nods. There's sympathy in his eyes. 'I gather something happened?'

I tell him about the legal trouble I had with that awful company, and he listens with compassion.

'I can see why that left a scar,' he says, getting it immediately. 'Something similar happened to a writer friend of mine. He paid to have his work critiqued, and next thing he knew it was published on the Internet – he said he felt like he'd been burgled.'

I nod. It's exactly like that: ideas stolen and sold, only to end up who knows where.

'How long's it been since you enjoyed drawing?'

I think for a moment. 'About four years.'

'Then Gillian's right, you should draw again. And there *are* good companies out there; you just need to be wary.'

I take another sip of my whiskey. He's right, and if I want

to try drawing again, this place has pedigree. Maybe this is even why Fate sent me here? I smile at Joe, and put the art materials to one side, but my fingers stray to the bottle of ink and the pencils. Surprisingly, the feeling of nausea I usually get when I think about the whole episode is muted. I stroke the brushes in wonder, and wish I could do something as meaningful for Gillian, but I wouldn't know where to start.

'Did Gillian have any hobbies and interests?' Though now I say it, the words 'hobbies' and 'Gillian' don't sound right together. 'Or close friends we could ask to visit?' I ask, changing tack. 'Gareth said this place used to be a hive of activity.'

'It did. Unfortunately, she's alienated most people. As for hobbies . . .' Joe frowns and Gillian's distant snoring fills the gap.

'What did she do in her spare time?' I ask, trying to help.

'Her photography took a lot of time, of course – she was very much in demand and the go-to person for a lot of magazine editors. She was often off on assignments.'

'Was she?'

Joe nods. 'She was very well travelled, and her photos turned up in the glossies all the time. She was really highly thought of. Her pictures caught something real. I'd almost say warts and all, except they were more beautiful than that. They reach in and grab your soul, somehow.'

'Really? I mean, I knew she was a photographer, but I just assumed she was one of a myriad of photographers offering stock shots and photos for puff pieces.'

'Oh no, she was good. Why, haven't you ever seen any of her pictures?'

I shake my head, and for a second Joe looks shocked, then he takes out his phone and types in Gillian's name. He taps the images icon and hands it to me. I start to scroll through.

The first image is taken outside in India as the first monsoon raindrops hit the dry ground, and it's of a grandmother in a wheelchair, her grandchild on her knee, with both their faces and arms raised to the sky in delight. In the background, an adult is running bent almost double to fetch them in. It's simply called *Rain*.

'She won a competition for that one,' says Joe quietly.

The second captures a potter at his wheel at the exact moment the massive bowl he's throwing tears itself apart thanks to its weight and the wheel's centrifugal force. The potter's nose is wrinkled and his teeth are bared, but there's also a hint of amusement and inevitability in his expression. He knows he's pushed it too far. *Gone to Pot*, reads the title.

The third is of an extremely fit double amputee on her running blades, caught mid-enormous jump. A child looks on amazed, and the caption reads, *When I Grow Up . . .*

The next is of a beautiful actress, hair pinned under a skullcap ready for a wig, face white with make-up, and her expression is blank as she looks into the camera via a mirror. The title is *Blank Canvas*.

By contrast, the next is of an actor, famous for playing villains, his reading glasses perched on the end of his nose, frowning at the chessboard as his daughter, aged about ten, grips her bottom lip between her teeth, eyes wide with excitement, watching him search the chessboard. *Check Mate*.

There's one of a ballet dancer sitting on the floor with arms and legs bent like a spider tugging on its gossamer, wincing as she pulls off her ballet shoe. It's called *The Point*. Another shows a professional kitchen in uproar, circled around a smashed plate; the expensive layers of garnish and caviar a disjointed mess on the floor, surrounded by shards of crockery. The head chef is the only one looking up, his fingers bent into furious claws, and his bottom teeth jutting out. The caption reads, *Massacre*.

There's one of children, their faces puckered as a zookeeper shows them a giant millipede, all except for one little girl, her face beautiful in its complete delight. The title reads, *Worth It*, and I look up to find Joe watching me.

He smiles. 'Your aunt has some *serious* talent.'

'I had no idea!' I flick through a few more. A conductor squatting flat-footed with a score on the ground between his feet, his baton a blur as he hears the music in his head. *Beatnik*, reads the title. A ballet dancer dressed in tights and a leotard, scrabbling to pull her legs out of motorbike leathers. *Metamorphosis*.

I hand his phone back. 'And doing this is how she met Mike?'

'Yes, a journalist was doing an article on him, and they sent her to photograph Mike in action, as it were.'

'Was it love at first sight?'

Joe's eyes widen and he laughs, but not unkindly. 'Nothing so simple, I'm afraid. He took issue with one of her photographs.'

'What was wrong with it?'

'She'd photographed him looking dangerously angry with himself, scrubbing at a wrong brushstroke with a white-spirit-soaked rag. Apparently, the strength of rage on his face was almost frightening, so he forbade her from using it.'

'What happened?'

'She published it.'

'Against his will?'

Joe looks down and grins at his glass. 'No, Gillian gave it the title, *The Inner Turmoil of a True Artist*. I gather it spoke to his inner narcissist, and not long after, he commissioned her to take twelve more. It was that second visit that led to them seeing each other.'

'Love at second sight?'

'Or perhaps it all came down to how she captioned the moment.' Joe smiles at me. 'After that, she moved up here and they were a done deal.'

'And what happened once she moved here?'

'I don't think much changed as far as her photography and his painting went. They co-existed, but she also kept Mike going – and me, too, come to that.'

'And what about friends?'

Joe shrugs. 'She got on with everyone.'

'Really?'

Joe chuckles at my incredulity. 'She was just as straight-speaking,' he concedes, 'but back then she had time for people, and she listened, so people often dropped by for advice and a mug of tea.'

Thinking of Gillian's stark and oddly reassuring assessments, and how I go to Vivienne for just that kind of straight talking, I can believe it. 'And close friends?'

'Out of everyone, Bridget was her best friend.'

'And did Bridget try to help Gillian after Mike died?'

Joe blows out a breath. 'Yes, out of everyone, I believe Bridget persisted longest, but in the end I think Gillian hurt her feelings more than anyone's . . . at least, Gillian pushed her away so hard that Bridget stayed away, which I wouldn't have thought possible.'

'So what are our chances of convincing Bridget to come and see Gillian?'

His mouth twists. 'Put it this way: she's just as bloody-minded as Gillian, and if Gillian offended her . . .?' Joe shakes his head. 'Although, Bridget *was* the one who told me about Gillian being in hospital, so maybe there's hope.'

'OK, well let's see what we can do about that. And Petra mentioned Seren?'

'Now that *is* a good idea – she's lovely and she'll happily come and visit Gillian. Even Gillian wouldn't be rude to Seren.'

I have to drown a small voice that protests at his admiration of Seren. I take a deep breath and grin at him. 'Are you sure? Because I reckon Gillian could be rude to the Pope.'

Joe grins. 'Pretty sure, and even if she is, Seren will forgive her.'

'OK, then. Let's try Bridget and Seren.'

'Great idea.' He puts aside his glass and levers himself out of his chair, and Pompom gets up and gives herself a little shake. I stand, too, and Joe and I are suddenly very close together. So much so, I can feel the heat coming off him. By rights, he should step back as I have the sofa behind me, but he doesn't. He looks down at me with the gentlest expression, and I suddenly very much want to both kiss and draw him. In fact, if I stood on tiptoes, our lips would meet.

I look into his eyes trying to determine if that's what he wants when a clap and a hiss from the back door tell us Pompom has just surprised Bozz coming in through the catflap. Delighted, she races back and leaps around our feet, doing a good impression of the erratic turn my heart just took. Joe bends to pick her up, and while he's not looking, I kick-start my breathing.

'See you tomorrow?' asks Joe, amused as Bozz slinks in and glares at us.

'Absolutely,' I agree. I follow him to the front door and stand in the doorway as he walks across the yard. Pompom leaps out of his arms into the back seat. He waves and I hold up my hand, but I only close the front door once his taillights have disappeared down the hill. I lean against the door and let my breathing slow to the sound of Gillian's snores.

Why didn't he kiss me? I mean, I know we haven't known each other that long, but still! Bloody Hell! It was the perfect moment.

I return to the kitchen, give Bozz a stroke, and curse again before I turn out the lights.

17

Bare Bones and Bare Feet

The next morning it takes me and Gillian a while to get her up, but thankfully she's managing more herself, and after minimal help dressing and a bathroom visit, she hobbles into the kitchen unaided and dumps herself in the armchair. I hold up a mug and she nods.

'You're handy to have about, I'll give you that,' she says with a tired smile.

'People employ staff for a reason,' I point out good-naturedly.

'I know, but . . .' Gillian fiddles with the bandage on her wrist. 'Well, you've met your mother.'

'I have,' I agree, taking her point. Mum's version of offering you a cup of tea is telling you where the kettle is. 'Did you ever get on?' I ask, suddenly curious.

'We got on fine when we were young.' Gillian smiles at my raised eyebrow. 'Oh, I'm sure you've heard different. The parents favoured her, of course, but she was the youngest and did as she was told, so I never held that against her: it was the easiest path to take. But up until I moved in with Mike, she never had a problem with me. Why would she? I was the foil against which she shone.'

This doesn't match up with what Mum said at all. I sit

opposite Gillian, and carefully place her mug within reach. 'Then what went wrong?'

'I'm not sure. She came to stay here at about the age you are now, supposedly to barter some kind of truce between me and your grandparents. But since we both knew that was a lost cause, we put it to one side and concentrated on having a nice time. And to begin with, she seemed to really like the place—'

'Mum did?'

Gillian nods. 'What wasn't there to like? It was the height of summer, with glorious long days and the place was bustling with artists. She seemed to love the atmosphere, settled in with everyone, tried her hand at painting, let her hair hang loose and walked around barefoot. Honestly, she took to the place like a teenager to Glastonbury. She was having a whale of a time, and then . . .' Gillian stops.

'And then what?'

Gillian looks at me. 'I've no idea,' she says, shrugging. 'One morning, she tied her hair back in a tight chignon, put on her shoes and walked out with barely a word.'

'Do you have any idea what happened?'

'None, but whatever it was made her furious with me. At first she spouted a whole load of crap about me trying to drag her down to my level and ruin her life the way I'd ruined mine, but then that stopped. She cut all contact, but why – I don't know.' Gillian holds out her good hand helplessly.

'So you haven't really spoken to each other in over thirty years?'

Gillian shakes her head. 'I thought our relationship might improve after our parents died, but when Mum finally went fifteen years ago, all we managed were a few stilted phone calls about probate, which, given the nature of the letter Mum left for me, I almost wish we hadn't bothered with.

But then, if we hadn't made that small amount of contact, I wouldn't have called Marion from hospital and you wouldn't be here now.'

'Yes, why *did* you call her from hospital?' It's a question that's been bugging me since I discovered she could have called Joe.

Gillian purses her lips and finally shrugs. 'I thought I'd see if Marion had an ounce of family feeling left in her. And to be honest, when she said you might, though probably wouldn't come, I thought she was fobbing me off. That's why I was so surprised to see you at the foot of my hospital bed.' Gillian chuckles as she sips her tea.

'But you never found out what happened thirty years ago?'

Gillian shakes her head. 'No, and when you were born eighteen months later, that was the last I heard from her for a long time.' She frowns. 'You look disappointed.'

I bite my lip. 'I don't know, I guess I was just hoping for some clue about who my father is, but if she wasn't even speaking to you at the time . . .'

Gillian shakes her head sadly. 'Sorry, she just sent a terse card announcing your birth. She never mentioned who your father is.'

'It was a long shot.' I smile to hide my disappointment, but Gillian isn't fooled.

'Let's have some breakfast,' she says kindly. 'Sometimes food's the best medicine.' I get out a pan and set about making us some scrambled eggs on toast, and as I crack the eggs I firmly close the chapter on finding out about my dad.

We've barely finished breakfast when there's a loud knock at the front door, and I open it to find a health visitor standing on the doorstep. Hearing the health visitor introduce herself, Gillian mutters an oath, which proves to be only the start of a long, bad-tempered visit. The health visitor's stance

throughout seems to be one of disapproval, while her accus-
ations that neither of us is doing enough has me guilt-ridden
and Gillian outraged. Luckily, Joe lets himself in just as the
health visitor is dressing me down for the third time, and
plucks the exercise leaflet from my hand.

He studies it and asks questions with such disarming
sincerity the health visitor almost melts. After that, I leave
her to Joe and head off to collect the car, and only join him
again at the front door as her car beetles off down the track.

'Sorry I was late. I reached an exciting bit with my writing.'
He grins, more thrilled than apologetic.

'I'm just glad you came – I couldn't say a thing right.'

'No, well, it's difficult once Gillian has put their backs up.'

'I did no such thing!' Gillian shouts through. 'If anything,
it was the other way around; wrenching me around like a
piece of meat. It was bloody excruciating, and now I need
the loo!' Joe pulls a face. 'And don't you make that face,
young Joe – I can hear it from here!'

I laugh. 'She's got you there.'

He leans in close. 'Always did. She would have made a
terrifying teacher,' he whispers, and I giggle. Petra pulls into
the yard in front of us, and I nudge him. Joe sighs irritably.
'Oh, and I was going to say Petra might pop by. I'll go in
and see to her ladyship.' He brushes past me, and I'm still
smiling a little too widely as I greet Petra.

'Hi. Tea?' I offer.

'Herbal, if you have any.' We wait for Gillian and Joe to
make their way through to the bathroom, and go into the
kitchen. Petra selects a kitchen chair and sits down, not taking
her eyes off me.

'I'm not sure we have any herbal tea. There might be
some at the back of one of the cupboards?'

Petra's eyes widen. 'Ordinary will do.'

'It might be safer,' I agree.

I make us all a cup, put one in front of Petra, and after taking Gillian and Joe's through – Gillian having decided she needs a lie-down after the ministrations of the health visitor, while Joe massages her cramping calf – I sit down opposite Petra, cupping my mug in my hands.

'So, how's the cottage coming along?' I ask to cover Gillian's carrying oaths, then wish I hadn't because I don't want to bring it up within Gillian's hearing.

'Fine – there's not much to sort out, to tell the truth. It's pretty spartan.' Her eyes graze over the kitchen, which is better than it was when I arrived, but certainly isn't spartan, and Bozz sitting on the dresser, his legs splayed as he washes his chest, is hardly a fine ornament.

'How come Mike had the cottage as well as this place?'

'Not sure. I think he bought it to rent out, or maybe even for Joe? Either way, it's no longer needed for its original purpose, so . . .' she smiles sweetly.

She clearly has no qualms about it. I force a smile, unsure what to say.

Petra scoots forward on her chair. 'I actually came to arrange for us to go out. You know, like we discussed?' I struggle not to roll my eyes. 'I was thinking about tomorrow night? Head for town, find a bar, get to know Gareth a little better?' Her eyebrows dance suggestively. 'He likes you, you know.'

'No, he doesn't. He just can't help flirting. That kind can't.'

'Don't put yourself down!' cries Petra.

'I wasn't,' I say, surprised. If anything, I was putting him down.

'Well, don't ruin this for me; I'm desperate for a night out, and since Joe's only interested in some "big new idea" to do with his writing, I'm going stir crazy! Please say yes.' Her eyes are so huge it's like trying to turn down a puppy. 'Please?'

'Actually, I'm pretty busy with Gillian and sorting out the house.'

Petra glances around. 'And when you're not slaving away . . .? It's not like there's a TV! Come on, I know you must be just as bored as I am?'

I look around. Is that what happened to Gillian? Did Gillian spend too long alone, dwelling on the might-have-beens, missing Mike? Did she go stir crazy? It might explain the mess, but not her sudden withdrawal, and something tells me I really need to get to the bottom of that.

'Ella?' prompts Petra. 'You deserve a night out.'

'I'm sorry, I can't.' I try to look regretful, but any excuse to avoid Gareth's flirting.

'Can't what?' asks Joe, coming in.

Petra pouts. 'Ella says she can't go out with me tomorrow night because she has to *be here* for Gillian.'

Joe frowns at me. 'Don't be silly, I'll look after Gillian.' I widen my eyes to show he isn't helping. 'Honestly, you'd be doing me a favour. I hate going out, don't I, Petra?'

'All he does is write,' she agrees.

'It's true.' He tries to look repentant, but it doesn't come off. 'So, if you girls go and have a lovely evening, you'll be doing me a favour. I might even get some writing done if I manage a dull enough monotone.' He winks at me to share the joke, but I'm not amused.

'Oh, come on, Ella.' Petra turns her puppy-dog eyes on me, and Joe crouches down beside her and lets out a Pompom-type whimper. I can't help laughing, for all that I'm irritated with the pair of them.

'Oh, all right!' I say ungraciously. 'But I think you're both bullies.'

Petra high-fives Joe, who isn't expecting it, and has to do some good fielding. With her mission accomplished, she gets up.

'So we'll pick you up at seven,' she says.

She rewards Joe with a kiss on the cheek, and he stares

after her as she flounces out. Joe takes her seat, and we sit in thoughtful silence as her car pulls away. She hasn't touched her tea, and as I get up to take it to the sink, Joe's eyes meet mine.

'You're in big trouble,' I tell him.

Joe smirks. 'You could have said no.'

'I tried! And I was doing quite well until you joined in!' I glare at him. 'How's Gillian doing? Recovered?'

'Complaining like hell that the health visitor broke all her remaining limbs, but fine, I think. I left her nose deep in your e-reader. She's behaving like Gollum over it.'

'At least it keeps her entertained.'

Joe scowls condemningly. 'That's what bad parents say when they plonk their kids in front of the TV.'

'E-readers are different,' I say sternly. 'It's reading, which is good for you, but you're right, we should sort out some visitors. You mentioned Seren and Bridget?' Joe nods. 'And what about Gareth's mam down at the pub? She said she might drop by.'

'Dolores?' Joe hesitates. 'Not sure they ever had much to do with each other . . . which is odd, considering how small the place is.' He pauses. 'But thinking about it, perhaps we should start with just one or two. Gillian will kick like a mule if she thinks we're trying to organise her.'

He has a point.

'In that case, let's get on with lunch before we have to start using code-words, Resistance style.'

'I know where the resistance will be coming from—' begins Joe, just as Gillian hobbles in from the bedroom.

She leans on her crutch. 'All I can hear is you two sniggering like school children.'

Joe winks at me, and I hide my smile by opening the fridge.

* * *

'So, I was thinking I'd take Ella up the valley this afternoon.' Joe's eyes meet mine across our plates of pesto pasta and cheese. 'You'll be all right for an hour or two, won't you, Gillian?'

Gillian gives him a look that would paralyse most dictators. 'I managed for eighteen months without any help from you. I'm sure I can manage a couple of hours.'

'Good.'

'I'm in the middle of a good book, anyway.'

'Great,' he says, his eyes crinkling at the corners.

'So I wasn't wanting your interference,' she adds.

'Excellent,' says Joe, his eyes sparkling with amusement.

Gillian looks from him to me and huffs out a breath. 'Oh, just leave me with some tea and biscuits and I'll be fine!'

I break Joe's gaze. 'Are you sure?' but the sternness of her expression surprises me.

'I just said so, didn't I? You go and do whatever it is you're up to, because I know you're up to something! Just don't expect me to like it.'

Joe smiles into his pasta. 'I'd *never* expect that,' he says quietly, and we finish our lunch in silence.

Afterwards, I make sure Gillian has tea and biscuits to hand, and Joe takes her to the toilet. Then, to make her point, Gillian picks up the e-reader and dismisses us with a flick of her good hand.

Joe smiles. 'Grab a coat, it's chilly.'

'Inside or out?' I ask, glancing significantly at Gillian, and plucking my coat off the peg, I follow him out.

18

Friends in High Places

Joe drives carefully around the worst of the potholes and I raise a hand to Bryn as we bounce past his gate. Typical to form, Bryn doesn't respond, which strangely makes me smile, and I glance over at Joe. 'For someone who's self-interred themselves for the last eighteen months, Gillian doesn't like being left on her own much.'

'No,' he agrees. 'It's odd, isn't it? Perhaps the fall shook her more than we thought?'

'Maybe.' Although the scratch marks on the studio door, the flat tyres and all the other things might also be the cause. It's almost like someone's trying to scare her . . .

At the main road, Joe turns up the valley rather than down towards the pub and the bridge.

'So where are we really going?' I ask, because February, drizzle and this valley don't exactly lend themselves to sight-seeing.

'To see Bridget, and brace yourself, because I'm not expecting a warm welcome.'

'Why? Her argument's not with you, is it?'

'No, but people have a habit of shooting the messenger, and with Bridget I'm expecting a cannon and boiling oil.'

'Sounds messy. But didn't you say she told you about Gillian's accident?'

Joe nods. 'Yes, but in the nature of a human telegram, and as soon as she'd given me the salient points, she left.'

'Just how offensive *was* Gillian?'

'I'd hazard "very", because Bridget wouldn't give up otherwise, but even then . . .' Joe blows out a breath and shakes his head. 'I wouldn't have thought rudeness would faze Bridget for a second. If anything, she'd give as good as she got, so for her to give up . . .'

'It must have been pretty bad?'

'Yes,' he agrees.

We meander along the road and take a turning up the other side of the valley to a row of four cottages. One has smoke coming out of the chimney, but the others look like they've been shut up for a while. Even so, they're quite sweet and I take a quick photo with my phone, while we park on the muddy verge behind an old green Ford. Joe gives the cottage a distrustful glance and leads me to the front door and knocks.

A striking woman, straight-backed, keen-eyed and with a long plait of iron-grey hair pinned up at the back, opens the door and looks over her glasses at him. She switches her focus briefly to me, and without uttering a word, holds the door open for us.

'So, Gillian,' she says once we're in the small hall. It seems we're welcome no further. 'How is she?'

'Recovering,' says Joe. 'Slowly. It was a nasty fall, but there's no permanent damage.'

Bridget dips her head. 'Good. And you're here because you want me to visit her.' It's not a question. She glances at me. 'Girlfriend?' she asks, still addressing Joe.

I hold out my hand. 'No, I'm Ella, Gillian's niece. Pleased to meet you.'

Bridget turns to me, but leaves my hand hanging in mid-air. 'Why?'

I slowly put my hand in my pocket. 'Novelty?' I suggest. What else is there?

Bridget's head tips, but just as I think she's going to ball me out, she nods minutely. 'Yes, I'm not your run-of-the-mill old codger.' Satisfied, she turns back to Joe. 'It won't do any good. Gillian won't see me. It's her decision, and fair enough in my opinion. Did you want anything else, or is that it?'

She's succinct, I'll give her that.

Joe adjusts his pose. 'Is there really nothing you can do? You used to be such good friends and she needs friends and company. Can't you put aside whatever happened? Apologise, if necessary, and come and see her?'

Bridget lets out an exasperated breath, and droops slightly as if she was holding herself rigid with it. 'If it were up to me, yes, but it's not for me to decide, Joe. This is something *she* has to come to terms with, and when you add grief to that, who knows how long it will take? Trust me, there's nothing I can do or say to change this.'

'I refuse to accept that, and to be honest, I'm surprised *you* do!'

Bridget's eyes shy away from Joe's. 'Well, I do.'

'Then get over it: she needs you.'

Bridget's lips purse. 'It's more complicated than you realise, Joe. You should leave it alone.'

'What – so you can both hide away at opposite ends of the valley and fester in your own self-pity?'

Bridget's knuckles whiten, but she doesn't respond.

'Do you miss her?' I ask quietly.

Bridget's eyes snap up, suddenly fierce with anger. 'What damned fool kind of question is that? Of course I bloody miss her!'

'Do you think she misses you?'

My question hangs in the air like a rudely rung bell and her face gains years and pain in equal measure.

'I wouldn't know, would I?' she says quietly, and closes her eyes.

It's like I've struck her. I can't look at Joe, so I turn to examine the picture beside me. It's a collage of the row of cottages we're standing in done in some kind of textile; the threads so fine that the wispy fibres act almost like brush strokes. I focus on them, unsure what to say, but the more I look at how the delicate strands have been teased into clouds, mountains, stones and window frames, the more impressed I am. It isn't like any kind of felting I've seen before. It's extraordinary.

'This is amazing. What is it made from?'

'Wool.' Bridget's tone is flat and accusing.

Joe shifts impatiently, but I ignore him. 'You made this?'

Bridget sighs, but she nods.

'And it's a form of felting?'

'Yes.'

'Locally sourced?'

'Of course it's bloody locally sourced – look at the hills! They're covered in sheep!'

'Do they sell well? The pictures, I mean.'

Bridget looks perplexedly at Joe, then sighs heavily. 'Not so you'd notice, no.'

'Hmm. They should, you know. They're beautiful.'

Bridget folds her arms exaggeratedly. 'Have you quite finished, or would you like a tour around the rest of the cottage as well?' I wonder how angry she'd be if I said yes, but my hesitation provides enough ammunition. 'I wasn't being serious, you stupid girl!' She turns back to Joe. 'And as for Gillian, there's nothing I can do, and you should know she *won't* thank you for coming here, so if you have any sense you won't mention it! So, if you're done raking up the past, I have things to be getting on with.'

She opens the front door and stands beside it. I take her

cue and go to wait by Joe's car. Joe, however, hangs back. She glances at me and expectantly back at him.

He smiles at her. 'Just so you know, Ella went to art college in London, so she knows what she's talking about,' and as he walks towards me, Bridget's gaze strays in my direction.

'That'll get her thinking,' he says quietly as we pull away, and I don't know if he just did something very clever, or very kind. But one thing's for sure: he left her with more to think about than just her argument with Gillian.

'So that was Bridget,' says Joe as we bump back down the track.

'She's a tough cookie.'

Joe glances at me. 'Yes, like Gillian, but I reckon they need each other. We just need one of them to admit it.'

'Hmm, not the easiest task!'

'No,' he agrees, letting out a sigh. 'And if it goes wrong, we could end up with a crater a mile wide.'

I picture the valley razed and burnt, with two smouldering, glowering women fuming at its base.

We meet the main road, but rather than turning back to Gillian's, Joe heads up another track with grass up the middle. In the distance is a set of farm buildings.

'Are we going to see Huw and Seren?' I ask.

'Yes,' he says, and as we pull into the yard, it's immediately obvious we're on a working farm, because unlike Gillian's yard, there's mud everywhere, spattered quad bikes, excited dogs to avoid and the barns edging the yard are fenced off with hurdles.

As we get out, Huw comes out of one of the barns dressed in a padded shirt, waterproof trousers and wellies, and shouts for the dogs to calm down. He wipes his hand on his shirt before offering it to Joe, and two boys, aged about six and eight, dressed in red wellies, tracksuit bottoms, coats and woolly hats, run out behind him. They swing and jump off the hurdles and bales.

'Wondered how long it would be before we saw you,' Huw says cheerfully, and the two boys run back into the barn giggling. Huw grins at me. 'Jack and Ben. Half term,' he explains. 'Seren'll be proper pleased to see you, Ella. She's been dying to meet you, but we wanted to leave you and Gillian to settle in.'

Joe gestures at the barn. 'How are things going? Looks busy.'

'Crazy-busy. Lambing,' says Huw for my benefit, and both men nod in reverence. 'I'd love a hand, Joe, if you've got a minute? I've got one straining with twins, but to no good. Do you mind?' Huw smiles at me. 'Seren's in the house if you're all right showing yourself in?'

'She won't mind?' I ask.

'Not at all, but use the back door – we only use the front for posh. Oh, and tell her Joe's here.'

Glad of an excuse to get out of the cold, but not sure how I feel about walking uninvited into the house of someone I've never met, I walk around the farmhouse and through the back-garden gate. The back garden has a comforting disarray of tricycles, trampoline and a climbing frame, and I knock on the door.

'It's open,' calls a woman's voice from inside, and I open it onto a muddy welly drop-off point, and peer through the open doorway into the wonderfully warm and welcoming kitchen beyond.

'I can't get up, I'm feeding,' calls the voice, and I follow it round to where a Pre-Raphaelite beauty, dressed in dungarees and bright, loose-weave cardy, is sitting on a kitchen chair bottle-feeding a lamb. A baby girl, immobilised in a bouncer in the far doorway, is bouncing furiously behind her, uttering what is probably baby-swearing at the lamb suckling on a bottle.

'Hi?' says the woman, smiling at me as the lamb guzzles so demandingly it almost yanks the bottle out of her hand. She adjusts her grip.

'Hi, I'm Ella. I'm here with Joe? He just stopped off in the barn to help Huw.'

Her face relaxes instantly into a wide grin. 'Fantastic, I've been dying to meet you! Huw told me straight away that we'd get on, he did. Have a seat. I'm Seren. That's Bethan,' she says, indicating the red-faced baby. 'And this is Daf,' she adds as a burly old farmer sidles around the bouncing toddler, sending her twirling. He nods at me and puts the kettle on. 'Huw's dad,' Seren whispers, and gestures for me to sit on one of the free kitchen chairs.

Daf holds up a mug.

'Make one for Joe, too,' says Seren. 'He's in the barn with Huw,' and she smiles at me as she sets the lamb on the floor. The lamb takes a few uncertain steps and butts my leg with a surprisingly hard little head.

Seren winces. 'Sorry, he's a boy,' she says, as if that explains everything.

'Do all boys butt things?'

Daf lets out an amused 'Heh' and chucks an uncounted number of teabags into a tannin-stained teapot, but I notice he keeps a careful eye on the lamb as he moves about.

'Most of them,' agrees Seren. 'You have to hope the headache cures them, but it doesn't seem to be working with you, does it, boyo!' The lamb makes a second attempt, misses my leg, and butts the table leg instead. This time, I wince for the lamb, but Seren laughs as it sits down, bemused. 'Let's hope that does the trick for a bit. If not, we'll call him Bill, after the billy-goat he's trying to be.'

I laugh and look around at the kitchen. It's a glorious disarray, with bright crockery, a rich red, deep yellow and maroon tile splashback, pine table and units and a massive red Rayburn. It smells heavenly, too – probably something to do with the tempting array of herbs and spices on the massive spice rack, but there's more to it than that. There's a wonderfully convivial feel to the room that's completely absent from Gillian's. Something to do with the lovingly chosen items and the happiness of the people living here, which if Joe's to be believed, Gillian's used to have.

'It's a mess, but it's home,' says Seren anxiously.

'I *love* it!' I say immediately, and Seren grins, knowing I mean it.

'Thanks.' She reaches out and pats my hand. 'I'm so glad you came! I was starting to feel left out, what with Daf seeing you in the pub and Huw meeting you on the bridge. Both of them said we'd get on and that I was all set to come down and see you, when . . .' Seren holds her hands out helplessly. '. . . life happened.' Daf smiles and nods. 'But tell me, how is Gillian? We've been that worried about her, haven't we, Daf?' Seren's voice is fervent, and Daf's grunt is particularly earnest. 'We didn't like that she wasn't letting anyone in, but grief's difficult.' Her eyes stray tellingly to Daf, who busies himself with the teapot and kettle. 'We were tempted to muscle our way in and do the best we could for her, but Gillian's not the sort of person you can strong-arm. She'd have told us to bugger off, and no mistake.'

'Heh!' grunts Daf, amused.

I lean forward. 'I reckon I almost ended up sleeping in my car when she saw what I'd done to her kitchen! But Gareth's mam offered me a room if it comes to it.'

Daf gives Seren a sharp look. 'You don't need to do that!' she says quickly. 'Come and stay here if you need to,' and Daf nods to confirm it's the right thing to do.

I look from one to the other of them. 'Don't worry, it won't come to that. We're actually getting on surprisingly well, and she's definitely doing better than she was in hospital.'

'Has there been much swearing?'

'Tons, but she hasn't actually told me to bugger off, despite quite a few challenging moments.'

Seren giggles. 'I wouldn't have lasted two seconds!'

I can't help laughing. 'That's not what Joe said. He said you'd make an excellent visitor, and –' I make a face – 'I was wondering if you wouldn't mind coming to see her?'

'Of course I don't mind! So long as Huw or Daf can look after the kids?' She looks at Daf, who nods. 'I just didn't want to intrude, that's all. And when she was sending everyone away, I didn't want to add to the problem.'

Daf hands me two mugs and winks, and puts the other mugs on a tray. I put ours on the table and hop up to get the back door for him, but have to do some nifty fielding as the lamb makes a dash for freedom.

'Well managed,' says Seren as I close the door. 'That little bugger had me out there for twenty minutes the other morning. Daf got him in the end.'

'A man of few words, but great skill?'

'When it comes to sheep – definitely. But now you mention it, he never spoke much, even when his wife was alive. Not that they weren't close. Heart-broken, he was, when she died. A lot like Gillian, I expect. Except with farming you have to keep going. Huw and I had to move in in the end. It wasn't what we planned, but I wouldn't change it now we're here.'

I smile at her. 'It's strange how life turns out, isn't it?'

'Tell me about it! Speaking of which, how did you come to be up here?'

'It all began with a yoghurt!' and I tell her everything that led to me coming here. 'So here I am, four hours from London, looking after Gillian and all because I got fed up of someone stealing my yoghurts.'

Seren shakes her head. 'Mad to think if any one of those

things hadn't happened, you wouldn't be sat in my kitchen right now.'

'Yes,' I agree. 'And it's even weirder to think Fate made all those things happen to me just to make sure Gillian would be OK.'

Seren laughs. 'I don't think Fate works on just one level, or just one project at a time – she's cleverer than that.'

'So my coming here might benefit me, too, you think?'

'Gillian, you, me, who knows? Call it a collective bonus, because I'd *love* another friend up here.' Her eyebrows flick up enticingly. 'And heaven knows we could all do with a bit more excitement – it's been hell-of-a quiet since Mike died.'

'Yes, a few people have said that. Some people even seem to blame Gillian, which seems a bit unfair, and I'm worried it's making her more isolated. I want to do something to help, but I'm not sure I know enough to do anything lasting. I mean, what's it like for you living up here?'

Seren frowns. 'Fine, mostly. Farming isn't what it was, and we've had to diversify, so now we dye wool to sell to felters and spinning workshops. We're also a bit off the beaten track, so we have to be sensible with shopping – no nipping out for the odd thing, and the kids have to be collected for school by taxi.'

'A lovely place to grow up, though. I heard Huw and Joe loved it.'

She smiles. 'Yes, always getting into scrapes, they were, but also good at lending a hand when there was hay turning, wall mending or lambing to be done.'

I smile at the thought of those two spending their childhoods tearing around the hills. 'How did you meet Huw? Are you local, too?'

'Next valley over. I met Huw at school. Childhood sweethearts, we were. Seems like only yesterday, and here I am a farmer's wife with three kids!' She shakes her head, amazed by it all. 'I'm very lucky. But you must have a glamorous life in London?'

'Not really.'

'But there are galleries, museums, shows and clubs. I thought that was why people lived in London?'

'It's why people *go* to London. When you live there, you work late, stand like zombies on the tube, eat ready-meals and doze off in front of the TV with a glass of wine.'

Seren nods sadly. 'I know what you mean. People come from all over to walk the hills, but I only go up to fetch or feed the sheep.'

'It's human nature to take what you have for granted.'

'Now, there's true!' She toasts me with her tea. 'And it takes something major to shock us out of it.'

'Like losing your job.'

'Or divorce or death, and then you have to confront how lucky you were.'

'Or weren't,' I muse, thinking back over my last few years.

Seren laughs. 'Which brings us back to Gillian.'

'Yes. I was wondering what Gillian was like before Mike died – what her interests were, who she spent time with . . .?'

Seren shrugs. 'Bridget knew her best.'

I nod. 'We tried her on the way here, but . . .' I pull a face.

Seren shakes her head. 'Those two need their heads knocking together.' I smile at the image, and Seren frowns as she tries to think. 'There was Gillian's photography, of course, but I'm afraid I never knew her that well. You see, Daf wasn't that keen on Mike.'

That's interesting! I assume a polite expression, but Seren shrugs.

'All I know is what Huw told me: how she flew around the world taking photographs, but she always made sure she was home for Joe's holidays. At least, that's what Huw said.'

'I gather he was here a lot?'

'Yes, his parents were always happy enough to dump him and Petra, but from what Huw says, Gillian thought Joe should have a proper home, so she made sure he had one.'

'Does he see much of his parents?' I ask, sidetracked.

'No. They have some swanky retreat in the Caribbean, but I don't think he visits much. He always preferred coming here. At least, he did, until Mike died.'

'And what was Mike like?' I ask, hoping to find out why Daf didn't like him.

Seren's mouth twists. 'Single-minded. The few times I spoke to him, I found him friendly, but abrupt, or distracted maybe – probably because he was always in the middle of a painting. But most people seemed to like him. Their place was always busy, and people bought up all the little cottages around the valley like it was some kind of artistic Mecca. You couldn't herd sheep for tripping over artists clinging to their easels in the wind and rain.'

'Wow.'

Seren nods. 'Of course, it calmed down as they got older, but people still came to recharge their batteries. Then, when Mike died, it all stopped, and the valley . . . well, it seemed to die with him.' Bethan grizzles like an angry little engine, and Seren lifts her out of the bouncer and pops her on the floor, and she makes an immediate beeline for Bill. 'Even from up here, it was like the circus leaving town. I hate to think what it was like for Gillian.'

'Hmm,' I say thoughtfully. 'So, you think visitors would be a good first step?'

'Definitely!' says Seren, and we chink tea mugs as Joe, Huw and Daf all erupt through the back door on a tide of cold air.

Seren scoops up Bethan, and I grab Bill around his firm, woolly middle and lift him out of harm's way just before the two boys rush through, shedding coats and hats. Joe raises his eyebrows at the lamb on my lap, and a TV ramps into action in another room.

'Wash your hands!' yells Seren and, after a moment's pause, there's a rumble of feet up the stairs.

'Another two healthy lambs,' Huw tells Seren, and sighs as he plunges his hands under the hot tap. 'So what have you two been plotting?'

'We're trying to think how to get Gillian more involved with everyone again,' says Seren.

''Bout time,' says Daf, and Joe nods, taking his turn at the sink.

'That's what we thought,' agrees Joe. He dries his hands and puts a surprisingly warm hand on my shoulder.

Seren looks up at Joe, a smile curling her lips. 'I'm going to come and visit her,' she says. She looks from me to Joe and sips her tea, her beaming smile not quite hidden behind her mug. Nor is the sparkle in her eyes, and as the discussion moves on to farming, I notice she looks at the two of us quite often.

19

Get In, Get Out

On the way back, I ask Joe about Mike's legacy.

'I think the arts centre was just some pipe dream he had. I don't think he put any real thought into it, or what would act as a draw without him being here.'

'So there aren't any plans or stipulations?' I check.

'Not as far as I know: just some money and a general idea. Why?'

I pull a face. 'I just wondered, after what Seren said about Gillian's and Mike's being a hive of activity, whether it might be a way to get Gillian back involved with the valley? Even if it just got some artists up here for a bit, maybe it would help everyone.'

Joe glances at me as we bounce past Bryn's unmanned gate, and I can see I've got him wondering. 'There's not much to go on, as far as I remember.'

'But doesn't that mean we get free rein? Even if Gillian just holds an exhibition of Mike's work in the studio, she might get past whatever's been keeping her away from everyone. I suppose it depends on the terms.'

Joe nods. 'I have a funny feeling he wanted it to be inspirational or something, but beyond that . . .' He shrugs. 'And it wouldn't hurt to take a look at the studio. In fact, it'll give me a chance to check if anything's missing.' He has a point –

I wouldn't know if there were originally double the number of paintings in there.

As we let ourselves in, Gillian's eyes lift from the e-reader just long enough to check we're not burglars, and then settle back on her book. 'You were gone a while,' she comments.

'Yes, we went to visit Seren and Huw. Would you like a fresh one?' I offer, taking her empty mug and plate to the sink.

'No – I'll be in and out of the toilet like I'm doing the hokey cokey.'

'In that case, shall we take a quick look at the studio?' suggests Joe.

Gillian looks up sharply, her mouth taut, and her gaze wraps around him for a second. 'And why would you be doing that?'

'I thought Ella should see some of Mike's work,' says Joe.

Gillian's eyes flick to me. 'She's already seen it.'

'Not really, I found the hall one pretty quickly,' I point out. 'I'd love to see more.'

'You can come, too, if you like?' Joe offers. 'A bit of fresh air might do you good.'

Gillian's mouth clamps tight, but there's uncertainty in her eyes. 'Knock yourselves out,' she says after a moment's thought, but there are undertones she might mean it literally.

Joe takes the keys from the back door and I follow him out, wondering if he feels as awkward under her suspicious glare as I do.

'Mike's studio,' says Joe dramatically as he unlocks the door and pushes it open.

Of course I've been in here before, but the bright contrast with the house is still astonishing. 'It is a glorious space.'

'Isn't it,' he agrees. 'I reckon it's why he bought the farm, although he must have had vision, because it wasn't like this. He knocked the walls through, installed the roof lights and the concrete floor and boarded it out.'

'And without that it's just a poky set of outbuildings.' I nip over to the stored canvasses and start flipping through. There are dozens of mountain-scapes, seascapes, cottages and creatures. There are kestrels, badgers, foxes and pheasants, all dead, with studies of claws, wings, feet and beaks arrayed around the central picture. It makes me shudder to think what's in the freezer, but the body of work is impressive. 'So many paintings!' I breathe.

Joe nods. 'He spent a lot of time both in here and out on the hill.'

'And Gillian?'

'They weren't the kind of couple who were joined at the hip. They appreciated their space, and during the day they did their own thing – he painted, and she did her photography, walked in the hills, baked, visited friends, and in the evenings they met up to eat, drink, play chess and put the world to rights. And boy, could they talk – all the way into the small hours.'

'It sounds comfortable . . . homely, even.'

Joe nods sadly. 'It was.'

I stand back to look at the room as a whole. The light's perfect because it comes from the North, and the colours on the canvasses are crisp and clear. 'I bet people loved coming here for art classes.'

'They did. His classes were very popular. Of course Mike's reputation drew them in, but there was also something charismatic about him that kept them coming.' Joe shrugs at my questioning glance. 'I don't know, it was like a gift, because even though he'd ball out his students and be very forthright in his criticism, they'd emerge shell-shocked and muttering how brilliant he was, despite having had their painting styles hung, drawn and quartered.'

'Really?' I ask sceptically, thinking of all the thin-skinned artists I've known.

Joe shrugs. 'Well, OK, the odd one stormed out and flung their canvas over the wall, but then Gillian took them inside, fed them tea and cake and soothed their ruffled feathers, until even *they* grudgingly admitted he was a genius.'

'Wow. That's quite an accomplishment in itself.'

'She had this knack of seeing people's insecurities and they responded to that, which is lucky because she had to deal with all sorts over the years, from adoring, infatuated fans through to the hopeless and the artistically stuck. Mike had no patience with them – he taught his art classes and strode off over the hills – but she would sit them down in the kitchen, see something good in them and bring it out.'

'Perhaps that ability to see the good in people is what shines through in her photographs?'

Joe nods. 'You might be right, and Mike would certainly have upset a lot more people without her.'

I flick through a few more paintings trying to get a handle on the man who painted them, but there's something impersonal about landscapes, unless you're attached to the particular view. Gillian's photographs, by contrast, tell me about her sense of humour and humanity, and her deep understanding of her subjects through how she captured their personalities, expressions and body language.

'He didn't paint many portraits,' I say, looking around.

'No,' agrees Joe. 'Not many still lives either, unless you count dead wildlife.'

I leaf through a few seascapes, which are rich and evocative of the day, and yet tell me little about Mike except how invested he was in his art, which is already evident from the sheer body of work. I lean the paintings back the way I found them.

'Seen enough?' asks Joe.

I look around at the studio – at its light, its potential and all of Mike's work. 'Yes, I think so.' I follow Joe out.

'What are you thinking?' he asks as he locks up.

'I don't know, just that there must be *some* way of making this arts centre of Mike's work for Gillian,' I confess. 'It's too good a space, and he's left so much work behind and it feels like the valley's crying out for something. I just wish I could put my finger on what it is – but it's like I can't until I know more.'

'Like what?'

'Like why Gillian shut everyone out, what's going on with the studio door, what Mike wanted done with his legacy . . .' Joe's looking at me intently. 'What?'

'You're very passionate about others, for someone your age,' he says with a smile.

'I'm thirty in May!' I say indignantly. 'Why, how old are you?'

'Thirty-five. Don't get me wrong; it's a compliment. It's just most people are focused on themselves, but here you are determined to help Gillian. It's nice.' He smiles down at me. 'Let's get some ideas together.'

But as I follow him into the kitchen, I freeze. Gillian's eyes are on me, and they are colder than they have ever been.

'Find what you're looking for?' she asks. Her tone tells me to be careful.

'We found Mike's paintings, if that's what you mean, and they're wonderful.' I smile, but it doesn't cut any ice and Joe looks as puzzled as I feel.

'And?' There's so much accusation in her eyes, I hesitate. It's clear we've crossed some sort of line, but I've no idea what.

'And . . . he was very talented?' I try.

Gillian's anger bubbles over. 'I heard you outside the studio just now.'

I glance at the kitchen window, and it's true, we were just on the other side of it, but what did we say that was so bad?

'There's nothing sinister going on. I was just trying to figure out if there's any way to fulfil that clause in Mike's will.'

'And I told you: I'm not bloody interested!' She's staring at me, both furious and betrayed. 'I don't want an arts centre! I don't want to remember Mike! You will stop.'

I glance at Joe, but he looks just as shocked as I am. 'I'm sorry. We won't pursue it if you don't want us to.' I had no idea she felt this strongly about it.

'Except you will! You'll say it's for my own good, and you'll meddle in things that are none of your business, and all to salve your own consciences and serve your own needs! So let me spell it out for you: I'm *not* going to be saddled with some stupid concept Mike left in lieu of his great and almighty self! I'm *not* going to work my fingers to the bone just so his name can live on! And Mike can go whistle if he thinks he can force me to pander after all his bloody hangers on, servicing them like some maidservant until I die, while they all laugh, because Gillian's so God-damned stupid!'

I feel myself go hot and cold in shock. 'No one thinks that,' I say quietly.

'How would you know?' she hisses. 'You don't know the people around here. You don't know what they're thinking.'

'Gillian, Ella's right, no one thinks that—' starts Joe, and Gillian turns angrily. Behind her I shake my head vigorously and mouth 'Bridget', to make sure he doesn't mention her.

'Petra does,' she says icily. 'She thinks I don't see what's going on.' They stare at each other, locked in battle, Joe's mouth opening and closing, but unable to contradict her. 'Oh, for God's sake! Get out, Joe. I'm in no mood for you or your family!'

'Gillian, this wasn't down to Joe, it was me—' I say, trying to summon her fire.

'Then you can get out, too. Pack your things. I can manage perfectly well without either of you. In fact, I never asked either of you in the first place!' Gillian's eyes are hard and unyielding.

Joe shakes his head. 'You're being unfair, Gillian, and you know it.'

Gillian looks like she's about to say something she might regret, then looks away. 'Get out. I'm done with the pair of you.'

'Gillian—' starts Joe.

'I mean it. Get out!'

Joe looks from her to me, shocked.

'I'll go and pack,' I say quietly.

'And you can run back to Petra and tell her you'll sell the cottage,' says Gillian acidly, but Joe returns an expression almost as formidable as hers.

'That's not your choice to make,' he says, and taking his coat he sweeps out of the kitchen. I follow him into the hall and he grabs my hand and pulls me close. He carefully closes the kitchen door, his face inches from mine, and he looks oddly jubilant.

'Don't be too quick to pack – you gave me an idea,' he whispers. I'm about to ask what it is when he gives me a quick and firm kiss on the lips like it's the most natural thing in the world.

I look up at him, astonished, and he smiles down at me.

'Don't go before morning,' he adds. He kisses me again, and walks out the door leaving me starry-eyed behind him.

20

Last of the Elderberry Wine

An hour and a half later, with most of my things packed and piled in the hall and having just made a start on a clean sketch of Bryn, there's a knock at the front door. I expect it to be Joe, unsure about letting himself in after the argument, but it's Bridget standing on the doorstep with an unlabelled bottle of something that looks suspiciously home-made.

She looks me in the eye. 'I'm Bridget,' she says, making sure I understand we've never met. 'I thought I'd come and see how Gillian's doing.'

This must be Joe's plan, but how he's convinced her, or to what end, I don't know.

'Err, come in,' I stutter, shunting my tote bag out of the way with my foot. I open the kitchen door to show her in, but Bridget stops dead in the doorway and the air freezes as if there are drawn blades in the room. Even Bozz seems to sense it, and plops down off the dresser and disappears out of the catflap.

'Bridget is here,' I say brightly, and turn to go.

'No, stay,' says Gillian, not like she wants me here, but like I'm expected to witness the consequences now that I've let Bridget in.

Bridget and Gillian eye one another like warring cats. I

want to bolt, but I can't, and as neither of them speaks, I feel obligated to fill the void.

'Tea?' I offer.

'Homemade elderberry,' says Bridget. She holds out the bottle, but maintains eye contact with Gillian.

Gillian's eyebrows shoot up. 'The good stuff?'

'The very best,' Bridget agrees.

Gillian nods gravely. 'I'm honoured.'

'You should be: it's the last bottle.' Bridget progresses slowly and carefully sits on the edge of the sofa. 'So who's this?'

'My niece, Ella.'

'Really?' Bridget sounds unimpressed. 'Come to help, I imagine?'

'Yes,' concedes Gillian. 'Though she has her own agenda.'

Hardly! I frown at Gillian, but she's too focused on Bridget to notice.

'Sounds like you should thank your lucky stars, Gillian. Unless you're the kind to look a gift-horse in the mouth, of course,' and Bridget's cool glance tells me Joe has told her exactly what's happened.

'You can't be too careful. Look what happened at Troy,' says Gillian.

They stare at each other, and I swear I can smell burning.

'So, how long are you staying?' asks Bridget, turning to me, and although this has been the refrain of the whole valley since I got here, the significance of her question isn't lost on me. Especially since I'm not about to say I have ten days left when it might actually be hours or even minutes.

'Umm, I'm not sure?' I look at Gillian, whose eyes narrow. She looks from me to Bridget.

'As long as she wants, it would seem,' says Gillian, and a flicker of a smile touches Bridget's mouth. 'Wasn't there wine on offer, or was I mistaken?' adds Gillian harshly, and I retreat to rummage in the cupboard for some glasses. As I pop back up, I'm glad to see Bridget is no longer perched, and has sat back on the sofa.

'So, to what do I owe the pleasure?' Gillian asks Bridget as I pour the wine and pass each of them a glass. Gillian swirls hers and holds it up to the light.

'I think it's time to clear the air; turn it blue if necessary, don't you?' Bridget's determination challenges Gillian's scowl. 'We used to be friends.'

'We *used* to be,' agrees Gillian, and the air almost crackles.

I feel I should leave them to it, and glance at the door.

'Stay where you are,' insists Gillian without looking at me.

'But if it's private . . .' There's an unintended quaver in my voice, but Gillian's adamant.

'Sit. Down,' she says firmly, and putting the wine bottle on the table, I sit quietly in the other armchair. But as I do so, Bridget glances in dismay at the room and her mouth slowly drops open.

'Jesus, Gillian! What the hell have you done to the place? It's like a bloody mausoleum in here.' Bridget colours a little at her unfortunate choice of words. 'I mean—'

Her shock cracks the atmosphere like an egg, and Gillian sighs. 'I know *exactly* what you mean, but you of all people should know why I can't stand any of their stuff around me any more. Particularly as you were one of them!'

Bridget's eyes dart to me before returning to Gillian. 'Yes, I was . . . in a sense . . . a long time ago,' she agrees. 'But not the way you think! And I can explain . . .' She looks at me again. '. . . but perhaps you're right, Ella. This should remain private?'

Gillian assesses me and shakes her head. 'Do you know, Bridget? I don't *care* any more if the whole world knows. If they condemn me as stupid, so be it. All I know is I'm heartily sick of the whole bloody thing!' Gillian turns to me, and after a heavy pause, breathes in. 'Mike cheated on me.'

'Oh God!' I blurt. I look from Gillian to Bridget, because it must have been with Bridget.

'Yes, and not just with Bridget,' adds Gillian, and my heart goes out to her.

'Not with Bridget at all, actually. Not really,' corrects Bridget, with a fierce and defensive look, but despite her protests, Gillian's 'gullible and double angry' suddenly makes a lot of sense.

'How did you find out?' I ask.

Gillian looks into her glass and Bridget sips her wine. 'I was hit between the eyes with it at Mike's funeral.'

'How?' I ask, picturing a troop of lovesick mourners.

'Orchids,' she says flatly.

I'm no clearer. 'Orchids?' Gillian slumps back and rubs her forehead. She nods for Bridget to continue.

'There were all these women,' says Bridget. 'Ex-models, students, friends—'

'I knew most of them,' says Gillian. 'Some had posed for his classes, and others bought paintings . . .' Gillian shakes her head.

'And each of them carried an orchid,' says Bridget, finishing for her, and shaking her head in quiet disgust.

'"Precious and unique,"' mutters Gillian. 'That's what Mike used to say about them. But it turns out none of us were so sodding unique after all!'

'No,' agrees Bridget.

'And as for *precious* . . .?' The word hangs in the air as if on a gibbet. 'There used to be orchids on every damned windowsill in the place. I watered the bloody things, and every so often a flower stem would disappear. "I've just taken it to the studio to draw. Just some sketches," he'd say, and perhaps I should have put two and two together, because I never saw a single damned drawing of a bloody orchid!'

She's right: of all the paintings I looked through in the

studio, there wasn't a single orchid. But what it does explain is the graveyard of smashed plant pots in the corner of the garden – Gillian must have flung them there after the funeral.

'Did you take one to the funeral?' I ask Bridget.

'God no! I wouldn't have done something like that to Gillian!'

'So how——?' I ask.

Gillian inhales. 'I stood there, like a mug, mourning him and feeling lost without him, when all around me I see these bloody women carrying orchids. There they all were, giving each other furtive looks, and suddenly I knew. I knew it as well as if the whole sordid truth landed in my lap, and just like that, the bottom dropped out of my world. I looked at Bridget, and when I saw the sympathy in her eyes, I realised she knew exactly what those orchids meant.' Gillian pauses miserably, her eyes fixed on Bridget. 'And the only way she could know—'

'Was if I was one of them,' Bridget finishes for her.

It must have been ghastly. I want to hug Gillian, but she's like a cactus with a 'bugger off' sign. 'Shit!' I mumble insufficiently.

'A flipping large lorry-load of it,' agrees Gillian, her eyes still on Bridget. 'How could you?' she asks, but not in accusation. She's pleading for an answer.

'I didn't, not really – not in the way you think, and I didn't do it on purpose,' says Bridget with quiet dignity. 'What's more, I never slept with him. I want you to know that.'

'But you wanted to?'

Bridget's mouth twists. She breathes in, then lets out the air in a sudden spurt. 'I did . . . at first.' Her eyes flick to me. 'You see, I met him twenty-five years ago at a course he was teaching over in France. I had no idea he was even attached, and when he said he desperately wanted to paint me, well . . . I was flattered. He made me feel beautiful and attractive, instead of middle-aged and lonely, and as he sketched me, we talked about art and the future, my hopes and dreams. After a while it was like he really knew me. So much so, when he asked me to pose nude, it didn't feel wrong. I thought, why not?' She takes a deep breath. 'Then, when he said he'd love to paint me again and perhaps I could come to his classes in Wales, I was delighted, because who wouldn't want to spend time with someone who understood them and brought out all their creativity and vibrancy? I made plans and thought I'd surprise him. I thought I was being vital and spontaneous . . .' Bridget's eyes drop. '. . . but in truth, I was being bloody naive. And on arriving here, when *you* opened the door –' she looks at Gillian, '– I felt the ripest idiot. I promise you, Gillian, at that moment I stopped pursuing him – and there was never anything more than what was in my own head.' Bridget shakes her head sadly.

'But you stayed. You bought a house,' Gillian accuses.

'Yes.'

'Why?'

'Because the strangest thing happened – that very first time we met, you asked me in, you gave me tea, asked about my art, showed me your photographs, and just like that we slipped into a firm friendship. And that week, as I came to see you each day, I realised I loved it here . . . and since Mike made everything seem perfectly all right. He was very charming,' she adds for my benefit. 'But the truth is I stayed because of you, Gillian; because we became friends. Proper friends, and I hadn't had that in a very long time.'

'But not enough of a friend to tell me?' asks Gillian.

'No, actually: you were too much of a friend. I was afraid to lose you.' There's desperation in Bridget's voice. 'Would you have told me, if our positions were reversed?'

'No, probably not,' Gillian admits grudgingly. 'But that doesn't stop me from being bloody furious with you, Bridget.'

'I know,' she agrees. 'But you have to admit that unwittingly coveting Mike *before* I knew you, is very different from cheating on you afterwards.'

Gillian leaves a long silence.

'So, don't you think we should still be friends?' asks Bridget, quite daringly in my opinion. 'I know it won't be easy, and there are things we're both going to have to come to terms with, but surely our friendship's worth it?'

Gillian sips her wine and looks into the glass. 'The betrayal was the worst thing . . . but if you're saying that was never the case?'

Bridget shakes her head. 'I bitterly regret you ever even thought that.'

'So, where did the orchids come in?' I can't help asking.

Bridget's tongue touches her bottom lip. 'You know how artists have their trademarks? Picasso's Blue Period, Warhol's soup cans etc.? Mike said his was the orchid.'

Gillian hefts out a sigh. 'I thought it was something like that. But how sentimentally arrogant of them all to bring them to the funeral and flaunt his infidelity like that.'

Bridget nods.

'We can only hope they were horrified to discover they weren't half as precious or unique as *they* thought they were,' I point out.

Gillian looks down, but a small smile creeps onto her face. 'I damned well hope so.'

'Apparently two women tried to rip each other's hair out in the pub car park after the wake,' says Bridget with a smile. 'And when Dolores went out to break it up, she came back with a black eye!'

'Good!' Gillian smirks, and they give each other a silent toast.

'Pour some more wine,' suggests Bridget. 'And get yourself a glass.' She gives me a wink.

'Bloody good idea,' agrees Gillian, and I refill their glasses and fetch one for myself.

After Bridget's gone home and I've helped Gillian into bed, she watches me fold her clothes.

'You know, Joe can never hear about any of this,' she says carefully. I stop folding and look at her. 'It would hurt him too much – he loved Mike.'

'He loves you, too, you know, and he's been really worried.'

Gillian sighs. 'I know, but you mustn't forget that Mike was his *real* family. Joe would feel responsible, and he'd take it on himself to make amends, which would put unnecessary pressure on him to stay.'

'But isn't that what you want?' I ask, surprised.

'No. I've been thinking about it, and I want him to stay because he wants to.'

I square up the folded clothes. 'But what if it's the nudge he needs? I can't help thinking he wants to be here, deep down.'

Gillian shrugs. 'We can't know that. Perhaps he feels like that in Exeter, too, and much though I'd love him to stay, I can't emotionally blackmail him into doing that.' I give her a straight look. 'All right, I *thought* I could,' she admits, 'but it turns out I can't. So . . . for now at least, this stays between us.'

'Do you want me to warn Bridget?'

Gillian chuffs out a laugh. 'Bridget will take it to the grave if that's what I want. She's a far better friend than I gave her credit for.'

'OK, I'll keep quiet. For now at least . . . as long as you stop thinking the worst about us, because we're just trying to get you back on your feet.'

Gillian considers this. 'All right, but in return you have to include me in any plans that concern me.'

'OK.' I hand her the e-reader, and in a moment of daring, I lean in and kiss her cheek.

She pats my hand. 'And leave off the will,' she says gently, but firmly.

'I will,' I agree, and thanks to the potency of the elderberry wine, I wobble up to bed.

21

Box Clever

The sun pierces through the gap in the curtains and I pull the covers over my head like a cocoon, but there's no denying I need the toilet. I sit up and a headache sings across my skull. Wow, that wine of Bridget's packs a punch.

Downstairs, Gillian is also a bit groggy, and well she might be considering she and Bridget knocked back twice the amount I did. In slow, mutual sympathy, we get her up and into the kitchen.

Joe walks in to find us eating breakfast in absolute and necessary silence.

'Hello,' he says, looking from me to Gillian. 'Am I allowed in, or am I still banished?'

Gillian lifts her eyes. 'You can come in, if you're quiet.'

'A little tender, are we?' he asks.

Gillian gives him a dirty look before continuing with her toast and marmalade, wincing at each crunch. Joe grins at me, but he doesn't come over to kiss me as I expected. In fact, he doesn't show any change in how he feels about me at all.

'Everything all right?' he asks.

'Yes,' I say lightly, pushing down my disappointment. 'We had a lovely evening, and we had a visitor.'

'Oh? Who?'

I don't think his innocence fools Gillian for a second, but I still answer. 'Bridget.'

'Oh, how lovely. I haven't see Bridget in ages. How is she?'

'Very well. Her homemade elderberry is pretty lethal, though.' I rub my temples.

Gillian grunts. 'Lightweight,' she mutters.

'Don't pretend you aren't suffering, too,' I growl.

'So, what's the plan for today? Or isn't there one?' Joe asks diplomatically.

And I must admit, the way I'm feeling, I'm tempted to sit back and take the day off, but after Bridget's shock at the joyless state of the place, I know exactly what we need to do.

'I reckon we should make this place a little more homely.' I look at Gillian, more as a courtesy than because I actually want her opinion.

'Homely,' she shudders. 'Cutesy, saccharine, syrupy nonsense.'

'I was thinking more along the lines of decent, comfortable and tidy, but if you're fine with insanitary and . . .' I struggle for another word. ' . . . soulless—'

'All right!' She winces. 'What were you thinking of?' she says more quietly.

I massage my forehead to clear the fog that's clouding my thoughts. 'Well, when I was trying to find the spare room, I saw a lot of throws, cushions and other items that I assume came from down here?'

'Yes, things I removed for a reason,' she points out.

'Which was?' asks Joe.

I look at Gillian, because there's no way I can answer that – not without bringing up Mike and the orchid women.

'That they're reminders of people I don't want to remember,' she says coldly.

Joe frowns.

'The trouble is, this place looks like a case for social services,' I say, moving swiftly on.

'And you think a few cushions and throws will change that?' Her tone rings with contempt.

'Yes, I do.'

'Well, I don't, and social services can stay out on the doorstep for all I care.'

'What about your friends?' I ask.

Joe folds his arms and raises an eyebrow. 'Yes, do you want them to think you've given in to grief and self-pity?'

Gillian's eyes glitter dangerously and her jaw tightens. 'I haven't given in to self-pity, Joe!' I give her a sceptical look. 'I haven't!'

'Then prove it. I'm not saying you should put *everything* back, just a few things you like . . . and if you don't like any of it, buy something new! Do you remember what we talked about in the hall?' Gillian's mouth is clamped tight, which is worrying. 'Something old or something new?' I prompt, then stop because that's worryingly close to the wedding rhyme.

'Oh, hang from the bloody light fittings in rhinestone knickers if you want, just don't accuse me of self-pity!'

There's a bald silence, broken by Bozz sneezing.

'Well, I'm game if no one else is,' says Joe.

I grin at him, and even Gillian's lip twitches.

'How about you do that,' I suggest, 'while I see if we can do anything to make this place a bit more cheerful.'

'So what's the plan?' Gillian's tone is resigned.

I pluck my e-reader from Gillian's fingers despite her indignant squawk, find *The Life-Changing Magic of Tidying* by Marie Kondo, find the section on sparking joy, and hand it back. 'Homework,' I say significantly.

'A self-help manual?' she asks. 'I remember when people

went gaga for Feng Shui, afraid their fortunes would wash away if they didn't put their toilet lid down. I didn't fall for that, and I won't fall for this.'

'Just read it.'

Gillian opens her mouth, but I hold up a finger to show I won't accept another word. She closes it again and starts to read as I clear the breakfast things.

Joe joins me at the sink and leans in. 'Nicely managed, but what are you doing?'

'Making her consider what she wants, think how she feels about the past and take a look at her surroundings,' I say firmly.

Joe blows out a breath. 'Won't that make her more depressed?'

'Well, hiding from it hasn't done her any good.' His eyebrows flick up as he takes my point. 'And I think she wants to face it. At least, that's the impression I got last night.'

'Fine, but if this backfires, I'm hiding behind you.' I threaten him with the soggy sponge. 'Hey, I said I'm one hundred per cent behind you.'

'Using me as a human shield!' I agree. 'Make yourself useful and get a box down from upstairs.'

'My old bedroom?'

'No, I'm in that one. The stuff is dumped in the other one.'

'Good to know,' he says, and a smile touches his lips, while the area around his eyes crinkles in that way I find almost irresistible. But before I can think of anything suitably flirty to say, he goes to collect the first box.

He's gone a few minutes, but when he comes back he places the box on the floor, and Gillian puts aside the e-reader. We all stare at it like it's a trigger-happy jack-in-the-box.

I laugh, kneel beside it and look up at Gillian. 'May I?' I ask.

'There's nothing to hide,' she agrees, and I lift the flaps.

There are some lovely things, but they've all been thrown in without care or packaging, and I extract a broken William Morris pattern mug and set it aside. I hand Gillian a large pottery bowl, patterned with hand-painted tulips, but as she looks down at it her lips become a hard line.

'Nope,' she says, handing it back, and without asking why, I wrap it in some newspaper Joe hands me. I take out a small but gorgeous felting picture, which I instantly recognise as one of Bridget's, and pass it to her. Her face softens and with the minutest nod, I put it to one side. We progress in this way, keeping some things and carefully packing away others until, at the end of an hour, Gillian lets out a breath and looks at the three carefully packed boxes and the pile of items we've liberated.

'Well, that was harrowing. What do we do next?' she asks.

'We choose where to put them, and the place looks less like an abandoned house in a nuclear disaster zone.'

'Flatterer,' she says without rancour. 'And do we dispose of that lot?'

'Normally, yes, but I think you should take another look in a few years' time.'

'You think I'll feel differently?' she asks severely.

'Not necessarily, but given the circumstances . . .' I glance unintentionally at Joe and look down. 'I don't think you should do anything rash.'

'I know my own mind,' Gillian says firmly.

'Yes, but two days ago you'd have got rid of Bridget's pictures.'

Gillian glances at the pile, which has two of Bridget's pictures in it; one of this house and another of the end of the valley, and nods. 'True.' She frowns heavily at Joe, who's looking suspiciously at me, and I imbue my expression with everything I can to show he shouldn't ask about it.

His brow descends in concern, but he half smiles. 'Lunchtime?' he asks.

'Bloody good idea,' agrees Gillian, and she returns to her reading while Joe follows me into the small back hall, where I make a start on folding the washing.

He leans against the wall and watches me for a second. 'You will need to tell me what happened,' he says very quietly.

I glance up at him. 'I promised Gillian I wouldn't.'

He looks at the floor for a second then back at me. 'Is it something I should know?' Both his acceptance and perceptiveness surprise me.

I smile regretfully. 'I'll try and persuade her,' I promise.

'Thanks.' He brushes my cheek with the back of his fingers. It's intimate and familiar, but over in a second, and I can't figure out if there's something more serious than mild affection behind it. He did kiss me last night, after all. Perhaps if I make some move towards him – maybe take his hand or kiss his cheek to show him I'm interested – that might prompt him into showing me how he feels?

I join him in the kitchen where he's making a start on some sandwiches, but he smiles as if nothing happened and I chicken out.

After lunch, Joe takes Gillian through her exercises, and afterwards we sort through a few more boxes. It's tiring work, and while Gillian takes a nap, Joe puts up Bridget's pictures and I put a gorgeous blanket over the sofa and arrange some pretty crockery on the dresser. It transforms the room. So much so that even Gillian gives a faint nod of approval when she comes in, and Joe grins at me as we carry the boxes of Gillian's rejects out to the studio.

'I wouldn't have thought it was possible,' he confesses as

we leave the studio. I look back at him smugly, but Joe nods at the lane. 'You have a visitor.'

Bryn is leaning on his stick with his collie at his side, watching us from the yard gate. I'm not sure he's here for me, but I walk over, while Joe goes inside to collect the last box.

'Hello, Bryn.' I smile, and Bryn tips his cap.

'I saw Bridget came up here last night,' he comments.

'Yes.'

He nods towards the house to indicate Gillian. 'Friends again, are they?'

'If that's what you call an evening with Bridget and a bottle of her homemade elderberry wine,' I agree.

'The good stuff?' he asks, startled.

'Yes.'

Bryn grunts, either surprised or impressed. 'And Daf said you're friendly with Seren?'

'Yes, she's lovely!' I agree wholeheartedly, and Bryn nods, giving the impression I've passed some kind of test.

'You been down those steps?' He nods his head at the steps that lead down to the overgrown front garden-come-field that separates Gillian's land from Bryn's.

'No, I've only been in the back garden.'

'Watch yourself. That's where Gillian fell.' He looks me in the eyes to make sure I've got the message.

'OK,' I say, and with a nod to himself, he heads back down the lane.

Puzzled, I cross the yard and look down at the hard slate steps. It wouldn't be any fun falling down those, and mindful of Bryn's warning I make my way down them carefully. I reach the bottom without incident. As far as I can see, they're just steps, and the garden at the bottom is just as badly kept as the house was, though there are a few daffodils and snowdrops bravely holding up their heads. But apart from the overgrown pea and bean frames, the rest of the patch is hummocky grass and gnarly fruit trees.

I jump as Bryn clears his throat. He's by the wall that separates the garden from the lane. 'Be careful on those steps,' he repeats like a doom-laden Welsh soothsayer, and I glance up them. 'Give them a good scrubbing,' he advises, and with that, he continues down to his bungalow.

Was there blood? Is that what he's getting at? Surely the Welsh weather would have done a good enough job without me getting down on my hands and knees? I examine the steps – they're slate slabs, well set in, decently spaced and have probably been there for years, only . . . I touch the soil in the corner and rub my fingers together. There's a shiny residue. Oil?

I look down the track. Bryn is almost at his gate, and tips his head, satisfied I've found what he's directed me towards.

Joe, having come to see where I've got to, smiles down the steps at me.

I hold up my finger. 'What do you make of this? I found it in the corner of the steps.' Joe comes down the steps and goes through the same motions I did.

'Oil of some kind?' he asks. 'How did you notice this?'

'Bryn told me to scrub the steps.' I frown down at his bungalow. 'But how would he know it was here?'

'When Bridget told me about Gillian's accident, she told me Bryn saw Gillian fall and rang the ambulance. He must have noticed it then.'

'But wouldn't that make the steps slippery?'

Joe nods.

I bite my lip. 'You realise this changes things . . . unless Gillian spilt the oil herself.'

'That seems unlikely. But if she didn't, someone did this on purpose, and that's nasty.'

I nod, and feel my stomach churn. 'But how would

someone know she'd come down these steps? She's *clearly* not been gardening!'

Joe shrugs. 'Good point, but I still don't like it,' and as I stare around the garden at the innocuous daffodils I'm suddenly reminded of the orchid women. I sigh and wish I could tell him the whole of it.

'We have to tell her,' I say gently. 'Put her on her guard.'

Joe wipes his fingers on his jeans and looks into my eyes, taking my concern seriously. 'List *everything* you're worried about.'

I hold out my thumb and start counting them off on my fingers. 'Too much junk mail, sales calls, the fact that she installed the yard light, why her tyres have been flat often enough for Huw to bring it up, why Bryn feels the need to vet every person who comes up the lane, and last but not least, the scratches on the studio door.'

Joe frowns at the six fingers I'm holding out. 'Jesus! And to crown it all there's the steps. Are you going to ask her about it all, or shall I?' he asks, silently acknowledging that I know more than he does, but also offering me a get-out.

'I'll do it,' I say. 'But I think I need to do it on my own.' That way, if it's anything to do with the orchid women, she can tell me.

He looks at me for a long moment. 'Fine, I'll go home and do some writing to give you time to bring it up, but I need to know what's going on – especially if it puts either of you in danger.'

I don't miss that he included me in his concern, and I feel bad for excluding him, but I don't see what else I can do. 'I'll tell you what I can,' I agree, and follow him up the steps. I bite my lip as he gets in his car and rolls down his window.

'I'll be back tonight to look after Gillian – it's your night out with my sister and Gareth,' he reminds me, when I look confused.

'Shit!' It's the last thing I need just now.

He smiles. 'It might do you good to get out of here for a bit. It's been quite tense lately.' That's an understatement, but I still don't want to go. 'And Petra's been looking forward to it,' he adds, making me feel guilty.

'All right,' I concede. 'I'll see you later.' And with one last smile he drives off, while I head inside, trying to figure out how to broach the subject with Gillian.

Gillian gives me a keen-eyed stare over the e-reader. 'That took you both a while. Did I hear Joe drive off?'

'Yes,' I say, and I realise the only thing to do is come out with it. 'We found something worrying on the garden steps and he's giving me time to talk to you about it.'

She turns off the e-reader. 'What kind of thing?'

'There something spilt on them. It looks like oil. Do you know anything about that?'

Gillian breathes out through her nose as if I've unveiled some dark secret. '*That's* what Bryn was looking at when I fell. I thought he was worried I'd damaged the steps. But oil? I guess that explains why my feet disappeared from under me so fast.'

'Do you know why it was there?'

Gillian shakes her head. 'I've no idea. Why, is that what you and Joe were discussing outside? I could hear he wasn't happy.'

I've got to remember that she hears almost everything, but actually, she's taking it more calmly than I expected. 'He's worried. We both are.'

'Why?'

'Because he's seen the scratches on the studio door, and Huw mentioned you've had a lot of flat tyres. We also wondered why you needed the billion-watt yard light?'

'Ah,' she says, and there's vulnerability in her eyes. 'Well, yes. That does amount to a hill of beans, doesn't it?'

'What's been going on?' I ask gently.

'Someone's been playing silly-buggers, that's all. It's been going on for a while.'

'How long?'

'Since the funeral.'

'Do you know who it is?'

Gillian watches me sit down, and shrugs. 'Given the timing, it's probably one of Mike's . . . many . . . orchid women. Or perhaps an angry husband? Or maybe it has nothing to do with Mike at all, and I've upset someone?'

'Tell me what's been going on.'

Gillian drops her eyes and picks at her compression bandage. 'Various things. Tradesmen arrive saying they've been asked to give a quote or inspect something or other, the phone rings off the hook with double glazing and PPI quotes, the post is full of junk mail, plus the other things you mentioned – the flat tyres, someone trying to get into the studio, as well as rocks left on the front path, plant pots moving, dead animals left on the front doorstep. I had the yard light installed hoping to put a stop to it, but that kept triggering, and after a while I thought I was going mad through lack of sleep . . . but oil? You can't imagine oil, can you?' She almost looks relieved.

'No,' I agree quietly. 'Someone's being vindictive. Have you any idea who?'

Gillian shakes her head.

'Is anyone particularly upset with you?'

'Only Petra, and she's already working her own angle through the cottage and the will.'

'And I don't get the feeling she'd be this nasty, either.'

Gillian gives me a sharp look, but grudgingly nods. 'No, you're right.'

'So who *would* do something like this?'

Gillian shrugs, and the sadness and upset in her eyes yanks at my heart.

'OK, let's work our way down the valley. Bryn?' I offer.

'It's not Bryn! For the last eighteen months, Bryn has hardly said a word to me, but he's left things on the doorstep just about every day. He's also kept tabs on who comes up the track, he fed Bozz when I couldn't, and he was quick to sort me out when I fell.'

'What kind of things does he leave?' I ask, intrigued.

'Oranges, tins of soup, milk, pots of jam, chutney, cat food. He basically kept me going and, knowing I didn't want to see anyone, he turned people away – including quite a few contractors, I might add.'

'But he doesn't even say hello?'

'He has his reasons.' Gillian raises her eyebrows as she waits for the penny to drop.

Oh God. 'Not Bryn's wife? Did Mike—?'

Gillian holds up a hand to stop me. 'I don't know. But when she suddenly left, Mike never questioned it. That spoke volumes once I allowed myself to think about it.'

'But Bryn still looks out for you?'

Gillian nods. 'Only since Mike died. And he never says a word. In fact, I wouldn't even know it was him if I weren't such a bad sleeper.'

Guilt floods through me for even considering him. Not that it isn't a whole basketful of odd, but I strike him off my suspect list. 'Dolores?' I ask.

'To begin with Dolores was overly attentive, truth be told – offering to do shopping, cleaning and cook casseroles. But what I don't get is why she would be bothering me now?'

'What about her husband, George?'

'No, not George. He's an honourable man. It's not him.'

'Are you sure?' I can't help asking after the chilling reception he gave me at the pub. Gillian nods, so I let it drop. 'Gareth?' I ask, and Gillian shakes her head.

'Why would he bother with an old lady?'

'I don't know, but who else is there?'

Gillian shrugs. 'There is no one else. Seren, Huw and Daf are all lovely, and Bridget – well you can see it wasn't her. That's why I came to the conclusion I must be imagining it.'

'Except you're not.' I pause significantly. 'What about the people in the summer cottages?'

'They've all been empty at one time or another when my tyres have been let down.'

'So, by a process of elimination, it has to be someone from outside the valley?'

Gillian shakes her head sadly. 'And then it's not so easy.'

I sigh heavily. 'No.' I sit back in reluctant defeat. 'The best clue we have is the oil. Do you have any idea when it was put there?'

'I fell nearly two weeks ago, but I hadn't been down there in months.'

I look at her. 'Why *did* you go down there?'

Gillian thinks for a moment. 'Bozz was caught in the netting under the pea frames. He was yowling fit to bust,' but as my expression changes, hers does, too. 'Oh,' she says, realising. 'He was bait, because Bozz in trouble would get me down those steps when very little else would.'

'And you wouldn't be careful, either,' I agree, chilled at the depth of premeditation behind it.

Gillian looks upset. 'Poor cat, but at least Bryn freed him in the end.'

I wish I could ask Bryn whether Bozz was caught in a snare. 'Did he say anything?'

'Beyond that Bozz was fine and I shouldn't move until the ambulance arrived? No, he said nothing.'

We sit in silence, and I assess Gillian, trying to gauge how my next suggestion will go down.

'What?' she asks flatly.

'I want you to tell Joe about all of this, even about Mike. It's no longer fair not to.'

'It'll break his heart,' she warns, but that's not a 'no'.

'It won't,' I say, and I know I'm right. I also know it won't be pleasant for either of them. 'Tell him this evening. You'll have the place to yourselves because I have to go out with Petra and Gareth.' I struggle not to sound bitter, but at least this way, my going out will serve a purpose.

'You should get out for a bit. It'll do you good,' she says, but I reckon it's her who needs me to get out for a bit. Since I don't want her to say it, I get up and try to figure out what we should have for dinner, while Gillian stares off anxiously into the distance.

22

A Stag in the Dark

My fingers are stained black with mascara. It's almost like it knows I'd much rather stay here, drink whiskey with Gillian and Joe, and pretend to clear up the kitchen while Joe reads to Gillian. The only thing that's stopping me from crying off is knowing they need time to talk.

I use soap and my thumbnail to scrape away the smeared mascara. I dry my hands, roll on some lip gloss and stand on tiptoes to get a limited view of my sparkly top and jeans in the bathroom mirror. I'll do. And besides, Gareth and Petra will be here any minute, and so will Joe. I pick up my jacket and purse from the edge of the bath and join Gillian in kitchen.

She's settled in her armchair, doing her best not to look worried, but I know she's still affected by our talk earlier. She puts down the e-reader and raises an eyebrow at me. 'What are you looking so gloomy about?'

'Nothing,' but I undermine my answer with a heavy sigh.

'All this palaver over a night out. Honestly! If I were you, I'd be out there with the best of them.'

'So you're telling me, if it weren't for your fall, *you'd* be up for a night out with Petra and Gareth?'

Gillian smiles. 'Well, no, a drink down the pub with Bridget, Bryn and Daf is more my level.'

'That's hardly the same,' I say with feeling.

'No,' she concedes. 'There is something about Gareth and Petra that's a little . . . ?' she flaps her good hand.

'Excessive?' I offer, and Gillian laughs.

'I was going to say superficial. But I'm sure they know how to have a good time, and you'll feel better after a good bop.'

I look at her doubtfully. 'Bop?' I ask, laughter spilling out.

'Dance, boogie, whatever it is you call it these days. Go out and shake your tail feathers.' She grins at me. 'I bet Gareth knows a move or two.'

'I bet he does,' I agree darkly, but I'm saved from further comment by Joe letting himself in. Pompom trots ahead of him and darts under the kitchen table in search of Bozz. A yowl and some hissing tells us she's found him.

Joe smiles at me as he pockets his keys, and frowns as Pompom emerges unscathed. 'Gareth pulled in behind me. You look great, by the way.'

I blush. 'Thanks. Where's Petra?'

Joe pulls a face. 'Petra has bailed on you, I'm afraid.'

My mouth drops open. 'You have to be kidding me! I only agreed to go because she made such a fuss about how bored she is!'

'What can I tell you? She's had a hyper-sensitive stomach for the last few weeks and she's back at the cottage throwing up, so I think you have to give her this one.'

'Typical! I didn't want to go in the first— Oh, hi, Gareth,' I say as he walks in, and Joe bites back a smile, while Gillian's eyes shine with amusement.

Gareth nods at us all. 'Hi, Ella, Joe, Gillian.' He's shaved, put on a shirt and trousers, and his hands are stuffed in his pockets. 'Petra just rang me to say she's not well, so I'm afraid it's just us?' He looks so hopefully at me that, even though I don't want to go, I can't bail on him.

'No, of course I don't mind,' I agree, and his shoulders relax a little.

'Great. Ready?' he asks, and I scoop up my jacket and purse. 'Bye,' he says to Joe and Gillian.

'Don't do anything we wouldn't,' Gillian calls after us, but I'm too far down the hall to give an appropriate gesture, so I grind my teeth.

The air outside is chilly. Gareth opens the door of his souped-up Ford Fiesta ST for me. I get in, and smile as Gareth gets in beside me.

'Ready to see the sights?' he asks. 'How about a nightclub?'

'Yes,' I say brightly. I'm about to ask what the local town's like when he turns the ignition key and loud music blares out of the speakers. It's too loud for us to talk, but rather than turning it down, he smiles at me and nods along to the music with one hand on the steering wheel. Teenage girls would probably wet themselves at how cool he is, but for me the word 'plonker' springs to mind.

Left with no conversation, appalling music and an excess of aftershave, I settle back into the seat and watch the villages slide by. At least Joe and Gillian can get on with their awkward conversation, and thank heaven I'm not Petra throwing up in her cottage, possibly with food poisoning . . . that's been going on for weeks . . . Oh my God! I groan, but luckily Gareth doesn't hear over the music. Now I think about it, it's bloody obvious – the rumless Coke, herbal tea, the sickness? She's pregnant!

But I don't think Joe's realised, going by his clueless comment about Petra's weight the other day . . . but Gillian's anger afterwards? Gillian knows, and I guess that also explains Petra's hurry to put the cottage on the market. She probably needs the money, because despite Mum's bravery about it, I know parenthood isn't the easiest thing to do by yourself.

We drive through more villages, past the supermarket I used the other day and keep going out the other side of town. We're just pulling into the large car park of an old industrial unit dressed up as a nightclub, when Gareth hits the brakes so hard I almost go through the windscreen, so it takes me a second or two to notice the entrance isn't buzzing with music and strobes, but police and anxious teenagers.

I jump as a policewoman taps loudly on my window. I wind it down and Gareth turns off the CD. I smile, my heart hammering almost as loudly as the policewoman's knock.

'Here to pick someone up, are you?' she asks.

'Yes,' says Gareth at the exact same instant I say, 'No.'

Gareth glares at me, and the policewoman, who's younger than me, looks pointedly at my sparkly top and Gareth's shirt like we're drug pushers. But it isn't like we can scoop up some random teenager just to make Gareth's 'yes' true. She waits for an explanation.

'We're just looking for an evening out,' I say apologetically. 'Not that this looks like our thing,' I start to say, but she's already hailing over a colleague with a dog. She gives the policeman with the dog a flick of her eyebrows, and opens my door.

'If you wouldn't mind stepping out of the vehicle, please, madam, sir?' There's a steely look in her eyes, and Gareth grumbles quietly as the dog scrambles over his upholstery and sniffs here, there and everywhere. It jumps out, sniffs my crotch – I really would wet myself if it barked there – and the policeman, losing interest, waves us on our way.

'That was exciting,' I say as we get back in, trying to alleviate the atmosphere Gareth's scowl is creating. 'I've never been in a drugs bust before.' Gareth, though, doesn't seem inclined to take it with good nature, and he grips the steering wheel. 'What's the matter?'

'Nothing,' he mutters. 'Cinema?' he suggests, and I nod, but as he pulls into the cinema down the road, he gets out and brushes pointlessly at the seats as if to rid his car of invisible dog residue. I assess the two-screen cinema's billboards and there's a zombie horror and a children's movie.

'God!' he says, looking up at them.

'We could try the zombie movie?' but Gareth checks his watch and shakes his head.

'It doesn't start for another hour.'

Given how sulky he's being, I'm tempted to suggest the children's movie, but I don't want to walk back to Gillian's, so I bite my tongue and summon a pleasant expression. 'Any ideas?'

Gareth stares into the distance in moody contemplation. 'I know somewhere you'll like,' he says, his mood lifting as suddenly as it descended, and we get in the car.

We drive into the town centre, pass an Italian restaurant (which would be fine), a few takeaways (which would be OK, so long as we find somewhere with a decent view to eat), and some pubs with the youth of the area standing about outside (admittedly I'm less keen, but they might be all right inside, especially if they have a pool table). Gareth pulls into a small private car park behind an electrical shop, and waves away my questions about the private sign.

'We're not in London now – no one cares here, and it's the closest place to the bar. Come on – you'll love it!'

I'm glad he's regained his enthusiasm, so I follow him down the street to a doorway with a neon sign. He pushes through the group of scantily clad teenagers around the door, and walks up the dimly lit stairs towards the pulsating music above. Gareth grins confidently as we make our way through to the bar, and after buying us drinks, he leads me to a small, circular table strapped at waist-height around what looks to be a pole-dancing pole. I try a few bellowed questions, but it's useless, so Gareth nods to the music and watches the local girls as I sip my drink.

To be fair, they're worth watching. The prevailing fashion

is long hair straightened down their backs, exotic make-up, boob-tubes and miniskirts. I've never worn a boob-tube in my life, even when I was their age – I'd have been too frightened of it slipping or being yanked down, but here, along with short skirts or shorts, strappy high heels and a lace choker, they're the norm. So much so, I feel very out of place in my jeans and top. At least if Petra were here, her bubbly personality would carry us along, but without her we're as flat as a pancake.

I smile at Gareth and he smiles back, but this is terrible.

'Another drink?' mouths Gareth. He indicates my half-full glass.

I shake my head and lean in to him. 'Shall we call tonight a bust?' I shout.

His eyes stray across the teen flesh on display, but he nods. It's not like he has a chance with me in tow, so we finish our drinks, I pick up my jacket and we head out into the chill air. Gareth slides his arm around my shoulders and it seems churlish to shrug it off, but as we round the corner to the car park, just one look at the sticker on his windscreen tells us he's been clamped.

'Fuck!' growls Gareth. His arm slides off my shoulders and he storms up to the driver's side. He rips the sticker from the window and holds it up to show me. 'What were they doing – waiting around the corner?' he demands. He kicks out angrily at the yellow triangle chained to his front wheel, and I watch in fascination as his mouth slowly forms an anguished 'O', and he clutches his foot and hops around the car park. It would be quite funny if it wasn't so cold, but it is, and I take my phone out of my pocket and pray that Gillian's phone is plugged in.

Joe picks up. 'Hello?'

'Hi, it's me,' I half whisper.

'Checking up on us?' Joe's amused. 'You've hardly been gone an hour.'

I cup the area between my mouth and the phone as Gareth downgrades his hopping to a staggered foot-dragging limp, accompanied by jerky swearing and air-punching. 'No, I'm calling to say I might be late.'

'Oh?'

'Yes, Gareth's car has been clamped and I think he might have broken his toe.'

'Not really?'

Gareth leans on the car with one hand and glares at me, gripping his injured foot with his other.

'Yes,' I say quietly. The last thing I need is to rile the sulky beast. 'Can you stay with Gillian until I get back?'

'Where are you?'

There's a street sign on the side of the electrical shop, so I tell him.

'Hold tight. I'll come and get you.'

'But what about Gillian?' I ask urgently. The last thing I need is for her to be left alone after everything we found out this afternoon.

'Don't worry about Gillian. I'll make sure she's fine. I'll be about forty minutes?'

'Great, thanks.'

'No worries,' says Joe.

I hang up, and Gareth mutters a string of swear words at the wheel clamp.

'Joe's coming to get us,' I tell him, and Gareth grunts. 'We might as well wait in the car – he'll be a while.'

Gareth's hard, malevolent glower hovers on me for a moment, but he unlocks the car and whimpers as he slumps into his seat. After a second or two he unlocks my door, too, and we sit in silence, his angry breathing misting up the car.

I'm about to take out my phone and play a game on it when Gareth reaches into the footwell and peels off his shoe and sock. He peers into the darkness and pokes at his toe, while the smell of sweaty boy's bedroom fills the car. I try to hold my breath, but it's impossible to get away from.

He looks at me. 'Can you check if it's broken?'

There's nothing I'd rather do less, but I don't want to seem rude. I shake my head sadly, trying not to let my horror show on my face. 'Even if it is, there's nothing I can do. You could dip it in an icy puddle to slow the swelling, though. I know it sounds ridiculous, but it's sound medical thinking.' *And it might rinse away the smell*, I add silently.

Disgusted, Gareth lifts his foot, clonks me in my shoulder with his knee, and peers at his toe in the half-light. 'The least you could do is check it,' he complains.

But his turn of phrase snags on my last nerve. 'What do you mean "the least I could do"?'

'Well . . . considering I've taken you out, like Petra and Mam wanted.'

Anger and betrayal flashes through me in a hot wave. 'They *told* you to take me out?'

He dips his head. 'Mam said you'd be missing London, and I should show you a good time. She even offered to look after Gillian – told me to phone her if Gillian was by herself! And then Petra went on about how guilty she felt, letting us down, and made me promise still to take you out.'

'And as a consequence, you're trying to blame *me* for all this? For Petra being ill, the drugs bust and your wheel clamp? Because, if I remember correctly, I asked *you* if it was OK to park here, and you said yes!' I shake my head in disbelief. 'Next you'll be saying I made you kick the wheel clamp.'

'Well, I didn't do it because I was having a crap evening with the wheel clamp, now, did I!'

I wait for him to apologise, but he doesn't, so I get out of the car and pace about in the icy air, keeping myself warm by swearing judiciously and glaring at his car. By the time

Joe arrives, Gareth and I haven't spoken in half an hour and I think my extremities have turned blue.

Joe pulls up next to me and winds down his window. 'All right?' he asks, and Pompom stuffs her nose out behind his head and pants happily at me.

'Not even slightly,' I say as I stroke her nose, while on the other side of the car park, Gareth slams his car door and locks it. He swears and hobbles over with a scowl aimed at me.

'Can I get in the back with Pompom?' I ask Joe, and he nods.

'Get in the back and give her a cuddle while I deal with Prince Charming.'

I get in and Pompom rushes to and fro, excited to have someone in the back with her, while Joe waits for Gareth to manoeuvre himself slowly and painfully into the front seat.

'Hi, Joe,' he says gruffly. 'Could you drop me off at the hospital. I think I've broken my toe.'

'Sure thing,' says Joe cheerfully, and we pull away.

We drive in silence to A&E, where Gareth gets out and gives Joe a curt nod, and me not even that, and we watch him hobble in through the sliding hospital doors.

'So, nice evening?' asks Joe, giving me time to get in the front and strap myself in. I can tell he's amused.

'Put it this way: it would have made a great stag do. There was a drugs bust, plenty of near-naked women and a hospital visit, but as a night out . . .?' I shake my head in disbelief.

'Bad?' asks Joe.

'You wouldn't believe how awful it was!' I explode. 'And embarrassing! Did you know Petra and Dolores *told* him to take me out! What were they thinking? I've never been so bloody mortified in my life!'

'Maybe they just thought you needed a bit of fun?' suggests Joe.

'Well, THAT was not fun! The highlight of the evening

was when Gareth offered to show me his toe! And to be honest, I'd rather tackle Gillian's freezer!'

'Steady on!' chuckles Joe.

I glare at him. 'Stop laughing.'

'Look, I'm trying, but you have to admit it's quite funny.'

I stare hard at him, but as the ridiculousness of it sinks in, I have to giggle.

'It was *seriously* disastrous. But don't think I'll forget Petra's role in all of this! If it weren't for her, I could have spent a lovely evening with you instead.' Joe's eyes dart my way in surprise and, realising what I just implied, I quickly look down and clear my throat, blushing feverishly. 'I mean . . . with you and Gillian.' I bite my lip. Why didn't I say that in the first place? I feel like an idiot. Pompom nudges my elbow with her nose, and I stroke her head. 'So is Bridget looking after Gillian?' I say, more to break the awkward silence than anything, and he finally returns his attention to the road.

'No, I couldn't get hold of her. I left her a message, but then Seren said she'd come instead.'

'Oh?' I ask.

'Yes, she told me to set off, and said she'd be straight down. She also said she hoped you were OK.' He glances at me again, but I still can't quite look at him.

'That's really kind of her, especially considering it's lambing time. Did she say how it's going?' and we move onto the safe subject of the times Joe and Huw helped with lambing when they were kids.

In much less time than it seemed to take with Gareth, we turn up the hill towards Gillian's, and Joe pulls into the suddenly blindingly lit yard and parks between Seren and Huw's 4x4 and Bridget's green Ford.

I sigh, relieved to be back, but as Joe turns off the engine, I can see he wants to say something.

'Ella. I've been thinking about what you said . . .'

I'm about to say 'yes?', but the intensity in his eyes stops me. I try to smile, but even that seems difficult.

He looks down for a second, bites his lips together, then slowly and deliberately takes my face in his hands, and very gently kisses me full on the lips. For a whole second I'm afraid to breathe, but as my eyes close against the harsh yard light, leaving just the touch of his lips and the feel of his hands cradling my cheeks, I let myself fall into the wonderfully warm deliciousness of it. The warmth of the car cocoons us, and as he pulls away, smiling and wanting to see how I've taken his advance, Pompom pushes her head up between us.

'Well, somebody wants to make sure she's not forgotten,' he says, amused, but there's a small crease between his eyebrows, which I want to smooth away with my finger. 'Was that OK?' he asks uncertainly.

'Yes, that was fine.' What am I saying? I grin at him. He laughs, and so do I.

He strokes my cheek with his thumb. 'Good. But I'm afraid I should get back to see how Petra's doing. Will you be all right going in by yourself?'

A small pang of guilt plucks at my conscience, but even in my fuzzy state I know it's not my place to tell him about her. 'Yes, fine. I'll see you tomorrow?' I ask, even though it sounds needy.

'Count on it,' he agrees. He kisses me again, and as I fall straight back into the warm comforting seclusion of it, he pulls me a little closer before he pulls away. I smile at him, and with reluctance I get out and walk to the front door. I wave as he drives off, but as I watch his tail lights round the corner, I realise I have forgotten to say thanks . . . unless the kiss counts? And smiling to myself, I let myself in.

23

Making Waves

I close the front door and lean against the coats to collect myself. Who'd have thought a terrible night out with Gareth could end up with a glorious kiss from Joe? I allow myself a few seconds to revel in the feeling, because there's no way on earth that was just a friendly peck, or him being carried away by enthusiasm – *that* was the real deal.

There's a contented chatter coming from the kitchen and I can just make out each of Gillian's, Bridget's and Seren's voices, and a smile spreads across my face. Whether it was planned this way or not, Gillian has visitors! I pull myself upright and push open the kitchen door. To my surprise, a cheer goes up, and for an embarrassing second I think they know about the kiss, but with Gillian sitting in her usual armchair, Bridget reclining in the other armchair, and Seren sitting on the sofa swathed in the most amazing patchwork quilt that she's sewing, I realise there's no way any of them were looking out of the window.

'Hello,' I say cheerfully, then take in the full glory of Seren's quilt. 'Wow!' I say, bending down to examine it.

It's a swirl of beautiful blues in a glorious wave. There's not a square patch in sight, and the stitching follows the edges of the shaped sections of material, adding to the effect of moving water. Seren's busy adding sequins and what look like seed pearls to it, giving it a sense of frothiness, while nestled, almost hidden at the far end of this fantastic piece of work, is baby Bethan, curled up and sleeping within the amazing folds.

'You like it?' asks Seren, popping her needle into a pin cushion and giving me a one-armed hug.

'It's gorgeous!' I gush. 'Bethan's gorgeous, too, of course,' I add, and Seren grins.

'Let sleeping babies lie. But tell us what happened? Where were you stranded?'

Bridget nods. 'Yes, what happened? We've all been speculating outrageously!'

Gillian's trying to curb her grin, so I can only imagine how outlandish their guesswork has been, but seeing as it's led to a lovely evening for her, I'm no longer so annoyed.

'First things first: tea or whiskey?' I ask, both because no one has a drink, and also because I'd appreciate a moment to gather myself, because who knew a kiss could be so heady?

'Whiskey all round,' decrees Gillian.

'Tea for me,' calls Seren, and I put the kettle on and add some glasses to a tray.

'So?' prompts Gillian.

'Well, as you know, it all began with Petra crying off,' and I tell them about the car journey, the drugs bust, the cinema and the bar, and by the time I hand around the teas and whiskies, everyone's roaring with laughter at Gareth hopping around the car park, swearing and wanting me to look at his toe.

I pull out a kitchen chair and sketchily describe my relief when Joe got there. 'So, we dropped off Gareth at A&E and here I am.' Gillian gives me a shrewd look, and I cast around for a change of subject. 'But tell me, how long did this quilt take?' I crouch down next to Seren to get out from under Gillian's interrogatory gaze.

'Hours and hours. So many, I'd hate to admit the real number, but this is a double. The children's ones are quicker.' She pulls out her phone and shows me photos of a gorgeous knight in corduroy chainmail, with feather plumes erupting from his helmet and a lion rampant on his red shield. She swipes to another of a princess in a pale-blue satin gown with a jewel-encrusted bodice and conical headdress; the strands of her hair individually embroidered and sequinned. Then there's a double covered in a kaleidoscope of blue butterflies and a fourth of a sweeping willow; each leaf picked out in various fabrics.

'How do you have the patience?' I ask, picking up the nearest corner of the quilt. It's made up of five different pieces of material that come together at a piped edge.

'Oh, I enjoy it. I wouldn't make them if I didn't.'

'Do you make much money from them?' I stretch my mouth in shame as Seren looks to Bridget. 'Sorry, I'm being rude.'

'Oh, don't worry. Not much, truth be told. I just enjoy making them. It's the process that's fun, so I mainly sell them to friends for the price of the fabric.'

I stare at her, outraged.

Bridget shakes her head. 'I've told her for years she should sell them in London,' which I guess explains the look that passed between them.

'But it takes so much work to find anyone willing to sell them,' says Seren.

'But once they're in place, you're set,' I point out. 'Or you could set up a website? People love this sort of thing – a true artisan product, properly handmade, unique and full of creativity. I bet they'd sell for at least a thousand,' I get in quickly before Seren can demur.

Seren looks from me to Bridget. 'But I wouldn't know where to start! Websites take so much time to set up and there's never enough time as it is, what with the kids and the farm. And I can't go down to London to trawl the shops to see if they'd sell them, because even if they did, I'd never have the time to make them in the quantities they'd want.'

She has a point, and as soon as you add time pressures to a hobby the whole dynamic changes. I examine the beading Seren has already applied, and have an idea.

'But what if you had a website where people could follow your progress and bid on the quilt as you make it? That way, you could still do it for relaxation, and the whole point is you're *not* rushing it or doing it on a commercial scale. And there's the added benefit that, by the time it's finished, the new owner already feels attached to it.'

'But what if people pinched her ideas?' asks Gillian.

'You'd have to think of a point of difference. Didn't you say you dyed wool for felting?'

'Yes,' say Seren and Bridget in unison.

'Maybe you could dye some fabric and print a design on it that's unique to you, and incorporate it in the quilt? Or make some sort of label . . . I don't know, something distinctive like the Steiff bear button; something that declares it's an original Seren Quilt. Then you could keep a catalogue of all your designs, and if the pictures are all over the Internet, there would be no doubt where the original designs came from.'

'It's a good idea,' says Gillian, looking impressed.

'It's a bloody excellent idea,' decrees Bridget. 'What about me! You said you liked my felting pictures – any ideas?'

'Hmm, felting. I don't know much about it, to be honest with you, but I'd love to see more of what you do.' Bridget tries not to let her face fall, but I can see she's disappointed. 'Have you thought of putting your work on show?'

'No swanky art gallery's going to want my scruffy wisps of wool,' says Bridget sadly.

'I was thinking more of you doing a show up here. People love locally made stuff, especially in tourist spots.'

'Such as?' asks Gillian.

'Seaside towns, maybe that place with the longest place name, the visitor centre at the top of Snowdon?' I reel off, but Bridget doesn't look enthusiastic. 'Or,' I say stalling. 'Off the top of my head . . . I'd say most people don't know you can make more than toys and garish caps from felt, and given that crafting is so massive in the hobby-stakes these days, perhaps you could create a "how to" website all about felting? You might need to do some research, but you could show different techniques, together with what's possible with practice and maybe even market Seren's felting supplies?' Bridget glances at Seren, who nods. 'Then put a gallery on the website, with some how-to pictures and works in progress, together with skeins of "genuine Welsh wool, as used in your pictures" in a beautiful array of colours. You could give the colours mad names like . . .' I search for inspiration. '. . . Bethan Blue? Boswell Black?'

'Compost Green,' suggests Bridget. 'Bovine Brown.'

'They're more the colours we tend to get,' agrees Seren, laughing.

I nod vigorously, glad they're seeing the fun side of it. 'And then, if you linked it to an online retailer, perhaps with some of your work, I'd say you could be onto a winner.'

'I wouldn't know where to start,' says Bridget anxiously.

'Ask Petra: she's doing it already,' I say. Bridget doesn't look convinced, but luckily Seren butts in.

'But what about the wool? Don't they say consistency is everything, and dyeing isn't a very consistent process – it doesn't always come out exactly the same shade.'

'State it up front. Make it a feature – for example, you could sell them as the Compost Range, and there's every chance, if people are using them like Bridget does, they'll appreciate the variety.'

Bridget shakes her head, open-mouthed. 'What I wouldn't have given for this advice years ago!'

'She's good,' admits Gillian, nodding appreciatively at me.

'And maybe Gillian could do some photographs for your websites?' I add.

'Steady on. This isn't about me!'

'But that's my point – it could be about all of you!' I hesitate for just a fraction of a second and decide to plunge on. 'Especially if you make it meet the criteria of Mike's legacy?'

It's daring. Seren and Bridget shrink at the mention of Mike's name, and for a second I'm frightened I've gone too far, but I hold my nerve, and Gillian's gaze.

Gillian raises her eyebrows at me, but gives in with a heavy sigh. 'All right, Ella.' She turns to Seren and Bridget. 'Mike left this clause in his will about setting up an artistic retreat and workshops here at the studio. Something to do with living on in posterity, inspiring artists of the future with his name over the door. The reason Ella's mentioned it is that he left some money to carry it out.'

'And . . .' I prompt.

'. . . and if I don't do something about it soon, Petra will get her grubby hands on it.' I look sharply at Gillian, but she just shrugs. 'I don't see why she should muscle in on another hundred grand when she already has half the cottage, which by rights should have been Joe's.' I suppose she has a point.

Bridget leans forward. 'So what you're saying is, if we can somehow . . . I don't know . . . incorporate a few retreat weekends or some workshops, we could maybe set up something to help us all along?'

I nod.

'Wouldn't that be wrong?' asks Seren. 'If he was wanting to inspire artists?'

'You are artists,' I point out. 'And he liked the Arts and Crafts movement, so I'm sure he thought of all creativity under one bracket.' Gillian murmurs agreement.

'It certainly wouldn't harm to check the wording of the will,' says Bridget.

'You'd need to work together with Gillian,' I say quickly.

'Well, I'm game,' says Bridget. 'What do you think, Seren?'

'If it looks like it will fit in with Mike's wishes, I'll do what I can to help,' she agrees.

We look at Gillian. She shakes her head at me, half in irritation, half in submission. 'If you can make it work, I'll provide the where-with-all and the studio.'

That's not quite the engagement I was hoping for, but it's a start, and I feel like whooping. We sip our drinks as the possibilities sink in, and Bethan starts to grizzle.

Seren checks her watch. 'Sorry, I should get her back to her cot.'

'And I should be getting off, too,' says Bridget, watching Seren swaddle Bethan in what could be an exceedingly expensive quilt. 'I'll jot down a few ideas,' she adds, downing her whiskey with the serious look of someone with the bit between their teeth.

'Great – and thanks for coming to the rescue, both of you,' I say, getting up.

'Silly really, when I would have been fine,' disagrees Gillian. 'Joe was just fussing.'

Bridget gives me a wry smile. 'No need to thank me. You've more than repaid me in ideas, and I have a feeling this is the start of something good.' Bridget turns a stern eye on Gillian. 'And before you say anything, Gillian, we *are* going to work together on this.'

Gillian opens her mouth and closes it again. She might have met her match.

'Cheerio, all.' Bridget flaps her hands to show I should stay with Gillian and she will escort Seren and Bethan out to their car. I wave them off from the front door, and return to Gillian.

'What have you started?' she demands, but there's no anger in her words.

'I'm not quite sure,' I admit with a sheepish smile.

'Still, one good thing – we've found out what you're passionate about.'

'What?' I ask, coming out of my own sea of thoughts.

'Your face lit up when you were looking at Seren's quilt, *and* when you were talking about art and figuring out how they could make money from the stuff they produce.'

'I do love seeing new things and having a go at different crafts, and . . . yes, I love helping people come up with ideas,' I realise. 'But I'm not sure how that becomes a job.'

'Hmm, something to think about,' says Gillian with a rare hopeful smile. 'It's my bedtime. Nice evening though,' she says, holding out her hand for me to help her up.

'Yes, wasn't it?' I agree, and I realise one thing for certain: Dolores was wrong. I don't miss London at all – not even a little bit. I'd much rather spend the evening here with Seren, Bridget and Gillian. And Joe, of course, but I'm starting to think that goes without saying.

24

Trouble at 'Pub

Gillian and I have finished breakfast, and I'm about to start on the washing-up when Bridget pulls into the yard just ahead of Joe. I open the door to them both, and Bridget makes it up the path first and thrusts a sheaf of papers into my hands.

'I couldn't sleep,' she says by way of explanation, 'so I wrote everything down. Then I went on my computer and did some research. I think this idea has legs!'

'Legs?' asks Joe from behind her. He puts Pompom on the ground and she trots through to the kitchen.

Bridget gives him a stern look. 'Yes! Our girl here came up with some excellent ideas last night, and I think we'd be idiots not to act on them.'

Bridget strides into the kitchen, and Joe raises his eyebrows at me, but I'm just as surprised by the 'our girl' as he is.

'How's Petra feeling?' I ask quickly, stalling him.

'Better, but she's going back down to Exeter today to keep her business going.'

'Or to stay out of my way?' I suggest, and Joe's lip twitches, but he doesn't lean in and kiss me, just smiles and makes his way into the kitchen. I follow him, a little disappointed.

'Right,' says Bridget, seeing us come in. 'Get the kettle on, Joe, there's things we need to discuss,' and she plonks herself in the armchair opposite Gillian.

Joe flicks the switch on the kettle, and careful of Pompom, who is snuffling for toast crumbs under the table, pulls out a kitchen chair and prepares to listen.

I perch on the edge of the sofa and Bridget turns to me. 'Now, you know all the ideas you gave Seren and me over our work last night? Imagine what other people would give for that kind of advice. I'm reckoning they'd pay quite a bit, and rightly so.'

Joe's eyes meet mine. 'What kind of advice?'

Bridget leans on the arm of the chair. 'Imagine you're a struggling artist, and imagine being able to come away for a weekend and not only have a break in the Welsh hills, but also have people look at your work, and give you fresh ideas on how to turn your painting or crafting business into something more viable. After all, people try and fail to do that every year; each of them making the same mistakes, feeling terrified as their plans slide and willing to try almost anything to avoid going back to standard employment. They'd leap at the chance to have a break and a chat with people who can give them real ideas, maybe even help them set up something new.'

'So they'd get . . . business ideas?' I check.

'Not just business ideas! Kinship, inspiration and maybe even people to collaborate with.'

'So it would be a kind of collective?' I ask.

Bridget tips her head from side to side. 'Think of it more as a guild, with a bit of the Arts and Crafts movement thrown in.' Gillian suppresses a smile. 'Think of it as a way to develop, refresh and rejuvenate artistic businesses. After all, everyone gets stuck in a rut at one time or another.' My eyes flick involuntarily to Joe, and he grins at me. 'Our aim would be to jump-start them out of the rut.'

Joe looks at Gillian with interest. 'So this would be to do with that clause in Mike's will?'

Bridget smiles. 'That's the idea. Of course, we'd need to check the wording and make sure it qualifies, but what do you think so far?'

Gillian strokes her chin. 'You'd need to make sure it's worthwhile for you and Seren.'

'We'll open up our websites to other artists, once we've set them up. The more the merrier, and sales breed sales. And if there are weekend retreats, maybe we could give masterclasses in quilting and felting?'

Gillian nods. 'And you'd need to convince the solicitor. I expect he'd need a proper business plan after Petra's discontented mutterings about the money. It's just . . .' She lets out a discontented sigh. '. . . I still have my reservations about pandering to Mike's demands.'

Joe's eyes dart questioningly to mine. It seems Gillian didn't tell him about Mike last night, and Bridget looks swiftly my way, too. I shake my head minutely at her, and Joe's gaze becomes so insistent I guiltily bite my lip.

Bridget smiles awkwardly at him before continuing. 'That's no reason not to get the best out of it,' she points out. 'And it would be good for us to work together, don't you think?'

Gillian shakes her head. 'This is your baby, not mine. Or maybe yours, Ella's and Seren's.'

I hold up my hands. 'I've got to start my new job in nine days,' I say regretfully, wishing I could stay and see this through. It sounds exciting, new and innovative. It would be working with artists and crafters; no day would be the same. But then the real world comes crashing back in – bills, rent, food – and I push the idea from my mind.

Bridget purses her lips and turns her beady eyes on us. 'If the money's going to disappear if it's not used, we might as well give it a try. Put on a couple of workshops, maybe set up a weekend retreat or two, and see what we can do?

It's not like we have anything to lose. And if they stay in the valley, it would help George and Dolores, and maybe Bryn, too.'

'What are your ideas for the workshops?' I ask, because even if I can't be here, this is a good idea for Gillian, whether she realises it or not.

Bridget leafs through her papers and pulls out a list. 'We could get people in to talk about building websites, getting business loans, teaching, selling on eBay and approaching shops. Hell, people could come to teach each other their crafts, to give each other ideas and learn if they like teaching. And if push comes to shove, they could paint in the hills and treat it like a painting holiday. What do you think?'

We all look at Gillian.

'It's not the worst idea I've ever heard,' she concedes. 'But I don't see why you need me? I could just sign over the money.'

'You're the link,' says Joe, coming to our rescue. 'Without you, this is just some wannabes hanging off Mike's name. With you, it's a commemorative act. Plus, your photography skills would be a huge asset, and Ella would need somewhere to stay on the weekends she needs to be here.' He smiles at me, and my heart turns over. 'Plus, if this is going to happen, you won't be able to ignore it, Gillian. The studio will be busy and the yard full of cars, people will drop in and others will think this is where they need to register.'

Gillian raises her eyebrows at me. 'And you would come back and help?'

It's a loaded question. If *I* turn it down, *she* will – but who am I kidding? I'd love to be involved, even if only at a distance.

'Yes, I'd love to be a part of it,' I agree fervently.

Bridget's nodding. 'And Joe's right – your skills with a camera would come in extremely handy, Gillian. It would make the websites look professional and help with advertising . . .'

'If you're up to it?' Joe asks gently.

'Of course I'm bloody up to it,' retorts Gillian, and Joe does his best not to smirk. 'It just seems like a lot of work. And if you advertise it and no one comes . . . ?'

'No harm, no foul,' says Bridget.

'And what if more people turn up than you can accommodate?' challenges Gillian.

'We set a fixed number of places and allocate them on a first-come, first-serve basis,' Bridget replies readily. 'And that's probably going to be dictated by the number of people we can comfortably fit in the studio, or maybe how many can be put up at the pub.' She looks thoughtful for a moment, then seizes her papers. 'These are mainly ideas for my and Seren's websites, but give me a day or two and I'll have this retreat thing mapped out. In fact, I might pop in on George and Dolores and sound them out.'

'You don't waste time,' I say, taken aback but delighted by her enthusiasm.

'No point,' she says, and sweeps out of the door leaving only dancing dust motes behind her.

'I thought age had withered her and staled her infinite variety,' misquotes Gillian, 'but clearly I was wrong. You won't stop her now.'

'Is that a problem?' I ask.

Gillian shrugs. 'We'll have to wait and see. If it's viable, she'll make it work. If not, she'll bludgeon it six ways to Sunday until it does.'

Joe smiles and shakes his head in wonder.

'What?' I ask him.

'I miss one evening and you transform everyone,' he accuses. 'Though why I'm surprised, I don't know. Every time I walk back in here something's different, and I'm here every day!'

I feel my face heat up. 'But this time it wasn't just me,' I protest.

'It was, you know,' says Gillian. 'And what's worse, I reckon I've been railroaded.'

Joe gives her a stern look. 'It's good for you.'

'I had a nasty feeling it was,' she agrees. 'Now, you two go and look at the studio and make a list of what needs doing. You might as well; Bridget will be back asking you to do just that soon enough. And Joe, before you go, look in that dresser drawer and hand me Mike's will. I'll check the wording.'

Joe searches the drawer and hands her the will.

'Go on,' she prompts. 'Go and sort out the studio,' and collecting the keys and a pen and paper, we go outside.

Joe unlocks the studio, pushes the door wide, and as soon as we're safely inside, he closes the door behind us and turns slowly to face me.

It's the first time we've been alone since last night, and I feel almost shy. I don't know whether to be light and breezy or try for alluring, but as he steps towards me, cups my jaw in his hand, and looks deeply into my eyes, I settle for love-sick teenager. Pathetic, I know, but as his lips meet mine, I don't even care. I smile up at him as he pulls away and he kisses me again, but this time my arms wrap around him, my hands just under his shoulder blades and I pull him closer. Our lips move apart and the kiss becomes even more passionate. My eyes close, my head swims, and after a minute or two, we break apart and he looks deep into my eyes.

'I'm so glad you're coming back,' he says softly.

Is that why he's been so reticent? He didn't want to start something that wouldn't last beyond two weeks?

'It looks like I have quite a few reasons to come back,' I agree happily. 'The workshops . . . you . . . making sure Gillian's OK,' I list playfully. But as I say the last one, he looks down, lets out a breath and his forehead comes to rest gently against mine. Shit, I've just inadvertently spoiled the moment.

'Yes.' His mouth twists regretfully. 'And I'm afraid I must ask you what's going on with Gillian . . .' He screws up his eyes for a second. 'I know it has something to do with Mike, and no one wants to tell me, but I think I need to know.'

'I know you do, but it's not my place to say.'

'Nevertheless, I'm sorry, but I need you to tell me.'

Joe's looking at me intently, imploringly, even. Would it be so bad for me to tell him? . . . to prepare the ground? . . . get him over the initial shock? I stare into his eyes, unsure what to do.

'Please? I've tried to be patient, but from what was said inside, it's clear Bridget knows, and something tells me it'll affect the decisions we have to make.'

He's right, it will. I look at the floor and pray I'm doing the right thing. 'There's a possibility . . .' I begin, trying to figure out how to soften it.

'That . . .?' he prompts.

I look up at him. '. . . that Mike cheated on Gillian.'

The curiosity in his eyes changes to wariness, and he lets out a breath as if he's been winded. 'Oh God. When did she find out?'

'On the day of the funeral.'

His eyes clench closed, and he slowly starts to nod. 'Tell me everything,' and I explain about the women and the orchids and Gillian shutting herself away. I even tell him about Bridget.

'Jesus! Why didn't she say something?'

'She was afraid of spoiling your memory of Mike, and

also she didn't want to force you to keep the cottage through some misplaced sense of obligation.'

He shakes his head, and the muscles in his jaw stand out. 'And also, I don't think she knew *how* to tell you.'

Joe sits down heavily on Mike's paint-spattered stool and stares blindly at the concrete floor. 'And that's why she shut me out and shut herself away . . . and why she doesn't want to, as she put it, pander to his demands?'

I nod. 'And it might also help explain the nasty tricks.'

Joe's head jerks up. 'You think one of these orchid women might be behind it?'

'I don't know, but it's possible. Unless it's an angry husband?'

Joe pushes his hands through his hair. 'Jesus! I knew there was something off, but this?'

'I'm *really* sorry,' I say quietly, but he gets up and takes me in his arms. There's nothing sexual about it, it's just warm, comforting and all-enveloping, with my face pressed into his shirt.

'You have nothing at all to be sorry about,' he says firmly. He rests his check on my hair. 'Thank you for telling me, but I'm afraid I am going to have to talk to Gillian.'

'I know,' I mumble into his shirt, hoping she'll forgive me.

'I'll go in and do it while I take her through her exercises, if you're all right with that? At least then she can't run away,' he adds with a poor attempt at humour.

'Let me know if I'm evicted.'

'I will. Will you be OK out here?' His eyes search my face, and I get the feeling he's checking I won't just sit in here worrying.

I look at the pen and notepad. 'I'll make a list of everything that needs doing, and pretend nothing scary is going on.'

He smiles. 'Make sure you add "clear out", "store paintings" and "clean".'

'Tell me something I don't know!' I say sardonically.

He looks into my eyes with such unwavering determination that I have no choice but to look into his. 'That I don't know what I'd do if you weren't here.' His mouth twists into a smile. And with me probably looking stunned, he pecks me on the lips and goes out through the door before I manage to gather myself together enough to respond.

I stare after him, my fingers touching my lips. He thinks I've made a difference and that my being here has made things better. It's a lovely feeling: almost as good as being kissed. With a small smile on my face, I put the notepad and pen on the stool, and make a start on collecting together Mike's untidy pile of belongings, and put them with the boxes of unwanted items we brought in yesterday.

Three quarters of an hour later, Bridget marches into the studio and glares at me. 'That *bloody* woman!' she says with emphasis.

I look up, startled, and remember that I propped the door open to air the place. 'Who?' I ask as she looks around the studio and tips back a few paintings.

'What? Oh, bloody Dolores! She thinks hosting workshops up here isn't a "good idea". She reckons the whole thing should be held down in their events room. George was just as shocked as I was! He kept saying, "But Dolores—" and each time he said it she elbowed him. Looked like it hurt, too!'

'Is their events room any good?' I ask.

Bridget picks up a paint-clogged paintbrush and pokes it angrily back in its pot. 'No! The light's rubbish, but Dolores wouldn't budge. Went so far as to say we'd have problems finding accommodation elsewhere, and I should go away and think about it!'

'But I thought they'd leap at the chance of some extra business?'

'So did I! Like I said – bloody woman!' I grab the pen and pad just before Bridget plonks herself down on the painting stool. 'I can only imagine they're worse off than I thought, but like I told her, what's the point of throttling the life out of the idea by losing the Mike connection?'

'Do you think George will talk her around, if he was as surprised as you said?'

Bridget snorts angrily. 'We can only hope! What's the situation here?'

I hold out my hand. 'Paintings, art equipment, good floor space and light, no damp, but also no decent tables or chairs.'

'I'd have asked the pub if we could borrow theirs, but . . .' Bridget flaps her hand. 'By the way, Joe and Gillian sent me out here to find you – told me to bring you in for a break.'

They probably sent her out here so they could finish their discussion. I take my time locking up, and make plenty of noise as we walk into the hall. Joe gives me a flicker of a smile as we come in and retreats to make tea, while Gillian struggles to let go of her scowl. I get out some mugs and Bridget, who's either oblivious or just very good at ignoring atmosphere, kicks off the conversation with a dressing-down of Dolores using the same expletives she did with me.

'So,' continues Bridget, her rant over. 'What's the news on the will?'

Gillian gestures to the folded papers on the coffee table. 'He wanted an arts venture with his name on it, where artists can swap ideas and produce work together.'

'We can work with that,' says Bridget thoughtfully.

'Even the fatuousness of him wanting his name on it?'

'To be vulgar, Gillian, if he supplies the funds, it's fair enough. More bloody reasonable than Dolores, anyway,' she mutters. 'What are we going to *do* about the woman?'

'Leave it to George,' advises Gillian. 'He'll make sure the right thing happens.'

This doesn't marry with my impression of him, but Gillian's certain and Bridget nods.

'So, names,' says Bridget. 'I liked the sound of Kick Start Art, but I looked it up and it's already been used several times over, so how about "Hill Start Art"? If we tag on "at the Mike Masters Studio", that should cover the name aspect, don't you think?'

'I like it,' says Gillian.

Joe's eyebrows flick up. 'Really?' he asks.

Gillian nods. 'It suggests a difficult manoeuvre, has hills and art in it, and if you shift the spacing you get Hills Tart, which suits Mike down to the ground.'

'Oh,' says Bridget flatly, and I can't help laughing as Joe's mouth works around the start of several words.

'It would be memorable, and it's not like you have to give everyone the full meaning,' I point out.

'I suppose not,' says Joe cautiously.

'And it would make a memorable hash-tag,' I add, to Bridget's bafflement.

'Excellent,' says Gillian, like it's signed and sealed.

'Hmm,' says Bridget, and moves on. 'So how about we do a trial run, perhaps start with a few friends – ones who will give us proper feedback and help us jolly along any dissenters. I thought we might run one at Easter.'

'But that's only a few weeks away!' I blurt.

'It is pretty soon,' agrees Gillian, looking worried.

'I'm not talking residential. Just a trial run of a workshop or two to get things moving, get some photos for a website, that kind of thing?' Bridget smiles anxiously. 'Surely, the sooner we sort out the will the better, and if we have Joe and Ella here to help –' I nod at her questioning glance – 'we'd be in good time to make the most of the summer.'

She has a point. Joe looks purposefully at Gillian, and back at me. He reckons it will be good for her. 'Are you up for the challenge?' he asks her.

'Bloody cheek! Are you up for it? Because if you think you're going to slouch off to Exeter, you can think again!'

'I wouldn't dream of it,' he says, his eyes meeting mine. 'Not when there's so much to keep me here.' I grin at him, and Gillian gives the pair of us a fierce look, making me blush.

'Excellent,' says Bridget. 'In that case, we have plenty for you to do.'

'Clearing the studio?' I ask.

'For a start,' agrees Bridget, and she's so determined I can't see how Dolores can possibly hold out against her.

25

Take a Running Jump

The next few days are a buzz of activity. While Bridget looks into just about every aspect of running workshops and arts businesses, both online and in the real world, Joe and I catalogue all the paintings in the studio and make a photographic record of both them and all Mike's sketch pads and notebooks. It's actually quite rewarding as amongst Mike's sketches are some gorgeous pencil drawings of Joe when he was young. They're almost like E. H. Shepard's original *Winnie the Pooh* line drawings, and are just as Joe described – of him playing on the kitchen floor with Gillian in the background.

Joe and I also help Gillian sort through the rest of the items in the spare room. We get the house back to some semblance of a comfortable home and box up all the unwanted reminders so they're not lurking ready to burn her, like Mr Rochester's wife.

In the gaps in between, Joe switches between bouts of work on his novel and helping me with Gillian and her exercises, and sometimes, while Joe jots down notes for his book or works through his edits, he lets me sketch him. So far I've drawn a number of studies trying to catch those amazing laughter lines and that look he has when he's amused, but not quite smiling. And as I work, I find other expressions that fascinate me, including his fierce look of concentration when a thought eludes him, or those moments when he's picturing something and gazing unfocused into the far distance.

When he's not there, I work on the sketch of Bryn, as well as new ones of Gillian reading my e-reader and Bridget's cottage, complete with old Ford. I'm loving it: not having the strain of creating it for any purpose other than that I feel like it, and not feeling the necessity to 'stay true' to any kind of style is very freeing.

My friendship with Seren is also going from strength to strength – I phone and visit when I can, particularly when Gillian or Bridget get too much. I've become adept at fielding the lamb, now officially called Bill, and also Bethan, who is a dab hand at leg clinging, and I've taken some lovely photos of them both, where her rugby-like tackles of Bill look affectionate. I'm looking forward to turning them into drawings.

As for me and Joe, there's the odd snatched kiss and cuddle in the studio, and I love that a smile comes into his eyes when he looks at me, but what's really wonderful is we're getting to know each other. We discuss art, Gillian, childhoods, books, just about anything. Joe even talks freely and with excitement about his new plot; his poor detective, anxious to retire, tormented by people needing him in ways that breach his ethics, but also desperate to help. I love that Joe's enthusiasm brims over as he speaks, and how, even though he proclaims never to talk about his books to people, he seems so comfortable doing so with me. So much so, I almost feel I know his detective as well as if I'd read his books, which hopefully I soon will as he's promised to lend me some. But also, other small things have changed, like whenever he's near me, the gap between us is far less than it used be. Then there are the evenings when he stays late and sits and reads so I can sketch him. Often as not, he loses interest in his book and just watches me. The smile that curls his lips then is so captivating that I almost lose concentration. 'Stop it,' I say, and he laughs. In those moments I think I could live here forever.

The one persistent thorn in everyone's side is Dolores. She either wants the entire event held at the pub, or not at all, and no matter what anyone says, she refuses to back down. None of us can understand it, and everyone's trying to puzzle out why she is being so difficult, except Gillian. Gillian seems to think it's par for the course, which makes not just me suspicious.

'Why aren't you more annoyed about this?' demands Bridget one evening after Joe has gone home to write, so it's just her, me and Gillian sitting in the kitchen.

'Truth be told, we've never seen eye to eye,' says Gillian.

I look up. 'But she told me she did her best to help you after Mike died?'

'She was certainly up here a lot,' agrees Gillian crossly. 'Probably hoping for a "For Sale" sign.'

Bridget frowns. 'But I thought she and Bryn didn't want the farm? That's why their parents sold it.'

Gillian purses her lips. 'No, I think she was just hoping to get rid of me.'

'Why?' I ask, tensing.

Gillian shrugs. 'I believe there was a mild flirtation between her and Mike before I arrived here, back when Mike first bought the house. Nothing serious. It was just after she married George, and long before she had Gareth.' Her thumb rubs her wrist and there's a groove carved between her eyebrows.

'So you've never got on?' I check. I think back over Dolores' apparent concern back when I met her in the pub and try to understand it.

'Nothing so strong as that. We just kept our distance, that's all. Good manners, pure and simple.'

Bridget glances warily at Gillian. 'Is that why she's being so difficult?'

Gillian's shoulders rise a fraction. 'I don't know, but it might be worth sticking to day courses, if it's an issue.'

Bridget smiles like Gillian's suggested a cunning tactic. 'Yes, I bet she'll back down if I say that to her: tell her we're nearly ready with the studio, and we're going to do a trial run without accommodation. She'll leap at the chance of some extra income if she sees it slipping away. In fact, I feel a gin and tonic coming on,' she adds gleefully. 'I could ask Daf to pass some information to Seren in Dolores' hearing.'

Gillian shakes her head. 'I'll be surprised if it works.'

'Hmm, we'll see,' and with a sly smile, Bridget picks up her coat and heads out into the night on her mission.

A chill gust sweeps through the room, and Gillian massages her wrist.

I watch her for almost a minute, but Gillian doesn't look at me. 'Did Dolores have an orchid at the funeral?' I ask finally.

Gillian's eyes meet mine sadly. 'No, she didn't.'

'Is it possible she's the one who's been causing you problems?'

Gillian looks around the room, frowning. 'I did think of her, but considering she's had well over thirty years to take any revenge, I don't see why she'd start now. Also, why would she have a problem with me? She's more likely to have had an issue with Mike.' She has a point, but even before I knew all this there was something about Dolores that made me feel uneasy.

'Is it possible she's being so difficult about the workshops because they're being held in his memory?'

Gillian regards me for a long second. 'I don't know. I suppose it's possible, but then, she might just be after more money,' and she picks up the e-reader to show the topic is closed.

I collect my drawing pad and, using some photos I've taken on my phone of Bethan reaching for Bill (though the shot looks for all the world like she's stroking him), I settle down to do a small pen-and-ink drawing to give to Seren. But as I make the rough sketch, I have to agree with Gillian: I can't think of a better reason for Dolores refusing our business than that she believes she can make more by holding us to ransom.

Half an hour later and my mobile rings. It's Bridget.

'Hi, Bridget,' I say, and Gillian looks up.

'No dice,' Bridget says succinctly. 'Gillian was right, Dolores said the studio should be left as a homage to Mike, and that he wouldn't have wanted his workspace invaded by amateurs.'

'But it's in his will!'

'That's what I told her. I said she'd be denying him his last wishes. I laid it on thick, but she maintained the pub would be better. Why traipse people up the track, she said, when they can stay in the comfort and warmth of the pub.'

'And George?'

'He stood behind her shaking his head to show he couldn't do anything.' Bridget lets out a pent-up breath. 'The woman's just greedy.'

'Yes,' I agree absently. That certainly fits with what Gillian said. 'But we could stick to day courses? At least for now.'

'Maybe, but it's a long way for people to come, and aren't these things usually residential? Dolores said as much, so I told her we'd bed people down in the studio on camp beds if necessary.'

'Wouldn't that breach health and safety laws?' I say quickly.

'Probably. I was just goading her, but it looks like we need to have a rethink in the morning.'

'OK, thanks, Bridget.'

'Just thought you should know. Speak tomorrow.'

I put my phone down and Gillian lifts her eyebrows. 'Like you said – greedy.'

Gillian's lips draw tight, but she nods. It's exactly what she was expecting. 'I think it's time for bed, don't you?' and I help her out of her chair.

I can't settle. I've been in bed for a while, but everything's circling inside my head like skaters doing figures of eight – from Dolores to Gillian's tormentor, and from the work-shops to whether I can manage some sort of long-distance relationship with Joe – it seems like a lot to sort out with only six days left before my job starts.

I curl up on my side and try to focus on my breathing and—

—there's a knocking sound. Not a door knocking sound, no . . . it's coming from outside. It's the wobbly slab step outside the studio!

I listen hard, my heart thumping, but I don't hear anything else. I scramble out of bed and lift the curtain, but the studio door is too close to the house to see. The yard light hasn't been triggered, so . . . could it be Bozz? It's probably Bozz, and yet I'm not sure he's weighty enough.

I pull on a jumper and tiptoe down the stairs.

'Ella?' Gillian whispers as loudly as she can.

'Yes?' I whisper back.

She hasn't turned on her lamp, so I creep in using the moonlight from the small living-room window. She's sitting up in bed and beckons me into the room.

'I think someone's outside,' she says.

So do I, but I don't want to alarm her. 'It's probably just Bozz.'

'You'd think so, wouldn't you?' agrees Gillian. 'Except

you're up, and so am I, and neither of us have turned on any lights.'

We look at each other. 'I'm going out to have a look,' I decide.

Gillian hesitates. 'Put on a coat and some wellies, and scream fit to bust if anyone's out there.'

I nod. 'And I'll use the back door,' I add.

'So you can catch Bozz unawares if he's up to no good,' she says drily.

I let out a breathy laugh, pluck a coat off the pegs and slip on Gillian's gritty wellies. But as I tiptoe through the kitchen, open the back door and quietly lock it behind me, it's no longer funny. I pocket the keys and listen. A dull thud comes from somewhere around the front of the house. There's definitely someone out here. With my heart racing, I hurry around the side of the house and there's a hooded figure trying to jemmy the studio door. They slowly turn against the moonlight, the crowbar glinting in their hand, and both of us freeze.

Then, as if in slow motion, they glance at their weapon. I hold my breath, ready to leap out of the way and scream, when, with a sudden jerk, they take off towards the lane. My heart's thumping, and it takes me a second to recover, but I give chase. I round the corner into the lane and they're stumbling and lurching down the road ahead of me. They're not the fastest runner, and my strides are bigger, so I quickly catch up. I reach out to grab them, but just as my fingers touch their coat, my foot catches on the edge of a pothole, my other foot slams hard into the ground and my hands fly out to save me. I stumble, stagger, and almost right myself except my other boot snags on a rock and I'm pitched head first into a shockingly icy puddle. I land with one arm caught between me and the ground, knocking the air out of me and my head hits something hard. I roll over, spluttering, the sky a channel between walls above me, and a nauseous pain lances up across my left cheekbone to my temple where it slowly ramps itself into double-vision. I strain my eyes wide as the footsteps pound away.

'Oh, Jesus!' I mutter. I think I'm going to be sick.

Some footsteps crunch back towards me and I flinch, ready for the blow.

26

Queen, King and Castle

'There, now, you're all right,' says a man's soft Welsh voice. A hand lands on my shoulder, but not hard. 'Where does it hurt?' and as the collie nudges my hand and whines, I realise it's Bryn, only he's never spoken to me this softly before.

'My head.'

'I thought so.'

'They got away,' I murmur pathetically. 'They were trying to get into the studio.'

'Nothin' to be done about that now. Can you get up?'

I try to nod, but it bloody hurts.

'Right, then, up we go.' His arm circles my back and he hoists me up with surprising strength given his spindly frame. We stagger in through his gate and into the rude light of his bungalow where, with his help, I limp into his kitchen. It smells of tea and something rich, sweet and inviting I can't pin down, and as he levers out a kitchen chair with his foot and sits me down, for the first time I notice he's similarly dressed to me in pyjamas, coat and boots. He watches me for a second to check I don't keel over, then takes a roll of kitchen towel off its spindle, tears off a sheet, and dampens it under the tap.

He takes a seat next to me and, lifting the tissue slowly so as not to startle me, wipes some mud from my cheek. As he concentrates on what he's doing, I examine his face. Now I look at him, I'm not sure my sketch did him justice – it's too severe. It's not the weathered face of a farmer; it's not reddened by the wind, but softer somehow, and his skin has creased around laughter lines, which suggests a kind nature.

'There we are,' he says, pulling away. 'There's the damage,' and he moves over to the freezer and takes out some frozen peas. He wraps them in a tea towel and hands them to me. 'That should help.'

'Thanks,' I mumble, pressing them to my temple.

He sits back down and looks at me, and annoyingly tears start to tumble down my cheeks without my permission.

'What's this now?' he asks, surprised, and he pours me a whiskey and puts it on the table in front of me. 'Very brave, you were. Gillian will be proud.'

'Thanks.' I manage a wobbly smile and take a sip of the whiskey. It burns, but I feel a little better.

'She's had a lot of trouble up there,' he adds, his eyes taking on an angry gleam. 'Did you get a look at who it was?'

I have my suspicions, but I daren't say them to Bryn. 'No, but they weren't tall and not great at running.' I smile ruefully. 'Although I was worse.'

Bryn nods sadly, and pours himself a whiskey as I look around.

One half of the kitchen is sparse and masculine; everything in its place down to the labelled coffee, tea and sugar jars by the kettle, but the other half is completely given over to wood carving. There's a chair next to a section of counter holding a neat array of chisels and bradawls, and over to one side are lumps of wood carefully stacked on a pallet to keep them off the floor as they dry. Even from here I can see there's a variety of different types of wood. Above them is a shelf of power tools, and under the chair is a dustpan and brush ready to clear up at the end of each session. I half turn and behind the kitchen door there's a set of floor-to-ceiling shelves holding a vast array of carvings.

'Are they all yours?' I ask.

'Well, they should be considerin' I carved them.'

I'm desperate to see, but I'm still shaky. 'Can I look?'

Bryn hesitates diffidently. 'I don't show them to people as a rule.'

'Oh, OK.'

'But seein' as you chased off a robber, you can have a quick look so long as you don't go criticisin' and judgin'.'

'I wouldn't!' I try shaking my head, but that isn't a good idea.

'Come now, we'll move your chair,' and supporting me with one hand and lifting the chair with his other, he moves me gently to sit beside the shelves.

'Can I touch them?' I ask.

'They're sealed,' he agrees. 'I use beeswax.'

That probably accounts for the lovely rich smell in the room.

There's a set of four small intricate ogres in the hear, see, speak no evil poses, looking bemused and confused, with lovely warty flat feet, and the fourth less-seen 'do no evil' is curled up fast asleep clutching a teddy with his thumb in his mouth. I carefully pick him up and marvel at his carved leather garments and lopsided horned helmet.

'Rosewood,' says Bryn, watching me, but I don't know whether it's for my reaction or my carefulness.

'And you use chisels?'

'And Dremels, drills and sandpaper.' Bryn takes down a piece from one of the higher shelves, and hands it to me.

It's a smooth, dark egg, about the size of a large duck egg, with one side carved open to reveal a baby dragon staring out from inside. It's beautiful. It's tactile. It's compelling. I stare into the dragon's beady black eyes, and I could swear it's looking back at me, waiting for me to put it down so it can go back to sleep.

'It's extraordinary,' I breathe.

Bryn hands me another. This one's a pale wood whale with its mouth open wide and on its tongue is a man sitting on a raft, straight from one of Kipling's *Just So Stories*. I can see the panic on his tiny face as he clings to the raft's thin mast.

Taking down another carving, Bryn exchanges the whale for the head of a beautiful girl, but it's not her face that attracts my attention; it's the dozens of plaits, painstakingly carved and so bumpy yet soft to the touch that it's impossible not to run your fingers over them.

I smile up at Bryn.

'And these are my favourite,' he says, his voice a reverent whisper. He takes down an Everlast shoebox and removes the lid. Inside, each item is wrapped in tissue paper and as he opens them I see they're chess pieces, faintly reminiscent of the Isle of Lewis chess set. He lines them up on the shelf in front of me, but as I examine them I see they're quite different. These pieces have personalities and expressions that hint at a sense of humour I never suspected in Bryn. The white king looks weedy and scared, while the queen has a hint of steely-eyed Gillian about her. One of the black knights has a hobby horse, while the other only has a mop and a deeply envious expression.

I grin at Bryn. 'They're amazing!'

Smiling properly for the first time, he takes out several more – a pawn with a finger up his nose, another taking photos, a third on the toilet and a fourth showing his bum. He carefully wraps them back up.

'Does anyone know about these?' I ask.

'No, I do them for me, and since I don't want to sell them, I don't see how they're anyone's business but my own.'

'But they're amazing, and even if you don't want to sell them, you should display them.'

There's a beautiful bust further along the shelf. It's of a woman, her head tipped to one side, looking down wistfully, almost sadly, and with her curly hair radiating out in bouncy splendour, taking full advantage of the gorgeous swirls in the grain.

'English wych-elm,' says Bryn, and a stillness settles over him.

'Who is she?'

'My wife, Mair.' There's quiet sadness to his words.

'Did she die?' The words slip out before I can stop them.

'No, no.' He almost laughs. 'She left. Her dreams were bigger than the valley – and bigger than me, it seems. It wasn't right to stop her.'

'Couldn't you go, too?'

He spreads his hands to show there wasn't a choice. 'My parents were old. They needed me.'

'I'm sorry.'

'Don't be. She's happy enough,' he says, not realising I wasn't thinking of Mair. He hands me another sculpture. It's of the collie, sitting keen and tall.

'Your dog,' I say, surprised.

'Idris,' he agrees, and Idris looks up.

'Did you ever farm?' I ask, curious for the first time that he has a sheepdog and yet no farm.

'No, no, and nor did Idris, really. He was a runt. No temperament for it. Didn't like the other dogs, and when Daf whistled he sat down and wouldn't move. Daf said he was useless as a farm dog and passed him on to me. We've been happy enough, though, haven't we, Idris?'

We all jump at a knock at the door, followed by another without any time for Bryn to answer.

'Bryn?' Joe shouts from outside, and as Bryn opens the

door, Joe's words tumble out. 'Have you seen— oh, there you are,' he says, spotting me, and the breath gushes out of him. He supports himself on the doorframe and drags in a few deep breaths. 'Gillian said you went haring off after an intruder and didn't come back.'

My hand shoots to my mouth. Poor Gillian! 'I'm so sorry, I didn't think! I fell.'

'Come in, come in,' says Bryn, and Joe steps inside, and looks around with interest.

'Is she all right?' Joe asks him.

'She'll do fine,' confirms Bryn. 'Bit of a bump, that's all.'

'Thank God!' Joe takes out his phone and holds it to his ear. 'Gillian? She's fine. In with Bryn . . .' He looks at me. 'Yes, in his house.' He looks nervously at Bryn, who smiles at Joe's disbelief. 'I'll bring her up,' and Bryn nods in agreement.

'You'll be all right now, then?' Bryn asks me, and I grin at him as I hand him his peas.

'Yes, thanks – and thank you for showing me your beautiful carvings.'

Bryn dips his head, and Joe's eyes widen as he spots the shelves behind me.

I struggle upright and with a little help from both of them we make it out of Bryn's bungalow. I give Bryn a little wave with my free hand, and Joe and I hobble out of the gate and up the hill together.

After a minute or two Joe looks at me. 'What is it about you and getting into people's houses? I haven't been in Bryn's house since his parents died.'

'Regular hermits' hideaway you've got going on up here,' I comment.

'Hmm, except where it comes to you. You seem to get in where no one else can. Why is that?'

'I fell . . . and Gillian fell.' I frown. 'Maybe that's the key?'

'Hmm.' Joe doesn't sound convinced, but as we round the corner into the yard, all thoughts fall away as I spot Gillian waiting in the doorway. She's propped on one crutch and launches into a barrage of questions about what happened, who it was, was there any damage, how I'm feeling, all as Joe supports me into the kitchen and deposits me carefully on the sofa. He grins at me, before leaving me at Gillian's mercy, and goes back outside.

'Well?' demands Gillian.

I struggle to assemble answers. 'Erm, I'm not sure who it was – they fared better on the lane than I did. I was just about to catch them when I fell, and Bryn took me in, and I'm fine,' I say shortly. 'Does that cover it?'

Gillian purses her lips, but more with worry than anger, I think, and looks at Joe as he comes back in.

'They didn't get into the studio,' he says. 'But there's a few fresh gouge marks on the door, and whoever it was snipped the wire to the yard light.'

'Sods!' mutters Gillian.

I look at Joe. 'Someone seriously wants to get into that studio.'

Gillian frowns. 'But why? There's only Mike's paintings and equipment in there.'

'They must want Mike's paintings, then. You said they sold for quite a bit?' I ask.

Joe and Gillian look at one another, but not like they're convinced. More like they can't think of a better reason.

Joe sits down next to me and takes a look at my bruised cheek. 'Whatever's going on, I think we should move the paintings into the house. That way you can keep a better eye on them.'

'But won't that make them want to break in here?' I ask.

Gillian glowers. 'I'd like to see them try,' she says, but Joe sighs, taking my point.

'All right, let's think about it in the morning. I doubt they'll try again tonight, but I'll sleep on the sofa, just in case.'

The sofa doesn't look very comfortable to sleep on, not when there's a bed we could share upstairs. 'I don't think you'll get a good night's sleep,' I hazard.

'I'm not here for a good night's sleep,' he points out. I keep my eyes fixed on him, willing him to understand, and his expression softens. He smiles and strokes my cheek. 'And you need to go to bed with some painkillers and get some rest,' he says, touching my cheekbone with gentle fingers. 'I'll be fine.' I feel myself flush at his gentle rebuff, and daren't look at Gillian.

'Off to bed, Ella,' she says firmly. 'Joe knows where the sheets are,' and taking myself upstairs, I don't bother to stay awake to see if Joe joins me: I know he isn't coming.

27

Out of Sorts

Before I know it, it's morning, and I've slept like a log, but now I'm awake I want coffee. I reach in my handbag for my compact mirror and find a lovely purple bruise on my cheekbone, but luckily I don't have a black eye. I put it away and look in surprise at the Lloyd Loom chair. No Bozz! I put on my strangely fur-free clothes and tiptoe downstairs. Gillian's still fast asleep and Joe is curled up on the sofa, snuggled under the blankets, and Bozz is cosy behind his knees. Joe looks peaceful, his face free of worry lines, and he looks younger somehow, perhaps because of how his eyelashes brush his cheek. Bozz, however, looks furious at my arrival, although I'm starting to think that's his natural expression.

I switch on the kettle and Joe wakes with the noise of it boiling and watches me with a slight smile.

'How's the head?' he asks, stretching as luxuriantly as if he slept in a king-size bed, and Bozz jumps down in high dudgeon.

'Better. Would you like a coffee?'

'Lovely!'

Joe settles back into the cushions to watch me and strangely it's not unnerving at all. If anything, it's flattering. I smile as I bring over our mugs. Joe takes a sip and sighs contentedly, and I sit in one of the armchairs and tuck my feet up to get them off the floor.

Joe looks speculatively at me over the rim of his mug. 'How often do you think you'll be coming up here? Gillian will really miss you when you've gone, you know.'

I hope he's asking for more than just Gillian, but each time I think we're on track to something meaningful it seems to stall. I look around the kitchen at Bridget's pictures, the woven Peruvian throw Gillian brought back from a photography trip, and the various items of bright pottery made by friends. I know all their stories and now I think about it, I realise I feel more at home here than I do at Mum's.

'Quite often, I think. Don't forget, I've promised Bridget I'll help with the workshops.'

'In that case – woe betide you if you let her down!' he says playfully.

'Quite,' I agree, sipping my coffee.

'But I was thinking last night, when I saw you at Bryn's, how you really fit in here.'

'Do you really think so?' I almost laugh, but it means more than he knows. I love it here.

'Yes! I've brought girlfriends here before, and even though none of them had to face the level of squalor you did, they couldn't see past the basic facilities and the remoteness.'

I try not to frown as I picture him with a stream of glamorous girlfriends in sequined party dresses, tiptoeing around the potholes in their Jimmy Choos. I suppose that would explain his words to me on that first night about not expecting mod cons, but it also leads me to question, if they are his type, where that leaves me?

'And yet you,' he continues, 'get on with it regardless, and you have a knack for fitting in with the people here. They like you and feel better for knowing you.'

I try to push past the feeling that I might look sensible and even frumpy next to his gorgeous exes and take the compliment as he intends it. 'Well, thanks. That means a lot because I don't feel like I fit in anywhere in London, except maybe with my friend Vivienne.'

His eyes hold mine. 'Maybe that's because you belong here.'

All that's missing from that sentence is 'with me'. I search his eyes for the words, but in the other room Gillian lets out a loud groan.

'All right,' she calls. 'Who's going to help an old lady to get up?'

Joe's still looking at me, intent. I almost want to reach out and grab his hand, and insist he tells me how he feels, and whether he wants me. 'Think about it,' he says quietly. 'They'd love to have you here more of the time.'

I love that he thinks that, but I also want to take him by the shoulders and shake him. *How about you? How do you feel?* 'I should go and help Gillian,' I say instead.

Joe shakes his head. 'You have your coffee. I'll go.' He swings himself upright, letting his bare feet touch the stone flags and the blanket slips off his bare torso, the muscles moving beneath his skin as he leans to pick up his T-shirt. His eyes twinkle as his head emerges through his collar and he catches me watching. I look away, and quickly pick up a book from the coffee table as he gets up to pull on his jeans. I can feel myself smiling, though.

'It's upside down,' he whispers.

I snatch a breath, but he's kidding. The book is the right way up.

'Made you look,' he says, and I narrow my eyes at him, but he surprises me by kissing the top of my head. Honestly, I don't know if I'm coming or going, whether we're 'something' or not. The only thing I know is that I want us to be, because my heart's cannoning around my ribcage like a squash ball.

'Is anyone coming, or am I going to have to do this by myself?' shouts Gillian.

'Coming!' Joe calls, doing up his belt, and with a radiant smile, he leaves me to drink my coffee in thoughtful, frustrated and ambiguous reverie.

After breakfast and another curse-laden set of Gillian's exercises, we discuss what we should do about the attempted break-in. Gillian immediately vetoes Joe's suggestion of calling the police.

'What's the point? Nothing's missing and they're hardly going to issue a police guard,' she points out.

Joe pulls a face, but has to agree. 'Fine, let's install another deadlock? That would strengthen the door, at least.'

'Or we could move the paintings inside, like you said last night,' I suggest.

Gillian sighs. 'All right, for lack of any better ideas, you and Joe can move the paintings up to the spare room.'

'Thanks,' says Joe drily. 'And while we're doing that . . .?'

'I'll be reading,' she agrees. Her smugness makes me laugh. 'Big strong lad like you with two strong hips, and a good strong lass with . . .' Gillian chuckles as my eyes narrow. '. . . a go-getting attitude. You'll be done in no time.'

Joe shakes his head at her. 'Slugabed,' he mutters and, smirking, she retreats into the e-reader.

One thing's for sure: Mike painted a *lot* of pictures. It takes what feels like hundreds of trips up and down the stairs, and it's lucky we sorted through the stuff Gillian dumped up here or there wouldn't be enough space to stack them all.

As we complete the last trip, I can't help but marvel at

the huge investment in time and effort it all represents, considering each canvas probably took at least twenty hours of Mike's life.

'I've been thinking we should get Gillian down the pub,' says Joe, his thoughts running in a different direction to mine. 'What do you think?'

I hesitate. On the one hand, I'd love for her life to get back to normal, but on the other, what if something happens while we're out?

'In principle I think it's a great idea, but perhaps I should stay here?'

Joe lines up the canvasses a little more neatly. 'You could do that – hunker down and batten down the hatches. But how is that different from what Gillian's been doing for the last eighteen months?'

He's right. 'It does seem like someone has been deliberately doing petty things to keep her running scared,' I agree.

'Exactly, so what if we show them it's not working?'

'You mean, all go?'

Joe nods. 'I'd rather Gillian looked strong. And it would give us a chance to look everyone in the eye; see if anyone flinches.'

He has a point – I'd like to look Dolores in the eye. 'I think it's an excellent idea, and it will do Gillian good to see everyone.'

'That's what I thought,' he agrees. 'I thought I'd call Seren, Huw and Bridget.' He smiles and brushes some stray hair off my face, and for a second my insides flutter. 'So shall I set it up?' he asks.

I swallow so my voice comes out naturally. 'Sure.'

'Brilliant,' and taking out his phone, he calls Huw.

It's a busy afternoon. I go food shopping and Joe looks after Gillian, then I make Gillian and me dinner, while Joe goes back to his cottage for a shower and a change, and throughout it all Gillian is in an excellent mood. So much so, that I can tell I'm not the only one pleased she's finally going out. She fusses and demands that I brush her hair and find a particular jumper from upstairs, along with a patterned batik scarf that I have to search every drawer for. I don't mind, but as I pop in some earrings it still feels wrong to leave the house empty. I just wish I could know for sure it was the right thing to do.

I take a two-pence piece out of my purse and check both sides.

'Should we go out tonight?' I flip the coin, catch it on the back of my hand and cover it. 'Heads for yes, tails for no,' I quickly clarify, and uncover it.

Heads. Trouble is, I specified the sides after I'd flipped it, so I'm not sure it counts. Though heads is always yes, isn't it? Maybe I'll just double-check.

I look up at the glow stars as I try to formulate a question that will allay my fears.

'Will someone try to break in while we're out?' I flip the coin.

Heads. Shit.

'Are you messing with me?' I flip again, but this time fluff up the catch and the coin rolls under the bed. I'm ducked down trying to find it when Gillian calls for me to please remember the time. I have no choice but to leave it under there and go downstairs.

Gillian must be looking forward to it because she even manages the palaver of getting into Vivienne's car with only moderate good-tempered swearing, and as we start down the track she's nodding to herself.

'An outing,' she says, as I avoid as many potholes as I can. 'Haven't had one of those in a while.'

'No,' I agree. 'Everyone's really looking forward to seeing you.'

Gillian surveys the fields as we pass and comments on the state of the seasons, almost like a normal person, but as we enter the pub car park, I feel uneasy. It's partly because I really want this to go well, but also because I have a sudden urge to dash back.

'Problem?' asks Gillian shrewdly.

I relax my face into a smile. 'Of course not. Just hoping we can get you out OK.'

'Hmm,' murmurs Gillian, unconvinced, but she gives barely a whimper as I help her out, and as we hobble inside a shout of approval goes up as everyone, including Gareth, Huw and Seren, Bryn and Bridget and a few old gents from the lower valley, greets Gillian and offers to buy her a pint. Even George, behind the bar, has a hesitant smile – until he spots me, and Gillian flaps her good hand and tells them not to be silly, but lets them help her to a table near the bar and supply her with a drink.

I smile at Bryn, who dips his head, and I look around for Joe. He doesn't seem to be here yet, but seeing Gareth, I go over to make my peace and ask about his toe. He tells me how they didn't even X-ray it, and sent him home with it bandaged to the next toe. It also cost him sixty quid to get his car unclamped. I try to look sympathetic and make him feel better by telling him about a friend who paid two hundred pounds once, but it doesn't help, so I head over to join Seren. It's as I walk over that I realise I can't see Dolores anywhere, although I thought I saw her as we came in.

I waylay Huw, who's coming back from another table with two stools. 'Did you see Dolores at the bar?'

'Yes, briefly.' He sets down a stool for me and one for Seren before he looks at the bar. 'Perhaps she's changing a barrel.'

'That must be it,' I agree, and even though my stomach twists anxiously, I grin at him and try to act normally. I chat to Seren, who's pleased to have a night out thanks to Daf babysitting. Bridget joins us and we talk about the workshops, and it's great to see Gillian soak up the attention and listen to everyone's news after her long stint out of circulation, but even so, the uneasy feeling in my stomach doesn't dissipate. I can't relax, and I find my eyes darting both to the bar and also to the door in search of Joe.

But as I look yet again for Dolores, the look George gives me sends a chill down my spine. It isn't hostile exactly; but it's so direct it's like a shout across the room.

Excusing myself, I go to George and lean in as close as the bar will allow.

'Dolores hasn't come back,' he whispers. I look up at him and the concern in his eyes confirms all my fears that Gillian's problems are down to Dolores. I nod, and head back to the table. Behind me, Bryn calls to George.

'Problem?' asks Seren as I look around for Joe, but he still hasn't arrived.

'I forgot something,' I whisper to Seren and pull on my coat. 'Tell Joe to look after Gillian.'

Seren agrees, but grabs my hand. 'Do you want someone to come with you?' I must look as worried as I feel for her to offer.

I shake my head. 'I'll be back soon. Just tell Joe to look after Gillian.'

'Of course!' and unsure whether it's a good idea or not, I leave the pub.

28

Unfriendly Fire

I have to admit I'm a little bit scared, but excited, too, and even though it's ridiculously SAS, I drive back very slowly with the headlights off. I've also checked the wind direction, and as it's coming down the valley, I'm hoping she won't hear the car, but even so, I pull into a field gateway about halfway up the track and apply the handbrake. I get out and look up at the house. All I can see is the top floor, but that's the point – if I can't see her; she can't see me. I nudge the door closed and listen.

I don't hear anything, so I hurry up the track like I'm on some covert op, except, unlike them, I have to stop for a breather in Bryn's gateway. I catch my breath, hurry on past the two fields and peek over the wall by the yard gate.

I can just make out the cut floodlight wire splaying out from the wall, and sure enough, there's someone working away at the studio door. They're short, wrapped in a heavy coat, and worryingly, there's a petrol can at their feet.

I step out. 'What are you doing, Dolores?' I keep my voice calm, but I'm careful to keep well out of range of any crowbar throw.

Dolores turns, but keeps the crowbar behind her back. 'Oh, hello, Ella. I didn't know you were here.' She sounds friendly.

'No, I gathered that,' I agree, and she titters.

'I know this looks odd, but I didn't want to bother your aunt. Not when I just wanted a memento.' She says it like it's the most natural thing in the world. Jesus, she's even smiling.

I walk slowly to one side so she can make a break for it without cracking my skull open. 'A memento of what?'

'Mike, of course! Gillian probably didn't tell you, but before she came, Mike and I were together. Crazy about each other, we were. Long time ago, now, but I wanted a keepsake before she leaves.'

'But Gillian isn't going anywhere.'

Dolores shakes her head. 'There was an estate agent up here valuing the place a few weeks ago, so even if she hasn't said so, I think she is,' she says knowingly.

I stare at her and light dawns. 'Oh, you mean the estate agent who came to value Joe and Petra's cottage?' Her head jerks, showing her first sign of uncertainty. 'Yes, Gareth was surprised when Petra said it was her cottage the man was talking about. Didn't he tell you?'

'No,' she says quietly.

'So, you thought you'd bring a trusty crowbar to pick up . . . what exactly?'

Even in the moonlight I see her expression change. 'Just a painting. Gillian has so many, she'll barely notice if I take one, and they're just sitting in the studio, not being looked at. She doesn't want them,' she adds, like that makes a difference.

I stare at Dolores. 'So you thought you would, what? Break in and take your pick? Why not ask Gillian for one, or buy one?'

'I didn't want to drag up the past. That would be cruel.'

'Whereas breaking and entering? Twice? That's kind?' I ask. 'Because it *was you* I chased down the track last night.'

Dolores folds her arms, no longer hiding the crowbar,

and loses her polite expression. 'I just want a picture. It's important to me. Why does it matter to you?'

'I think the more important question is why it matters so much to you?'

She laughs, and there's a bitter edge to the sound. 'You've never been in love, have you, Ella? If you had, you wouldn't need to ask.'

'So explain it to me.' I've tried to keep it light, but her eyes narrow at my tone.

'Gillian ruined Mike's memory for everyone. She practically buried his pictures with him. I tried to make her see sense. I asked to see them, and even offered to put them up in the pub, but she wouldn't even consider it. No, she wanted him to rot, so she left me no choice.'

She stands four-square and self-righteous, but I shake my head. 'I don't buy it,' I say calmly.

'What do you mean, you "don't buy it"?' she almost spits.

'I mean, I don't believe you; about cherishing Mike's memory and about not wanting to hurt Gillian, because, for one thing, you won't allow the workshops to go ahead even though it was Mike's last wish, and for another, you've been persecuting Gillian.'

'Rubbish!' she hisses.

'Is it?' I leave a long silence and the cold wind billows through the gap between us. 'I know you're behind the endless junk mail, the sales calls and contractors. I know you've lurked up here at night and let her tyres down, and, if I'm not mistaken, you're the reason Gillian went to hospital.'

'Prove it!' she hisses.

'Oh, I can't, but I *can* prove you're here now with a crowbar and a can of petrol.'

I feel in my pocket for my phone, but as I glance down to take it out, she launches at me, crowbar in hand, I lift my arm and—

'DOLORES!' yells someone behind me.

It's as if they've shot her – her eyes dart behind me, her mouth falls open and her hand drops. I back away from her, and as soon as I'm at a safe distance I look behind me to find Bryn leaning on his stick in the gateway, as implacable and furious as a storm. I've never been so glad to see an angry person in my life.

'This doesn't concern you, Bryn,' tries Dolores, but her voice shakes.

'Funny that, because I *am* concerned,' he says, and his eyes flick to me and I sidle cautiously towards him.

'Well, it's not your business, then.'

'I'm not so sure about that.' He glances my way and almost imperceptibly indicates I should get behind him. 'This isn't right, Dolores. You know it isn't,' he says gently.

'And what Mike did *was*?' she demands, her voice rising in anguish.

'I'm not saying that; I know you were hurt when Gillian arrived, and since he died I know you've been trying to get Gillian to leave – I put that much together when I found the oil on the steps and realised it was you who's been doing all those unkind things to Gillian.'

'So what if I have? I just wanted it over! I wanted her gone,' cries Dolores. I can hear the anger in her voice, but there's also pain, and as I watch, tears tumble down her face. I almost feel sorry for her.

Bryn shakes his head sadly. 'I know, but it's gone too far, Dolores. You must be able to see that? You put Gillian in hospital! And when I figured that out, I couldn't let you do anything else. That's why I asked George to tell me each and every time you left the pub. He didn't even ask me why, Dolores. He just did it, so I think he knows, or at least suspects.'

'Are you telling me that's how, when Gillian was out of

the way, you were always at the gate when I came up here?' demands Dolores, and Bryn nods. 'My own husband and brother working against me!' Her expression hardens at their betrayal.

Bryn points at the petrol can with his stick. 'And for good reason, it seems. Were you seriously going to burn the studio with all his life's work in it?'

She swipes away her tears and looks defiant again. 'Yes, and why shouldn't I? It was our family that built it, and if it weren't for Gillian it would be mine.'

'But it isn't yours, Dolores; it's Gillian's. And what if someone gets hurt? Can you live with that?'

My guess is yes, but I'm not about to interrupt.

She gives a tinkling little laugh that makes me shiver. 'Stop being so melodramatic, Bryn. It's just a bloody outbuilding. Call the fire brigade if you want to. No one's going to get hurt, but I have to do this.' She moves back towards the petrol can.

'What about the firemen? What about Gillian when she finds the paintings are gone?'

Dolores looks back at us. 'She'll get money from the insurance.'

'That's not the same and you know it!'

I look from Bryn to Dolores as she slowly turns back and shakes her head at him. 'Why are you protecting Gillian, Bryn? You should hate her and Mike as much as I do.'

Bryn's eyes flick to me. 'Because she's decent.' His words ring with conviction. 'And because what happened with Mair wasn't her fault,' he adds sadly. 'And nor was what happened between you and Mike. If anything, Gillian's suffered more than anyone.'

'How dare you! Mike hurt me *more*! What did *I* do to deserve that!'

Bryn peers at her. 'Have you forgotten you're married,

Dolores? What were you thinking would happen? That Mike would beg you to leave George and you'd live happily ever after up here as his mistress and his model?'

The silence is both sickening and telling.

'Shut up, Bryn! Mike *loved* me, then *she* came and . . .' She closes her eyes, her hands gripping and twisting on the crowbar.

Bryn gestures for me to back away. 'Dolores, it ended a long time ago.'

'Says the old man who can't get over his wife leaving him! And not even for someone else! No, because you were boring, Bryn! That's why she left!' Her words are like venom, but Bryn doesn't retaliate.

'It's over, Dolores. I won't let you do this,' he says calmly.

Dolores looks at me. 'What about her?'

Bryn looks at me. 'Nothing's going to happen to Ella, and tomorrow this is all going to come out, so I suggest you go back and talk to George and Gareth.'

She grits her teeth and looks down at the crowbar in her hands. For a dreadful second, I think she's going to use it—

'No need, I heard enough,' says George quietly, from behind us.

Joe and Huw are with him, and Joe moves to my side and takes my hand. Huw walks over to Dolores and holds out his hand for the crowbar. Dolores looks at him, wide-eyed, and hands it over, but the anger still hasn't died in her eyes.

She laughs harshly. 'I wasn't going to do anything.'

'That's not true, is it?' says George. 'Like it wasn't true when you went out for long walks, or when you came up here to feed the cat Bryn was already feeding, or when Mike first moved here and you were up here more than you should be. We deserved better, Dolores.'

'Did you?' demands Dolores. 'Then why don't we tell

everyone why you're protecting her, George? Fancy her, don't you? Don't deny it; I've always known!'

George shakes his head. 'I've always admired Gillian, but that's as far as it went. I never did anything about it, whereas you and Mike . . . You think I didn't know? If anything, I was grateful when Gillian arrived. I thought we might make a fresh start.'

'But that's what I wanted, too. I just needed this to be over,' she says hopelessly.

'What?' asks George. 'You and Mike? You torturing Gillian? . . . Us?' he asks quietly, and somehow his sadness is more final than any amount of anger would have been. 'They're all over.'

'What do you mean?' asks Dolores in a pitifully small voice, and I snuggle in to Joe.

'I think it's time you left,' says George. Dolores' mouth drops open, and Bryn nods with slow deliberation. 'Before someone calls the police.'

She looks from George to Bryn, her face disbelieving. 'You wouldn't do that.'

'*I* would,' I say, so they don't have to answer.

'So would I,' says Joe firmly.

'Me, too,' agrees Huw.

Dolores' face is a bitter nest of shadows as George shakes his head dejectedly. 'You've crossed the line, Dolores. You've gone too far. I want you out. I want you gone.'

Dolores' eyes flick between us like a snared fox. 'You can't mean it! It's my pub! I grew up here!' But George shakes his head.

'You can't do what you've done and stay.'

'It's time to go, Dolores,' agrees Bryn.

She walks towards us and glares with hurt and fury at us each in turn. It's heart-rending and horrible, until she comes to me and it morphs into loathing.

'Pleased with yourself?' she demands.

'More than you'll ever know,' I agree, matching her fury as I remember all the things she's done to Gillian.

Joe steps between us and she turns and walks down the track, leaving us staring after her. I let out a breath and Joe puts his arm around me, practically holding me up. Bryn tips his cap at me and heads off down the hill.

'Jesus! That was horrible,' I mumble. 'Who's with Gillian,' I ask, suddenly realising we've just sent Dolores back in her direction.

'Seren,' says Joe, and I pull my phone out of my pocket and dial her number.

'What's happened?' asks Seren, picking up immediately.

'Dolores caused the problems. She's coming back to the pub. Can you get Gillian out before she gets there?'

'Absolutely, we're just getting her in the car,' she says. 'The place emptied so Gillian wanted to come back, anyway.'

'Thanks, Seren.'

'No problem,' she says, and hangs up.

The rest of us look at each other.

'You realise this is still a police matter,' Joe says quietly to George.

George nods. 'I'll go along with whatever Gillian wants. Tell her I'm sorry.'

'She'll be here in a minute. Seren's bringing her up,' I tell him, but George shakes his head.

'I'll come another time. Right now, I need to think,' and turning on his heel, he stumps off down the track after his wife.

29

Inference and Implication

I bury my head in Joe's chest, and Huw tactfully strolls to the top of the track to wait for Seren. After a few seconds I pull away, take the keys out of my pocket and unlock the front door. I turn on the kitchen lights with Joe just behind me.

Bozz is on the kitchen table. I give him a stroke and take a steadying breath, unable to stop thinking about how I could be lying bleeding in the yard if it weren't for Bryn, and Joe puts his arms around me from behind and holds me. I rest my head against his shoulder and feel his cheek resting on the top of my head. He's warm after the chill wind outside.

'You OK?' he asks.

I want to turn around and bury myself in his hug, but lights swing around in the yard.

'That'll be Seren with Gillian,' he says. I nod and he gently lets go and goes to help Gillian in. They're followed in by Bridget, looking more anxious than I've ever seen her, and while Joe helps Gillian to her usual chair, I give Seren a hug, and wave off her and Huw, who go back to relieve Daf and no doubt tell him about the excitement.

I come back in, and Gillian lets out a long slow breath and looks up at me.

'So, what happened?' she asks.

I glance at Joe, and he nods, so I explain all about Dolores trying to get into the studio, the petrol can and how Bryn arrived in the nick of time.

'Bryn saw you leave the pub, and followed you out,' agrees Bridget. 'I've never seen him move so fast. Then George got one of the old blokes from the lower valley to look after the bar—'

'I bet that cost him a few pints,' mutters Gillian.

'—and left, too. That's when Joe came in, asked where you were, got his coat on and he and Huw left,' says Bridget. 'Within seconds the pub was almost empty.'

'So, why was she trying to get into the studio?' asks Gillian.

I look at Joe. 'She said she wanted a memento.'

'And you need a petrol can for that, do you?' demands Bridget.

I shrug. 'My best guess is she wanted to burn all Mike's pictures, but . . .'

'What?' asks Gillian.

'I don't know. There's something I can't put my finger on. She said she asked to look through them after Mike died?'

Gillian's eyebrows shoot up. 'Pph! That's one way of putting it. One day I found her in there, pawing through his pictures. She told me some garbage about wanting to display them in the pub and needing measurements. I told her I wasn't interested and sent her on her way, but I took the studio key out from under the plant pot by the door after that. But now I think about it, that's when the pranks started.'

'Pranks?' asks Bridget, and I give her an abridged version of all the nasty things Dolores did, and how Bryn and possibly also George have been thwarting her. Bridget is outraged. 'What horrible things to do to someone!'

'You should have called the police from the start,' says Joe reproachfully.

'Do you think so?' asks Gillian. 'When it could have been my imagination and I had no proof? They'd have written me off as a crank.'

'But you suspected it might be Dolores?' I ask.

Gillian hesitates. 'I thought it *might* be,' she concedes. 'But if I'd been wrong it would have hurt George, Gareth and Bryn. They didn't need any more problems, not when Bryn had already lost Mair, and George, well . . . who knows what George had put up with over the years.'

'So you tried to protect them,' I realise. She nods. 'And all while they tried to protect you?' She nods again.

In a twisted kind of way, it makes sense. It also puts a very different spin on my first days here; from George's insistence I stay with Gillian so she wouldn't be left alone, to Bryn and George asking how long I would stay so they'd know when Gillian was vulnerable, not to mention Bryn's attendance at the gate. Poor man must have been on super-high alert the entire time Gillian was in hospital.

'You still should have told someone,' maintains Joe.

Gillian pats his arm. 'Who? I'd cut myself off from everyone, and I really wondered if I was losing my mind.'

'But you *should* have told *me*,' he persists.

Gillian's eyes are full of pity as she looks at him. 'I couldn't, because if I wasn't imagining it, no matter which way I looked at it, Mike caused this.'

'So you thought you should take responsibility for the fallout?' Joe demands incredulously.

'Not directly, but, I suppose, in a way . . .' Her eyes implore him to understand.

'Mike was a bloody idiot ever to do anything to hurt you,' he says gruffly.

Gillian shrugs. 'I doubt he ever thought it would come to this. He thought it would remain secret.'

'So what are you going to do about Dolores?' I ask Gillian.

Gillian looks at Joe. 'I'm going to let Bryn and George handle it.'

Joe's jaw tightens. 'If she does anything else, I'm reporting her,' he warns.

We look at each other awkwardly, and Gillian gestures to the bottle of whiskey I bought this afternoon. I get out some glasses.

'But that still doesn't explain what she wanted in the studio,' Bridget says into the brooding silence.

She has a point. 'No, it doesn't,' I agree. 'And she must have been desperate to get in there considering all the times she tried: creeping up here at night, injuring Gillian on the steps, even telling Gareth to let her know if Gillian was by herself the night we went out.'

There's silence as we realise how lucky it was Bryn figured out what Dolores was up to and kept an eye on the track all this time, and that everyone came up that particular night.

Joe looks at Bridget like she's the world authority on Mike's infidelity. 'Any ideas?'

Luckily Bridget doesn't take offence. 'None, but then I never came to the studio. Mike painted me while I was on a painting course he was giving in France.'

'How did he paint you?' asks Joe, suddenly intent.

'It was barely even a nude. It was just a head and torso, really, with my elbows propped on a table and my hands under my chin. I was looking directly at him.'

'Do you still have the painting?' Joe seems to be going off on some tangent of his own, but understanding radiates across Bridget's face.

'No, Mike kept it!'

'Oh!' I say, finally getting it. Joe nods at me and turns to Gillian.

'And have *you* ever seen the portrait of Bridget?' he asks.

'No,' says Gillian. 'I would have remembered, as I would have done if I'd seen any paintings of Dolores or anyone else, come to that.'

Joe slowly nods. 'So that could explain what Dolores has been looking for and why she's been so determined about it? Particularly if it was a nude.'

Gillian lets out a sigh. 'And to think, when I found her going through Mike's paintings after he died, I thought she was after a quick buck. It never occurred to me that she might actually be looking for something in particular.'

'It's not the first conclusion you'd leap to,' I agree.

'There's just one problem,' says Joe. 'We've checked all the canvases and there are no nudes.'

'Is it possible Mike destroyed them?' I ask.

Gillian purses her lips in thought. 'No, I don't think he'd do that. If he disliked a picture, he painted over it.' She shakes her head in confusion. 'But what I don't get is why now? It's eighteen months since Mike died, and although Dolores tried to get in initially, she soon stopped and just played nasty tricks. What made her start trying to break in and injure me this last month?'

'She thought you were selling up,' I explain. I glance at Joe, and he nods. 'Petra had an estate agent up to value the cottage, but she couldn't get here with the keys. He visited the pub afterwards, complaining the woman who owned the place couldn't let him in, and Dolores thought he was talking about you.'

Joe shakes his head at the unwitting role Petra played. 'Dolores probably rationalised that if you hadn't found the painting yet, you would if you moved.'

'And I guess that also explains why she was so set against us using the studio for the workshops,' says Bridget. 'If we cleaned the place out, we were bound to find them.' She cringes. 'And I told her we were doing that the same day

Ella fell in the lane chasing someone. She must have been trying to get in before we found them!'

'That still doesn't explain where they are,' says Joe. 'Unless Mike painted over them.'

'There'd be tell-tale signs. We might spot them if we're looking for them?' I suggest.

Everyone looks at me, but Gillian shakes her head. 'We'll look in the morning,' she says. 'I'm not up to a series of nude reveals tonight. Joe, open up the whiskey,' and while Joe peels the whiskey's plastic shield and pours it, Bridget tactfully moves the conversation on to plans for the workshops.

30

For the Love of Mike

The next morning, Joe arrives with bags under his eyes, while Gillian looks exhausted and fragile. I'm no better, and I've taken to the coffee like it's ambrosia – and I don't mean the rice pudding kind.

Joe and Gillian keep her exercise session short, but as she comes in for a well-earned cup of tea and some breakfast, she glances at me anxiously.

'Ready for the day ahead?' she asks.

'Yes. How are you feeling about it?'

She wrinkles her nose slightly and bites into her toast and marmalade, but the slow way she chews it suggests it's turned to ashes in her mouth.

Joe sips his coffee and we stand in uneasy silence as we wait for Gillian to finish.

'Ready?' Joe asks Gillian as she swallows the last of her tea, and she nods.

The procession up the stairs is an odd one. Joe helps Gillian carefully up each step, while I follow with a kitchen chair, and we set her up in front of the paintings. So as not to waste time, we've also set her the task of deciding which ones she wants to keep, but none of us are fooled as to why we're here. Luckily, we quickly fall into a rhythm where Joe selects a painting, Gillian decides if she loves it or if it can be sold, and last of all I check it by the window to see if it's been painted over. The task quickly loses its anxious edge, and by the end of the morning, we have a stack of paintings to keep, a stack to sell, and a small group that Gillian doesn't want up, but also can't bear to part with. As for my part, I only found a couple of redone landscapes, and not a single portrait.

None of us is quite sure if this is a good thing or not, and we troop, grubby and tired, back downstairs to have lunch.

Munching a sandwich, Joe gives Gillian a long look. 'You honestly don't think he destroyed them?'

Gillian rubs her eyes. 'No, he was an egotist. So much so, he even considered his failures a valuable learning experience. He'd leave them on display and go back and glare at them day after day until he fixed it, or, in a fit of impatience, whitewashed over it.'

'Then where are they?' asks Joe, his impatience showing. 'It's not like canvasses are the easiest things to hide – they tend to be quite big!'

'Unless they're removed from their stretchers,' I point out. 'Then they can roll up . . . or fold, although that's considered sacrilege, so I doubt Mike would have done that.'

Joe blows out a breath. 'But that still doesn't solve the problem of where they are.'

Gillian pulls a face. 'I doubt they're in the house.'

'Which leaves the studio,' says Joe.

'And considering that's where Dolores thinks they are . . .' I pause suggestively.

Joe frowns at me. 'It's practically a blank box except for Mike's art equipment and shelving . . .' Joe smiles. '. . . and the daybed!'

Gillian's eyes dart warily to mine. 'I want that thing out of there,' she says. 'But I don't think I can bear to be in there when you sort everything out.' It's either too raw, too Mike or too betraying, but I take her point.

'How about we pack everything up, measure up for Bridget, *dispose* of the daybed, and if we find anything in there we let you know?' I offer.

Gillian lets out a relieved sigh and smiles.

Gillian's had enough, that much is clear, but after lunch Joe and I start on the studio by ourselves. The shelves are of such a simple construction that they can't hide anything, and dismantling the daybed doesn't yield an ounce of flesh – just more washing. Frustrated, I fold up the easels and put all Mike's painting stuff in boxes, while Joe measures up to see how many trestle tables will fit in.

I fold closed the last cardboard box and put a folded easel on top to keep it closed, but I don't know whether to be glad or disappointed that we haven't found anything.

Joe does some calculations on a scrap of paper, paces the floor and looks around. 'What do you think to fitting twelve tables and a dais in here?'

'Seems reasonable,' I agree, and I pick up a broom and work my way down the room to where the daybed was.

'Did Gillian have some work done?' I ask suddenly.

Joe looks up. 'I don't think so. Why?'

'Because this section of plasterboard is scuffed, and I think it's been unscrewed.'

Joe joins me where the daybed was. He bends down to examine the screws and indicates some oil paint smudges.

'Could you get Gillian, while I find a screwdriver?' he asks, and his eyes meet mine for a second.

'Sure. You think it might *be* something?'

'Could be,' he agrees.

I hurry into the house and call Gillian, and Gillian lumbers out on my arm and gives the room a revolted look. She inspects the wall and nods. 'Unscrew it,' she says. I collect the paint-spattered stool for her and we stand back nervously as Joe removes each screw and lifts aside the piece of plasterboard.

Strangely, it's light behind there and crouching down I can see there's an extra six feet to the end of the barn, lit by the skylight that extends even into this extra six-foot section.

Joe crawls in on his hands and knees. 'There's something in here,' he calls, and there's a scraping sound as he backs out.

Gillian glances apprehensively at me, possibly having similar anxious body-in-the-wall type thoughts, which weirdly, in a sense, is what we're looking for, and Joe drags out a large, roughly hewn fibreboard box covered in a plastic sheet. He steps back from it and looks at Gillian.

Her eyes flick briefly to me and she nods. 'Do it,' she says, and we all hold our breath as Joe lifts off the plastic and pulls one of the paintings from inside the box.

It's of a nude, sitting on a chair, wearing a single orchid blossom behind her ear, the purple clashing dramatically with her dyed-red hair.

'Who is she?' asks Joe. 'I don't remember her.'

Gillian sighs heavily. 'A dreadful woman called Carmen; all floaty scarves and pouting lipstick. She was a potter, as I remember. Didn't stay long.'

Joe lets it slide back down and at Gillian's say-so lifts another. He peers around at the front of the canvas as we stare at the woman sitting with her back to us, a flock of inked birds flying across her back, and with Mike's signature orchid flower woven into her French plait. It's unnerving that she's posed on the very stool Gillian's sitting on.

Gillian shifts uncomfortably. 'She was a mouse of a girl – I didn't know she had a tattoo. Can't remember her name, but I think she was into etching and lino printing.'

Joe pulls up a third painting and we freeze, unsure what to say. It's Dolores, much younger, and it's shockingly explicit, not because of her body – no, it's worse than that – it's because her expression is so adoring it surpasses adulation into something more frightening. So much so, I want to stand in front of Gillian just to shield her from it, and yet all that yearning holds me transfixed, like I'm staring into an abyss. I've never seen anything come so close to pure rapture.

'Cover the poor woman up,' says Gillian, her voice a croaky combination of sadness and disgust, but Joe is examining the reverse. 'What have you found?'

Joe's head jerks up at the sharpness of her tone. 'Mike wrote notes on the back,' he says quietly.

Gillian closes her eyes. 'What did he write?'

'This one says, "Dolores in the throes of passion, detailing the joys of love-making."'

None of us dare comment.

Joe slides the painting back into the box and lifts up another, also of Dolores, but this time her expression is distant; her mouth taught.

'Has he written anything?' asks Gillian.

Joe examines the back. '"Dolores asks if I still feel the same."' Every dash of buried hurt, fear and reproach is painted into Dolores' face.

Gillian folds her bottom lip into her mouth, and nods for Joe to push it down.

The next painting is just of Dolores' face and hands: her eyes angry, betrayed and raw and her fingertips digging into her cheeks as she cradles her face. Gillian looks at Joe.

'It says, "Paint me, paint me like this, you bastard. Look at me and remember what you've done. Paint me like this, you bastard, and never speak to me again."'

Her anger stares out fiercely at us: vivid, severe and potent. It's almost putrid.

'It's like *The Picture of Dorian Gray*,' I whisper bewildered.

'All her despair on show,' agrees Gillian. 'He really dug into that poor woman's emotions, and I'm starting to see why she wanted to burn the place down – I wouldn't want anyone to see me like that, either.' Gillian pulls herself upright and stares at Dolores. 'But, you have to admit it's an amazing piece of painting. Let her down,' she says quietly, and Joe pushes it back in and lifts a painting of a beautiful and yet very dissatisfied woman, staring off into the distance caught in her own thoughts.

'Mair,' says Gillian, and I recognise her from Bryn's carving.

Joe tilts the painting slightly so he can read the back. '"I still love him, but I can't take another moment of his parents – their gripes, their moans, how nothing is ever good enough. There's no good end to this."'

Disappointment radiates from the painting. It seems Bryn's marriage was doomed by his parents. Poor Bryn.

Joe slides the painting back down and brings up one of Bridget. It's just of her head and chest, her arms covering her breasts and her chin propped in her hands like she's framed in a window. The orchid is on the sill in front of her, and she would look wistful if it weren't for the directness of her gaze and the uncertainty in her eyes. It's like she's afraid there's been some dreadful mistake. Gillian looks at Joe.

'"Of course I'm flattered,"' he reads out. '"I just don't understand why you want to paint me. There are so many more beautiful women, but if you really want to . . ."'

Gillian looks away, and I don't blame her. There's something intrusive about seeing an iron-clad woman like Bridget look so vulnerable.

'Put it back,' whispers Gillian, and Joe slides it down.

'How many more are there?' I ask. The bared souls are . . . too much, somehow. They don't seem to end, but just as I think Joe's taken my hint, he peels something off the side of the crate. He reads the single word written on the front and hands the envelope to Gillian.

A look of deep sadness crosses her face. She slips her finger under the envelope flap and takes out the letter inside.

'He wrote this ten years ago,' she says dully. She reads it through, nods once and takes a deep breath.

'*Dear Gillian,*' she reads out.

'Are you sure you want to—?' I begin, but Gillian raises a hand for me to be quiet.

'If you're reading this, it's because you have found my hoard of nudes. I always knew it was a possibility, but in case you found them when I was out on the hill, I thought I had better leave a letter of explanation. So first: let me assure you there's no need for concern. None at all.

Yes, these are my paintings. They are not the landscapes I sell, they are the paintings that keep me sane; the paintings that strive for something more, because despite all the heart and soul the critics say is in my use of paint, I'm no longer excited by the massive canvases I churn out for the galleries, and what's more, I haven't been for a very long time.

My enthusiasm waned even before I met you. Even by then they had become a formula; a way to make money, and I was desperate for something different – something real and more challenging: something worthwhile. So I visited the galleries in Liverpool to figure out what I was missing, and I found the nudes on the walls of the Walker Art Gallery. Some had emotion and engendered feelings, while others were remote and expressionless. I could tell instantly which artists had empathy with their sitters, and which had purely studied their anatomy. The difference fascinated me, and I decided to try my hand at capturing real emotions and securing that raw intensity of feeling in my work. The problem was I needed models. Not paid models: bored and cold, clocking up the hours, faces as dull as dishwater. No, I needed real people, invested in the process, frightened of being caught, exhilarated, shy and defiant. I wanted those feelings to shine through in my paintings, and that's when I found Dolores—'

Gillian cocks an eyebrow at us both, takes a deep breath and continues.

'—It was just after I arrived in the area, and I didn't know many people, but there was Dolores. She was always popping up, desperate for some peace and quiet from the pub she and her husband were renovating, and more than willing to be my artist's muse.

Of all the women I painted, she was the only one I slept with. I thought it would help, but what a mistake that was! To begin with, it was exhilarating and fun, and I thought we were on the same page – after all, she was married – but soon it was fraught with problems. Not artistically: she was a rich and luxuriant cornucopia of emotions – but personally, it was clear she was in too deep, and unfortunately for her, that's when I met you, dear Gillian.

I felt terrible as I explained to her that it was just a bit of fun, that I didn't want her to leave George, but she was adamant we were meant to be together. All too soon, with the exception of a few good paintings, I wish I'd never touched her. Her threats and cajoling went on for months. I couldn't keep up with her, but the one thing she was always adamant about was not having her pictures on show. So that's how I finally shut her up: I said as long as she stayed away from us, I would keep her paintings safe and secret. She agreed on the proviso that I stuck to landscapes and still lives, and made a particular point that she'd never forgive me if I painted a nude of you. She said it was "our special thing", and that's why I didn't. I didn't want to tar you with the same brush, and it's why every painting contains an orchid (a loose interpretation of still life, but needs must). It's also why every one of these paintings had to be done in secret, because Dolores would have raised hell if she found out.

So after that, though I talked to my models, and encouraged them to share their ideas, hopes, and fears, and sometimes even helped them come to a few life-changing revelations of their own, I never slept with any of them. And though it had to be kept secret, to be fair it suited me well, as I was able to keep this branch of my art for myself, rather than have it ruined by commercialism.

So, don't be angry or upset. Instead, know I love you, keep your head, look through the paintings if you wish (I'd love to have your opinion), but leave my clothes in the drawers. I'll see you later,

Mike x'

Gillian folds the letter and puts it back in its envelope. For a split second, I think she's going to cry, but our eyes meet, and I can see that her teeth are clenched and her eyes are fierce.

'What a *bloody idiot!*' she exclaims. Her eyes flick to Joe. 'Sorry!' she says. 'But for all that he could paint like a master, Mike had no sodding clue. He thought he could just delve into them, mine their innermost feelings, slap them down on canvas and walk away. Hell, I almost feel sorry for them – even Dolores!'

I picture Dolores' bitter festering hate, Mair leaving Bryn as maybe she would have done anyway, but who knows? And Bridget, so desperate for a meaningful relationship she trailed up here after him, and take her point.

'But at least he says he didn't sleep with them once he was with you. That has to stand for something. He didn't betray you, after all,' I say, but Gillian shakes her head.

'The trouble is that, even if he didn't, *they* felt they had a relationship with him, and I'm not sure if that's more disturbing. I only hope he didn't unwittingly inflict too much damage on them.'

I glance at Joe, but he doesn't seem to know what to say either.

Gillian beckons to Joe. 'Come on. Let's get the rest over with.'

Joe hesitates, his eyes on me, but none of us want to string this out. He pulls up another painting, and we work our way through; Gillian naming them as Joe lifts them up and reads the captions on the back. There are a couple more of Dolores in various states of mental undress, and many more of artists and friends who visited or stopped visiting over the years. The pool of naked women grows, and it's almost like we're becoming immune, until Joe raises one of the last pictures and—

Gillian and I freeze.

On the canvas is a much younger and more lithe version of Mum. She's not fully naked; she's clasping a shawl together with an orchid flower to her chest, but she's not focused on the orchid. She's staring straight at us, looking more relaxed and lovely than I've ever seen her, but also more . . . alluring.

Joe pulls back slightly at our reaction. 'What?' he asks, and peers around at the front of the painting.

'Marion,' whispers Gillian, her voice deadened.

I feel sick and yet I can't stop staring at Mum's keen glance – the way her lips are slightly parted, and how her beautifully painted fingers loosely grasp the shawl that covers her modesty. It looks ready to drop away.

'Who?' he asks.

'My mum,' I explain, and his mouth drops open.

Gillian stares at the floor, not so much in shock as defeated, and my stomach turns over like it's been ploughed.

'I'm so sorry, Gillian,' I breathe. It's hardly adequate, but what can I say?

Gillian swallows. 'What does it say on the back?' she asks, not looking at me, while the painting won't stop staring at us both.

Joe studies the back. '"I've felt so trapped, living under the weight of our parents' expectations. It's been hard being the good sister all these years. I've been so angry, but now I'm here I see why she lives the way she does. Anything is possible and I'm free to be me. I'm allowed to be beautiful and vibrant, and I'm ready."'

'Ready' for what? I look into Mum's painted eyes and I know exactly what she's ready for. But how could she do that to Gillian? I'm so angry I want to slap her, so I walk up to Joe and ram the painting back into the crate.

'Well, that's that,' says Gillian very quietly. She levers herself up off the stool and her gaze finally meets mine. 'She never opened up to anyone. If she opened up to him . . .' She closes her eyes, unable to finish. 'When is your birthday?' Gillian stares at the concrete floor.

'You don't think . . .' I laugh. 'No, you can't mean . . .' I stare at her aghast. 'I was born eighteen months later. You said so yourself.'

'When is your birthday?' she repeats, her tone is so flat it scares me.

'May twelfth.'

Gillian looks at me in such an agony of sympathy, I can't refute it. 'I did wonder, when you said she wouldn't say who your father was, and when I overheard you say you're almost thirty . . .' That was the day she tried to send me home, and it suddenly makes sense why she was so angry. 'I really hoped I was wrong, but I don't think I am. Why else would it be such a secret?'

I glance at Joe and back at Gillian. 'But I was born eighteen months later,' I insist.

She shakes her head. 'No,' she finally manages. 'You were born in May. Marion told me about your birth in a Christmas card.'

Joe's mouth drops open. He looks as horrified as I feel.

'But . . .' All the pieces start to fall into place. I count up the months between August and May. I count again. 'But he said he didn't sleep with any of them.'

Gillian shakes her head. 'I'm so sorry. It looks like he lied.'

I steady myself on the traitorous crate, and snatch my hand off it.

'Did you know . . .' I have to force the words out. '. . . before I came?'

'No, I didn't. And when you said you were thirty soon . . . I prayed I was just scaring myself, but now, what with the painting—'

My legs give way, and as I sit down on the studio floor, the sorrow in Gillian's eyes almost chokes me.

'Joe, get her a whiskey,' Gillian says quietly. Joe doesn't move.

'But . . . he can't be.' My words seem to be in another room. 'That doesn't work.' I glance at Joe. He's looking down at me in anguish.

'Joe, get her inside. Joe!' says Gillian more sharply.

He snaps to his senses and lifts me off the floor. But as he supports me inside, his arms are shaking, which could be to do with my weight, but something tells me it isn't.

Gillian limps along behind. I want to tell him to put me down and help her, but I can't.

'Put her on the sofa,' she instructs, and as I land on the cushions, his eyes meet mine for a second before he pulls away. Gillian hobbles to the kitchen table and sloshes a large measure of whiskey into a tumbler.

'Get that down you,' she orders, stumping over with it.

I shake my head.

'Take it,' she orders, and Joe takes it from her, hands it to me so he can help her into her chair. She glances from me to Joe. It's like she can see every hope I had regarding him being abrasively and forcefully scrubbed away.

'I'm so sorry,' she whispers.

I sip the whiskey, which restores my composure if nothing else.

'I guess we're related,' says Joe. His words are hollow and his smile doesn't reach his eyes.

'Yes.' My voice is scratchy.

'You should go home, Joe,' says Gillian as Joe lingers, not knowing what to say to either of us. 'Go home,' she repeats more gently, and after laying a hand on my shoulder, he picks up his coat and sweeps out of the door.

31

Burnt Bridges

Even before the front door closes, tears tumble down my cheeks, and Gillian heaves herself out of her chair and hobbles over to slump onto the sofa next to me. She pulls me hard into her side, and I start sobbing.

She doesn't say a word, just gently rubs my back as great hiccoughing convulsions erupt through me, heaving out one after another, like there's an endless sea of them waiting to come in. I don't know how long she holds me, but by the time I stop, a lot of the light has drained from the room and I'm exhausted. I slump back against the end of the sofa, and heaving herself up, Gillian retrieves her stick and turns on the lights.

'A nasty shock, and not what you were expecting,' she says quietly.

I nod, and her world-weary expression makes me feel young, naive and overly dramatic. 'I'm so sorry. You've been betrayed by your sister and your partner. I should be the one comforting you.'

She flaps her hand. 'It wasn't sprung on me . . . not really. In fact, I think I've been waiting for it, all these years. Or perhaps hiding from it would be a better description. The way she left – I knew it wasn't right. But I never thought you were part of the equation. If I had . . .? Well, you can't fix the past. But I guess that answers the question of who your father is.'

I nod numbly. 'I expected to feel relieved. Especially after working through all the stupid stories Mum came out with.'

'Such as?' asks Gillian.

'To begin with he was a sperm donor especially chosen by science for his intelligence and attractiveness.' Gillian gives me a look. 'I know, I know, it was more likely to be some spotty student trying to earn a few quid, but when I was little I thought it was all done in smart futuristic laboratories, with Adonises on tap.' Gillian smirks, and I can't help smiling at the visual, too. 'Then it was a friend or colleague of my mum's, selflessly helping her have a baby. Then it was "leave it alone". But the one thing she always maintained was it was her choice. Trouble is she holds babies like ticking time bombs, so it never rang true.'

'Yes, well, she did decide to keep you, so maybe, in that sense, it was her choice,' says Gillian softly.

'I suppose.' I stare at the floor, still feeling side-swiped by it all. 'The ridiculous thing is I thought I would be immune, not care even, who he was. I thought it was just a matter of interest, or curiosity, and yet here I am sobbing all over you even though you've been more betrayed than I have.'

Gillian half smiles. 'You forget – I've already done my trials of angst over family, not to mention the hours of wretchedness over Mike.'

'But still . . .'

'What's done is done,' she says firmly. 'I tried to send you away before you found out, but that was silly, because we can't change it.' She looks at me for a long second. 'But I am sorry about Joe. I knew you got on well and I tried to warn him to keep a little distance between you, but I hadn't realised you had grown so close, and it wasn't until I saw your faces that I realised just how much Mike had ruined things.'

I stare at the grooves between the stone flags, and will myself not to cry. 'Luckily, it hadn't gone anywhere.' Not physically anyway, probably because of what Gillian said to him and thank God for that.

She takes my hand and holds it. 'Whiskey,' she says suddenly, 'and cheese and biscuits.'

'Good idea,' I agree, and get to my feet as wobbly as an invalid.

We work together to make what amounts to reinforcement and ballast, but as we sit down and start munching, the cheese and biscuits are reassuringly comforting.

'Better?' she asks, and I smile ruefully, because we both know better is a relative term.

'How about you?' I ask. 'This must all have been difficult for you, especially seeing the paintings?'

Gillian shrugs. 'Perhaps I should have expected it. He had this charisma that drew people to him. He dazzled them and made them feel special. It was almost like magic. Even when not in close proximity, he shook them up, inspired them and made them do bigger and better art, but then he lost interest. He'd send them on their way slightly bereft, but I honestly don't think he knew the effect he was having.' Gillian's mouth twists. 'I don't know if that makes him any less culpable, but I'm starting to see just what a mess he made . . . especially for you, little that he knew it at the time.'

'Is that what happened to Mum, do you think?'

Gillian presses her lips together. 'I expect so.'

'It could explain why Mum's so anti-art, anti-you and anti-anything to do with this place. And why she has a big problem with orchids,' I add as an afterthought.

'Don't we all, now?' agrees Gillian drily, but she doesn't look annoyed.

I take another sip of my whiskey, and look Gillian in the eye.

'I'm sorry I stirred it all up. If I hadn't come, maybe none of this would have come out and . . .'

'And what?' Gillian asks quietly.

'And I'm sorry that the biggest threat to your happiness wasn't Petra, or Bridget, or Dolores . . . I'm sorry it was me.' I look into her eyes, imploring her to see how regretful I am.

Gillian half laughs. 'Oh Ella, it was never you! Don't you remember I was "gullible and double angry" before you even arrived? And you coming here made me see that Bridget, Joe, Seren and Bryn, and everyone except Dolores, are genuine, kind and decent, and I'm lucky to have them.' She takes my hand again. 'And for that, I thank you.'

I smile at her. 'And what about Mike?'

Gillian sighs. 'I'm still angry with him, and I guess his actions are something I'm going to have to come to terms with, but overall,' she looks around the room, 'I wouldn't want to be anywhere else. And I don't think I would have wanted to miss out on the life I had with him, either. He made me strong and gave me the confidence to be who I am.'

'But weren't you strong before? You must have been to cut ties with everyone and come here.'

'You make it sound easy. It wasn't.' Gillian examines the back of her bruised hand and smiles. 'In truth, after meeting him, I went back to London and dithered. I didn't know if Mike was serious about me, or if I'd ever see him again. I certainly didn't know if I could trust how I felt about him, so I took on some work and went on as usual.'

'What swung it for you?'

Gillian looks at me. 'A chance encounter; a bit like you and your busker. I was doing a photo shoot of the London boat race: some lovely shots of the Oxbridge crews and their boats, boats crossing the line, and some ghastly shots of dignitaries hobnobbing. I was snapping away, doing broad shots of the crowd, when a man hurried over, looked at my camera, looked at me and laughed awkwardly. I asked him if there was a problem and he grinned at me. "How many scruples do you have?" he asked.' Gillian smiles at the memory. '"About my own behaviour, or other people's?" I asked him. "Both," he replied, and it was such an odd question, I answered him honestly.'

'What did you say?' I ask, already absorbed.

'I answered that "I have some scruples about my own behaviour, not that my family would believe it, but so long as I can look myself in the eye at the final reckoning, I'll be happy." He laughed and told me he liked my thinking. "As for other people," I said, "so long as no one gets hurt – their business, their consciences." "Good answer," he replied, so I asked him about his scruples. "Near enough none, but with an underlying core of decency," he said, and I liked him immediately. "Glad we sorted that out. What do you need?" I asked, and he looked worriedly at my camera. "One of the photos you took. My lady-friend would prefer it remained undisclosed that we were here together." "You're not the husband?" I guessed. "Not even the boyfriend. More disreputable and injurious than either, I'm afraid." But he didn't say it like he was ashamed. He said it with relish, and I couldn't help laughing.

'"I'd be happy to help, but it's on a reel with some shots I'd rather keep," I said. "I can destroy the negative, though," and I remember him glancing anxiously over his shoulder to a woman I recognised from the newspapers. "Could I come to your studio, just to reassure my friend that the negative has been destroyed? . . . Although, now I say it, that's not great for you: strange man, with a dodgy reputation. Suggest somewhere public, we'll wear mackintoshes and you can bring the negative in a brown paper envelope?"

He smiled at me with such mischief and fun, I almost agreed. Then I don't know why I did it, but I gave him my address.'

I breathe in.

'Yes, I know, not something I'd advise, but the next day he came to look at the photographs and there was nothing to worry about. He was genuinely interested and very complimentary, and gave me a hefty reward from his lady-friend for the incriminating negative, which I tried to decline, but he insisted I kept.'

'So how did that make you come here?' I ask.

Gillian purses her lips. 'Actually it was quite odd. He was on his way out when he spotted my half-unpacked bags by the door. He immediately said, "You want to be somewhere else," and the way he said it, made me realise just how right he was. Seeing my surprise, he asked me to tell him about it, so I did. I explained all about Mike, how he made me happy, angry and amused like no one else; how we fitted together and yet didn't need to live in each other's pockets and how neither of us believed in marriage. I explained it seemed like a wonderful, interesting and exciting opportunity, but if I chose him, my family would almost certainly disown me – not that they hadn't already, really, but that this would be the final and determining coffin nail, with no turning back.'

'And what did he say?' I ask, riveted.

'He asked me whether my family made me happy, and I said no. He asked whether the choices they made, made my life better, and I said no. "Are they tolerant, far-seeing and kind?" he asked and I remember laughing. "No," I said. "Then how come they get to choose?" I remember the shock. Then he said, "Forget your family; even forget this man for a moment, and ask yourself whether you'd rather be the person who goes and fails, or the one that stays here and doesn't risk it?" So that's what I did, and that was the night I moved to Wales.'

'Because of a man you met at a regatta?' I check.

'Because of a man I met at a regatta,' she confirms. 'His name was Donald.'

'Do you regret it?'

She breathes in, then stops, and a small smile touches her mouth. 'No.'

'Even considering all this?'

Her eyes meet mine, and her forehead relaxes. 'I couldn't have done anything else – not really. I never felt the same about anyone else,' she admits.

'You loved him.'

'More than anyone,' she agrees. 'And perhaps I should remember that, even though it's going to be hard to recon-cile with all this.'

'And can you forgive him for . . . me?' I don't know how else to put it.

'If I didn't know you, that would be one thing, but now that I do?' She looks into my eyes. 'Perhaps I should be grateful for you, because who knows where I would have ended up without you.'

'Probably in police custody having brained Gwenda with a bedpan.'

Gillian laughs. 'Probably,' she agrees. 'What about you? How are you feeling about it, now that it's sunk in?'

I shake my head. 'Honestly, I don't know. Everything's still too close, somehow. I think I need to go back to London just to process it.' As I say it the weight of my impending return to the city weighs heavier on me than ever, but I know it's the right thing to do.

'Is it because you're worried what people will think? Because if it is, they'd rather you stayed, you know.'

I shake my head. 'That's something to think about, but

no. I need to get my head around this and I can't do it here.'
Not with Joe so near, I add silently. And I need to talk to
Mum. I take a deep breath. 'I need to go.'

Gillian nods sadly. 'You'll be missed.'

I think of Joe. God knows what he's thinking. And Seren,
and Bridget, and Petra. 'Can you explain for me?'

'I'll tell Bridget, but you should tell Seren. She'll be
concerned, and I have a soft spot for that girl . . . almost as
big as the one I have for you.'

Her sad smile almost brings tears to my eyes. 'Don't start
me off again, please!'

'Heavens! You'll wrinkle up like a prune. Let's make some
tea. But first, I've got to go through the palaver of a visit to
the toilet. Coming?' she asks.

'Of course,' I agree, and getting up off the sofa, we work
together to make ourselves more comfortable.

32

Goodbye, Wales

Terrible doesn't even begin to describe how badly I slept. To start with I couldn't get to sleep, so after an hour of restlessness with everything pulsing through my head, I got up and packed, even though I had to tiptoe around so as not to wake Gillian. Not that I think she was asleep, because when I put a bag on the landing, there was a faint glow coming from downstairs, but since we've said all that can be said, I left her to the e-reader. After that, I lay awake with everything Mum ever said about my parentage scrolling through my head. I must have fallen asleep eventually, but I woke up all too early this morning still in full possession of the miserable facts. The main fact being that, the truth, which, if I'd heard it two weeks ago by myself, would have made very little difference to me, is now devastating. It hurts Gillian, Mum, me, and it drowns all possibility of a relationship with Joe as effectively as if I hit an iceberg at full speed. Though, I suppose I should be grateful our intimacy didn't go any further than it did.

I sigh and pull the blanket off my face and heave myself out of bed. I get dressed and lumber downstairs with one of my bags. In the bathroom, I use the shock of the cold water to brace myself for the day ahead, and go and make us some tea.

Gillian isn't asleep either. She's sitting up in bed with my e-reader, calm but exhausted, and gives only a flicker of a smile as I put a mug down next to her.

'Bad night?' she asks, eyeing the bags under my eyes.

'Not the best. You?'

She frowns at the e-reader. 'I read a whole book, but now I'm thinking that *The Picture of Dorian Gray* possibly wasn't the best choice. Still leaving?' she asks lightly.

I pull a face. 'I was thinking it might be better if I slide off before Joe gets here.' *If he gets here.*

Gillian pats my hand. 'Call Bridget. She'll understand, and what's more, she'll be awake.' Gillian looks significantly at her clock, which shows it's only just past 7a.m. 'She always was an early riser.'

'Thanks.'

Gillian dips her head and I go into the kitchen to ring Bridget.

Bridget picks up almost immediately, and perhaps because she can hear the strain in my voice, says she'll be right over.

I help Gillian up and load my car as we wait, then make up a tray of coffee and biscuits, neither of which Gillian and I can face.

Bridget comes straight in, and raises an eyebrow. 'What's happened?' and with a commendable succinctness Gillian tells her exactly what we found in the studio. 'I'm just hoping that Marion was the only one apart from Dolores that Mike slept with,' says Gillian. My eyes dart to her in dismay. I hadn't even thought of that! 'But poor Ella here might be his progeny.'

'Bloody hell,' says Bridget, her eyes wide as she chomps into a ginger nut. 'He just keeps on throwing punches, doesn't he?'

'And I'm not sure I can roll with this one,' I admit.

'Well, I'm afraid it's about to get more interesting,' Bridget says, and she nods towards the window to where Petra is parking up.

'Hell,' growls Gillian as the front door slams and Petra marches into the kitchen and glares at us with her arms crossed.

'What the bloody hell have you done to Joe?' she demands. 'And you'd better make it good, or so help me there's going to be some trouble!'

I stare at her, unsure what to say.

'Petra, this isn't any of your—' begins Gillian, but Petra turns on her.

'The hell it isn't! I know you don't want us to sell the cottage, and that you don't think we deserve it, but Mike left it to *us* in his will, not Ella, and it's *our* choice what we do with it, so whatever leverage you've used on Joe, stop it!'

'What?' I ask, flummoxed.

'Joe came back yesterday saying we should sign it over to you!' Petra's eyes bore into mine. 'I don't know what you two have said, but you've done a real number on him. He's a mess!'

I close my eyes, but it only makes me see him more vividly so I open them again. 'Petra, I didn't ask for the cottage and I don't want it.' She doesn't look convinced. 'I never did want it and I won't accept it,' I add.

'Then why is Joe so determined you should have it?'

I glance at Gillian and she nods. 'Because we think Mike might be my father.'

Her eyes widen and she looks from me, to Gillian, to Bridget and sits down with a woomph on the sofa. Dust motes dance around her.

'But I thought you and Joe were . . .?' She stops. 'Did you know?'

I swallow uncomfortably. 'I didn't even suspect.'

Petra's eyes stray to Gillian and back to me. 'How did you find out?'

'We found a painting of Mum in the studio, and I came along nine months later.'

'But that doesn't mean . . .' She looks at everyone. 'That's not proof. I mean, there are DNA tests and things?'

'Her mother acted very oddly when she left here,' says Gillian.

'But . . .?' Petra is having just as much trouble with this as the rest of us. 'But you and Joe?' she says again, looking at me.

I shake my head, blinking back tears.

'Shit!' she says succinctly, and slumps back on the sofa. 'I'm sorry I . . . Oh, I don't know. I'm just . . . sorry, I suppose.' She looks at me anxiously, not realising that I actually think more of her for being upset about Joe than she realises.

I smile weakly. 'This has nothing to do with the cottage, and I don't want it. That's just Joe overreacting; being all honourable.'

Petra gets up. 'I can see that,' she says, nodding. 'In that case, I'll leave you to it. I'm sorry for butting in,' and she sounds like she means it.

I shake my head to show it doesn't matter, and Bridget and Gillian and I watch each other as Petra lets herself out and drives away.

'Well, that gave her something to think about and no mistake,' says Bridget. 'Ginger nut,' she offers, holding out the packet. 'Good for queasiness,' she adds, so I take one.

'Best thing you can do right now is go over and see Seren,' Gillian says. 'Get some fresh air, but call in on your way back. I don't want you heading back to London without saying goodbye.' She fixes me with a look, and I nod contritely. Bridget pats me on the shoulder as I pass, and after a reassuring nod from both of them, I pick up my keys and jacket.

The drive up to Seren's is beautiful in the early morning sunshine. The first lambs are in the fields and the daffodils nod at the roadside, defying my first dark, dank impression of the valley. I pull into their yard and I'm serenaded by their dogs in their kennels, but there's very little warmth in the sun, and I do up my jacket.

Seren opens the back door at my first knock and grins at me. The whole family are at the kitchen table eating breakfast and Huw calls through for me to join them. It looks comfortable and homely, but it takes Seren just one glance to see that something's wrong.

'Come on, let's get some fresh air,' she says. She pushes her feet into some wellies, takes my hand and leads me outside. We walk over to the section of yard wall that overlooks the entire valley. I can even see Gillian's from here.

'I have to go home,' I tell her without preamble.

Seren keeps a tight hold on my hand. 'What's happened?' she asks gently, and I tell her. I tell her about the paintings, about Mum and about Petra this morning.

Seren shakes her head. 'I can't believe it. After everything with Dolores, I thought we were done with nasty surprises.'

I take a deep breath. 'As it turns out, she was just the tip of the iceberg. I almost wish for Gillian's sake that I never came.'

'Don't say that!' says Seren, squeezing my hand. 'You've done so much – you got Gillian back in the land of the living, and Bryn, too, from what Joe said. You made Bridget's and my lives a hundred times better and Joe and Gillian are speaking again. Can't you see you made everything better? In fact, it's been exciting from the moment you got here. I'm a little scared of how dull it's going to be without you.'

I give her an empty smile. 'Hill Start Art will take off and the place will be busier than ever, you'll see.'

'Maybe, but it's not the same as having a best friend here.' Seren bites her lip. 'Cup of tea?' she asks hopefully, and her smile drops as I shake my head.

I can't pretend to be happy right now.

'What a mess,' says Seren miserably and pulls me into a hug. 'I wish you weren't going. I'll really miss you, but I can see that you need to go.'

'Thanks. I'll miss you, too,' I mumble into her shoulder.

She half lets go and we stare down the valley arm in arm. I can see Bryn's bungalow, the pub, even Bridget's cottage from here. Further up, there are more cottages. One of them must be Petra and Joe's. One has smoke coming out of a chimney, so I guess it must be that one. He's probably inside struggling with this just as much as I am, and I feel bad for leaving without talking it through, but I don't know what else to do. I can't make it better and I can't change it.

I smile at Seren. 'Come on, I have something for you,' and I lead her over to the car. I lean in and take out the sketch I did of Bethan and Bill the lamb, and hand it to her. 'A goodbye present,' I say, and she shakes her head in wonder at it.

'I love it!' She gives me a fierce one-armed hug, grips tight and lets go, and looks at the drawing again. She smiles delightedly. 'You've got them exactly!'

I stare along the valley at the small dots of lambs gambolling around the ewes and sniff to stave off the tears. 'I'll miss you all.'

Seren gives me another squeeze. 'Don't let this stop you visiting. It's more reason, not less, if you're proper family.' But she knows it changes everything.

I nod and she hugs me again. 'Bloody Mike,' she mutters

and, smiling sadly, she watches me get in the car and waves me off.

I pull into Gillian's yard, and I don't know whether to be relieved or upset that Joe's estate isn't parked beside Bridget's old green Ford. I vowed as I left Seren's that Fate should decide whether I talk to him before I leave, but now I'm back here, I don't know if I left her enough time to get him up, in the car and over here. But then, if she needed time, I'm sure Fate would have found some way of taking it, so maybe it's for the best.

Bridget and Gillian look up sympathetically as I come in.

'Everything all right with Seren?' asks Gillian.

I nod jerkily, like a Thunderbird puppet. 'I might as well make a move.'

'Sure you don't want any breakfast?' It's pure politeness. Gillian knows I can't eat, but I appreciate it all the same.

'No, thanks. Will you two be all right until Joe gets here?'

'Of course we will,' says Bridget.

'And can you ask Huw or Joe to rewire the floodlight?' I ask her. 'I know everything should be fine now, but just for peace of mind.'

'Of course,' agrees Bridget.

I hold it together as I hug them, and Gillian makes slow, laborious progress to the front door to watch me get in the car and drive out of the yard. I even lower the window and shout goodbyes as I drive out the gate, but as I pass Gillian's garden dotted with daffodils, pass Bryn at his gate, who surprisingly raises his hand, it feels more and more like I'm trying to swallow past a bar of soap, until tears jolt down my face as I jerk in and out of the potholes.

At the junction I pause to wipe my face and take one last look at the valley, crowned with clouds, while the sun pierces through with rays of sunshine. It's stark, but utterly beautiful;

almost unbearably so. I turn past the pub, which is mercifully quiet and go over the humpback bridge, where Bozz is sitting on the wall.

I slow and we look into each other's eyes. It's like he knows. I gulp at the lump in my throat as I pass him and it feels a hell of a lot like I'm driving in the wrong direction, but what choice do I have? I'm being chased from the valley by the memory of a ghost, and it's the only way I can go, so I dry my face on my sleeve and get on with it.

33

Hello to London

It's a long drive back, with too much time to think about being Mike's daughter. I've tried to feel happy, or sad, or even angry about it, but I feel no connection with him at all. Perhaps it's because I never met him, or maybe it's as a consequence of knowing what he did to Gillian, Bridget, Mum and Dolores and feeling unable to be anything but disapproving of him. I don't know, but if anything he's just a collection of stories, like a myth or a legend . . . or maybe even the bogeyman. Perhaps, I'd feel differently if I'd seen a photograph of him or felt more of a connection with his paintings, but as it is, I feel nothing. All my grief is attached to Gillian and Joe, Mum and Seren, and having to leave the valley. Hell, I even feel more of a connection with Bozz! And what's worse, I see no up-side of knowing . . . although I suppose it explains where I got my artistic tendencies . . . and it explains all the snide comments Mum made about Gillian all these years, *and* why she's avoided telling me who my father is. In fact, from that perspective, it explains a lot.

Except where that leaves me.

Do I carry on as before? Sweep it under the carpet and act like I don't know . . . or do I confront Mum? They say let sleeping dogs lie, but what if they've savaged half the household in the night?

I pull up in front of the flat emotionally exhausted, and my flatmate greets me with a smile that, if she was one of Mike's paintings, would have a note on the back saying 'Oh God! There goes our blissful privacy.'

'Hi,' I say.

Her boyfriend is spread-eagled over the entire length of our sofa, and shows no sign of moving. I carry my things through and silently pass them as I go back for a second trip, aware I'm even more of an intruder than when I left. I plonk the last few things down on my bed, sit on it with my back against the wall, and call Vivienne.

'Hi, I'm back.'

'But you don't want to be, I'm guessing?' asks Vivienne, amused at my flat tone.

'Well, who'd choose to go back to work at their old job?' I can't keep the tremor out of my voice.

'Oh Ella. That's not the whole story, is it? You're back three days early. What happened?'

I do my best to keep my voice level. 'Everyone's fine. Joe's looking after Gillian; Bridget and Seren are busy with Hill Start Art; and George and Bryn are set to have their businesses augmented by the people coming into the valley. It's practically sorted. They don't need me.'

Vivienne hesitates. 'So, you're telling me, that from being a founder member of this brilliant Hill Start Art thing and a vital support for Gillian, with a budding relationship to boot, you're no longer needed?' Her incredulity radiates down the phone line.

'It . . . well . . . something happened.'

'I guessed that. And it had better be something major because otherwise I think you're a complete dunce for coming back.'

I draw my knees up and hug them. 'We found some paintings and it seems that I might actually be—' I take a deep breath '—Mike's daughter.'

'Holy cow!' Her astonishment hits my ear, and I flinch.
'Quite.'

'Which makes you and Joe . . .?'

'Cousins.'

'Shit! Come over,' she orders. 'We've got wine.'

I love her, but I just can't do company right now. I take
a deep breath. 'No, I'm fine. I have washing to do, and a
few things to sort out.'

'You have plenty of time for that. Come over.'

'What I really mean is I want to curl up into a ball and
sleep 'til Monday.'

Vivienne hesitates, and I'm so touched at her obvious
concern it almost undoes me. 'All right, but let me know if
you need me.' Her voice is firm.

'OK.'

'Day or night,' she adds.

'OK,' I promise, even though I won't, and as Vivienne
hangs up, I let the phone fall into my lap.

I stare at my bookshelf full of films and books, many of
them about real-life people who made radical and wonderful
changes to their lives: people who achieved fulfilment and
happiness. None of them had to contend with something
like this – their paths were set for success. But then, I suppose
they wouldn't have written their books or made their films
if they hadn't made it, because the people who fail just chalk
it up to experience, say it wasn't meant to be, and quietly
move on.

So why can't I shake the feeling it *was* meant to be?
Relatives, relationships, best friends and art? It all looked so
promising.

I rake my fingers across my scalp.

Maybe I should resign myself to the fact that Fate's plan
really *was* just about Gillian from the start. After all, she's
no longer alone, she's no longer hiding from what Mike did,

and she's no longer contending with Dolores, so maybe I shouldn't be surprised Fate has landed me back on the same square I was on before I left – 'Do not pass go. Do not collect £200.' And, to be fair, what have I actually lost? ('Better to have loved and lost, than . . .' Oh, shut up!)

Maybe this is the kick up the bum I need to sort myself out?

I try to feel positive about that, but as I glance at my bags by the door, I'm reminded of what Gillian's regatta friend said: 'You want to be somewhere else.' Yes, I do. But since I can't go there, perhaps it's time to trawl the Internet for a new flat and a new job, because if there's one thing I've learnt, it's that I don't belong here.

34

A Hard Day's Day

I've been back for over a week and I still haven't talked to Mum. Truth is, I don't know how to ask, but also I'm a little scared of opening up old wounds and even more scared of hearing her confirm it's true.

As for everything else, I've settled into my old routine with an inevitability that's depressing. So much so, if it weren't for the drawings I'm doing in the evenings, the research on job possibilities, and all the ideas I keep having for Hill Start Art, it would almost be like the last few weeks never happened. But they did, and it's occurred to me that, even though I'm not up there, there's nothing to stop me forwarding a whole set of ideas to Bridget, because I like the idea of helping, even if only from a distance.

It doesn't stop me missing everybody, though. Especially when I flick back through the sketchbook at all the pictures I did when I was there. From the drawing of Bryn and the one of Gillian absorbed in my e-reader, to all the pictures of Joe, one or two of which, where he was looking straight at me, I still have to skip past. And like a glutton for punishment, I've also been reading Joe's thrillers, which are excellent, if a little gory in places. I cling to them every night, reading voraciously, and go to sleep imagining Joe typing away on his laptop in between shifts helping Gillian. And it doesn't help that Vivienne, who's of the firm opinion I should go back, keeps sending me sheep emojis.

But oddly, one of the things I find I'm missing most is me. I was different there. Here, I mill through the days in a torpor of politeness and manners tempered against the background radiation of angry call centre calls. There, I bounced off Gillian's acerbic retorts and stringent opinions, thrived on Seren's enthusiasm and kindness, enjoyed Bridget's implacability, and was reassured by Bryn's presence at the gate. As for Joe's honesty, genuine care and thoughtfulness . . . well, I miss everyone's clean-cut sincerity and reality.

Then there are the little things. I miss Gillian cutting through the crap and Joe telling me how his detective is getting on. I miss hearing the tennis-like banter between him and Gillian. I miss knowing he'll be there when I get back, or the certainty that he'll come and get me if I'm stranded. I miss the surprise of a cup of tea landing next to me. I miss hearing him read aloud and I miss seeing him in the armchair, deep in a book, with that look of concentration in his eyes and the smile playing on his mouth. When I close my eyes I can still see it.

But then I remind myself why I left. Because despite missing them like crazy, the guilt over Mike doesn't seem to be lessening. It's like an ugly, underdeveloped chick; all claws, half-formed wings and beak, turning over inside my stomach, becoming angrier and spikier by the day.

It even bothers me here at work. I almost snapped at someone yesterday when they asked me what I was going to do about their account, which isn't like me at all. I used to be patience personified, but now, I feel like at any minute I could—

My manager taps my partition. It's her usual reprimand for chatting, but I'm not – I'm tapping through plan options, trying to get a particularly harassed mum onto a better payment plan. I look up in irritation, but to my surprise she hands me a note. I take it and read it as the mum I'm on a call with fends off her small offspring. Apparently, I have a personal call waiting on another line, which almost never happens, and my manager doesn't like that it's happened now. She taps her watch to show I should be quick about it, and my heart races as I switch the lady's plan and try to hurry her grateful thanks. I smooth my hands on my trousers and press the extension number.

'Hello?' I ask tentatively, hoping against hope—

'Hi, Ella, it's Petra.'

Petra? Several ghastly possibilities involving Gillian, or Joe, or . . . 'Hi, Petra?'

'Hi. Your flatmate gave me your number and I know it's weird I'm calling—'

'No, no, it's fine,' I hastily assure her. 'What's up?'

'Well, I talked to Joe and even Gillian about the possibility of you being Mike's daughter and, well, to be honest . . . they told me to leave it alone, but I've thought long and hard about this and . . . I really don't think you are!'

For a second my stomach floats, then sinks back into place. 'Petra, I really wish I wasn't, but I'm afraid it looks pretty likely.'

'But are you sure?' she persists. 'Only, Joe said Mike wrote in his letter that he never slept with any of those women, except Dolores, so what makes you think he slept with your mum?'

'Don't you think he'd have lied about that?' I ask gently.

'No, actually, I don't.'

Her childlike conviction is endearing, but since even Gillian suspects I'm Mike's daughter . . . 'Look, Petra, whatever happens, I'm not going to challenge you over the cottage—'

She tuts impatiently. 'I know that, and I'm not talking

about the cottage. I'm pointing out that he said he *didn't* sleep with any of them.'

I can't believe I'm going to have to explain this. 'Look, Petra, he wouldn't have wanted to look bad, and he didn't want Gillian to burn his clothes and chuck him out. Can't you see he had plenty of reasons to lie?'

'But what if he didn't?'

I leave a long pause. 'What do you mean, what if he didn't?'

'What if he told the truth?'

'Then there's still the nine months gap between Mum's visit and my birth to explain, and also the rift between her and Gillian to factor in.'

My manager taps her watch again, and I give her an awkward smile.

Petra sighs like I'm being stubborn. 'But he didn't believe in lying.'

I stare at my keyboard in disbelief. 'What do you mean he didn't *believe* in it?'

Petra exhales. 'When I was small I went to stay with Gillian and Mike. I hated it, and I lied about how bad it was to my parents. I made it sound terrible; I said they hated me, laughed at me and only played with Joe. Mum was furious and was straight on the phone to Mike. Of course he put her straight, but afterwards he gave me a good talking to. He told me I should never lie; "leave things out, or stay quiet if you must," he said, "but lies always bite you in the bum." He made me promise, and in return he promised me he would never lie, either.'

I almost laugh. 'But he was talking to a child. That's the kind of thing people say to small children.'

'Except he never spoke down to us like that. Gillian didn't either. They expected us to take responsibility for our actions, which I found unnerving – still do, to be fair,' she says with that turn of humour that makes me like her, almost despite myself.

'There were so many women, though,' I point out.

'But he didn't sleep with them. I know because I spoke to them at the funeral.'

'What?'

'I saw all the women carrying orchids and I wanted to know why, so I spoke to them at the wake. They each said Mike changed their lives. One said she travelled the world thanks to him, another said she started making amphorae, which she's now world famous for, a third said she designs fabric, but they all said he challenged their belief in themselves and made them see what they truly wanted. That's why they paid tribute to him with the orchids – they wanted to thank him, nothing more. At the time, I just thought it was a nice gesture.'

Could it really be that simple? Just a case of mixed messages? Apart from Dolores, of course. 'Have you told Gillian this?'

'You think she'd listen to me?' Petra scoffs. 'But you see my point: if Mike didn't lie, then . . .' I so desperately want to believe her, but I'm also almost scared to hope.

'. . . I might not be his daughter,' I say finally, heat zinging through me.

'No, so can you check?'

'Check?'

'Ask your mum if it's true.'

I fall silent. She doesn't know what she's asking. You can't casually ask someone if they had sex with their sister's partner. I should know, I've been putting it off for over a week.

'Please?' adds Petra. 'This place has been like a morgue since you left. All Gillian does is read, Joe's been brooding and glares at his laptop rather than writing, Seren flutters around trying to make sure everyone's all right, but she's not happy, and Bridget has been bossing us about like a sergeant major, so even she's missing you. So can you make sure it's true before you turn your back on them all?'

I feel bad for not seeing her good motives, and I really don't like the image of me turning my back on them. 'It isn't an easy thing to ask someone,' I point out.

'I know, and I wouldn't ask except . . .' She sighs and comes to a decision. 'When Joe came here and I went to stay in London all those years ago he wrote me loads of letters telling me all the things he and Huw got up to; from tadpoles to wall mending, from building dams to digging for Welsh gold. And do you know what? I envied him. Not that I wanted to do any of it, but I envied how happy he was. But as he got older, he lost that happiness. I thought it was a normal part of growing up, but then you arrived and suddenly he was like that again. He was like that about his writing, about Gillian, about seeing Seren and Huw – and about you. So *please* can you check? For me?'

I swallow hard as my manager leans on my partition. I mouth 'sorry' at her and 'family emergency' for good measure. 'I'll think about it,' I say quietly to Petra.

'Thanks,' she says meekly.

'But there's every possibility you're still related to me,' I warn her. After all, who else could my father be?

'That's not a problem – I always suspected we'd end up related one way or another,' and hearing the smile in her voice, I smile too.

I hold up a finger to denote one minute, and my manager walks off. 'Can I ask you something, in the spirit of a concerned relation?'

'Yes?'

I hesitate for only a fraction of a second. 'Are you pregnant?'

There's a gasp at the other end of the line. 'How did you—?'

'Morning sickness the night I went out with Gareth, am I right? No alcohol at the pub, and also your need to sell the cottage.'

'Yes,' she says with dismay. 'Does Joe know?'

'I don't think so, but Gillian does, so you should tell him.'

'Are you sure? She didn't say anything,' she says, surprised.

'No. I think she reckoned it was your business, but you should tell Joe.' My manager taps on my partition and I nod briskly. 'Sorry Petra, I *really* have to go.' I inject as much regret into my voice as I can, so she knows it isn't by choice. 'Tell Joe.'

'And ask your mum,' she says, and with a hurried goodbye, I hang up as my manager holds her distinctly frosty expression for a charged ten seconds, and moves on down the room, not happy, but satisfied. I, on the other hand, feel like I've eaten five packets of marshmallows, drunk two giant Cokes and just felt the roller-coaster safety-bar clamp down.

Shit. How the hell am I going to ask Mum?

I know I'm delaying the inevitable, but on my way back, I detour to my old tube stop. I considered visiting Vivienne, but I already know what she thinks, and I'm not sure I want to admit the possibility of Mike not being my father until I know there's any validity to it – I couldn't take the let-down and if-onlys later on. But a kind stranger? No recourse, no consequences.

I follow the sound of 'Here Comes the Sun' and find the tattooed busker and his dog in the same spot I saw them last time.

He smiles at me and strums the final chords. 'Not often I get a return visit. Did Fate find you?' He looks pointedly at my work clothes.

'She did, actually. I went to Wales, met a relation who turned my life upside down, and came back.'

'I'm impressed – apart from the coming back part.'

'Well, that was sort of forced on me,' I admit.

'Did you want more advice?' he dangles teasingly.

'I'm not sure, really, but what I've been wondering is: what made you choose this life?'

'Ah, my guidance qualifications,' he translates with a laugh. I want to deny it, but I guess that is what I'm asking. He puts his guitar down in its case. He lets the lid fall closed and crouches down to stroke his dog. 'I was a stockbroker; worked all the hours God sent. It was my life and my meaning, and one day I looked at my Rolex Submariner and realised it represented the futility of my life, because its purpose wasn't to tell me the time; its purpose was to intimidate and subjugate my colleagues, who I didn't like, and who, in turn, didn't like, value or respect me. Don't get me wrong, they liked, valued and respected the position I held, but *I* wasn't important. Anyone could be me. I was just the one wearing the watch and only as good as my last day's trading, and if I dropped by the wayside, someone would replace me without blinking, and what would be left? Nothing, because as a person, I was empty, so I quit. I sold everything, donated the money, and now, in the evenings, I work with kids in a youth centre, and during the day I do this,' he says, indicating his guitar, 'to remind me how far I've come.'

'Are you happy?'

'Yes, I can honestly say I am. I have twenty-seven kids who do better because of me, I have enough money to get by, and every so often, I meet someone worth talking to.' He smiles at me. 'So what are you grappling with?'

I take a deep breath. 'I have to ask somebody something awful, and I'm scared.'

'Because it will hurt them?'

'Yes, and because it could hurt a lot of other people, depending on the answer.'

'You included?' he asks perceptively.

I bite my lip and nod.

'Is it your business?'

His eyes are both kind and concerned, and he *is* a youth worker, so he must have heard this kind of thing before. 'I need to ask my mum who my father is.'

'Wow. That's your business, all right.' He nods thoughtfully. 'OK, how about this: can you live with not asking?'

'No,' I realise. 'I have to know, but I'm scared of the answer.'

'And you think that's a reason not to ask?'

I shake my head. 'No. I'm just scared.'

'Scared of what?'

'Everything changing?'

He looks at me sympathetically. 'Everything changes whether you want it to or not.'

And as he says it, I realise he's right. I'm afraid of losing my relationship with Mum, but I'm already avoiding her. I'm afraid of losing everyone in Wales, but I already left. And I'm scared of being stuck here forever, unloved and unmotivated – all of which I am right now. Everything I'm scared of has already come to pass. I haven't got anything left to lose!

'You're right,' I say out loud. 'I'll ask her. Thanks.' I grin at him.

'Any time,' and giving him a little wave, I head back to the flat with him playing me out to 'Any Time at All'.

35

Tea and Sympathy, Coffee and . . .?

Lindi and her boyfriend fall silent as I walk into the kitchen. I don't think they mean to make me feel unwelcome, but they do nonetheless, so I make myself a cup of tea and a sandwich and go back to my room. I chew slowly and look at my phone between bites.

I have to do it face to face, so this is just a call to meet for coffee, but that doesn't stop me feeling seriously apprehensive. Putting my plate aside, I hoist my feet up onto my bed, scroll through my list of phone contacts and press the green icon. I squeeze my eyes closed and let the ringing sound drill through me and I almost drop the phone when she answers.

'Hi, Mum,' I say, getting a better grip on my phone.

'Ah, back in the land of the living? Is the job going OK?

'Yes, thanks.' I could back out and just have a casual chat, but what would be the point? I'd just find myself having to go through all this again. 'Umm, Mum, do you think we could meet up for coffee some time? I have something I want to ask you.'

Mum laughs. 'Sounds ominous.'

It's not too late – I could still back out. 'I need to ask you about something.' I try not to sound too serious, but Mum loses her cheerful tone.

'All right. How about tomorrow? It's Saturday, so I could meet you somewhere in town around eleven?' and we settle on a lovely little coffee shop I know that sells excellent éclairs.

I've arrived early, but considering my nerves have been ramping up ever since our call, I didn't see the point in waiting at the flat any longer. I take a seat, pleased that the coffee shop isn't that busy, and easily spot Mum as she walks in. She waves at me, and gestures that she's going to order coffee.

Stood at the counter, she looks smaller and more vulnerable than I remember her and I get up and hug her as soon as she comes over.

'I've ordered plenty of éclairs,' she says sitting down. 'I have a feeling we're going to need them. Right, where do you want to start?' She doesn't look as cross as I expected, just resigned.

I clear my throat. 'While I was at Gillian's, we found a picture . . . umm . . . painted by Mike? . . . of you in a shawl?'

'Oh, that!' Mum laughs. 'It was just some painting Mike did when I visited once. I'm surprised Gillian kept it.' She seems relieved it's just that, so much so I almost don't want to disappoint her, but I can't back out now.

'Was that visit nine months before I was born?' My words sit between us, and Mum folds in her lips and looks down at the table as the waitress arrives with a pot of coffee and a plate of éclairs. I shift back slightly so she can slide a plate in front of me, but my eyes don't move from Mum.

'Where are you going with this?' she asks as soon as the waitress leaves. All the lightness has fallen out of the conversation like rain.

I lick my lips, but my tongue is dry. 'Is Mike my father, Mum?'

There's a brief silence. Mum forces out a laugh. 'No! I'm surprised you'd even think that. With my own sister's partner?' She sounds scandalised, but I can feel her unease. There's something not quite right.

'Then *please* tell me what happened.'

Mum looks nervously at me, helps herself to an éclair, takes a bite and chews it thoughtfully before answering. 'Mike wanted to paint me. That's all there was to it.'

That isn't anywhere near all, I can feel it. 'Mum, I saw the painting. It tells a story . . . A story about someone who wanted more than to be painted . . . And whether he's my father or not, isn't it about time you told me who is?' My voice is calm, but I'm shaking inside.

Mum blows out a long sigh and pokes at the cream oozing from the choux. 'What the hell,' she mutters under her breath. 'You're probably right. It is time you knew, but I want you to know I'm not proud of it.' She takes a deep breath. 'I did want more, and I thought Mike did, too, but what you have to understand is, he had a way of focusing on you that made you feel like the centre of the universe. That, together with his enthusiasm and energy while he was painting me, made me think it was the start of something.'

'But he and Gillian—?'

'I know,' she cuts in sadly. 'But at the time, in my head, I reasoned that he wouldn't marry her, so he couldn't feel that strongly about her. Then, when he painted me and asked such deep, personal, core-of-the-soul-type questions – the kind that people don't usually ask – he made me question everything, from who I was, to where I was going in life. I started to wonder whether Gillian was on the right track, and I should throw caution to the wind, and I'm ashamed to say . . . I had an aberration and offered myself to him.'

I hold very still, trying not to imagine it and not to judge. Instead, I try to imagine what Mum was like back then. She would have been about thirty? Long since qualified as a solicitor, single, alone, old enough to know better . . . Or maybe that's the point. Perhaps she was lonely, trapped and fed up – not so far from how I've been feeling lately.

'Anyway, long story short, he declined,' she says quietly. 'And as I stood there humiliated,' she gulps, and her face suffuses with colour, 'he said, "Let me paint you like that. Let me capture that emotion," and it woke me up like nothing else! I slapped his face and never spoke to him again. So, no, Mike is not your father!'

I take an éclair and bite into it, trying to hide the weird gush of emotion pulsing through me, and watch her slurp down some coffee. 'So who is?' I ask with commendable calm.

'What?' she asks, still distracted by her remembered humiliation.

'Who *is* my father?' I don't want to push her, but I don't know when I'll get another chance to ask.

Mum looks down. 'To be honest, I'm not sure, really. I had a lot of alcohol, and there was this man who ran the local campsite. I think his wife had just left him? Well, *he* was lonely, and *I* was drunk and embarrassed. One thing led to another, and the next morning I woke up and got out of there. I'm afraid I was only with him for one night, so no emotional connection, or romantic attachment.' She finally looks at me. 'Sorry if you were hoping for something more.'

But even as she watches me I can feel the heat of a flush rising up my neck. 'Was his name Bryn, Mum?' It's not like there are any other campsites around there.

'Umm . . . the name rings a bell . . . yes, that could have been his name,' she agrees.

I try to keep my mental balance on a pitching ship. Bryn.

Bryn of the bungalow, who stands at his gate, watching with his collie by his side . . .? She's still watching me.

'Mum, I've met him,' I say quietly.

'Did you like him?' she asks instantly.

I don't know why, but the question catches me off guard. I stare at her as I try to make sense of it.

Did I like Bryn? Bryn, who looked after Bozz and helped Gillian. Bryn, who left jars and other offerings on her doorstep, who picked me up when I fell . . . Bryn, of the utterly beautiful carvings. For a second I feel like the little man on the raft inside the whale's mouth. Or maybe the dragon waking up to find someone peering at him. OK. Bryn . . .

'Yes,' I say quietly, and Mum smiles. I picture her younger, pregnant, alone. 'But can I ask you one other thing that's always bothered me?' Mum nods. 'If Granny and Grandpa were so against Gillian living in sin, why didn't they shun you when you had me?'

Mum blushes uncomfortably and her mouth twists. 'Ah, that's another thing I'm not proud of. I implied I'd been led astray by Gillian. I didn't think it would make any difference to her, seeing as her relationship with our parents was already irretrievable, but I knew it would be enough for them to lay the blame firmly at her door and not send me packing.'

'Poor Gillian.'

Mum nods. 'I should probably apologise to her. Do you think she'll accept it?'

I smile at the thought of Gillian's relief at discovering Mike didn't betray her after all, and I take Mum's hand. 'I expect so. Underneath it all, she's very decent,' and taking another éclair each, we change the subject.

On the tube back, the truth of everything Mum said starts to hit me and seeing as the carriage is almost empty, I go against convention and call Vivienne. She listens avidly as I quietly tell her everything.

'But that's amazing!' she says as I reveal it's Bryn.

'Is it? I'm still digesting it.' That and several éclairs.

'Of course you are right now, but it's the missing piece of who you are. It's the answer to the question of where you're from.'

'I suppose it is.'

'You're damned right it is! And who was the first person you drew when you got to Wales?'

'Bryn!'

'And who's been like your aunt's fairy godmother . . . apart from you?'

I can't help laughing. 'Bryn.'

'For God's sake, he's honest, kind, loyal and he likes animals. You should be pleased, especially considering the alternative.'

I try to think straight. 'I am, I think. It's just he's so insular.'

'Wouldn't you be if your wife left you and your sister was a raving lunatic . . . oh God! Does that make her your aunt?'

Shit, it does. 'And Gareth, my cousin,' I add, and hearing the horror in my voice I laugh. 'I'm glad I never saw him in a romantic light.'

'Unlike Joe.'

Unlike Joe . . . 'Who's no blood relation at all,' I breathe. That thought's been pricking at me ever since Mum told me, but now that I'm free to admit it out loud a warmth spreads through me like a constriction bandage has been cut from my ribcage.

'You should tell him,' says Vivienne.

Yes, I should, but I didn't even say goodbye, so God knows what Joe thinks of me. I push the thought to the back of my mind. 'I should tell Gillian, and Seren and . . . Bryn.' I feel the first quaver of anxiety. 'Do you think he'll be pleased?'

'Who, Bryn? Of course he'll be pleased! Gorgeous girl like you, he'll consider himself damned lucky!'

'Thanks.' I laugh, but still feel uneasy: a daughter is a lot to land on someone.

'Now, get yourself together and make some plans to get back there.'

'To Wales?'

'Of course to Wales! It's where you belong, isn't it?'

I picture Gillian, glaring at me over the e-reader I left with her, Seren welcoming me into her kitchen and telling me to catch whichever errant child or animal is heading for the door, Bryn shyly showing me his carvings, Bridget bossing me about fondly, and Joe . . . Joe sitting quietly in one of Gillian's armchairs grinning at me as Gillian makes some particularly outrageous comment, and putting his book down to get us all a whiskey. I can almost feel the place wrap itself around me like a protective mantle . . . like a home.

'Yes. That's where I want to be. In fact, it's everything I ever wanted,' and, as I say it, I can feel the ringing truth of it.

'Everything? Then come and get the car!' orders Vivienne.

Hanging up, I get off at the next stop and change tube lines.

But as I take a seat on the next train, I wonder if that's actually true. I take out the list I wrote a few weeks ago and read it through. It seems like, back then, I didn't have a clue what I wanted, and seeing as I have a few stops before Notting Hill Gate, I take a pen from my purse and quickly correct it.

What do I want?

1. A place of my own. To be somewhere I feel at home – somewhere I'm welcomed and wanted, and where I make a difference.

2. ~~A career.~~ To do something I enjoy and earn my keep.
3. ~~Fulfilment? Or at least be able~~ to feel proud of myself. <u>And</u> help others achieve their dreams.
4. ~~To find some way of putting everything bad that happened with my drawing behind me.~~ To learn lessons from what happened to me and stop others from making the same mistakes.
5. ~~A man who actually wants to spend time with me, who's interested and interesting, and who's there when I need him, (or a cat).~~ Joe (and Bozz and Pompom).
6. ~~To find out who my dad is.~~ To find out Bryn is happy about me being his daughter.

I grin to myself. They're all achievable, and I have plans for number four, but one thing's clear – they all hinge on being in Wales, and if I'm fast, I might even make it there tonight.

36

My White Knight

Vivienne's encouragement and excitement has carried me a long way, but now I've sat in traffic for over three hours with a whiney voice inside my head asking 'What if Joe's angry I left without saying goodbye?', 'What if Bryn doesn't want a daughter?', 'What if Bridget resents my interference?' and worst of all, 'What if I can't make this work?' I have to admit I'm getting seriously anxious. The main thing keeping me going is the thought of Gillian's relief that Mike isn't my dad, and Seren's delight I've come back. But Joe . . . ? Bryn . . . ? How they'll feel, I have no idea.

I just keep reminding myself that there's very little in London to go back to. There's Vivienne and Clara, of course – they tried to *give* me their car, only reluctantly accepting my cheque at the last second, but apart from them the job's rubbish, and my flatmate's joy was almost insulting. Not, she kept telling me, because I was potentially leaving for good, but because she's never felt this way about a boyfriend before – and to be fair, she did her best to look sad as I threw my stuff into bags and boxes. She even kicked her boyfriend into helping me carry things down, and with his help, we strapped my wicker shelves to the car roof. It had seemed like a good idea at the time, but thanks to how they're tied through the windows, I'm now freezing and deaf from the whistling. I've also been praying it doesn't rain, because I don't fancy arriving trailing swirling bamboo like curling ribbon behind me, no matter how festive it looks. Luckily, even though it's now dark, it's stayed dry and I negotiate the humpbacked bridge with a surge of what could be either excitement or apprehension. But I'm glad to feel there's also some relief mixed in there, because even just being here, I know I don't want to go back to London.

I pass the well-lit pub and turn up the track, trying to keep my nerves under control, but as I roll in and out of the potholes, it's difficult to know if it's the poor road surface or my anxiety making me feel sick. I slow as I reach Bryn's gate. I crane my neck to see if he's around, but even though the kitchen light's on, there's no shift of the curtains. I picture him carving a chess piece in his kitchen, hearing my car trundle by, relieved he doesn't have to get up to check who it is any more. Not sure if I'm disappointed or not, I drive on and pull up on the verge outside Gillian's gate.

I get out, and recognise Huw and Seren's 4x4 and Bridget's Ford as well as Gillian's Land Rover in the yard. There's no sign of Joe's estate. Even so, fright zaps through me like an electric current, but it's too late to change my mind now. I walk meekly to the front door, triggering the yard light, and close my eyes as I knock. I count my breaths, out, in, out, in. There's the sound of muffled footsteps, Seren opens the door and squeals!

'Oh my God! It's Ella,' she shouts through to the kitchen and yanks me inside and straight into a hug.

'What?' asks Bridget coming into the hall, and her mouth falls open. 'It's her,' she confirms to Gillian, going back in.

'If it really is, tell her to damned well come in here!' Gillian shouts from the kitchen. 'I want to see her,' and Seren closes the front door, bustles me through and stares delightedly from me to Gillian to Bridget.

'Hi, Gillian,' I say warmly.

'Well knock me down with a feather,' says Bridget, subsiding onto the sofa like I've done just that, and Gillian frowns at her.

'Good to see you,' she says sternly, levering herself up from her chair, and she pulls me into a fierce hug. Bozz watches us from the dresser, giving me a disdainful where-have-you-been glare. 'Now, what's this all about?' she demands, letting go, and a smile sneaks onto her face.

'I have some news,' I say succinctly.

'I gathered that. What is it?'

I look from her, to Seren and Bridget. 'I'm not Mike's daughter.'

'. . . Not?' Gillian sits down heavily and takes a deep breath.

'No,' I say, bursting with happiness.

Gillian breathes hard. 'Are you sure?' she demands.

'Yes, I asked Mum.'

'Blimey, I'd never have dared!'

'No, well I nearly didn't, but Petra called me yesterday and convinced me I should.'

'Petra?'

'Yes. She was convinced Mike wouldn't lie, and said I should make sure, so I bit the bullet and contacted Mum. Turns out Mike turned her down and she . . . well, she slept with Bryn.'

Gillian takes a few more deep breaths and starts laughing.

I glare at her. 'It's not funny. The poor man has a daughter he doesn't know about!'

She's still laughing, but she manages to settle it enough to talk. 'Calm down, it's relief, and as far as Bryn's concerned . . . the poor man's lonely.' There's gentleness and affection in her voice. 'He loved his wife, he loved his parents, but they're gone and his sister's an absolute nightmare, as you well know. Actually, doesn't that make her your aunt?'

'Yes,' I say, resignedly. 'I'm clearly meant to have a loony aunt in my life, and since you turned out to be normal—'

'Don't count your chickens! One word about me being normal and I'll wear a foil hat and give everyone a glazed grin.'

'Interesting?' I try and Seren laughs.

'Better,' agrees Gillian.

'Eccentric?'

'Careful!' warns Bridget.

'Yes, yes, enough! Now, how long are you staying?' she asks.

I can't help pulling an anxious face. 'I've packed up everything and brought it with me, so if you're all right with it—?'

'Of course I'm bloody all right with it! I loved having you here!'

'I'll need to find a job.'

'Does administrator to the whims of Mike's pedantic sodding will sound good enough to you? I should warn you, it'll mean working with Bridget.'

I grin at Bridget. 'In which case, shouldn't you check with her first?'

Bridget flaps her hand. 'Are you joking? I'm bloody delighted. I've been telling them how we need someone like you around, with fresh ideas and a decent head on their shoulders.'

'The rest of us don't pass muster, apparently!' gripes Gillian.

'And Joe?' His name escapes before I can stop it.

'Don't get me started! He's been moping about, which he says he isn't, but he is and if I hear one more sigh I'll cosh him with the cat, *who*, by the way, has been waiting for you on the front doorstep with that ridiculous fluffball of a dog, Pompom, ever since you left!'

'Bozz has?' I glance at him, but he still looks furious.

'Yes! Used to be a decent animal before you came along. Now he spends half his time with Petra's ridiculous frou-frou dog, and the rest sleeping on your bed, like some dog on his dead master's grave—'

We all fall silent as a car pulls into the yard outside.

'Oh my God, that'll be Joe!' squeals Seren. Her eyes are wide and she's jumping about on the spot. 'This is so romantic!'

'Go out and surprise him,' suggests Gillian, and with my heart rocketing around my chest, I open the front door and find Joe standing in the middle of the blindingly lit yard staring back at where my car is parked.

Pompom rushes over, yapping, and jumps around me like she's on springs. Joe, finally hearing her, turns, and stops short. He stares at me.

'Surprise!' I say weakly.

His eyes hold mine as Pompom bounces around me. I crouch to give her a cuddle, and stand up with her in my arms.

Joe still hasn't moved. 'Here to visit?' he asks quietly.

'Here to stay,' I correct.

'Tell him your other news,' calls Gillian, leaning heavily on her walking stick in the kitchen doorway and she lumbers out, with Bridget and Seren hot on her tail.

'News?' asks Joe, his eyes warily meeting mine.

I take a deep breath. 'I'm not Mike's daughter, so I'm not your cousin.' A smile spreads unbidden across my face, then halts halfway because he's still frowning. He looks at Seren, who nods, then back at Gillian.

All of us are waiting for his reaction.

He looks at the ground. He strides over, takes my hand and holds it carefully in his. He looks down at it as if he's unsure what it is, takes a deep breath and slowly starts to nod.

'OK,' he says more firmly, and taking Pompom out of my

arms, he puts her gently on the ground, and without warning he lifts me up in the air and holds me there, and slowly swirls us round so that Bridget and Seren have to hop out of the way. As he lets me slither down, he kisses me, and all doubt about coming back washes away as it's replaced by a deep sense of rightness so strong it could lift me up in the air like Joe just did. We lose ourselves in the moment, wrapped up in each other, until Bridget clears her throat pointedly, and Seren snorts out a laugh.

We pull apart, our breathing uneven, and I'd be embarrassed except Joe won't let go of my hand, and he looks so overjoyed all I can do is beam.

'Bloody knew it,' says Gillian. 'Right, everyone inside, you're letting all the heat out.'

'Do you have somewhere to stay?' asks Joe, as we follow her inside, my hand still firmly in his.

'Yes, she damned well does,' says Gillian from in the kitchen, and Joe releases my hand so I can give her another hug, but takes it again as soon as he can.

'Damned glad that's sorted out,' she says briskly. 'You had me worried there for a minute,' she says sternly to Joe, and he grins.

'Pleased to have her back?' he asks her.

'Course I am. I've missed you,' she says to me, her eyebrows in a deep V like she's telling me off. 'Have you told your mother, yet?' An impish gleam comes into her eyes.

'Not yet,' I admit.

'Would you like me to do it?' she asks wickedly.

'We'll tell her together on speakerphone,' I concede. 'It'll be good to get them talking, no matter what their motives. 'Speaking of parents . . .' I bite my lip anxiously. 'I should go and see Bryn.'

Joe looks up curiously, then twigs and his mouth falls open. 'Bryn?' he sputters. 'Really?'

Gillian looks at me keenly. 'He should hear it from you – and the sooner the better. He's been a bit low.'

I take a deep breath. 'All right with everyone if I go and see him, now?'

Gillian nods. 'Good luck.'

Bridget pats my shoulder, but Joe gets up to go with me.

'I'll come as far as the gate,' he says, still holding my hand, and grabbing coats, with Pompom and Bozz following us, we start down the hill to see Bryn.

'I'm sorry I didn't say goodbye,' I say as soon as we're on the track.

He shakes his head. 'I'm sorry I didn't know what to say when it all went so horribly wrong. It was like all my impulses to take you in my arms were wrong, and I was lost as to what to do.'

'Me, too.'

We stop at Bryn's gate and Joe cups my face in both his hands and very delicately kisses me. For a fraction of a second I relax. 'Now, go do this,' he says gently, 'and I'll see you back at Gillian's.'

'Do you think he'll be pleased?' I can't help asking, my hand on the gate.

Joe smiles at me with calm confidence. 'Yes, I do.'

He waits for me to reach Bryn's door. I glance back at him and hold up my crossed fingers, but Joe grins and shakes his head to show I won't need luck for this one. He gives a small wave and sets off up the hill. Bracing myself, I uncross my fingers and knock.

Bryn opens the door and looks down at me with a pleasant half-smile.

'Hi, Bryn.'

He dips his head in greeting. 'Saw your car head up the hill. Shelves on top.'

He doesn't miss a thing. No wonder Dolores had such a

hard time getting past him. 'Yes. Umm, could I come in? I want to ask you about something.'

Standing back, he makes room for me to pass and I instinctively go into the kitchen and stare up at the shelves of carvings. Bryn comes in and stands beside me, but I have no idea how to start.

'Cup of tea?' he asks.

'Yes, please,' I say quickly, though I don't really want one.

Bryn bustles around the kitchen and gets out two mugs. He glances at me, but he doesn't say anything. He picks up the jar labelled 'tea', removes the lid and reaches inside.

'I've spoken to my mum,' I blurt, and Bryn's hand hovers over the mugs with teabags. '. . . and I was wondering if, thirty years ago, you and she might have . . . well, I wondered if you might be . . .' His eyes meet mine, and panic courses through my veins. What if it isn't him? What if it's someone else? After all, it was me who supplied Bryn's name—

'Thirty years ago?' he asks, letting the teabags fall in the mugs, and he lets out a long breath. 'I want to show you something,' he says, and leaves the room.

I don't know whether to take over making the tea, look at the carvings, or just sit down, but he comes back after only a few seconds carrying an old album. He carefully checks the kitchen table is dry before setting it down, and flicks through the pages. He stops and points at one of the photographs. I don't recognise the woman he's pointing at.

'That's my ma when she was young.'

She's a happy, pretty lady and the more I look, the more I see there's definitely something about the eyes and the forehead that's familiar.

Bryn's watching me. 'I saw the similarity the first time you stopped at my gate. I thought I was being an old fool, daring to think such a thing, but if you're here because . . .'

'Because my mum told me you and she . . .' I don't want

to say it. '. . . were *together*.' We both stare at the photograph. 'Then maybe . . .'

'Then maybe you are,' he agrees.

'Do you mind if I am?'

He lets out a juddery breath that's almost a laugh, and stops. 'Do you?' he asks.

'Not as long as you don't.'

A smile spreads across his face, and he pats my hand. 'Then no, I don't mind. That's the last thing—' He breaks off, takes a deep breath and I'm startled to see tears in his eyes.

I don't know whether to hug him, but he doesn't move, so I put my hand on top of his and squeeze gently.

'I'm going to be around for a bit. I'm moving in with Gillian and helping out with Hill Start Art, so I was wondering if . . . well, if it would be OK if we got to know each other?'

He removes his hand from under mine, and for a second I'm scared I've said something wrong, but he gets up and goes over to the shelves and takes down the Everlast box of chess pieces. He opens it, takes out the topmost wrapped piece and holds it out to me. I carefully unwrap it, and gasp, because it's me! It's me as a white knight holding a sword, and with Bozz at my feet. It's beautiful, and him depicting me as my own white knight couldn't be more perfect.

'You belong here,' he says firmly. 'You're family. Where else would you be?' and smiling to himself, he goes back to making the tea, calm and quiet, even though I think my heart will explode. I focus on the intricate carving and the details of my hair, my mouth and eyes, even down to my nails on my fingers clutching the sword. It must have taken hours.

'Thank you,' I say, *really* meaning it.

He dips his head and the collie in his basket lets out a snore. Bryn's hand grazes across his face and it comes away glistening. He puts my tea on the table and I take his hand again. He grips mine, and nods.

That nod tells me everything.

'I'll teach you to carve, if you like?' he offers after a minute or two.

'I'd love that.'

He gets up and picks up a small lump of wood. He turns it over and over in his hands, and as I sip my tea, he starts to explain about the grain, pointing out how it twists and how you work with the wood to make the most of it. It's comfortable and as he looks earnestly at the wood, and quietly at me, it's everything I'd ever hoped for, and after half an hour, I return to Gillian's with a massive grin on my face.

'Went all right, then?' asks Gillian, with a shrewd smile.

Joe smiles, Seren hugs me and Bridget chuckles, slapping me on the shoulder.

'Course it did,' says Bridget with absolute certainty that it could never have done anything else. 'Now, about these workshops,' she says, and Joe gets up to make everyone drinks, while Seren takes a seat.

'I have a whole host of notes in my car,' I assure her. 'And I wanted to talk to you about me doing a workshop on how artists can sell their work safely. I've done a lot of research.'

'I think that's an excellent idea!' says Bridget immediately. 'I'd come, and I have several friends who would, too.'

'Me, too,' agrees Seren.

Bridget's eyes narrow. 'What other ideas have you had?'

'Get the whiskey, Joe. We won't stop them now,' Gillian says, shaking her head at us.

'Not now that I've got someone with a decent head on their shoulders,' agrees Bridget with the determination of a terrier. And as we all settle in for a raucous and enjoyable evening, Bridget sets about trying to ferret out as many of my ideas as possible.

EPILOGUE

One evening, a few weeks later, Joe and I are up in the spare bedroom, storing Mike's paintings more neatly so Gillian can use it as a dark room.

'Bluebeard's dungeon,' decrees Joe, carefully turning the remaining orchid paintings towards the wall. The rest have already been picked up by their mostly grateful models, although, in Dolores' case, she burnt hers behind the pub, before leaving for a new job managing a pub near Cardiff.

My hands are grubby so I wipe some loose hair off my face with my shoulder. 'Or Pandora's box with the demons neatly stacked, packed and catalogued?' I offer.

'Isn't that worse?'

I indicate Gillian's photographic equipment and folders. 'Not if you consider there was hope in Pandora's box as well as evil. And if you ask me, that secret space in the studio was far more sinister.'

'I suppose,' agrees Joe. He picks up a tripod, puts it down again and looks at me. 'Are you glad you moved here?'

'I'm loving it. You know I am,' I say with surprise.

And I am. I work each day (and some evenings) with Bridget, Seren and Gillian ready for our first retreat weekend, where I'll be giving one of the first workshops on copyright and Internet safety. I see Joe most evenings, sometimes staying over at his cottage, while Bryn is now a frequent visitor, and in any spare moments I get, I'm drawing.

It's like everything's fallen into place. And not just for me, because the formidable woman George hired from the lower valley has everything well in hand at the pub; her massive extended family seeming to possess every trade and skill known to man for the upgrade of the rooms and any catering that will be needed, and the place is buzzing. The whole lower valley is frequenting the place thanks to her, and she even has a daughter who's smitten with Gareth. They park around on the valley tracks smooching, and on the few occasions I've been down the pub, I've also caught George watching Gillian with a speculative expression. Gillian says I'm talking nonsense, but she looks at George with a lot more interest since I mentioned it.

Vivienne and Clara look set to be a part of everything, too. They came up to stay last weekend and enthused over our plans, envied us Mike's studio and promptly asked Bridget to craft ten exotic bird pictures from wool and commissioned twelve cushion covers from Seren with the promise they'd sell any quilts she made going forward. As for Vivienne and Gillian, they took one look at each other and raucously deconstructed the art of the last half century over a bottle of whiskey, while Clara, Joe and I watched in amused awe.

Even Petra has come into her own, agreeing to help set up any websites and buying platforms, on the provisos that firstly, I work with her instead of Bridget and secondly, that I be her birthing partner. Part honour, part terrifying!

'Why do you ask?' I ask Joe now.

'I've made a decision, and Petra's agreed,' he says, taking my hand. 'That as soon as I receive my next royalty payment, I'm buying her out of her half of the cottage.'

'Because of Gillian?'

'No,' he says with a half-smile. 'You were right about that.

I have to do what I want, and given that the cottage suits me, and I'm writing better than I ever have and . . .' He looks into my eyes, tilts my chin up with his forefinger and kisses me gently. '. . . you're here. I've decided this is where I want to be.'

'When did you decide?'

'A few weeks ago. Around the time you turned up on Gillian's doorstep again.' He grins. 'Also, I thought I might help with Hill Start Art – maybe even run a few writing courses, or writers' retreat weekends. What do you think?'

I kiss the end of his nose. 'You'll have to ask Bridget and Gillian. I'm just the lackey.'

He kisses me much more deeply, and my stomach somer-saults. 'The power behind the twin thrones, more like. I'm asking for *your* opinion. Would Hill Start Art like a literary edge on occasion?' and he kisses me again.

'I think it's a great idea,' I say softly, pleased I remember the question.

'So there's room for a writer in the mix?'

'Definitely. Ooh! And you could start a magazine. You know, like the original Arts and Crafts movement? It could have poems and a short story section, and showcase people's work, advertise courses—'

'With photos by Gillian?'

'Of course. She could take ones of people crafting, maybe even one or two of us lot, and we could print ones of Mike, too, that is, if Gillian doesn't mind.'

'Maybe even the ones she took when she first came here,' he agrees.

I stop dead and look at him. 'Do you know, even though you've all spoken about them, I've never seen them? In fact, I've never seen a photograph of Mike.'

'Well, they must be here somewhere.' Joe picks up some albums.

'What are you two doing up there?' Gillian shouts from downstairs. 'More work, less canoodling!'

I giggle. 'I was just saying, I've never seen a photo of Mike,' I shout down.

Silence.

'That's shut her up,' whispers Joe.

'Bring down the navy portfolio,' she calls finally. 'They're the personal ones.'

'You're honoured,' says Joe, taking the navy folder from the large stack of black ones. I follow him down to the kitchen and he puts it ceremoniously on the empty table in front of Gillian. Joe and I look at each other, but Gillian unzips it without concern and flips through the huge pages, past ones of Joe when he was young; one of him with a lamb, the curls of wool wrapped around his fingers, another of him ankle-deep in a stream with a young Huw holding up an open-toed old boot dripping with water. There's one of the farmhouse against the night sky, the stars crisp and bright, and in the middle are a lot of loose photos. She hands me one of Mike. It has to be Mike. He's working on a painting of the hills in the studio, looking at her with a frown that says 'What are you up to?' and I'm surprised – he isn't at all what I expected. He isn't handsome. He doesn't look tall, or well-built. He's lean with stubble, and has a straggly, starving-artist vibe – more leprechaun than Norse God.

She hands me another of him looking straight down the lens, and suddenly I see it – it's in the clarity of his gaze. It has a smouldering intensity and it's almost like his dark eyes can see right through to my soul, all while holding a hint of mischief and daring. And this is just a photo. I can imagine that in real life he was devastating, and I finally understand why women opened up to him – they thought he already knew them; understood them better than anyone else. Little did they know he was merely embalming their emotions while he remained as untouched as a lake reflecting the view.

'He was a charming bugger,' says Gillian, looking down at the fury encapsulated in the fateful photograph that changed their lives forever. 'But maybe I should have trusted him more.'

'If he'd trusted you and told you what he was doing, maybe you would have done,' I point out. 'Trust goes both ways.'

She nods. 'True. And I loved him, in spite of it. That's why it hurt so much.'

'Hmm,' mutters Joe. 'He certainly left a mess behind. He almost destroyed you, and the valley with it.'

'And yet he left all the elements for success,' I say, shaking my head in wonder. Startled, Gillian and Joe turn to me. 'Well, if it weren't for him, none of us would be here, and nor would Bridget. We wouldn't have the farm, the cottage or the studio, or the means to make Hill Start Art happen, and I'd be stuck in London wondering what the hell to do with my life. In fact, no, I wouldn't even have existed!'

Gillian smiles at me, then at Joe. 'She's right, you know.'

Joe wraps an arm around me. 'But then, without you, none of it would have come together.' He rests his cheek on my head. 'It's like it was all waiting for you; waiting for you to come home and sort it out.'

I love that thought. I love the idea that not only do I belong here, but that I'm also a fundamental part of what happens here.

I smile up at him, and Gillian frowns at us both.

'But don't forget you would never have come here if it weren't for that yoghurt, and your busker,' says Gillian. 'Who do we have to thank for that? Fate?'

'Well, I'm very grateful to Fate for the yoghurt and the busker,' says Joe seriously.

'Yes, me too,' I agree.

'Well, let's toast her then,' says Gillian, but I don't picture Fate as we pour out the whiskey and chink glasses. Instead, somewhere deep in the recesses of a London tube tunnel I imagine my underground prophet playing a cover version of the Beatles' 'The End', before stroking his dog and moving on to someone else. I silently toast him, and then with a contented sigh, I snuggle up on the sofa with Joe.

ACKNOWLEDGEMENTS

This book has been great fun to write, and that is in no small part due to the support of a wonderful team of people.

I wish to thank my lovely literary agent, Jo Bell from The Bell Lomax Moreton Agency, who has been helpful and supportive throughout. I also owe my grateful thanks to my editor, Thorne Ryan, with whom it has been my very great pleasure to work with once again. She has been excellent and I thank both her and everyone at Hodder and Stoughton who helped make this book possible.

At home, I must thank my gorgeous husband and children for their unrelenting encouragement, tea and patience. I'm so glad you have been on this journey with me – you have been truly amazing.

I would also like to thank my grandmother, who was not at all like Gillian, but who was formidable, strong and possessed that wonderful gift of an enquiring mind. I will always be grateful for all the wonderful things she taught me.

**If you enjoyed *Leave It to Fate*,
you'll love Beth Corby's gorgeous novel
*Where There's a Will***

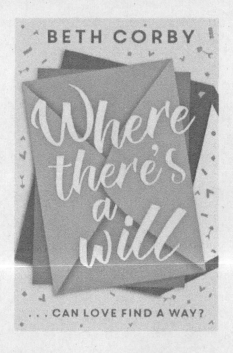

**Would you take the chance that could change
everything?**

Available now in paperback and ebook